SATURDAYS ARE GOLD

Pierre Van Rooyen

Endaxi Press
www.endaxipress.com

First published 2011 by Endaxi Press
Unit 11, Concord House, Main Avenue, Bridgend, CF31 2AG

www.endaxipress.com

ISBN 978-1-907375-65-1

Saturdays Are Gold copyright © Pierre Van Rooyen 2011

The right of Pierre Van Rooyen to be identified as the author of this work has been asserted by him in accordance with the Copyright, Designs and Patents Act, 1988

The characters and events portrayed in this book are entirely fictitious. Any similarity to real persons, living or dead, is purely coincidental and not intended.

All rights reserved. No part of this publication may be reproduced, stored in or introduced into a retrieval system, or transmitted, in any form, or by any means (electronic, mechanical, photocopying, recording or otherwise) without the prior written permission of the publisher. Any person who does any unauthorised act in relation to this publication may be liable to criminal prosecution and civil claims for damages.

1 3 5 7 9 10 8 6 4 2

British Library Cataloguing in Publication Data.
A catalogue record for this book is available from the British Library

Typeset by ReallyLoveYourBook Bridgend, South Wales.

Printed by Lightning Source, Milton Keynes.

This book is sold subject to the condition that it shall not, by way of trade or otherwise, be lent, re-sold, hired out, or otherwise circulated without the publisher's prior consent in any form or binding or cover other than that in which it is published and without a similar condition including this condition being imposed on the subsequent purchaser.

Acknowledgements

With heartfelt thanks to five wonderful people who supported me through thick and thin.

Judith Ryder, long time friend, in Wakkerstroom, South Africa who has spent a decade managing Faith's and my affairs while we sailed among Indian Ocean islands.

Charlotte Otter, author, journalist and professional writer in Heidelberg, Germany, who consistently pointed me in the right direction. Under Charlotte's direction I came of age. She writes a wonderful blog. Please visit her on
http://charlotteotter.wordpress.com

The late Gerry Dailey, editor extraordinaire, in Chicago, United States who scrutinised the manuscript and edited the fifth rewrite, working through the volume more than once. Wherever I went wrong Gerry put me back on the straight and narrow.

Michele and Andrew Brenton in Wales – their dream of what might be, incredibly innovative thinking, resolution and long hours of hard work, made it all happen.

For Faith, Brett and Ingrid.

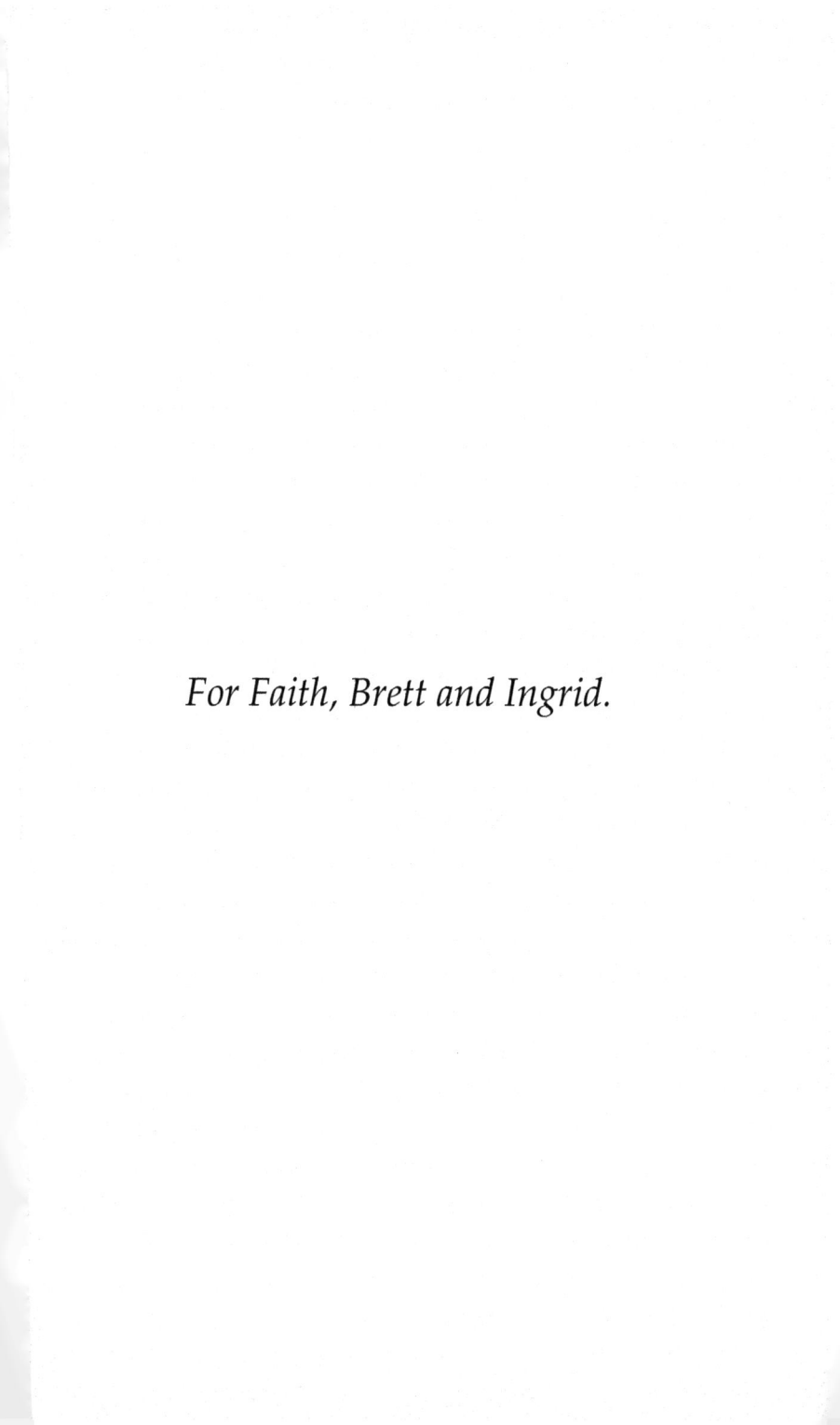

Chapter 1

One sad Thursday in 1944 our father brought Momma home and buried her. Or at least the funeral parlour did. Of the three of us kids, only Victor aged ten was at the service and burial. It was decided for me that as a little boy just six years of age I was too young to attend.

Our four-year-old sister Maudie was still under sedation. She'd tried to tell the family what caused the accident but all we'd heard was garbled nonsense issuing from her lips. Our family doctor had given her an injection and prescribed a tranquilliser and vitamins.

I can only imagine how Father took Momma's passing for he didn't speak to us children about his hurt. He was most kind to Maudie however and spent part of his evenings reading to her.

"Maudie sweetheart, let me tell you about Jock of the Bushveld tonight and find out how Jock chased the stray dog raiding the chicken coop..."

My sister sat on his lap listening and watching, but she didn't respond and she never said anything.

Maudie and I slept in the same room so I knew about her nightmares. I had enough of my own but my baby sister didn't sleep at all well and often I would get up in the night and hold her until she calmed down.

Then one Sunday morning after working on our battered old Chev's engine our father packed a picnic hamper and Primus stove, bundled Victor, Maudie and me into the back seat and put the picnic stuff on the front passenger floor. No one was allowed to sit in Momma's seat and the car had no boot, only an outside luggage carrier so it was easier to carry small things inside. He drove at twenty miles an hour to Gillooly's Farm, a local picnic spot popular with the families of Johannesburg.

A watercourse, not quite big enough to call a river, drifted through Gillooly's. I suppose it lay a quarter of a mile from the picnic sites and we could reach it by making our way across a pasture and down through the willow trees. We brought our costumes and Victor and I changed on the bank and plunged into the water. He was much bigger than me and known to everyone as Frog. I splashed about while he showed off his crawl stroke. Maudie did not swim. She sat on the bank in her faded orange dress, staring into space and bending a grass stem backwards and forwards.

Frog swam to the far shore, powered back with a great deal of to do and climbed out.

"I'm going back to Father. I've swum enough. You can do what you like," he mumbled, without looking at me.

"No, wait... don't leave us..." I ran after him, wanting him to stay as the spot was deserted.

He ignored me.

When I turned back toward the riverbank, our sister was gone.

"Maudie? Maudie?"

I dashed to where she had been sitting and noticed the broken stem of grass lying there. I peered upriver in case she had taken it into her head to go for a stroll. I checked downstream. No sign of her.

"Frog... Frog... where's Maudie?" I shouted. Either he didn't hear me or chose not to and he became smaller in the distance.

Perhaps two minutes had passed since I left Maudie. Instinct urged me to go to the edge of the bank and look down, but panic warned me not to because of what I might find.

Reluctantly I inched toward the bank. Even today as

an adult the horror of what I saw remains with me.

My sister was in the watercourse beneath the surface. Her little face looked up at me, her hair waving like seaweed and her old orange play dress floating up around her waist like a halo. She was a fair swimmer but was making no attempt to save herself.

"Maudie... no!"

I don't remember going in. I do remember her eyes watching me come for her.

Swimming above her I made a grab for her hair, snatched her shoulder and finally had both my arms around her. On the bank we fell in a heap. I rolled her onto her stomach and pounded her back. She retched up river water again and again. When at last she could breathe she started weeping. I stroked her sodden hair and hugged her as her sobs came in fits and starts. Eventually, she fell asleep while I sat there with her on the grass on the edge of the riverbank.

We stayed like that until Frog came looking for us, angry and fed up that our father had sent him on such an unimportant errand. "What's going on here?" he demanded. "Father and I've been waiting hours for you."

"Maudie slipped and fell in the water, that's all. We just drying her clothes."

My sister watched me during this exchange and although she didn't say anything, her eyes told me she was happy with what I said to Frog.

I never told the family about her near drowning.

By now I was attending junior grade at primary school, playing marbles with other boys and getting beaten up by the bullies. In the week I saw Maudie only in the afternoons. She spent her days playing in the fig tree but she wasn't absolutely alone during the mornings because Sampson kept an eye on her. Sampson was a saint. He was a Zulu man who accepted the role of housekeeper, cook, nursemaid and even seamstress. He came to us after Momma died and taught himself to use her Singer treadle sewing machine so he could patch Maudie's and my clothes. Frog's clothes never needed mending. So while Sampson busied himself with housework, he would also check the fig tree from one of the sash windows facing the backyard.

In the afternoons I played in the dirt under the fig tree, building mud forts for my five or six tin soldiers, often aware that my sister was watching me wistfully.

"Maudie...?"

I would glance up and she'd quickly turn her head away. This went on for nearly two years.

Then one day, while making my usual surreptitious search for her in the fig tree I saw something that made me chortle. Maudie had discarded her play dress and was wearing my old clothes. Boy's clothes. While I was at school she must have sorted through the few hand-me-downs I possessed and selected an old, torn pair of beige corduroys I had inherited from Frog but were now too small even for me. She'd also chosen a sleeveless shirt which I hadn't worn for weeks and had seen better days.

When she noticed my expression, she started giggling. My heart skipped a beat because it was difficult to communicate with her and here she was responding to my incredulity. I waited in trepidation terrified I might unnerve her.

It came as a shock to hear Maudie speak because I hadn't heard her voice in two years and didn't recognize it. Her speech was soft and weak, almost inaudible and full of despair.

"Tadpole," she murmured, "what's the use of praying?"

I didn't answer.

"I never stop praying," Maudie confided, "for Momma to come back."

I was silent. I had prayed many times for this too but God just ignored me.

"Maudie, what's happened, s'happened. Nobody can undo it. Not even God."

"You think I should give up praying?"

"Dunno, Sis. I gotta think."

I didn't know how to answer her especially as she had been hurt so badly. While I was racking my brains, she started speaking again. I still couldn't believe I was hearing her voice.

"I been thinking of giving up. But I scared if I stop praying the bottle 'n bag man's gonna take me away from the family."

Johannesburg teemed with bottle-and-bag men, swarthy individuals with unkempt hair and clothed in rags. They trundled their homemade pushcarts through the suburbs, picking up anything that could be sold for a few pennies. Glass bottles were popular as they could be redeemed at the city market.

"Tadpole, s'no use, I been praying to God for anything he got but he give me nothing."

I gathered that my baby sister had confidently started out with a considerable list. When nothing appeared at her bedside the next morning she progressively pared her requests.

Before long her list was halved. Then cut further until she decided that perhaps the right thing to do was to ask for only one gift. "P'raps God can't give his things away all at once."

She had spent weeks praying for the cheapest rag doll she had seen in town. Nothing happened. Concluding that she was still asking for too much but terrified the bottle-and-bag man would take her away, she reduced her request to a tickey, which is three-pence. That was three weeks' pocket money. In despair she cut that to a penny, then a ha'penny and finally a farthing. "Hang it, Tadpole, a farthing's worth nothing. It can only get the horriblest liquorice in the shop."

"Yah, Maudie. A penny's okay. It can buy two sucker-balls, but a farthing's no good to us. Lemme tell you, Sis, we wasting our time. Something from God's not gonna happen. I gave up praying long time back and I still here. The bottle 'n bag man's not gonna hear about it cos we not gonna tell anybody."

"S'what I wanta hear. If you not afraid, I not afraid also," Maudie grinned. "I never gonna ask for nothing more. I'll get it myself."

Once a week, kicking acorns along the pavement, we sauntered to Sunday school but never asked our Maker for anything. It was a matter of pride.

In 1946, my sister started going to school. She was speaking much better but still reticent and the august institution quickly became a problem for her. At the end of the first month, having been fetched by Sampson every day because she wasn't allowed out of the front gate on her own, she came crying to me where I was digging a pretend mine shaft in the shade of the fig tree.

"I never going back," she sobbed. "I finished with school."

"Tis the law, Maudie. We hafta go."

"Hmph, if you ask me, the law's plain crazy and school's miserable. I probably know everything already. School makes me wish I never was born."

"You dunno everything, Sis."

"Abe taught me lotsa things."

Only Maudie called our father Abe. She picked it up when Momma was alive. He was Abraham John. His friends called him AJ.

"The teacher thinks we still babies. Big A little a, bouncing b, cat's in the cupboard and can't see me. Have five apples then eat two, how many left? Does she think we stupid?"

"Can't be helped, Sis. You hafta go to school to learn

arithmetic and history and geography."

"P'raps, Tadpole, but the week's awful long, I probably gonna croak one day."

"Why don't you make signs you can stick up somewhere, just the names of the days so you can cross 'em off? On Wednesday, for instance, you can start looking forward to the weekend.

"Monday won't be so bad then because on Monday afternoon you can cross it off and you'll know the worst of the week's over."

She stared at me.

"I gotta think about that."

She went off and came back an hour later with seven strips of paper neatly torn out of an exercise book. Each had been painstakingly lettered with the name of one of the days of the week, all beautifully crafted in wax crayon.

"What you think?" she quizzed.

"Say, those're wonderful. I reckon you done a first class job."

She eyed me.

"Sure you not messing me about?"

"Never, Sis."

"P'raps we can pin today on the fig tree?"

She had lettered that day a Friday, in crimson. The following day Saturday, was a mixture of yellow and ochre.

"That's s'posed to be gold," she confided. To this day, I cannot visualize Saturday except in gold.

"This one's act'lly silver," she pointed out, showing me her *Sunday* sign. She had achieved the colour with a grey crayon over-lettered with a white one. My lifetime impression of Sunday is silver.

"And this one's Monday," she muttered, scowling. "The worsest day of my life."

I stared at her *Monday* sign and felt a chill run through my body. It wasn't blue. It was black.

As the weekdays progressed, my sister's colours

became brighter. *Tuesday*, a day of relief, was pink, a great change from *Monday*. *Wednesday* was green, *Thursday*, orange and *Friday*, of course, red.

"Why the different colours, Sis? I thought you'd do 'em all the same."

"Cos that's the way I am," she responded, hands on hips, gazing at me as if I was dumb.

"Monday I'm terrible black. I don't mean like Amos. He's not black he's brown but act'lly he's silver inside. Then on Tuesdays I'm pink. Don't you see, silly? By Saturday I'm gold."

I stared at her.

"Isn't everybody the same? Isn't Abe green on Wednesdays and orange on Thursdays?"

"Yah, Maudie, I think maybe you're right. I always thought the days were different colours, but I didn't know what ones."

"I s'pect that's cos you didn't have my crayons. Otherwise you woulda known the colours easy."

Every morning from that day on, my sister pinned the day of the week on the trunk of our fig tree and I think the rest of the household knew that Wednesdays were green and Saturdays, gold.

Chapter 2

In 1947 the future Queen of England drove up Roberts Avenue only six houses down from our house and passed within a hundred yards of the fig tree. Prancing on the pavement my sister and I waved and cheered until we were blue in the face.

"They seen us," Maudie hollered, putting two fingers in her mouth and wolf-whistling at the royal family. "I positive they seen us. Wave Tadpole so they know we seen 'em."

It was the year the British Royal Family toured South Africa: King George VI, Queen Elizabeth, Princesses Elizabeth and Margaret Rose. Multitudes lined the pavements, whipping their Union Jacks back and forth and cheering themselves hoarse. As the Royals drove through our suburb, they smiled from their drop-head Daimler and Maudie could hardly control her excitement.

"Now they seen us, maybe they gonna write us a letter. We better check the post everyday."

For months after that my sister made me play 'princesses' with her, although I have never seen another princess with untidy hair, dirty feet, beige cords and tattered shirt.

There were no Buicks, Lincolns or Cadillacs where we lived. Kensington was a working class suburb with Chevs and Fords from the '30s parked outside the houses or in the narrow driveways.

The houses were old and weatherworn. They'd been

repaired and repainted countless times but they were still old and weatherworn. The people had pride so their houses were reasonably neat. Once every five years our father repainted our roof or refurbished a peeling façade. He hired one of the black jobbing painters who made their rounds of the suburbs looking for work and the two of them tackled the task together.

Not everyone could afford a motorcar and those who could, bought second-hand. Our family pride and joy was a '34 Chev. Like every other car, it was drab black with the middle portion of the roof made of rubber. The Chev had a straight six motor and derived its life from a single side-draft carburettor. There was no boot. Where the boot might have been there was a luggage carrier that folded down when you wanted to use it. Our father tied our stuff onto the carrier with sash cord.

The back doors opened forwards and we stepped onto running boards. The spare wheel was strapped into a well in one of the front mudguards with a leather belt. There was only one windscreen wiper.

"It's gonna rain, Abe," Maudie observed. "Turn the scriper on. Aw pleeze do. I wanna see it go ziggity-zag slurp-slurp."

The scriper was in front of our father. So when it rained, we passengers never got to see where we were going. Only the driver could.

There were one or two Austins and Morris Eights. Some men back from the war in Europe and North Africa managed to buy surplus army lorries. These too stood outside the houses or in the narrow driveways. Those who couldn't afford to buy an army vehicle or a second-hand car commuted on the four-wheel double-decker trams. Or walked.

A handful of men owned motorcycles. There was the sprinkling of English bikes, Triumphs, Nortons, BSAs and Velocettes and one or two American Harleys. The women didn't like the motorcycles. The bikes were dirty and noisy and the wind messed their hair. Also it was unladylike climbing onto a pillion in a dress. So the women would rather their men didn't have bikes. They'd rather ride on the trams.

People wore hats. When they walked in the streets the men wore hats and the women wore hats, when they rode on the trams or went shopping and when they attended a sports meeting or went to the circus. Children wore hats too. Their best dress was their school uniform. Girls wore white panamas and boys pushed their school caps to jaunty angles at the backs of their heads.

Women never wore trousers, not on home territory anyway. Trousers were only permissible when touring in a motorcar or at a resort. Shorts were strictly reserved for the beach. Nowhere else. Strange as it seems, men never wore shorts either. They wore grey flannel longs with baggy crotches and turn-ups that measured twelve inches across. Women wore long skirts or dresses reaching halfway down their shins. They painted their lips cherry red. In our suburb none of the mothers had spending money to visit a hairdresser. On Saturday afternoons or Sunday mornings they visited among themselves and cut and permanent-waved each other's hair at home.

Back from the war, men worked in factories like our father did or got jobs in offices as clerks. Many worked in the mines where the hours were long and there were night shifts and day shifts. The women stayed at home to look after their children, feed them when they returned from school and see that they did their homework. They cooked the evening dinner, they vacuumed and kept house, they budgeted and bought groceries and they sewed, knitted and darned. On weekends they weeded their tiny gardens while their husbands mowed their minute lawns with push mowers or got on with painting jobs around the house.

There were suburbs worse off than ours. But not

many. Mrs Probert, a busybody across the street, looked down her nose at the families who lived in those suburbs and behind their backs called them terrible names.

"Ne'er-do-wells, poor-whites with no breeding who'll never amount to anything."

"What about the black people, Missus Probert?" Maudie asked. "They live in backyards and only got shanties or grass huts."

But Mrs Probert did not believe black people existed.

Our father called my sister and me something terrible too.

"When did the great unwashed last bath?" he teased.

"Aw gee, Abe," Maudie objected. "We not nearly as bad as the McCallum boys up the street. They only bath once a week."

People were superstitious. They wouldn't walk under a ladder through the triangle of death. Thirteen was unlucky and most wouldn't have anything to do with it. Six-six-six was not mentioned among the pious. Many made secret wishes if they saw a falling star.

"What about black cats, Tadpole? I believe they real important."

"Dunno, Sis. I can't figure out if they lucky or unlucky. We hafta just keep outta their way."

When we were taken to town, we had something else to worry about.

"Make sure not to step on the lines. Else the bears'll get us."

Our housekeeper had superstitions too. He filched twenty bricks from a building site, wrapped them in newspaper and placed five under each leg of his bed, raising it to waist level.

"Whatsa matter with your bed, Semp-Sonne?" asked Maudie, eyebrows raised. She could never quite get

Sampson's name right and it might have had something to do with her lapse in speaking.

"To save me from the Tokoloshe, little madam."

My sister pursed her lips at being called little madam but couldn't do anything about it because Sampson was her substitute mother.

We found out later that the Tokoloshe was a leprechaun that could reach up to you during the night. Hence Sampson's need to make a little more distance between his mattress and the floor.

Sampson's room was in the backyard and I was never sure what came through his windows at night, for his window, sash and fanlight were permanently closed. To stop any mythical creature peering in, he pasted brown wrapping paper over the glass.

Johannesburg bustled with trade. Black woman hawkers patrolled the streets.

"Greeeeeen... mealies," they hollered. Then white housewives ran out to buy succulent corncobs from them.

Black milkmen rattled their glass bottles with metal spikes used for removing cardboard tops. Black dustmen ran alongside dustcarts setting the neighbourhood dogs into a cacophony. Indian-owned horse-drawn greengrocer carts did business in the streets, grocery vans delivered to the houses and coal lorries with black coalmen poured massive dirty sacks of the stuff into backyard coal bins.

And of course the ragged bottle-and-bag man. Also black. This spectre was exploited by parents as a bogey man to scare children into doing something they resisted, for fear he would come and take them away. Our father never frightened us with such stories but older children did.

"We oughta hide," Maudie whispered, crawling under her bed. "The bottle 'n bag man's coming up our street."

Cats disappeared and the black dustmen were

blamed for stealing and eating them. On Sunday afternoons, black Pentecostal churches baptized their followers in the streams that flow through the city and suburbs. It was not unheard of for some poor convert to accidentally drown and meet his Maker a little sooner than he expected.

Prohibition was in force but only for people of colour. Europeans could become fighting drunk and they did too. However nobody else was supposed to touch the stuff. The law spawned a roaring trade in bootlegging, a profitable black market and hundreds of thousands of shebeens.

Occasionally The Star reported the disappearance of a child. Every afternoon the newspaper was tossed onto our garden path by a paperboy pelting down the pavement on a bicycle. My sister tumbled out of the fig tree and raced me to get the paper so we could read Curly Wee, a cartoon story about a piglet.

"Wait for me, Tadpole. You gotta give me a chance to get there first. You bigger'n me, you know. Wait... Oh phooey, s'not fair."

That's how we noticed the two or three inch columns about the missing children. Reports speculated on ritual murder by African sorcerers cutting out vital organs while the victim was still alive.

"We African people call it muti-murder," Sampson explained. "Very bad. The sorcerer makes himself invisible. Don't go out alone at night."

Lying in her bed just after the light was turned off that evening, Maudie must have been thinking about sorcerers.

"No way I gonna be afraid of a silly old Tokoloshe."

I stared into the darkness and didn't say anything.

Chapter 3

I think the best thing that happened to my sister was getting Hobo, the greatest dog that ever lived. It took her by surprise and launched her into ecstasy. Hobo was a heroine in quelling Maudie's memory flashbacks and soothing her trauma.

Secretive as usual, our father didn't let on what he was up to. This was quite normal for him. Whenever my sister and I overheard something we weren't supposed to and became inquisitive, he had a stock answer for us.

"Hares," he replied, with a grin.

"Hairs?"

"Yes, hares with long ears. The great unwashed have long ears like hares." Then he'd walk off chuckling.

Then one Saturday afternoon our father parked the Chev in the street when he returned from Saturday morning work. We were curious about this because he usually brought the Chev up the dirt drive to the corrugated iron garage. We didn't want him to tease us for being inquisitive so we pretended we hadn't noticed the Chev in the street.

After lunch Maudie in her cords and patched shirt retired to the fig tree and I scrounged around trying to find the forked handle of an old catapult our cousin Graham had left hanging on the fence. I had it in mind to repair it so I could ambush the grey rats that came down from the koppies and invaded our compost heap. Frog was perfecting his homework.

Our father slipped out, freewheeling down Good Hope Street before engaging the gear so we wouldn't hear the engine start. He drove to the SPCA on the other side of town and selected a pooch for Maudie. It cost him five shillings, which was more than a year's pocket money for my sister. Only much later did he tell us that because of overcrowding of strays the scruffy little animal had been scheduled to be put down. He had effectively rescued her.

"Abe's coming back," Maudie whispered on hearing the Chev roll up the drive. Our thirteen-year-old saloon stopped below the fig tree.

"I've brought you something, Maudie," called our father, putting his purchase on the ground.

My sister just about fell out of the fig tree, she came down so fast, and obliterated my fort at the bottom of her plummet.

"Why, that's a little hobo puppy," she squealed.

The third and newest member of the great unwashed was an off-white mongrel bulldog bitch, as dirty as doesn't matter anymore and wagging her whole backside, never mind just the tail.

"I think she's yours, sweetheart."

My sister's eyes flew open in astonishment. She spun her head around to see if she was being teased but our grinning father nodded and mouthed, "Y. E. S".

She glanced at the disreputable dog and began clapping her hands and jumping up and down on her toes.

"Oh Abe, I'm dancing. Lookit me... lookit me, I'm dancing."

She darted forwards and Hobo leapt into her arms. She knew who her new mistress was. The happy couple waltzed around and around the fig tree, Hobo's little tongue furiously wetting my sister's nose. Maudie ran to our father, pouring out her thanks.

"The best day of my life, Abe. This is so exciting. I got a friendly puppy. She gonna live with me in the fig tree."

When she couldn't think of anything else to say she let out a whoop of delight and the two friends collapsed in a heap on the ground.

Chapter 4

The night before Guy Fawkes, my sister experienced her first nightmare about the missing children. I woke to her yells. The clock that ticked in the passage sounded its carillon and chimed twice. Maudie squirmed in her bed. She slept under the window. I slipped out of my blanket and tiptoed across to her.

"Davy..." she groaned, "here am I.... see me above you.... you tied.... he gonna cut you.... aw, no...."

"Wake up Maudie," I murmured. "You're having a nightmare."

She sat up, dazed and shaking.

I hugged her and said, "S'okay Sis. You awake now."

But she was dazed.

"Tadpole, I getting scared. Davy's gone. I saw the sorcerer cut him. The drain. The stormwater drain by the park."

"S'alright Maudie. Forget about it. S'only a nightmare."

"He dumped him in the water pipe under the road. But his clothes're by the drain."

"S'okay Sis."

"You won't leave me, will you?"

"Do you wanna come in with me?" She nodded. We padded to my bed and climbed in together.

When daylight came, my sister remembered nothing of what happened during the night.

Guy Fawkes that year fell on a Saturday, a hot

November Saturday. All afternoon a thunderstorm built up along the southern man-made horizon and loomed threateningly over Johannesburg's enormous mine-dumps. Kite season was waning and kennetjie and cricket were on the way in. Maudie worked in the fig tree fixing planks so Hobo could negotiate the branches. She had long ago nailed tread-boards on the bole so her dog could join her up there. Our father came out of the garage.

"When you taking us to the fireworks, Abe?" Maudie pestered.

"Not till the great unwashed clean themselves up, sweetheart. My children look like waifs."

"Aw gee. We not's bad as the McCallum boys."

"True, but you're not much better either. Now off you go to the bathroom. And please use water. Don't just wipe your dirt onto a facecloth."

Maudie rolled her eyes.

Distant thunder rumbled, but we knew from the appearance of the sky that it wouldn't rain this Guy Fawkes evening. As usual Frog was in the dining room revising his homework.

Our brother's nickname was my fault. When I started school and was highly nervous, a sports master from the nearby high school stood in for our lady gym teacher away on leave. The man, a bristling English army captain called Collard was so intimidating I could hardly answer him. He coached us in cricket and was emphatic that we understood the game properly. Victor lazed on the other side of the field studying a book.

Collard became furious and turned to the nearest pupil who happened to be me.

"What's that boy's surname, the one behind the wicket reading a blasted book when he's supposed to be paying attention to the game?"

Our surname is Freyer, but I couldn't say it.

"Well come now boy, answer me."

"Fffrrr... Fffrrr... Fffrrr...," I stammered in front of the rest of the boys.

"Sir!" he bawled. "You address me as Sir!"

"Fffrrrehhhg..."

"Frog, you say? Frog, it is then."

In a voice that boomed across the playing fields, he thundered, "Frog, I'll strew your guts across the cricket pitch. Put that confounded book down and pay attention to the game, man."

To Victor's dismay the field roared with laughter. The name caught on immediately and by next morning my own name was Tadpole instead of Tom. Victor/Frog hardly ever spoke to me after that.

Our father went into the house and Maudie reached for the bole of the fig tree and took her yellow and ochre *Saturday* sign down.

"Snazzy, hey? We gonna see fireworks at the park tonight. I wanta sneak Hobo into the car so Abe don't know he's taking her."

Rhodes Park is at the bottom of the Kensington hill. Almost every street in Kensington goes up or down a hill. The suburb is built in, on, among, under, around and against many koppies and the natural vegetation ridges of these hills dominate the rooftops. If you are not ascending a hill you are descending one. Each house is built slightly above its neighbour on the one side and slightly below its neighbour on the other. One looks over a lot of roofs in Kensington. The suburb is crammed in among the koppies. Uphill backyards butt against their wild vegetation.

Side streets run into dead ends where footpaths commence tortuous routes up, down and across the slopes. The terrain is covered in scrub, bush and natural veld grass, dotted with granite outcrops, boulders, rock faces and caves. Nature's little creatures abound on these pinnacle and ridge-topped hillocks. Field mice, the odd snake, tock-tockies, a box shaped beetle that taps a tattoo on the ground with its abdomen, millipedes which our playmate Amos called shongololos, spiders, wild birds and many others are all there. Grey rats come down from the koppies to the houses and soon find the attraction of becoming house rats.

Tramps find crannies to sleep there, winos establish secret drinking places where they won't be disturbed, criminals creep out of sight, loot is stashed in caves and parents warn their children to stick to the paths and stay in sight of the houses.

Spectators began gathering for the fireworks show well before sunset. They brought their supper in wicker picnic baskets and spread blankets on the rugby field. Organizers put finishing touches to a display on a goal post. An improvised bandstand was set up and uniformed musicians played John Philip Sousa.

Young mothers parked their prams, excited toddlers raced around and fell over their own feet. Older children lobbed tennis balls and played eggie or stingers. Women opened flasks of tea and sipped from bakelite cups. Men reached for bottle openers and flicked the tops off quart bottles of Castle Lager. They filled tumblers until the froth stood above the rim. *Hands Across the Sea* pervaded the air.

"How on earth did Maudie's dog get here?" our father asked.

My sister shrugged.

"Dunno, Abe."

Frog joined his friends. Maudie and I messed about throwing a stick for Hobo.

For once it didn't rain on Guy Fawkes night. As *Stars and Stripes* began ringing out, a reddening sun dipped toward the water tower on the hill and sank into a bank of nimbus overhanging the city. A throng of spectators congregated on the field, waiting for the exhibition to begin. Some had arrived on trams, a few on bicycles. Many had walked. A scattering of cars, pickups and vans stood on the perimeter. Moses, a black man who worked for Trixie next door, wandered past and greeted our father.

"There's old grumble-bum," Maudie warned, indicating another man standing some distance away. "He never got anything nice to say about anybody."

I caught sight of Mr de Beer the local school housemaster and turned so he wouldn't notice me.

Selina, a neighbour's black housekeeper sat chatting and paying little attention as her eight-year-old son Amos ran around barefoot, in patched khaki shorts, wearing a dirty pullover without a shirt. Amos was born out of wedlock and had no father. On her meagre wages Selina paid his school fees. She clothed him by begging cast-offs from friends with older children. Amos lived with his grandmother in Sophiatown and visited his mama on weekends. Mr Sunshine, a black travelling salesman, sometimes gave Amos a ride in his rickshaw and occasionally in his Chrysler. The fancy car became a taxi during the week and a bridal limousine at weekends.

"You go'n invite Amos for bread and peanut butter, Tadpole and I'll tell Abe to make a extra helping."

I chased after our playmate. Amos was clever and articulate beyond his years but new to the city and naïve. Pint-sized and chubby with a voice like a miniature Louis Armstrong, he was a Zulu umfaan. We had heard him sing at a high school carol evening. He wasn't supposed to be singing. Some of the carols were for audience participation and others were to be sung by the choir alone.

Selina only had one ticket so there was no seat for Amos.

"Here's a stool my boy. You go find a place for yourself at the back," an official had told him.

Amos couldn't see the stage over everyone's heads so instead of sitting on the science lab stool he'd stood on it. He had no idea that only some of the carols were meant for audience participation. Starting with *Silent Night* and continuing through the program to the *Hallelujah Chorus*, he sang all the carols at the top of his umfaan voice.

The choir on the stage couldn't hear the vocalist at the back of the hall singing along with them and nobody in the audience had said a word, because half of them were embarrassed and the other half couldn't stop snickering.

I caught up with him running along steering a homemade wire motorcar he'd made himself. His creation fascinated me and I traded with him to drive his car. It had a long steering column so you could run behind, controlling it as you went.

"Hey, Amos," I called. "You wanna peanut butter sandwich?" Amos executed a u-turn and marched over to visit us, stepping in time to Sousa and grinning widely.

Our father didn't drink beer like the other men. He upended his mug of tea and spread butter onto hunks of bread.

"Plenty peanut butter for us, Abe. Make it thick. Specially for Amos."

Our father grinned. Amos accepted his portion standing erect while spreading his toes. His pullover was small for him, exposing his stomach.

Way back when my sister quizzed him about his past, she'd informed me, "Amos is a schoolboy, Tadpole. Not a playboy anymore."

The last notes of *Liberty Bell* faded. We jumped at the shattering report of a thunder-flash. Spectators shrieked. A crescendo of sibilance followed as a skyrocket took off.

Maudie's dog sat upright, staring rigidly at where the explosion had taken place. When the hissing rocket roared away into the heavens, she let out a wail of anguish and raced after it, bolting over picnickers' blankets, knocking over tea flasks and sending plates flying. People scrambled for their things.

"Darn dog," our father exclaimed. "Who sneaked her into the Chev?"

Maudie shrugged.

When Hobo reached open ground she streaked for the launch pad where she'd seen the rocket standing. She overshot it by thirty feet skidding to a halt, her neck craning upward as she caught sight of the crimson tail disappearing overhead.

"Blast," our father exclaimed. "I'll have to fetch her back." He sprang to his feet and charged after my sister's dog.

He came almost within reach as a second rocket left the ground. Hobo howled her outrage and galloped after it, ending on the opposite side of the display. She trotted around with her tongue out and peered up at the sky. Our father tried to catch her.

"Wanna hand, old man?"

People started laughing.

"You gonna hafta be quicker than that, fella."

The catcalls didn't stop.

"Maybe you better learn to swing a lasso."

"You gonna charge us for all this entertainment, mister?"

They wolf-whistled and made fun of him until amid catcalls, cheers and jeers, he returned to where we were sitting. Maudie hid her face in her hands.

For the next hour and a half Hobo amused the crowd. She sat in the circle of light, gazing intently as if the display was for her alone. She watched Catherine wheels, sparklers, jumping jacks and roman candles. When the display was rounded off with three rockets fanning upwards simultaneously, Maudie's dog went berserk, zigzagging at full gallop across the field. The band broke into *King Cotton* and then struck up *God Save the King*. Everybody stood to attention.

Hobo came running through their legs.

"Never again, sweetheart," I heard our father mutter under his breath. "Never again."

We strolled with our hamper and blanket. The evening sky glowed in the west where the city threw up its loom of light and a few neon signs.

"Ah, goodie, just what I was looking for. Musta got lucky," Maudie piped when she unstuck a wad of second-hand chewing gum under the seat of a seesaw. She shoved it in her mouth to taste if there was any flavour left.

"I want it when you finished," I pleaded.

A half-moon tinged the silhouettes of the maples silver. On the rugby field the crackling tailpipe of a Morgan three-wheeler sports car blasted into life. Its headlights flared and when the two-seater barrelled onto the street, they illuminated a black van parked in the shadows.

Behind us, children older than Maudie and me tossed firecrackers at people's legs then darted away to avoid a cuff on the ear.

A man strolled by smoking a pipe. He carried two wafer ice creams from the kiosk, making his way to a bench where a woman sat cradling a toddler.

"Yummy, Abe, look what they got. And we got nothing, you know," Maudie lamented, eyeing the purchase.

"Maudie my sweetheart, what have you done with your pocket money?"

"Spent it on sucker-balls."

"Well now you have your answer."

My sister was silent. She received a penny a week and although she stretched that piece of copper to its limit by breaking it down into ha'penny and farthing purchases, it was beyond her capability to make her allowance last longer than four days. So for the rest of the week Maudie was broke. I received a tickey which was three-pence but as I had no choice other than share my fortune with my sister, I was also penniless half the week. For some peculiar reason I never found out, our father gave us our pocket money on pink days but never on black ones.

On the way to the car park, we strolled along a terrace overlooking Rhodes Park Lake. It is not a large stretch of water by any means, maybe three acres in extent with an island thicket in the middle where waterfowl roost. Wild birds would glide from the sky to that haven too. Iron railings fenced the lake. Outside the railings a macadam promenade encircled it. There were lampposts adjacent to the fence and the water's edge was lit at night. Beyond the railings, clusters of reeds grew on the banks and in between the clusters were clearings where Sunday afternoon fishermen sat hopefully, children sailed their boats or dangled bent pins on the end of string chancing to catch a crab, while an artist attracted the curiosity of busybodies.

Although Maudie and I climbed through the fence, there was a gate leading to a jetty where people hired rowing boats. We never had enough money for that and even if we did, we wouldn't have squandered it in so short a time.

"No ways," my sister objected. "Two sucker-balls cost only a penny and we can make 'em last a half hour if we careful."

At night the boats were not for hire as the man who sold the tickets and handed you your oars went home at five o'clock. A Manx cat Maudie nicknamed Tsotsi lived under the jetty. My sister didn't know that *tsotsi* was a Zulu word meaning gangster. Neither did I.

A scary part of the lake on the far side lay diagonally opposite the jetty. It was overgrown, with swamp conditions and willows that hung down and touched the water. We'd heard from older children about underwater reeds that entangled your legs and dragged you down. We never swam in the lake because we'd seen crabs there as big as a man's fist. We were also a little more than respectful of the whiskered black catfish that splashed in the shallows. And because we couldn't see what else lurked in the muddy water, we especially avoided the scary side, not sailing our bark and leaf boats there and not dangling for crabs either in case we caught something we didn't want.

As we strolled along the terrace above the lake we noticed a commotion going on at the water's edge. People gathered. A man called and others joined him. Women and children followed until there was a crowd on the foreshore. A dog barked.

"Aw gee, I wanna know what's going on," Maudie pestered. "Please Abe, can we go see?"

"As long as your dog stays with me." Our father slipped a leash over Hobo's head. "Please sit," he instructed, pressing Hobo's rump with his foot. "You've caused enough trouble for one night."

"Son," he addressed me, "take your sister down there. And look after her. Victor and I will carry on to the car park. Please don't be long."

"Yes Daddy."

"Let's go," my sister urged.

With me following, she sprinted down the sloping lawns and raced across the promenade. We leapt for the railings of the fence to see for ourselves what was going on. There were families all around us. We clung to the top rail and looked around, puzzled. On the jetty a man in shirtsleeves clutched a sapling branch. He raised it to strike the water. People pressed behind him and others craned forward to get a better view. The jetty creaked under their weight.

The man with the branch swiped the weapon onto the water. He struck again, darting across the T-piece of the jetty, aiming at something on the move.

"For Chrisakes!" he bawled. "I can't seem to get the damned thing."

Maudie and I perched on the railing.

"What's going on?" my sister asked a girl clinging to the rail next to us.

"A big dangerous snake," her mother intervened.

"A cobra," the father explained. "It'll bite someone if we don't kill it, probably a child."

The cobra swam out of range and the man with the stick pushed his way off the jetty and raced along the shore inside the railings. He came toward us.

"There's it," Maudie whispered, a finger pointing at a cluster of reeds. "Ooh Tadpole, hold me. I getting scareder and scareder."

Then I saw the reptile. The head and eighteen inches of its body was raised clear of the water. From the diameter of its body there was probably another four feet on the surface, so the man with the stick had nearly six feet of cobra on his hands. It swam fast and rippled the surface as it came toward us leaving a wake trailing behind. The head was dirty yellow in the moonlight and it moved agitatedly from side to side. The eyes were black. The forked tongue darted in and out of its jaws.

"Kill it!" the woman next to me shrieked.

The cobra tried coming ashore causing a wail of yells from the crowd, some people making a break away from the fence with children scooped into their arms. Maudie and I were already as high as we could get without toppling over the uppermost railing.

"That's a damn big snake," my sister blurted.

The man with the stick pranced for another attack. He swiped the branch at the water and missed. The snake hesitated then tried coming ashore again. Again the man swung the branch and again he missed. The cobra didn't falter. In near frenzy he repeatedly swiped at the water. One attempt touched the snake's body. It shot away and swam along the perimeter of the lake, moving fast.

"Set the dogs onto it!" someone behind the fence shouted.

The man with the stick cursed and trailed the cobra

along the shore.

"Head the damned thing off!" he yelled at another man who had cut himself a staff too. "Chase it back here. I'll do the sodding thing in yet."

I was so engrossed in what was going on I didn't notice a new development to the drama until I heard someone call out sharply.

"Hey! Who's that idjit swimming out there in the dark?"

I peered at the lake and sure enough, there was someone in the water. The swimmer came our way.

"Damn fool," the woman next to me commented. She was one of those who had fled earlier when the cobra swam for the shore.

"Don't come here, buffoon. Clear out, damn it!" the man with the stick threatened, waving the swimmer away with his branch.

"I got a angry snake on the loose here. You come any closer my friend and you're dead meat, I tell ya. He'll get you for sure."

The head in the water edged toward the cobra.

"Get out of it, damn it! Didn't you hear? There's a snake in the water just in front of you."

The swimmer approached, gliding without disturbing the surface. I noticed now his head was protected by a panama hat, the genuine article crafted from screw-pine fronds. The pliant brim shielding his face, hung inches above the water.

Maudie grabbed my arm.

"That looks like Old Joseph, Tadpole. Whadya think? S'gotta be Old Joseph."

She put two fingers in her mouth, blew a piercing wolf-whistle and began waltzing on the railing.

Chapter 5

I stared in disbelief. Joseph was something of a recluse. He had already seen seventy-one summers and lived with his daughter Trixie in the house one up from ours in Good Hope Street. He didn't stay in the main house. The property was on a double stand with space for a conservatory. The old man had set himself up in a garden shed annexed to the conservatory and which he called his shack. He lived frugally. There was a narrow iron bedstead covered with a coir mattress. On this were two army surplus blankets, one to lie on and the other to cover him. Even during our cold high-veld winters I never knew Joseph to use an extra blanket. It might have been a discipline he learnt half a century earlier in the 1890s when he sailed the southern oceans in square-riggers.

Next to his bed neat and aligned so it lay where his feet would land when he rose, was a tiny Indian prayer rug. Joseph was not religious, as most people would define the word. He never went to church or preached religion. However more than once when Maudie and I sneaked away to his shack in the hope of hearing a story, we found him on his knees on that prayer rug. We were too ashamed of our own godlessness to disturb him and squatted on the ground until we heard him stirring inside.

"I've put the kettle on. You children want a cup of tea with me?" he chuckled, coming out of his shack.

"You don't mind tin mugs, do you?"

"Crikey, Old Joseph, don't you know? Tin mugs are the best."

Joseph had taken one of his daughter's kitchen

chairs which served him when he wanted to sit and read. If he had a guest he sat on his bed and offered his visitor the chair. Other than that he owned a small chest of drawers and a wooden table at which he wrote or did his scrimshaw and woodworking. A lion-skin karros adorned the wall above his bed.

Joseph was not a big man and his main physical characteristic was one of lithe slenderness. Gentle and serene, he had not enjoyed an easy life nor a pampered one and had survived violent exploits. He moved quietly. Even when Amos fell out of his walnut tree and plummeted through his glass conservatory, smashing thirty-six panes, he didn't say much.

"You sure caused some damage," was his only remark.

Born in 1876 in Grahamstown, Joseph Long tramped and hitched six hundred miles to Cape Town when he was fifteen. Down at the docks, he signed on as Titch to a three-mast, full-rigged sailing ship bound for Australia. Two years later he rounded Cape Horn on his way to England, surfing the greybeards at twenty knots under sail.

"You children know what a Titch is?"

We shook our heads.

"Titch is the youngest of the rawest greenhorn recruits on board a square-rigger. I was Titch once when I dropped a bucket overboard while my ship was lying at anchor in Table Bay. I was holy-stoning the teak deck and accidentally let the bucket slip. A simple rope handled wooden bucket which drifted away in the southeaster. The bo'sun called me names and yelled that either I went overboard to retrieve ship's property or he would dock a month's wages from my pay."

"Gee, that's not fair, Old Joseph."

"I didn't think so either, Maudie. I ripped off my shirt and before the bo'sun could stop me I dived two stories over the gunwale into the Atlantic. They told me later the entire ship's crew stopped work to see what was going to happen.

"Well I reached my bucket which wasn't easy in the southeaster chop. But now I was downwind a quarter of a mile from the ship and couldn't get back. Half an hour I tried, often going down and beginning to drown. The captain ordered a longboat launched and the oarsmen picked me up. I was only fifteen but I got my wages. The able seamen didn't say anything because I was only Titch but for that first voyage they grinned at me when they passed."

"You showed 'em Old Joseph, didn't you?" Maudie chortled. "I woulda done the same."

For a quarter of a century Joseph sailed aboard square-riggers by which time he turned thirty-eight years of age. We heard tales of what it was like to run before a sixty-knot gale in a sailing ship. Men clinging to the yards eighty foot above the deck, fighting iron-hard frozen canvas, fingernails ripped out and knuckles opened to the bone. Lying out thirty feet along the spar overhanging raging seas below. The ship careering at over twenty knots, two men lashed to the wheel fighting the rudder to prevent broaches. And astern, breaking seas overtaking the ship at thirty-five knots.

Joseph nodded

"Temperatures in the southern oceans drop below zero. We chipped away ice in the rigging with marlinspikes to stop our ship from capsizing. We rigged the decks with safety lines. Seas came aboard every few minutes and flooded the main deck chest deep. Our officers drove the ship in those gales. I was in the rigging once when an overtaking sea swept our poop deck and overran the ship. For maybe half a minute all I could see were masts and sails. White water covered the rest of the ship. The helmsmen roped to the wheel were chest deep until it drained away."

Steam overtook sail and in 1914 Joseph joined the South African forces against the Kaiser and was shipped to British East Africa. He had married by this time and was the father of five children. His wife taught music in Cape Town.

One of his peculiarities Maudie and I noticed was his left-handedness. We were intrigued that he did most things with his left hand and spared his right.

Then one steamy afternoon when we were very young and before Momma was taken from us, we surprised him working in his conservatory. He was barefoot, wearing a pair of ducks and had taken off his shirt. Maudie and I sauntered into his conservatory.

"Wot you dooning, Old Joseph?" My sister sang, announcing our arrival.

With the usual quiet smile on his face he turned toward us. I was unprepared for the sight of his injured right shoulder. It wasn't just his shoulder but the surrounding collar bone, chest and back too. Deep indentations where bone and flesh had been gouged out met our unashamed gaze. The skin over these areas was not his normal tan but rouge red.

"Ooh, Old Joseph. You done gone hurt yourself. I'll quickly fetch a ban'age for you," Maudie blurted, clasping her hands to her mouth in shock.

Joseph laughed and put his shirt on. He told us the story.

"No, my little girl. This happened a long time ago. I was a dispatch rider in East Africa during the First World War and rode a charger left over from an old cavalry unit. Late one afternoon with the grass casting shadows across my track, the sun sank below the Tanganykan thorn trees.

"A lioness in full view about seventy yards up ahead, padded onto my track. My horse skidded to a standstill nearly throwing me off and refused to budge. I was alarmed because we were close to the lioness. I reckoned though that if I turned him around my charger should be able to out distance her.

"What I didn't know was that a second lioness crouched dead still in the grass alongside waited for me.

I coaxed my horse to back up but as I did so she came out of the grass. She reared up on her hind legs, clamped her jaws over my shoulder and ripped me off my charger. My horse must have been terrified for the last I saw of him he galloped away as fast as his legs would carry him.

"With the decoy lioness following, she dragged me across the track into the grass. Her purring only inches from my ear deafened me. She had me by my right shoulder. My body dragged limp between her front legs. Every now and again she tripped over me. Once she dropped me and picked me again. I nearly passed out from the pain.

"Do you know how lions dispatch their prey, children?"

We shook our heads.

"They bite their heads off. I reached with my left hand for my revolver. My holster was empty. My sidearm had dropped out when the lioness dragged me off my horse. I had a knife, a cumbersome German trench knife I didn't think would do much more than infuriate her, but I decided on a last effort before she decapitated me. With my left hand I felt for my knife in its sheath, frightened I might drop it. I let my fingers unclip the strap and I clasped the hilt. Then cautiously I brought my trench knife around to her chest. My pain was excruciating but I drove my arm upwards, stabbing her."

"And then? Old Joseph?" my sister blurted.

"To my dismay, Maudie, she carried on as if nothing had happened. I became desperate and twisted the hilt, then wrenched the blade free. Her blood spewed from a severed artery. She carried me for a few paces, opened her jaws and dropped me in the grass. She stood over me bleeding onto my face, groaned and lay down. She started licking me with her rough tongue and died, her head propped on my chest.

"And then?"

"Then I started searching for a tree to climb. The sun had already set and nighttime is very dangerous in the African bush. What I saw was the decoy lioness waiting. I figured that the dominant female was the one who'd dragged me off my horse. As long as I stayed with her, adherence to hierarchy would keep the other female at bay. I waited. Twilight came and the other animal stood and stretched herself, roared and went to drink.

"I'd lost so much blood I couldn't stand. I dragged myself through the grass to the base of a tree, pulled myself up and slowly began climbing, making only inches with each effort. It was nearly dusk and I was barely ten feet off the ground when the lioness returned. I didn't have any more strength.

"Unfortunately she found me, stood on her hind legs and swiped into the tree with her forepaw. My legs were dangling and she'd have clawed them and pulled me down. I managed to lift them out of the way just in time. I balanced precariously. Inches below she raked the bark off the bole. The tree shook. My big problem was blacking out from loss of blood. I took my time clambering higher into the branches where I fastened myself with my webbing belt. Then I did pass out and kept doing so the whole night.

"The lioness kept vigil, repeatedly standing on her hind legs to torment me. By morning I had no strength left. But my charger saved my life. He returned to base riderless of course and at sunrise my unit sent out scouts. They came across signs of the scuffle where the lioness dragged me off my mount. Half an hour later they cut me down. I spent three months recovering in a military hospital. It took me a year to regain the use of my arm, but it was never the same again. My colleagues had the lioness I killed, skinned and made into a kaross by the local tribes-people. At the end of the campaign I brought my kaross and German trench knife home to South Africa."

"So you won the horrible lion," applauded Maudie

who was only three at the time.

However Joseph came back to great sadness. Joseph the adventurer, the youth who walked six hundred miles to Cape Town, who sailed the roaring forties fighting gales and ice, who fought in a world war, and who saved himself from being eaten by two lionesses, came home to a wife wasting from cancer.

"It broke my father," Trixie told us. "He watched my mother suffer a slow, painful death."

After that Joseph made his living on a trawler operating out of Cape Town. The marketing of fish put food on the table, paid for his children's education and settled the mortgage. He was forty two when the Great War ended.

He fished the Cape waters from 1919 until just after the Second World War when he turned seventy. Then he retired and came to Johannesburg to live with his daughter next door to us in Kensington.

Chapter 6

"You be careful, Old Joseph," Maudie shrieked, rocking her feet on the railing. "There's a damn big snake here. Don't let it getcha. I 'spect you gonna kill it with your lion knife?"

"Damned fool," the woman next to us muttered.

"Clear off nincompoop," yelled the man with the stick.

Someone threw a stone at the cobra.

With his wide brimmed panama covering his head, Joseph swam toward us. The crowd's attention was now divided between him and the snake. People began speculating what the cobra would do when it realized it was not alone in the water.

Joseph circled the snake, swimming with no perceptible movement. He looked like a self-propelled hat floating on the surface. He came inshore putting himself between the man with the stick and the reptile.

"Get out the way, you idjut."

"Yah, whatya think you doing?"

"You gonna get bitten mister."

The protests didn't stop.

Everyone at the fence offered advice, some of it hysterical, on how to kill the cobra but mostly the advice was to get out of the water. The old man swam away from them and closed with the snake. I held my breath. The cobra faced him inching forwards, its raised head investigating the brim of his panama.

"S'gonna get on his head," Maudie blurted.

She drew in her breath. As Joseph advanced so the cobra retreated. Then it turned away and began swimming ahead of him away from the crowd.

"What an arse," I heard a man curse. "Now we'll hafta start all over again and kill it round the other side."

Joseph coaxed the cobra to the middle of the lake and then manoeuvred the creature toward a deserted stretch of shore.

"He's gonna let it go," Maudie pointed out.

When the crowd realized what was happening, people began protesting.

"Dangerous thing, that," the man with the stick warned. "Bad tempered and vicious. It'll come back an' bite us if we don't kill it."

He led the group at a trot along the shore to be ready for the cobra. Two big dogs followed, barking and frolicking in and out of the water.

"Hey, quit it," my sister abruptly blurted, twisting around on the railing.

"What's the problem, Sis?"

"A man behind me... put his hand on my neck."

I glanced behind us. Many people crowded around.

"Now he's disappeared," Maudie said.

Joseph was occupied coaxing the cobra to a place of refuge and didn't notice the crowd racing across the lawns. When he had the reptile in shallow water, it was too late. The dogs bounded into the water, baying excitedly. One made a feint at the cobra. The snake struck with lightning speed, biting the dog in the shoulder. Then its upper body and head were up again ready for a second strike. The man with the stick rushed in and lunged with his branch half catching the snake's tail. The cobra turned and struck at Joseph.

As the reptile turned on him, the old man dipped the brim of his panama into the water. The fangs struck the crown. Then the cobra backed off to within range of the man with the stick. He swiped, catching the snake across its back. The cobra shot past Joseph, heading for the middle of the lake.

Patiently the old mariner followed. We watched

from the railings. This time he headed the cobra toward the opposite shore where the willows overhung the water. This was the overgrown, swampy section of shore, the spongy marsh inaccessible to the crowd unless it wanted to flounder in and out of knee-deep ooze.

"Confound him," the man with the stick cursed. "Just what's that interfering old fool think he's doing?" He jabbed the ground with his branch.

"Damn thing's gone for good. We'll never get it now."

He arced his stick over the water where it fell with a plop. He tramped away as the crowd began dispersing and the dogs bounded after their owners. One was limping. He would be dead within the hour.

"Old Joseph gave 'em the slip," Maudie giggled. "P'raps we better go and say hello."

"Race you there," I challenged and hared off to where he'd guided the cobra toward the deserted shore.

Maudie got left behind in the dark.

I sprinted like a maniac and found Joseph's old warpainted Harley Davidson and sidecar parked under the willows. I stroked the metal. It was a unique machine. Possibly because he himself was a man of serenity, he had stuffed his silencer with fifteen of his daughter's pot scourers. Trixie complained for six months about that. Every time she bought new pot scourers, Joseph pushed them up his exhaust pipe. The result was that the Harley's motor ran so silently it was difficult to hear when it was idling.

My sister arrived at a gallop and breathless.

"That man followed me," she complained, scanning the bank behind us.

I peered into the dark but saw nothing.

"But now he's gone again, like he made himself invisible."

Joseph waded waist-deep through algae. I saw him through the willows.

"Hullo, Old Joseph. You did a good job," Maudie bellowed.

"Yes," he called, chuckling. "The cobra's gone now. Silly of them to want to destroy one of God's creatures just because it exists. Don't you think?"

"Yah, I s'pose so," Maudie agreed.

Just then, Joseph stumbled and overbalanced. He went down and disappeared under the water. His panama floated off. When he surfaced spluttering, he grasped what looked like a deflated soccer ball in his hands.

In the moment before he dropped it in repulsion, I had the impression it resembled a child's head.

"What was that, that Old Joseph found?" Maudie asked.

I shivered which didn't help my stutter.

"Dunno, Maudie. Maybe just an old soccer ball. Don't pester Joseph."

The old man retrieved his panama and waded out of the water. He said nothing about his find.

"I – think it best – if you children – get on home now."

I grabbed Maudie's arm and we bolted back to the Chev.

"Where on earth have you been all this time?" our father demanded.

"There was a snake in the water, Daddy."

In our suburb, spread among the koppies, it was not unusual for snakes to come into the gardens. Grass snakes and mole snakes weren't poisonous and never bothered anyone. I didn't want him to know it was a cobra in case he made the park out of bounds to us. Maudie and I were frightened of the big snakes like puff-adders, ringhals, mambas and cobras, but we knew that if we kept out of their way, they would keep out of ours.

"Yah, Abe," Maudie boasted. "A 'normous, longly, wiggly-waggly snaky. Bigger'n the biggest one you ever seen."

"How long?" he asked suspiciously.

She drew in her breath and stretched her arms, pointing in opposite directions with her index fingers. She looked first at one arm then at the other to see if her estimate was long enough which I knew it wasn't.

"So long, I reckon."

I pinched her on her shoulder.

"Old Joseph saved it, Abe," she beamed. "He did, he really did. He went swimming with the snake. Tadpole and me saw him."

Our father already disbelieved her estimate and her further claim convinced him that she was making it up.

"You children have big imaginations," he muttered.

Chapter 7

With Frog and me and Maudie on the back seat there was no room for Hobo. The dog lay between our feet on the back floor of the Chev with Maudie's feet planted on its stomach.

"I been thinking," she sighed. "The Catherine wheels were best."

"Hobo liked the rockets," I pointed out.

"Yah, the rockets were amazing."

"Son, I trust you've done your homework," our father enquired. He was speaking to me. Frog always did his homework. He completed it the day it was allocated. Maudie didn't get any homework over the weekend.

"Yes, Daddy," I drawled. "S'nearly done."

"How much?"

"Maybe half."

He sighed. "First thing tomorrow, please complete the rest."

"Louis and Graham're coming tomorrow," Maudie reminded him.

"He can finish it before they come."

"You better finish it fast," she urged, nudging me in the ribs.

When we turned into our driveway in Good Hope Street, Maudie and I leapt out. It was our job to open the gates. Years before we lost the battle with Frog about whose job it was. I leapt first and landed with my feet in a mound of horse manure left by the hawker's horse earlier in the afternoon.

"Yuck," Maudie grimaced, seeing the look on my face. She peered past the running board before alighting.

"That horse again. Now Abe's gonna tell me I hafta fetch the shovel and spread it on the garden. Phooey."

She slammed the door and giggled at me. We opened the gates and sprang onto the running boards for the short ride up the drive.

I didn't go into the house with the others but sauntered down the drive. There were gaps in the corrugated iron fence. Trixie's property was higher than ours and the ground had burst the fence open in places. Moses crouched in his yard. He had lit a cooking fire next to the fence and scooped his maize porridge from a three-legged pot. He dipped the hard pap into a goat meat stew and chewed on it leisurely.

"Siyakubona, Moses." I greeted.

"I see you," he responded.

I hesitated at the garage and picked up a stone. Then I sneaked past the fig tree, squinting through the moonlight at the compost heap. Yeowing I charged, letting fly with my stone. It was my private war on the grey rats that burrowed into the compost. So far I hadn't managed a direct hit on the rodents although I was planning to repair Graham's catapult.

We sat down in the kitchen to eat. The Queen Mary had gone out. It was father's name for our slow combustion coal-stove, our only means of heating bath water. Nothing was insulated. The steel feeder tank stood in a corner. It was painted grey and supplied only one bath.

"Bucket bath tonight, Tadpole," Maudie groaned. "Water's cold. You gonna die of the friz."

"I aren't as dirty as you, Sis. You gonna double die."

Our father kept an old jam tin near the stove with a mixture of candle wax and paraffin. I dipped my finger in the lotion and smeared my chapped lips.

Saturday night fare was soft-boiled eggs with bread and butter. We'd just sat down when someone tripped over the washboard on the back veranda. Babs, our father's half sister fell in through the screen door. She was well oiled. I don't think Maudie noticed. Babs wore a man's sports jacket, trousers, open necked shirt and velskoens, raw leather bush shoes. She took a puff on the stub of her cigarette, leant back through the door and flicked the butt across the back veranda into the yard.

Babs was thirty. When she left high school she attended an agricultural college for two years. So she knew how to plough a field and bale hay. Somewhere along the line she also learned to fly bi-planes.

In 1939 when war broke out, Babs volunteered for duty and spent five years in North Africa opposing Rommel. Some time after she returned, the local evening newspaper The Star ran a competition with a prize of ten pounds. The competition could only be entered by ex-service men and women because the paper wanted a two thousand word essay on a personal experience encountered up north or in Europe during the war years.

Babs had spent the war in the desert. She once saved a supply convoy from annihilation by German armoured cars by hiding the convoy in a shallow depression while the enemy reconnoitred within a thousand yards of her position. So she wrote about that. She won the competition but was embarrassed because the whole of Johannesburg would see what she had written and might think she was bragging. The Star contacted her for biographical details they intended printing as an introduction to her essay. This appalled her. So she sent a facetious letter to the editor, thinking it would annoy him into selecting another winner.

Dear Sir, she wrote, *I was found under a cabbage on the morning of 1st April 1913. This was one of the contributing factors to The Great War breaking out the following year. At the age of six I was forcibly escorted to lower grade school. There I pulled faces at the teachers for five years before they discovered it was not my natural appearance. They never did discover what was my natural appearance.*

My father came from Alexandria in the Cape near Grahamstown. Anyway it was near there when he was a boy. My mother came from the 1820 Settlers. So I may have the dubious honour of ancestors who fought on both sides of the Anglo Boer War simultaneously. I wouldn't know as unfortunately they are all dead. What do you expect if they were so stupid? The only relic left to me is an old family bible weighing forty pounds and dated 1820. I read it and pray for forgiveness during bad thunderstorms and when letters from The Star arrive in the post.

By sending a petition to the government I managed to gain entrance to a farm school. I was the only woman there. For three years I used to walk through the maize fields, about forty yards behind the other students and the lecturer and thus out of earshot, throwing clods of earth at the students up front, who could hear the lecturer.

I nearly broke my thumbs milking cows at three a.m. in the morning. I don't know why they have to wake them up so early. I also sheared sheep with ordinary little clippers exactly the same as for trimming the edges of lawns. I'm now confused as to whether gardeners trim their lawns with sheep shears or whether farmers shear their sheep with lawn clippers. Perhaps you can tell me? I swear as long as I live I'll never shear another sheep again. My right hand is still deformed from shearing sheep. I graded fleeces, judged cattle, ploughed, harvested, baled hay, made silage, pruned fruit trees, got kicked by an ox and studied forestry.

I was rescued from my bewilderment by my husband. He wasn't my husband then and he isn't my husband now. That was an error I shan't be making again. He was at varsity doing a B. A. I don't have to tell you what that stands for. He's cleverer than me, that's why he didn't write an essay for the local rag. I once turned the garden hose on him through the bedroom window while he was still in bed.

I have been in and out of work since 1931. Once when I was out and not in I was walking down Commissioner Street looking for a job, when a tramp who wasn't looking for a job sidled up to me and said please lady can't you spare a shilling, you don't know what it's like to be in my position. Well my position was not much better than his position and I was down to my last shilling myself. So you work it out for yourself what I told him to go and do with his position.

What else do you want to know? I've done a lot of flying. In fact, if I had to talk about flying I'd have to send this letter to you in instalments. For instance, there was this nervous captain of a transport that used to fly in to Cairo. He was so nervous he would never allow his co-pilot to have any landings or takeoffs, until he relented one day and agreed to let his co-pilot fly the transport off the ground. But the captain was so nervous he couldn't keep his hand off the undercarriage lever and accidentally retracted the wheels while the plane was still on the ground doing ninety miles an hour. They shot right through the fence at the end of the runway giving the co-pilot a lot of experience.

Then there was the time coming in to Cairo one night in an Anson. The pilot set the altimeter for the runway he normally used. But the control tower told us to use another runway and he didn't check what high ground there was on this approach. The runway lights were still a mile away when they abruptly went out. The chap flying the Anson thought they'd been switched off on purpose. But the lights disappeared because there were sand dunes between us and the runway and we were lower than them. We accidentally landed on one and came to a stop so quickly we flipped tail over nose and I broke my front teeth. The worst however, was walking home through the desert in the middle of the freezing night.

I still do a bit of flying around Johannesburg, parachute jumping mainly. We spend eleven months of the year fixing up the old Moth and one month waiting for ideal jumping conditions. By then the plane's falling apart and we have to start fixing it up again.

I entered your essay competition to annoy your critic Major von Biljon. Tell me, does he look like his name sounds?

If I've left anything out I'll send you another letter.
Love and kisses,
(Signed) Babs Thomas.

To Babs' dismay, The Star published her letter in full together with her essay and sent her the ten pounds. She was blotto for weeks.

Her army training had to do with vehicle maintenance. Besides flying and I suppose how to milk cows, that's all Babs knew. So when she came back to civilian life she got a job with a garage driving the breakdown lorry, filling out job cards and helping in the workshop. I don't think the mechanics ever made a pass at Babs.

"Come in and join us," our father invited. "Maudie sweetheart, set a place for Babs please."

Our half aunt skidded a kitchen chair around, sat on it the wrong way and leaned on the backrest. Hobo sidled over to have her ears scratched. Maudie played some sort of game with her spoon, wiping yolk across her cheek into her hairline.

"You got egg everywhere except in your mouth," Babs teased.

"That's cos when I eat, my whole face enjoys my food."

Our aunt laughed.

"Missus Probert bitched to me that her cat disappeared."

"All the cats in our street're disappearing," I said.

"Good thing we don't own a cat," Maudie

commented, getting more egg in her hair.

"Missus Probert says it's been going on for weeks. Everyone's talking about it. The cats just disappear."

"The dustmen," I interjected, "they steal and eat 'em."

Frog pulled a face like he wanted to throw up. He banged his spoon down and let his egg get cold while he sat watching me, counting to ten. When he got to about a hundred he quizzed, "What was going on down at the lake this evening?"

"Nothing," I shrugged, remembering what Joseph might have found. "Just a snake in the water, that's all."

"Did they kill it?"

"Nah."

"Old Joseph swam and saved it," Maudie beamed. "He shooed it from the men trying to kill it so it could escape onto the koppies."

Frog didn't believe her. He pursed his lips and buttered another slice of bread.

"You've got grass in your hair," Babs told me.

"That's cos Frog feinted him," Maudie explained, referring to a punch he had landed in my stomach when no one was looking.

"That's rubbish. He thought it was funny to fall on the ground. I didn't drop him,"

Maudie and I never won an argument with Frog.

"When you taking us flying, Babs?" Maudie begged.

"One day, I suppose. But not for a couple of months. We're preparing a charity air show in December. If your father approves, maybe then."

"And Amos," Maudie reminded her. "Tadpole, me and Amos."

After supper, my sister and I were the first to use the bathroom.

"Yikes, come help quick, there's a baboon spider in the bath," she yowled.

"Well just poke him with your toothbrush, Sis."

When she bent down to prod the tarantula, it

jumped onto her head.

"Eeyowee... Get it off me, quick, before it's too late..."

I flicked the hairy spider away.

"S'okay Maudie, tee-hee, he scuttled under the bath."

"S'not funny. I was just picking him up friendly like. He didn't hafta jump on my head. Made me wet my pants."

When we were in bed with the light off, Maudie called out, "G'night everybody. G'night Abe, g'night Tadpole, g'night Babs. Not you Frog."

I lay in the dark pondering the newspaper report I'd read before I came to bed. The latch on the gate squealed. Sampson let himself in. He strolled up the drive wheeling his bicycle and crooning in Zulu. He would be wearing his tartan golfing cap that was so dear to him. And his knobkerrie would be tied to the crossbar of his bike.

Street noises subsided and neighbourhood dogs settled down. Over the back of the house a half-moon sank in the west. The roof cooled after the hot November day. Corrugated iron sheets contracted in starts and fits, emitting metallic rasps. Floorboards in the passage creaked and groaned.

Nobody else had noticed what I'd seen.

In the living room The Star lay discarded. I'd flipped the pages to Curly Wee. But before I'd reached the cartoon my eyes had been drawn to a headline.

"Child Missing. Parents Frantic. Seven-year-old David Nguni from Sophiatown went missing yesterday afternoon. Nobody has seen him since. Anyone knowing of David's whereabouts should telephone their nearest police station."

Someone walked over my grave. On Friday night my sister dreamt of a child being mutilated by an

African sorcerer. She'd said his name was Davy and told me where the atrocity took place.

Tadpole, I'm getting real scared. I seen the sorcerer cut him up bad. Davy's no more. The drain. The stormwater drain by the park.

Then she'd slept and lost all recollection of her nightmare.

Only I knew of David Nguni's whereabouts.

Chapter 8

Sunday morning found the sleepy suburb of Kensington reluctant to rise. The old houses, weathered and mended, worn and repaired, stood silent in the eastern sun. In the tiny gardens flowers turned their heads toward the warmth. Crickets crept away to hide under flowerpots and dried leaves. Earthworms burrowed down to where the soil remained moist and cool during the sunlit hours. Geckos appeared from cracks in brickwork and crevices in stone foundations and garden walls.

There were houses and gardens where the occupants had little or no pride. Usually there wasn't a motorcar standing outside in the street or in the driveway. Sometimes it was because the father drank. Sometimes because there was no father and the mother became the breadwinner, bringing home her meagre earnings to a house and household that demanded more attention than she could provide. Working and commuting and cooking and sewing and supervising and budgeting, left no time to paint the roof, seal the woodwork, weed the garden, mow the lawn, fix the fence or trim an overgrown hedge.

Sometimes it was because the wife had run off with a man of more promise leaving the man with less promise to struggle on in despair, raising his children with no maternal love. Those houses always needed more doing to them than their neighbours' and their neighbours looked over the dividing fences begrudgingly, wishing that some new family would move in next door.

"C'mon Hobo. Spelling's easy-peezy. You can easy

get ten out of ten like me. Just try again, my angel."

I stuck my head out of my blankets.

"What're you teaching your dog now?"

"Reading and writing. I think it's gonna take her a bit of time."

"We better get going, Sis. We hafta get up for Sunday school. And we already late."

Religion in our household was a funny thing. We'd been christened and went to weddings and funerals often enough to be familiar with the inside of a church. On forms requiring details, we professed to be Christians. But the family never went to church. Maudie and I were the only members of our household required to attend although it was only Sunday school. We each had a penny for the poor.

We dressed and trotted down the garden path. I swung the front gate open just as a rickshaw arrived. The spider-wheeled vehicle had whitewall tyres coloured with whitewash. The rims and hubs were painted silver to match the spokes festooned with red ribbon. The woodwork was painted yellow and the upholstery was shining black leather. The shafts were decorated with African beadwork and the Zulu man holding them wore tribal dress.

An immaculately attired African man lounged in the rickshaw. Dressed in a double-breasted blue suit and grey homburg, he beamed at Maudie and me. A suitcase big enough to fit a child inside lay at his feet. Sampson said he was a travelling salesman and kept samples inside his case. Good Hope Street is steep and the barefoot Zulu holding the shafts was puffing by the time he set them down outside our driveway.

The passenger stepped down from the rickshaw and retrieved his case. His face seemed to be the light from which all happiness flowed. I had never seen Mr Sunshine gloomy. He was eternally pleased with the world, with himself and with those around him. I don't know which came first, his cognomen or his temperament. He was especially pleased to speak to children but I didn't think anything of it at the time.

"Morning Mister Sunshine," Maudie piped.

"Lordy... Lordy... Lordy... it's the Freyer children on their way to church now. How's Miss Babs and everybody else?"

"They're fine, Mister Sunshine."

He hefted his suitcase and hesitated wanting to say something more but changed his mind. "Well... Lordy... Lordy, I have some business with Sampson. Is he inside?"

"Sure Mister Sunshine. Semp-Sonne's peeling vegetables for Sunday lunch."

He waved us off and with a grin and watched us skip down the sidewalk. When we turned the corner into Roberts Avenue, he was still gazing after us.

"What business do you think Mister Sunshine has with Semp-Sonne?" Maudie asked me. "He also goes next door to Moses, I been noticing, but never Amos's mama."

I kicked a brown acorn from the previous summer.

"Not sure, Sis. He and Sampson go into Sampson's room and close the door. I suppose they talk about business things. Like Sampson said, Mister Sunshine's a travelling salesman."

"What about that suitcase of his? Whadya think he got in that big case?"

I shrugged.

"We better keep an eye on him, Tadpole. I wanna see what he got inside."

We danced down the pavement. "You know, something I been wondering about Hobo."

"What about your dog?"

"If she's Christian like us? I mean, we don't know where Hobo came from before the SPCA found her. It would be funnier than anything if Hobo's a Jewish dog in a Christian family."

"Yah, Maudie, that would be funny wouldn't it?"

Sunday school was the usual, "Joy... joy... joy, my heart is bubbling over," which we shrieked at the tops of our voices. We handed over our pennies for the poor.

On the way home Maudie became thoughtful. "You know the man that touched my neck last night? What you think he was doing?"

"What man?"

"Don't you remember, silly? When the snake bit the dog, I felt a hand on my neck. I told you about it..."

"Yah, I remember now, Maudie."

"When I turned round he was gone, like he made himself invisible... But I smelled him."

"You smelt him, Sis? What did he smell of?"

"Dirty things, old tobacco, sacks and bags, maybe old rope... you know, those sort of things."

"How about snuff?"

"Yah, maybe something like that. Snuff... sweaty old clothes. He followed me around the lake."

"Followed you? Oh come on Maudie, you imagining this?"

"Nuh, not me. Remember, I told you last night at Old Joseph's Harley Davidson."

"Yah, I forgot, Sis."

"He ran funnier than a rubber man. Like a giraffe."

"A giraffe? You mean his neck went backwards and forwards when he ran?"

Maudie nodded. "He was gonna catch me but I ran like anything and managed to get away. You left me behind, Tadpole. You didn't wait for me. When Old Joseph came out the water, he disappeared like he made himself invisible."

"I wouldn't worry so much, Sis. You just imagining things."

We arrived home to find Sampson wielding a broomstick up the fig tree. Underneath clutching his carpenter's plane our father gesticulated and gave instructions.

"Can't you get her down?"

Sampson clicked his tongue and shook his head. He let go his broomstick and nearly toppled out of the tree. I heard a tittering from both sides of the yard. Amos hung onto the fence on one side and Moses peered over the corrugated iron sheets on the other.

The cause of the consternation was Maudie's dog. She wasn't in the fig tree but on the roof of the house standing proudly on the apex, clutching an abused tennis ball in her mouth.

"What a clever little angel," my sister encouraged.

Hobo wagged her stump of a tail.

"She'll fall off and break her neck if someone doesn't get her down," our father protested.

"Come my angel," Maudie cooed. "Bring your mama her ball."

Hobo was quite happy to come down now. She slid down the pitch onto the back veranda roof. The fig tree's branches overhung the veranda and this is how she got up in the first place. However she didn't go back the same way. Judging her distance she leapt the gap onto the garage roof. Then she hobbled with two feet in the gutter and two on the pitched slope until she reached the back wall dividing our property from the house behind. She had a good look into our neighbour's yard before springing onto the dividing wall and then onto the compost heap. Her little tail wagged furiously when she presented the ball to Maudie.

"Sweetheart, did you teach her to do that?" our father asked.

Maudie rolled her eyes at him and shrugged.

"Just one of her tricks, Abe."

"She'll break her neck one day," he warned, shaking the plane at her. "In any case, what will the neighbours think?"

Sampson clambered down the tree, giving a

disgruntled click of his tongue. I hurried to get my homework done before the twins arrived. Maudie changed into her fawn cords and whistled for Hobo. She arranged her rag doll, Little Meagan and a one armed pink monkey, Jackson on the tiny square of lawn. She made Hobo sit with the soft toys and gave the three of them a lesson in hygiene.

"Now don't fuss so much."

Maudie cleaned her dog's teeth with a broken toothbrush, soap powder and the garden hose. Hobo pulled all kinds of faces, foam pouring out of both sides of her mouth.

By the time I got halfway through my comprehension, Hobo was studying grooming. She sat obediently as a lady bulldog should, even if she was a mongrel.

Maudie cradled one of Hobo's front paws in her lap while clutching a bottle of Trixie's nail varnish and painting her dog's toenails bright red. Hobo eyed the work appreciatively.

I struggled with my last couple of sums while Maudie lifted Hobo into a rickety old doll's pram we'd found on the koppies. It only had three wheels. Hobo wore a baby's nappy around her hindquarters and one of my sister's vests around her body. She reclined in the pram with her feet sticking over the sides. My sister pushed her around and around the house, crooning lullabies.

An Alsatian that lived up the hill stood staring in through our front gate. Hobo could just see over the top of the pram. She had an aversion for large male dogs and when she caught sight of Bliksem she bounded out of the pram sending Maudie flying. Hobo rocketed through our father's roses, shot through a hole in the fence and appeared on the pavement, painted nails, nappy, vest, fragrant breath and all.

The Alsatian looked bemused at this apparition, but not for long. With Colgate-white teeth bared, Hobo charged. Bliksem jerked his throat out of the way, leaned back from the attack and wheeled away from the white bitch. Then he was gone, tail between his legs bolting up the street with Hobo galloping after him. She saw him off as far as Trixie's top boundary fence and came trotting back, the nappy slipping down her legs.

Chapter 9

Ever since Momma left us, Mrs Probert across the street took it upon her shoulders to see that we didn't become guttersnipes.

"I want to see you brought up and not dragged up."

"Interfering nag," our father muttered once she was gone. "I ought to make her a stable door."

Mrs Probert didn't approve of us playing with Amos because he was black.

"Mark my words Mr Freyer, that child's a bad influence on your two. They get their dreadful ways from him."

Her other aversion was to foreigners although this included everybody she didn't personally know. She had an inherent suspicion of anyone who wasn't Caucasian, English speaking, Church of England, Victorian breeding and working class, but somehow, Mrs Probert always said *middle*.

I glanced up to see her waddling across the street. When she walked she tottered from side to side. Women's shoes would no longer fit her and she had taken to wearing men's velskoens. However they wouldn't fit either so she cut holes in the uppers for her big toes to stick out. When Maudie saw her she packed her things and carted them around to the backyard.

Babs was unlucky enough to emerge onto the front veranda when Mrs Probert started up the stairs.

"Ah, bring me the bench, won't you, Babs? I'd like a cup of tea with you."

Our half aunt dutifully fetched the garden bench from the lawn. Mrs Probert didn't fit into our veranda chairs.

"I need to talk to you, Babs."

Babs strengthened her tea with a tot of brandy.

"As you know, my daughter Ruth's getting married next week. You work for a garage. Do you think you could get a bridal limousine for Ruth, you know, something nice?"

"Well I don't know, Missus Probert."

"Now don't beat about the bush, girl. I want something really fancy for my daughter."

"How about a Rolls Royce?"

Mrs Probert wasn't impressed.

"Even a De Soto costs money you know."

"Don't go off on a tandem now. Can you get me a limo or can't you?"

"Perhaps I can. Maybe I can get hold of a '46 Chrysler for you. I'll have to see if the car's free next Saturday. But it'll cost you a few quid, Missus Probert."

"Splendid. When will you let me know?"

Babs scratched her head. "Probably tomorrow evening after work."

"How much will it cost?"

"Five pounds, Missus Probert. Let me have the fiver and I'll arrange your limo."

"My limo... ah yes, I'll have the cash for you tomorrow evening. My limo..."

Maudie made the mistake of coming down the drive.

"Oh Maudie dear," Mrs Probert cooed. "Come sit with us awhile."

My sister dragged her feet up the veranda stairs and plopped on the parapet, swinging her legs.

"Maudie, where's your pretty Sunday dress I made you? Those old corduroys are ready for the next jumble sale."

"They the only trousers I got, Missus Probert. A dress's no good in the fig tree." My sister wiped her nose on her wrist.

Mrs Probert shook her head disapprovingly. "I've been thinking about that story you children told me about the Chinaman. And quite frankly I don't believe it."

"What Chinaman, Missus Probert?"

"The one who broke into that maternity home and killed those poor babies. It's an imposterous story."

My sister was flummoxed. "Maternity home? We said a germ got in the maternity home and killed the babies. We read it in the Star."

"Germ? Are you sure? I could have sworn you told me it was a German." Mrs Probert banged her teacup into her saucer. "Chinamen or Germans, they're all foreigners..."

I finished my homework and joined Maudie on the parapet.

"I hope you're wearing clean underpants, young man?" Mrs Probert pried. "As sure as God made little apples if you're not wearing clean underpants you'll be knocked down by a car and taken to hospital. Then what will the nurses think when they see your dirty underpants, young man?"

I didn't know the answer to that as I was wondering what the nurses would think when they found out I wasn't wearing any underpants at all.

"And just look at your hair. Such a mess. Did you comb it before you said your prayers last night?"

She'd got me on two offences. As it was impossible to look at my hair, I stared at my toes. I knew she was worried about the house falling down during the night. Then when the neighbours came to rescue me they'd notice I hadn't combed my hair. I had no idea what they would say about the omission.

"Cleanliness is next to Godliness," Mrs Probert droned but was interrupted by a hullabaloo coming down the street.

"Graham and Louis." Maudie whooped.

"Humph," Mrs Probert snorted. She had no time for our cousins, Uncle Stanley and Aunt Phoenie's twelve-year-old sons who boarded at Kiewietjie, a boys' hostel serving local schools. Stanley's widow farmed a hundred miles away and the twins went home to her during school holidays.

The housemaster ran the hostel like a detention class. His name was de Beer so the boys nicknamed him The Bear. He took medication for a nervous affliction. Graham and Louis were constantly on the point of being expelled. Every time they got up to mischief Mr de Beer complained to our father because he was the closest relative.

The twins were disparate. Their only similarity was that they both did poorly at school. Graham was the cleverer of the two. He was younger than Louis by fifteen minutes. Graham presented as the model of goodness. Tall, fair-haired, neatly groomed, baby-faced and manicured, knowledgeable in matters that a ringleader should be and charming to adults; when trouble was headed the twins' way, Graham sensed it before Louis did.

Louis, the elder brother by a quarter of an hour, was short, black-haired, tousled, rough in appearance, often scowling and with dirt under his fingernails. The dull one always taken in by his younger brother's cunning he still achieved better exam marks than Graham who convinced Louis to do not just his own homework but his lazy twin's as well.

"Wow, look everybody, they racing. Zoom-zoom. Last one's gonna be a squashed tomato, I bet you."

Maudie danced up and down the parapet, nearly falling off the veranda.

From the sound of the twins' yelling, they were coming down the hill fast. Graham led. He shot past our house whizzing down the tarmac on his roller skates.

A second later Louis came pelting down on his decrepit bicycle. He hurtled down the hill whooping like a Red Indian. Head and shoulders thrust forward, pedalling furiously. He had a spare bicycle tyre dangling from the handlebar.

"Come on Louis, faster." Maudie yelled.

As he flew past in a blur the chain derailed from the sprocket. In the ensuing lurch his foot hooked in the spare tyre yanking the handlebars around. Rider and machine parted. I screwed up my eyes. Louis became airborne. Behind him the bike cart-wheeled and slewed into the gutter, the rear wheel spinning crazily.

He hit the tarmac face first, legs and arms spread-eagled.

"Total wipe out," Maudie yowled. "Better go help him, fast."

We raced down the stairs. Our cousin hunched over his knees in the gutter, his face bloodied, his elbows raw, his shirt shredded and blackened.

"Gosh Louis, you came off second best again."

"Hell's bells, why me?"

Maudie put a hand on his head. "You hurt yourself real bad this time. Come with me, Louis. I'll fix you up proper."

"Why me always? For crying in a bucket s'always me, never Graham."

Maudie led him to our house and doctored his wounds with iodine. I picked up the bike and half-carried half-wheeled it up the drive to the garage. It needed fixing.

Mrs Probert needed to relieve herself, a logistical problem for her because our privy was in the backyard. Graham squeezed past the Chev parked under the side veranda and belched, a drawn out eructation for the benefit of Mrs Probert. She turned to see who had made the voidance. When she caught sight of Graham she turned her back on him so missed hearing his mutter.

"Jeez, I gotta go to the bog before I devastate the whole world." He bolted for the backyard leaving me dragging Louis's bike.

Mrs Probert heaved herself up. Her laborious journey through the house onto the back veranda down the kitchen stairs and across the backyard, brought her to our outhouse after Graham had already got there. She found the door open as he was in too much of a hurry to close it. Because of the sunlight and her myopia, she didn't make him out sitting there.

Mrs Probert, too broad to do an about turn inside the confines of our privy, turned around, hitched up her dress, dropped her bloomers and reversed in.

Graham was shocked. He didn't realize his arch enemy was unaware of his presence. He thought she was reciprocating in kind for his belch. After years of provocation, she had risen to his challenge and was employing a diabolical tactic to obliterate him once and for all with her weight. When her shadow fell across the doorway, he looked up in horror to see her monumental bottom descending on him.

This was the end of his short twelve years on earth. There was no escape. For all his bravado, this woman was meeting fire with fire. She had seen through him and was employing an unconventional method to deal with him once and for all.

Desperate he leaned back, brought his knees to his chest and lifted his feet to receive her two fleshy cheeks. As she lowered herself he put all his strength into his legs and launched her out the door.

She staggered forward, bemused. He leapt up clutching his trousers, squeezed past her and scrambled over the back wall into our neighbour's yard. He hid there until she went home and for weeks afterwards avoided her, acutely aware of the weapon she was prepared to use against him. She never said anything to Babs or our father and Graham assumed it was because she didn't want the other adults to know about her dastardly tactics.

Louis looking the worse for wear, limped down the back stairs.

"You know the chain comes off," he complained. "Why didn't you give me a chance to tighten it first?"

"Owhatanassiam," Graham retorted.

"Say again?"

"Owhatanassiam, chum. 'Tis a magic word. Say it after me...."

"O-what-an-ass-I-am. Damn it Graham. S'not funny. Look at me."

"You see, even you admit it," Graham guffawed. He snatched up a stone and flung it at the compost heap.

Louis scowled and upended his bicycle. He fetched spanners from the garage and unbolted the rear wheel. The tyre was down to canvas and the new tyre he'd brought wasn't exactly new. With his catapult sticking out of his pocket he went to work.

"Mind you don't pinch the tube," Graham warned, keeping an eye on the compost heap for any unwary rat.

Louis grunted and finally got the new tyre to fit. As Graham had ruined his bicycle pump by converting it into a flame-thrower, Louis fetched our father's tyre pump and inflated both tyres as hard as rocks.

"You'll shake your nuts off like that," Graham scoffed.

Amos climbed through the fence with his wire motorcar, making engine and gear-change noises. Maudie was playing with Hobo who was now being a horse having forfeited nappy and vest but still sporting painted toenails and a brilliant smile. Amos sat on the back veranda steps to watch as Maudie groomed her dog in dressage. She'd knotted together a string bridle and a wire bit Hobo kept trying to spit out.

"Come on my angel, I gotta teach you properly."

The jump was a stick laid across two upended bricks. Maudie led Hobo into the jump at a trot.

"Now keep your head high and tuck your feet in. Yah, that's right. Good work."

She wheeled Hobo around at the end of the rein and led her from the opposite end. She repeated this, jumping her dog to and fro, scolding poor Hobo if she knocked the jump over and cooing with delight when she cleared without a fault.

Where my sister learnt about riding horses I don't know. The only horses I'd ever seen were cart horses delivering green groceries, milk or firewood. Maudie always knew about things before I did.

Sampson came onto the back veranda.

"Lunch everybody. You wash first."

Other children had mothers to tell them what to do. We had Sampson.

Chapter 10

A magnificent Sunday afternoon. Thunderclouds above the Kensington koppies evaporated leaving majestic cumulus heads hanging over the suburb.

Sampson gave us coffee in tin mugs and Louis promptly burnt his lips.

"Darn it Sampson, do you hafta give me the blinking hottest and the blinking fullest?"

Our housekeeper chuckled.

"What we gonna do this afternoon?" Graham grumbled, kicking a fig across the yard.

"Visit Old Joseph," Maudie suggested.

I glimpsed him in Trixie's garden. He wore his panama under Johannesburg's midday sun and paced the garden with a divining rod clasped in his hands.

"Nah. What for?"

"He rescued a snake last night. Men with sticks tried to kill it cos it was trapped in Rhodes Park Lake. Every time it tried to get on land they bashed it. Old Joseph saw what they were doing and swam to save it."

"That's stupid. What happened, Maud?"

"He shooed the snake with his hat and swam after it to the scary shore so it could get away."

"What sorta snake? A mole snake?"

"Nah, Graham. A cobra... sixty foot long."

"Six foot," I corrected.

Graham glanced at me, not sure whether my sister was telling the truth.

"Not bad, for an old fogey like that."

"He's not a old fogey," Maudie protested. "He done lotsa things you couldn't do. He sailed round the world on sailing ships plenty times. He been to Australia and

South America and England and India. He won the First World War and killed a lion with his knife."

I laughed at her vehemence.

Louis reached under the kitchen windowsill for the gum he'd stuck there before lunch. Amos checked if there was any more.

Graham slumped in the dirt under Maudie's *Sunday* sign and strapped on his roller skates.

"I'm getting bored. Let's go to the park."

At the driveway gate I saw Joseph statue-still in Trixie's garden. The divining-rod quivered in his hands. He retreated two paces and approached the same spot. The rod shivered toward the ground.

"What you doing with that forked stick thing, Old Joseph?" My sister asked.

Joseph glanced up and eyed the five of us. He eased his hold on the divining rod and let it dangle in his left hand.

"Hello Maudie and all. I'm looking for water."

"What's wrong with the taps? The pipes're full of water."

Joseph chuckled.

"It's not the same, Maudie. You see I want natural water. I'm designing a lake system for Trixie's garden, miniature streams and ponds, waterfalls maybe and pools where fish can swim. I'm going to lead the watercourse through the conservatory into a pond with water lilies."

"Gee that's sugar and spice, Old Joseph. Can we come and paddle in your water and sail our boats?"

"I have to bring it to the surface first, Maudie. I always thought there was an underground stream here. Now I think I've found it. The divining-rod reacts strongly. I'm going to dig a hole until it fills with water. Then I'll siphon the water into my system. I'll have a pretty little lake system and," he gestured with his hands, 'tis all free."

Graham jabbed me in the back. "I'm bored. Let's go

to the park."

On the pavement he snatched Louis's catapult from his pocket, scooped a handful of gravel and peppered Mrs Probert's roof.

"Run for your life," Maudie shrieked.

We bolted down the street and around the corner into Roberts Avenue. Graham swung in at the high school leading us past the gymnasium to the rifle range. We hung on the fence while he crawled into the embrasures searching for spent cartridge cases.

"Doppies," he grinned at Louis. "Stacks of 'em for the cattie."

The shells whistled shrilly when launched from a catapult making it much more fun.

"Ah, lookee here," he exclaimed, holding up his hand. "Live ones also. All two-two's." He dropped the unused cartridges into his pocket.

"We'll experiment with these later, maybe in a fire. Or how about the tramlines? We can shoot up the whole of Kensington."

The traffic light at the bottom of Roberts Avenue had suffered its weekly Saturday night misadventure. The council brought their equipment on the back of a steam wagon. There were others like it in the city museum. The wagon was solid tyred and stood hissing quietly. The firebox glowed. The engine wheezed steam down the chassis. Smoke drifted from the chimney and when we passed I gasped on the sulphur fumes.

"Whewee, who let off?" Graham accused. "Musta been you, chum."

Louis guffawed and spun the rear wheel of the bike on the pavement.

An influx of Kensington residents crowded the park. Clad in white shirts, grey flannels, summer dresses, sandals and plimsolls, families strolled and children played. They spread blankets on the lawns, rocked prams and played games.

"Ah lookee there," Graham whooped, pouncing on

two Coke bottles for redemption at the kiosk.

The band on the covered stand played *The Blue Danube*. Maudie waltzed along the promenade. A din of shrieks and laughter came from inside the swimming pool enclosure. Amos pointed out a man going off the high board. A moment later we heard his body smack the water.

"Bellyflop!" Amos shouted.

From swings and merry-go-rounds came shrill cries of toddlers.

"Pip-squeaks," Amos cried. He leapt into the monkey rope and swung from handhold to handhold. Then he pelted across the lawn into the paddling-pond, kicking up spray as he went. He skirted the pond, running sideways so he could watch toy boats being pushed by their owners.

All four tennis courts were in use, the balls clearing the nets by yards. I saw quiet games of bowls being played on the greens beyond the tennis club. Amos skipped along alternatively serving imaginary tennis balls and bowling invisible woods.

A soccer match was in progress, a friendly game with mothers and fathers, brothers and sisters dribbling a ball. On another field, high school children flew a rubber-powered model airplane. A child tried to launch a kite but there wasn't enough breeze to keep it aloft.

The surface of the lake shone sky blue, broken only by drifting rowing boats. On the near shore the water reflected banks of cumulus. A flotilla of ducks paddled down the shoreline pecking at the grassy bank. On the reed-covered island wading birds stalked the shallows. Above, a pair of cormorants scouted for a place to alight. Fishermen dotted the near shore, motionless with their light rods and tackle.

We flopped on the lawn to watch.

"S'not fair," Maudie muttered. "We don't have a boat of our own."

"And we never got any dough to hire one," Amos

cut in.

"We can build our own," Graham suggested.

"Not me," Louis retorted, scowling at his brother. "I'll be doing all the work and you'll be riding in it."

"But why don't we?" I stuttered. "Lotsa junk behind our garage, bits of timber and corrugated roof sheets."

"Yah, why not?" Amos agreed. "I never been in a boat before."

"S'too late to start today," Graham pointed out. "What else can we do?"

"Old Joseph found a football in the water last night," Maudie said. "Tadpole's pretty sure its a ball. Maybe it's still there."

"Floating?" Graham asked.

"Nah," I interjected, "Sunk. Full of water. Probably punctured."

"Let's go get it right away. Jeez man we can fix it with my bro's puncture kit and kick it around."

We set off around the perimeter headed for the willows, the overgrown kikuyu grass, the slush and the algae.

"Sis, keep your eyes open," I warned. "This is where the cobra came ashore last night. Could be still holed up here."

"Okay, now where must we look for the ball?" Graham demanded.

We were alone under the willows. Other people didn't come to this part of the park. I pointed at the water.

"Out there Graham, waist-deep." I picked up a stone and tossed it where Joseph had stumbled.

"Just other side the splash."

He looked dubious.

"Bro," he called. "We need you to go in the water."

Louis scowled and protested but Graham persuaded him to remove his school shoes, hitch up his shorts and wade into the water.

"Feel with your feet, chum."

Louis shuffled through the algae staining his shorts. Twice he tripped flinging out his arms. For half an hour he found nothing.

"Come on Bro. Stop messing about. I woulda found it long ago."

Louis covered a big area when I heard him grunt. He bent down fouling his shirt and came up clasping what we thought was our soccer ball.

"At last, chum. What took you so long? Looksa funny shape to me. S'it full of water?"

Louis began screaming. We all saw what he clutched. A child's head. He dropped it in revulsion and staggered toward us, splashing through the algae. When he reached the bank he fell on his hands and knees and vomited up Sampson's lunch.

"Graham you bastard, you bastard, goddamn you."

I couldn't speak. Graham looked dazed. Amos sprinted ten yards and spun around to stare at us.

"Davy Nguni," Maudie murmured.

I went cold and glanced at her. Her eyes weren't focused and she might have been in a trance. In the confusion nobody else registered her words.

"What did you say, Sis?" I whispered.

She popped out of her stupor and frowned.

"I didn't say anything, Tadpole."

Two constables strode toward us; one white, one black. I thought we were going to get into trouble but they wanted to know what was wrong with Louis.

"Uh, he's okay," Graham assured them. "My bro's got a weak stomach that's all."

"Well you children better go on home. You've wandered onto a crime scene. We're cordoning off this side of the lake."

I glanced up at the constables. I needed to tell them about it. My seven-year-old sister knew more about the crime and the scene than they did. And she knew where the rest of Davy was hidden.

"I... I... think... maybe... I... can help..." I stuttered

before I realized I was making a fool of myself. I closed my mouth, took my sister's hand and led her away. Graham, Louis and Amos were already leaving.

It was over a mile back to the house but on the way Joseph's Harley Davidson pulled alongside. The old man eased the gear lever on the tank into neutral and let the big vee tick over quietly.

"You children want a ride back?" he invited.

"Ah sure, Old Joseph." Maudie enthused. "Good thinking, but how we all gonna fit on your motorbike?"

"No problem Maudie. You and your dog in the bottom of the sidecar. Amos and your brother on the seat. And you Graham, on the pillion."

"What about me?" asked Louis.

"What on earth have you been up to? You look a real mess. Anyway get on your bike and put your hand on your brother's shoulder. We'll give you a tow. I'll keep the Harley in second."

So that's how we got home that afternoon. Five people and a dog on an ex-army motorcycle combination towing Louis on his bicycle. We idled up the avenue at ten miles an hour pulling stares from pedestrians on the pavement.

That night Maudie woke me with her moaning. The house slept and I had no idea of the time. I threw my blankets aside and padded across to sit with her. She squirmed in her bed.

I stroked her arm.

"No don't... don't do it... leave me alone..."

"Maudie, s'me, Tadpole. You having a nightmare."

She woke with a start and reached for me.

"S'okay, Sis," I murmured. "S'only a dream."

She didn't respond.

"Sis, wake up properly. You mustn't go back to sleep thinking those things. The nighmare'll come back."

She squeezed my hand.

"Come with me," I urged. "I'll make space for you. Then your dream won't come back. I promise."

We crawled in together and slept soundly until the sun crept through our bedroom window.

Chapter 11

"Monday again, s'always Monday, s'never Saturday, oh puke." Maudie dragged herself out of bed.

It was a bad day and was to end with Hobo falling out of the fig tree and breaking her leg. The morning started at half past five with the milkmen rattling their milk bottles. They made their deliveries on bicycles with balloon tyres.

"Baboon tyres, Tadpole."

The front wheel was small. Fitted ahead of the handlebars was a wicker basket packed high with bottles. This made the bike unwieldy and accidents at speed when some poor rider lost control of his mount going downhill, were spectacular. Milk and glass flew in all directions and housewives rushed out with iodine and cotton wool.

The milkmen had a habit of rattling a metal spike inside their empty bottles. The spike was for removing the cardboard lids. Each morning Hobo lay in wait for our milkman. On his way down the drive tauntingly rattling our empties, Hobo allowed him to almost reach the gate. Then baying in excitement she charged after him giving him seconds to escape through the gate. They both liked that game.

Maudie's face looked like thunder as she found her black *Monday* sign and in a pique, pinned it to the fig tree. She remembered nothing of her nightmare.

"Frogs 'n snails 'n crogodile's tails," she muttered under her breath.

Our father breakfasted in the kitchen, discussing the day's chores with Sampson. Frog was in the bathroom combing his hair and Babs, in man's pyjamas, hurried outside to the privy.

Lizzie arrived. A Mozambique washerwoman who laundered clothes and linen for households in our neighbourhood, she came to our house every Monday. And every Tuesday her daughter Mary came to do the ironing. They scandal-mongered over the fence with Moses.

Our elder brother never walked to school with Maudie and me. "Frog's just a big smarty-pants," Maudie called after him, as we trailed behind him on the sidewalk, "but his nose in a rat trap, squashed flat."

Miss Meldrum made me stay in after school. Her habit of cluttering the blackboard with writing, floored me and I hadn't noticed all the homework she'd set and omitted to do my spelling.

I didn't care for Miss Meldrum because she made fun of me, mimicking the stuttering, facial twitching and rapid blinking which overcame me when I got flustered.

"I must not break what I cannot make," my sister had to write twenty times after she tried repairing a mock ship in the junior playground by kicking a loose board into place.

"I was only fixing the damn thing, Tadpole, that's all. That teacher got no brains."

We spent the afternoon in the fig tree, hammering planks into place between the branches to form the beginning of our tree house. We had just hoisted a new plank into the tree when Sampson leaned out of the kitchen window.

"Bath time. Your father will be home soon."

After bathing, Maudie dried herself in our bedroom. I was stepping into the tepid water when I heard Frog shouting. He leaned out the sash window in the kitchen and Sampson charged out the screen door onto the veranda. I caught a glimpse of Hobo in the fig tree. She had climbed Maudie's foot treads and out along a branch to our tree house. She balanced on our loose plank up there rocking backwards and forwards. Every time she moved the plank lurched.

"Don't move, you stupid dog," Frog shouted. "Keep still."

Sampson stumbled down the back veranda steps making for the trunk of the fig tree. Hobo found momentary equilibrium before our plank flipped upside down.

"Watch out," Frog yelled.

By this time neighbours peered out their windows. Amos had his head over the fence on his side of our backyard and Moses' face poked through the gaps in the corrugated iron on the other.

"Hobo my little angel, you gonna fall," Maudie bawled, hugging a towel to herself.

"Semp-Sonne... Semp-Sonne..."

Her dog pitched off the plank, clung to a branch with her fore paws for just long enough to swing upside down and plummeted out of the fig tree onto Sampson's head.

"Aiyee," he grunted as he went down.

Hobo thudded into the dirt, twisting a hind leg and squealing in pain.

"Hobo. My baby, my little angel." Maudie flew down the back stairs, clinging to her towel.

Hobo rolled her eyes at her mistress and gave a wag of her tail. She didn't get up.

"Humph," Sampson exclaimed, dusting himself off. Moses doubled over, laughing himself silly behind the corrugated sheets trying to stifle his mirth. On the other side of the backyard we heard a tee-heeing coming from Amos who was rocking to and fro. However, when Sampson turned around to glare at him, he lost his balance and fell off the fence. There was a muffled thud followed by whimpering. Sampson glared in his direction, dusting his hands for effect.

When our father arrived he laid newspaper on the kitchen table and placed Maudie's dog on that so he could examine her.

"Sweetheart, she's broken something," he pronounced, manipulating the poor dog's limbs. Hobo wet on the newspaper every time he touched her leg.

Hobo was terrified of the vet. She sat on the floor between Maudie and me and began shaking. Her little body shivered so much, her teeth began chattering. Her jaw rattled. Her teeth banging on each other made such a noise that people in the waiting room began looking at us. Even the lady behind the reception desk got up to see what was going on. Hobo couldn't stop. When the vet placed her on the examination table she wet on that too.

"Unfortunately her hind leg is fractured," she told our father. "I must immobilize the limb in plaster. Your pet will have to spend the night in the dog's hospital."

Hobo was out of action. For three weeks the milkman could rattle his bottles with impunity and there was nothing Maudie's dog was able to do about it. Except lie in her wooden box with her paws over her ears.

It was only after supper that I noticed the newspaper. The front page displayed a half-tone of police officers and detectives among the willows at Rhodes Park. Some had stripped and waded in the water.

The headline read, "Gruesome Find in Park."

Maudie trembled when she saw the report. I pretended not to show any interest. If our father found out it was us kids who'd made the discovery, he'd tan my hide.

I read that detectives had retrieved the head of a Johannesburg child from the shallows. They intended a wider search of the bottom, but needed their diving equipment. The victim was identified as David Nguni, seven years old. There was no trace of his torso. David's parents, who worked in the garment industry, were black and lived in Sophiatown. Their son was missing when they returned from work the previous Friday afternoon. After leaving school he had never reached home.

"Davy..." I whispered.

"A little black boy. His cut body's not gonna be found cos he's in a culvert under the road. I seen where his clothes're hidden. Under rubbish by the stormwater drain..."

"You crazy or something? What you talking about?" Maudie wanted to know.

I gazed at her and shook my head.

"Nothing Sis. Just something I was thinking. S'not important."

"The police found that thing real quick," Maudie whispered. "I wonder if Old Joseph told them."

"We didn't see him with 'em today," I breathed.

I read that detectives were searching for the rest of David Nguni's remains. There was speculation about it being muti-murder.

Speculation, I thought. *My sister knows it's muti-murder. They're searching for his body. And they won't find it. Unless Maudie tells them where. And she can't because she doesn't remember her nightmare.*

I put an arm around her as we read the report. Then we paged to Curly Wee and I felt her tension subside.

Muti is traditional African medicine. It is largely rendered from herbs, bulbs, roots, bark, leaves and other innocuous ingredients. It really does work and is no different from other cultures' home and farm remedies, going back to the time when people lived on the land.

Stronger muti, but perhaps with a great deal of hype

lauded by the shaman, takes the form of powdered antelope horn, ground wild animal fat, ground animal flesh and rendered bones or organs.

Sorcerer's muti is a different kettle of fish. Concocted from human organs and based on superstition, it is purported to be supernaturally powerful. Children are chosen by sorcerers because their organs are young. They are snatched and spirited to a quiet spot where the sorcerer slices out their organs while his victims are alive. The louder the victim screams the more potent the muti.

"Son, I think you and your sister had better keep away from the lake," our father told me after reading the front page story.

"Yah Abe, we'll be real good about it. Promise. Pray to God and hope to die if we tell a lie," Maudie responded.

I nodded in agreement. In any case, I wasn't that keen on the scary side of Rhodes Park Lake. I would stay away from the willows even without his warning.

That night I had a nightmare about Maudie gazing up at me through murky water. She sank further from my reach while I was held by an invisible force. I called to her but she didn't hear. Then she was gone and I woke trembling.

Chapter 12

Amos had begged a ride with Mr Sunshine to Sophiatown and was back with his grandmother. Hopefully he was at school. Maudie's pink Tuesday adorned the fig tree.

"When you gonna fix our box-cart, Tadpole?" she pestered after we trudged home from school.

I'd built it for her from old packing case planks nailed together. It resembled a go-kart with a box we sat in when we rode downhill. We steered holding two ropes tied to the front axle. The brake was a timber lever we dragged on the ground when we wanted to slow down. The wheels came from a discarded pram and their eight-inch-nail axles occasionally came loose. Then the wheels would fall off.

"Why don't we take the box-cart up the street and onto the koppies," Maudie suggested. "We can ride down that snazzy path. Then we can pull the cart up to the next street and come home that way."

"Now how about that, Sis? We haven't been on the koppies for donkeys' years, I reckon."

Good Hope Street was too steep for me to haul my sister's box-cart up the hill with her sitting in it. We tramped up the pavement towing her cart and squeezed past the cul-de-sac barrier at the top. Maudie climbed in. She made herself comfortable, lifted her feet onto the footrests and clutched the steering ropes. The path was steep and I raced after the bouncing cart.

Veld grass interspersed with bush and stunted trees covered the koppie. Scattered among the scrub were outcrops of yellow granite. I hauled my sister up the next slope and stopped to rest. It was lonely here. We had a quarter of a mile to cover before the path climbed toward houses on the ridge. Down the next slope Maudie cruised between grass verges. I chased behind, my head down checking her cart. At the bottom of the path we rounded a granite outcrop.

A sangoma squatting with his muti sack blocked our way. A sangoma is an African medicine woman or man, a shaman, herbalist, healer and diviner.

Maudie stared at the muti-man's sack. My reaction was to run but I couldn't leave my sister. We had spied on him before from a distance. This was the first time we'd come face to face and I caught a whiff of jute, or snuff, or perhaps hemp. I couldn't be sure.

Older children told us they had glimpsed inside his sack dried roots and bulbs, leaves, seeds, dead blooms, herbs, tubers, stems, berries and bark. At the bottom we heard, the old sangoma kept brains, hearts, livers and intestines of birds, cats and chameleons.

Once, in a seedy part of Johannesburg we had walked past a herbalist's shop, a dusty, dark interior. Hanging near the door I'd seen animal skulls, white and black feathers, dried skins, the mummified carcass of a mongoose and the hairy foreleg and foot complete with claws, of a jackal.

Maudie and I holed up in the grass, had spied on this sangoma a number of times. Sitting cross-legged, he jabbered away. Then he untied his knotted cloth and threw the bones for patients. Sometimes they revealed ancestral spirits had been angered. Then he advised his patients to appease the dead with offerings. Sometimes it emerged the patient was a victim of a sorcerer's spell. He exorcised this with protective medicines and amulets.

We watched all this from our hiding place on the koppie. One afternoon a woman suffering bruises from having walked into a moving lorry, limped up the path. The sangoma treated her with cow-dung poultices. Each day the patient reappeared for treatment and by the end of the week was cured.

A gangster came off second best in a knife fight. While blood pumped from a forearm, his sinister friends carried him up the koppie. The sangoma retrieved a rope of mopani sapling bark from his sack and applied it to the wound. The bleeding stopped and my sister and I opened our mouths in disbelief. He had chest wounds too, weeping infection until treated with the sap of an indigenous bush. One patient suffered pus-filled boils and was treated with antelope horn. Another, septic grazes which he bandaged with the leaves of an onion-like bulb.

"Siyakubona, little children, I see you."

I didn't know whether to flee but he motioned us to sit. I slumped down next to my sister. The sangoma placed his sack on the ground and arranged his blanket, squatting on his haunches and watching my sister intently.

"You have come at last? Isanusi has seen you in his visions."

"Who, me?"

The old man nodded.

Maudie appeared to be under his spell and I wondered whether the sangoma had hypnotized her. Words came out my sister's mouth in a drawl.

"Mister Isanusi, how many mutis do you have in your sack?"

My sister frightened me. This was not the way I thought things would go. I wanted to break contact as soon as politely possible. The herbalist chuckled at me.

"You've seen bees?"

Maudie nodded.

"And wild honey?"

We were city children who had never seen honey in the comb.

"Like wild bees around a hollow tree."

Maudie was enchanted. "How strong're the mutis in your sack, Mister Isanusi?"

"With liver of meerkat, Isanusi will turn a weak man

into a fierce warrior of great courage."

Maudie smiled.

"Isanusi's springbok fat will enable a man to run like a hare." He gestured with a hand and narrowed his eyes, staring into what might have been the distance, but in reality was the tall grass and granite rock about us.

"Fat which Isanusi has taken from the eagle will give a man eyes so sharp, nothing will be able to evade them."

I snorted and wanted to pull my sister away.

"Monkey flesh," he pursed his lips, gazing first at Maudie, then at me, "of which there is in Isanusi's sack, will make my patients crafty and cunning."

He paused, eyeing us up and down. "If I administer chameleon flesh, I'll make someone vanish before your eyes."

"Invisible?" Maudie muttered.

I shivered. It was time to be going.

As if reading my mind, Isanusi began watching me. "I could clean your blood," he offered. "There are many leaves and stems in Isanusi's sack for blood purifying."

I shook my head.

"Or what about your stomach? I have dug up a hundred different bulbs and roots from the soil."

I wanted to go home.

He reached and drew a finger across my forehead. "You have a pain here? Isanusi can cure all your pains."

I shook my head vigorously.

"Show us your magic bones, Mister Isanusi," my sister requested.

I screwed up my eyes.

The diviner complied. He emptied his bones onto the blanket, scooped them into his hands and held them out for Maudie and me to see, knuckles and anklebones and other things too. One was a hairy foreleg with paw and claws.

He spread the bones on the blanket, smoothing them over with his fingers. Among the knuckles, anklebones and foreleg, lay a bird's beak, a fragment of animal hoof, dried pumpkin pips, a rounded pebble, a shell of some kind and a square of carved wood.

He picked up one of the bones. "The lion... king of all beasts in Africa." Replacing it he selected another. "Hyena. Treachery and sorcery." Then he sought something else. "Kudu, observance and watchfulness."

I became anxious as he selected a shard of tortoise shell and held it up. What was going to happen?

He reached for the pumpkin pips. "Health and survival. Could be good, could be bad."

I watched him drop the pips onto the blanket and select a fragment of hoof. "This will inform Isanusi about the flocks."

Then scratching his forehead, he lifted another bone. "Baboon. Tells me about family matters. There is nothing Isanusi doesn't know."

He selected another from the blanket and pointed it at me. "This is steenbok. It knows only fear and nervousness."

The next item was a seashell, a strange thing four hundred miles inland. "Triumph over an enemy."

He then picked up a duiker bone. "So Isanusi will know if someone is going on a journey," he said, tossing it back and selecting a small bone. "Monkey this one, artful and sly." He shook his head, chuckling.

"This bone," he continued, picking up another, "is of the leopard, the one who hunts at night." He then lifted the rounded pebble. "A riverstone but not an ordinary riverstone. This one was found in the stomach of a crocodile." I wouldn't touch it, which amused him.

Isanusi indicated the bird's beak, the foreleg and claw. "These will point out where something yet to happen will take place." He noticed a little bone previously overlooked and fingered it cautiously. "The ant-bear," he murmured, frowning.

Later, I discovered from Sampson that the ant-bear is associated with the underworld and portends the end of life.

Maudie was mesmerized. "When do you throw your bones for somebody, Mister Isanusi?"

The shaman gazed at her. "To have their future told. Or perhaps if someone is troubled or bewitched and needs Isanusi to divine the cause of their trouble or sorcery,"

"S'not true, it's just superstition," I blurted.

Isanusi shook his head. "You saw the knife wounds healed, the bruises, the boils, the infection. You've seen Isanusi's muti work with your own eyes."

I was shaken. How did he know my sister and I spied on him?

He started replacing the bones in his cloth.

"Isanusi knows things white people laugh off. Evil forces that cause terrible harm. Do you know about the Impundulu Bird?"

I'd never heard of such a bird.

"We African people know it as the Lightning Bird or the Wind Bird, because it flies across the sky striking lightning and laying eggs in the flashes. Thunder comes from the Impundulu Bird's wings beating the air. It's an evil spirit and makes people do bad things."

I couldn't believe what I was hearing and I wanted to go.

Isanusi continued. "Last month at a funeral in Sophiatown, talk was that the deceased was bewitched and the body we saw was not his own. It changed into an Impundulu Bird. Before the coffin lid was closed, mourners saw the body moving."

Maudie screwed up her eyes.

"You've heard of the Tokoloshe?"

We nodded. Sampson warned us about this hairy dwarf.

"You children must be careful. The Tokoloshe is evil and walks the streets invisible. It can change its shape and become something else. It lives near water and is especially drawn to children. Beware."

"Have you seen the Tokoloshe, Mister Isanusi?"

"Aha, no. To meet the Tokoloshe face to face is to die."

Maudie glanced at me.

"What about the Mamlambo Snake?"

I shook my head.

"A river spirit that lives under water. It casts spells and changes into a human. A Mamlambo once turned itself into a beautiful young woman. A man made her one of his wives and took her back to his kraal. She cast a spell on his family. They fell sick and the husband became the Mamlambo Snake's slave."

"That's terrible," Maudie commented, "what about happy things like seeing the future?"

She clasped her hands together.

"Mister Isanusi, will you throw your bones for me and Tadpole?"

The diviner hesitated before undoing his dirty old cloth.

"Hold out your hands."

He clapped his fingers over ours, clasping Maudie's and mine in his. Then he brought his head forward, peering into our faces.

"Our spirits must work together."

We sat while he nodded and reached for his divining bones.

"Hold out your hands to receive the bones."

He emptied the contents of his cloth into our fingers. A shiver ran up my spine. I stared at the knuckles and anklebones in our hands, trying to remember which was the kudu and which the lion and which the baboon.

The hairy foreleg was on top, the amputated end touching my wrist. The tortoise shell slipped off the bird's beak exposing the crocodile stone. I stared at the pebble.

"Your two spirits have to leave your bodies now. They must leave your bodies and enter the bones."

My head spun.

He took the bones, cupped them in his hands, mumbled, leaned forward and blew his breath over them.

"Let Isanusi's spirit and the spirit of the ancestor of whom Isanusi is the favourite pass over these bones."

He pitched them onto the blanket. I drew in my breath.

"Look," he breathed. "Some are sleeping for they have lain on their sides."

He clicked his tongue. "These ones have become lazy for they are upside down. The sea-shell, the pip and the crocodile stone will tell me nothing."

"Aha, these upright ones will inform Isanusi about you children."

He ran his fingers over them, observing how the upright bones paired with others. I looked on in silence.

"The steenbok stands between the hyena and the ant-bear... next to the tortoise shell." He shook his head.

I tried to remember what the steenbok bone meant and the hyena and the tortoise shell. He never told us about the ant-bear.

Isanusi gazed at the bones.

"The kudu and springbok are also upright," he mumbled, shaking his head and narrowing his eyes.

We didn't move.

Isanusi stroked the bird's beak, gazed at my sister and took her wrists in his fingers.

"What'd the bones say?" I blurted.

He shook his head. "Isanusi is thinking."

I snorted.

"Be careful. Isanusi is advising you children to be on your guard."

The bones lay untouched.

"Please, Mister Isanusi. We hafta know," my sister pleaded.

"If it makes you unhappy?"

I hesitated. Bad news was something we could do without.

Maudie tugged at my arm. "We gotta know, Tadpole."

"Yah, Mister Isanusi," I replied. "Even bad news. We

hafta know what you read in the bones."

"Isanusi saw a warning in the bones. The signs are you children must be watchful like the kudu antelope."

We crouched around him.

"Isanusi is puzzled by how the bones fell. Many lay sleeping upside down, the crocodile stone and the pips and the sea-shell and others. They were the lazy ones and told me nothing. The upright bones are the ones I need, for they can tell me a lot. The steenbok stands between the hyena and ant-bear next to the tortoise shell. Nearby are the kudu and springbok, also upright."

We didn't interrupt.

"Fear and nervousness trapped between treachery, sorcery and – the underworld."

Neither of us moved.

"It is yet to happen." His gaze made me fidget.

"The bones also tell Isanusi you must be on the lookout."

His gaze fixed on me. "You have to be fleet-footed like the springbok gazelle. Otherwise your sister..."

He peered at Maudie and shook his head.

"What should we watch out for Mister Isanusi?" Maudie clasped her hands in her lap.

"Isanusi smells evil and sorcery. People are being deceived. This evil touches you children. It comes and goes. But there is sorcery too. They will catch up with you."

I sat bemused. My nostrils picked up a waft of dried hemp.

"That is what I have to tell you. Be careful where you go. Watch what you do. And beware who you speak to."

An African man came down the path. He wanted to consult with the sangoma.

"Come Maudie, we oughta go."

"Thank you, Mister Isanusi. We sure gonna take care."

"Hambani kahle. Go well."

We scrambled to our feet. Maudie grabbed her cart's

steering rope. We ran, towing her cart up the koppie path until we reached the barrier at the top of Good Hope Street and were among houses again.

"Don't listen to him, Maudie. S'only superstition."

My sister didn't answer.

"What'd you smell when he threw the bones?"

"Dagga, maybe..." She wrinkled her nose.

Dagga is cannabis. It is extracted from the hemp plant.

"How about snuff?"

"Maybe. Not sure. Can't tell the difference."

She rode her box-cart hell for leather down the middle of Good Hope Street. I hared after her hoping she wouldn't break her neck.

Hobo came home that evening. Our father fetched her on his way from work. She bobbed up and down on the back seat of the Chev in spite of her plaster cast. When we lifted her out, she began worrying the cast.

"I was afraid of that," our father admitted. "She'll chew it off by morning."

He disappeared into the garage and a moment later summoned Maudie. She came into the house, rummaged through her toy-box and emerged carrying her old seaside bucket. I followed, curious as to what was going on.

Our father cut the bottom out of the red, white and blue bucket.

"Aw gee Abe, now what am I gonna do?" Maudie moaned.

He filed the edges smooth and drilled holes around the perimeter just above where the bottom had been.

Maudie hung onto the end of the workbench, eyeing this wanton destruction of one of the few things she owned.

"Sweetheart, bring your dog," our father chuckled.

He slid the open-ended bucket over Hobo's head and wired it to her collar, passing the wire through the holes he had drilled.

Maudie's dog looked like a white body with a red, white and blue lampshade for a head. Only the tip of her muzzle protruded past the brim. She galloped circles in the backyard trying to throw it off. She could see where she was going and could eat and drink. However, she couldn't look to either side and it was impossible for her to touch her plaster cast with her muzzle. If we spoke to her, she had to spin around to face us.

"Crikey Moses, Hobo, you a crazy bronco now," Maudie cried in hysterics.

"Good," our father laughed. "That fixes that problem."

"What about my bucket, Abe?"

But our father was going into the house and a headless dog raced on three legs across the yard to terrorize a pigeon pecking porridge from her bowl.

Chapter 13

"Look at this, Tadpole."

I was engrossed in Curly Wee's adventures. Maudie nudged me to turn to The Star's front page. Wednesday evening's edition was the third issue covering the muti-murder. The gruesome find warranted the front page but was below the fold, two columns by five inches, continued on page two.

I learned that the police were looking for a killer, a black man who commuted between Sophiatown and Kensington. The two suburbs were five miles apart. One was white working class, the other a black shanty town and a haven for criminals. Investigating detectives had no leads to follow. Only my sister knew the truth. And that was buried in her subconscious. I wanted to reveal what Maudie had seen in her dreams but I knew my stutter made it impossible.

"This matter is becoming serious," our father warned. I don't want you two playing anywhere near that side of Rhodes Park Lake."

"Yah, Abe. That's the scary part anyways."

"And I suggest you stay off the koppies. They're not the safest of places."

"We promise, Abe, honest, swear to God and hope to die."

That evening, Mr de Beer invited himself to supper. I wondered what sort of trouble Graham and Louis had got themselves into this time.

"Those two hooligan nephews of yours damn near

burnt down Kiewietjie," he complained to our father. "I had to call the fire brigade."

Kiewietjie was named after the South African green plover but the hostel didn't do any credit to the bird. Our cousins might have done the neighbourhood of Belgravia a favour by razing it. Built in Victorian style in the 1890s it was a run down two-storey building. Originally the palace of a British gold mining magnate, but those days were gone. The Anglo-Boer War, two world wars and the 1929 depression had seen to that. Now in an unfashionable suburb it was too big and the rates and taxes too high for a working family to maintain. With forty schoolboys boarding with him, the housemaster found it difficult to give them three square meals a day.

Kiewietjie's walls peeled and the roof rusted. Victorian fireplaces remained cold because Mr de Beer couldn't afford the coal. Overgrown garden paths and hedges hadn't been trimmed in years. The property cried out for the loving touch of a woman but rumour had it that Mrs de Beer ran off with another man. Her husband resided with his African housekeeper-cum-cook Lucas and forty schoolboys, no part of the way they lived being tempered by a woman's touch.

"The fire brigade, Sir? Heavens, what happened?" our father asked the housemaster who pulled a medicine bottle from his jacket pocket, shook two tablets into his palm and swallowed them with a gulp of water from a tumbler.

"Its perplexing I tell you, because after I summoned the fire brigade the blaze just darn disappeared. I don't understand it."

"Go on."

"Except for your two nephews whom I don't believe anyway, none of the other boys seems to know anything about it. What I don't get, there's no evidence of any fire. Oh sure I saw it all right, six foot flames engulfing the boys' bathroom. I got such a shock I phoned the fire brigade. What happened afterwards is what makes me so furious with your nephews."

"Tell me. Maybe we can get to the bottom of this."

"Well, the truth is the business didn't start with the flames in the bathroom. It started with a loose floorboard in the dormitory. Your nephew Graham must have been eyeing the raised end of a board adjacent to the doorway, wondering how he could get some mileage out of it."

"What did he do?"

"The fiend pulled the loose brads out of the board, levered the end up and wedged a stone underneath. This prevented the door opening further than halfway."

Our father waited for the housemaster to continue.

"After lights out your nephew started a pillow fight and the dormitory got into an uproar. I raced down the corridor and flung their door open. Of course I was expecting to stride through, flick on their light and lambast the hooligans."

"I would've done the same."

"But I wasn't expecting the door to strike your nephew's floorboard, rebound and catch me in the face. All in the dark I tell you. I took a step back and swung the door again. The same thing happened. Then I reached in and switched the light on by the wall."

"So you now had light to see what was going on?"

"Well I tell you. I was so goddamn mad I kicked the door as hard as I could. It rebounded and slammed shut on me. Your nephew's doing mind you. Your nephew. I squeezed in and what do you think I saw?"

"All the boys back in bed?"

"Exactly. I ignored them and tried smoothing the floorboard with my foot. That didn't work. I put my weight on it. I didn't realise your nephew had jammed a stone there. So I went down on my hands and knees to discover why the offending board wouldn't lie down."

"Because of the stone?"

"Worse than that. Your nephew had stolen a bottle of ammonium sulphide solution from the high school science lab and stashed it under the floorboards. I just about gagged. You know how it stinks? Putrid eggs. Of course all the cherubs pretended to be asleep."

"Eh, eh, eh. Boys will be boys."

"I don't see the humour. I ordered them out of their beds and made them close windows and fanlights. I wanted everything closed so they could gag on their own fumes. I slammed the door and left them to it."

"I'll speak to Graham and Louis about it."

"No, I haven't told you about the fire yet."

Our father waited.

"I still can't work out what happened. My suite is at one end of the corridor on the first floor. The boys' area is at the opposite end. Halfway along the corridor is a pay-telephone for their use. Now I'm sometimes obliged to answer that phone when the boys are out."

"You're losing me."

"The phone rang. Nobody answered it and I went to do so myself. When I opened my study door I saw the boy's bathroom going up in flames. I rushed back into my suite and called the fire brigade."

"That sounds serious."

"Yes but you don't understand. When I hastened back into the corridor the fire had gone."

"Can't happen."

"Well I tell you it did. I raced to the bathroom expecting flames to shoot up again but sweet Fanny Adams. I don't know what to make of it."

"Surely woodwork was burnt, curtains singed, the ceiling smudged?"

Mr de Beer shook his head. "Clean as a whistle,"

"The reek of wood smoke? That would have been strong after the kind of blaze you describe."

"If there was I certainly didn't smell the aftermath." He held up his nicotine stained fingers.

"Didn't the fire officer inspect the premises?"

"Not exactly. I was so embarrassed at having called them out, all I wanted was for them to go away again."

Our father chuckled.

"They were very angry at me. Threatened prosecution and made me sign an affidavit that I'd called them out unnecessarily."

"I can't punish my nephews for something you yourself told the fire brigade didn't happen."

Mr de Beer snorted on a mouthful of food.

"I'll get to the bottom of it yet,"

I found out later that Graham had climbed onto the roof above the bathroom window. He'd led a length of wash-line through it to a baking tray on the concrete floor. He'd also led electrical flex through the window, its live and neutral ends twisted together so they would spark when electricity was fed to them.

Into the baking tray he'd poured a measured volume of petrol, already timed behind one of the outbuildings as being the exact amount that would blaze for thirty seconds before being depleted.

The rest of the hostel boys had played a ball game in the garden so the housemaster was under the impression they were all outside, while Graham perched on the roof and Louis strolled two blocks down the pavement to a public telephone booth.

Louis had dialled the number of the phone in the hostel's corridor. Waiting on the roof his brother heard the instrument trill nine times before The Bear flew out of his suite to answer it. The moment Graham had heard the door of the suite being opened he closed the electrical circuit allowing two hundred and twenty volts to spark over his tray of petrol.

Mr de Beer opened his study door to witness what appeared to be the entire east wing going up in flames. He was so shocked he spun on his heel and raced back into his suite, spent another half minute fumbling for the fire department's number and frantically spun the dial.

Graham had calmly counted down thirty seconds and pulled both the empty baking tray and the remains of his flex up to the roof. A minute or so later he was in the garden joining the ball game as Louis strolled up the pavement. Having summoned the fire brigade Mr de Beer had leaned out of his window yelling at the boys.

"Fire! Fire! Fire, everyone. For God's sake, hurry."

With his gown flying behind him he'd sprinted down the corridor. To his utter disbelief the second floor was as quiet as a church. He'd tiptoed to the bathroom, prepared to throw his hands up to protect his face when the flames gushed through the doorway again. They hadn't. Confused now but concerned for the safety of his hostel he darted down the corridor, snatching doors open and flinging them closed. He was thus occupied when the fire engine arrived and neighbours ran out of their houses into the street.

"I won't tell you what the fire officers said to me," he complained at the supper table.

Babs drank from a teacup fortified with brandy. Frog read Popular Science Magazine propped next to his plate. Maudie stuck peas to her fork with mashed potato.

In the lull that followed Frog looked up and told the adults (he never actually addressed Maudie or me), "It says here, the moon looks bigger when it's rising and setting than when it's overhead."

"Right," our father agreed.

"The question is, Father, which is the correct size? When it's near the horizon or when it's overhead?"

"That's obvious," Mr de Beer snapped. "When it's overhead."

"Why, Mister de Beer?"

"Surely you know that, boy. On the horizon we look through a lot of atmosphere that distorts everything, making it appear larger than it actually is."

"Wrong, Mister de Beer," Frog smirked.

The housemaster stiffened. Our father leaned forward. Babs gulped her bandy.

"The correct size according to Popular Science," Frog lectured, "is when the moon is near the horizon. We then see it straight on, accurately."

"I don't believe it," Mr de Beer contradicted.

"When the moon's overhead," Frog explained, "we swivel our eyes upwards. This distorts our eyeballs, making things appear smaller than they actually are."

"What rubbish," the housemaster retorted.

Our father frowned. "Have you read the article correctly, Victor?"

Frog glared at him and closed his magazine.

The adults rose and went through to the living room for coffee. After that I knew The Bear would challenge our father to a game of chess. He always beat the pants off our father. Maudie and I stayed in the dining room to finish our homework.

While we were there I overheard the housemaster relate a bizarre tale to our father and Babs.

"I was walking my Pekinese on the koppie near the Foster Caves," he began. "As no other dogs were about, I took the leash off Pikkie and he ran ahead of me. I didn't get a clear view but something came out of the scrub very fast sending Pikkie flying. The impact probably broke his back. I scrambled down the path to see the tail of a python disappearing into the grass. My dog was gone."

"I'm sorry to hear that," our father commiserated. "I wouldn't think there were pythons on the koppies in this day and age."

"Grass snakes in the koppies, yes. Maybe one or two poisonous types I can understand. But a python is a bit much. I mean, what does it feed on?"

Babs commented, "I don't think it's out of the question for an old python to be still up there. There are plenty small animals to feed it. Birds, lizards, grasshoppers, scorpions, frogs, rats, mice and even other snakes. Also one or two monkey troops up there. A monkey would make a good meal for a python."

"Pythons are not poisonous," our father added.

"No, but this one took my dog. It's quite capable of taking a child."

He excused himself to go to our outhouse. After he stepped down the back stairs into the yard, Maudie and I had a look at Hobo in her box on the back veranda. We were kneeling over her stroking her broken leg, when we heard the chain flushing in the corner of the yard. Mr de Beer pushed the door open.

Halfway across the yard he turned his face to the moon overhead. He hesitated, staring at the orb. Then glancing about the yard, he lay on his back on a tiny verge of lawn bordering a bed of violets. He shielded his eyes from the light coming out of the kitchen window and gazed at the moon.

"What's he doing?" Maudie whispered, holding my arm.

"I guess he's checking Frog's story. He's lying on his back so's he can look at the moon straight and not swivel his eyes."

Just then Bliksem the Alsatian from up the street trotted into our yard. The front gate must have been left unlatched. The dog was curious about the figure lying on the lawn and padded over to investigate.

"Voetsek," we heard the housemaster hiss. "Buzz off."

Bliksem stood over him, his muzzle inches from his face.

"Get away, damn dog."

Bliksem's tail erected, the hair on his back rose. He stood stiffly over the figure on the ground, sniffing his clothing cautiously.

"Go home," Mr de Beer ordered. He tried lifting his head but a growl erupted from Bliksem's throat.

The housemaster lay pinned to the ground while the dog continued sniffing him. Satisfied at last Bliksem casually lifted a leg, ejected a squirt of urine over The Bear and trotted out of the yard.

Maudie and I disappeared into the house before he could get off the ground. We raced to our bedroom, dived onto my bed and buried our faces in the pillow. A moment later the screen door on the back veranda slammed. The housemaster stormed down the passage. He stamped into the living room, accidentally on purpose flipped the chessboard with all its pieces onto the floor and grabbed his hat.

"I'm going," he snapped.

He slammed our front door, jumped into his Morris Eight and roared down the street.

Our father stared after him, frowning.

"There's something strange about that man," I heard him remark to Babs.

He came into our room looking troubled. "Son, I don't want you children playing anywhere near the Foster caves. They're not safe."

I nodded gloomily. There would soon be no place left where Maudie and I could play.

It was time for bed.

In her dreams that night, the bottle-and-bag man carried my sister off. He caught her and stuffed her inside his sack. David Nguni's head was in the sack with her. Davy warned her about mamlambo snakes, rubber necked sorcerers and broken car tyres.

Maudie surfaced from the inky interior of his sack and found herself standing at my bedside. She was sleep walking and mumbled what was inside the bottle-and-bag man's sack. She climbed under the blankets with me without waking.

Chapter 14

When you got used to my sister's coloured signs in the fig tree, you just knew Mondays were black. They were also lie-under-the-blankets-as long-as-you-can days.

"Wakey wakey, rise and shine. The great unwashed will get to school by nine," our father crooned at six a.m.

"Yah Abe, we know," Maudie groaned before disappearing to the bottom of her bed.

The clock in the passage ticked away. At the stroke of seven, she leapt from her covers and raced me to the bathroom. I lost and dashed into the yard to our outhouse. Maudie brushed and scrubbed and combed in the bathroom.

Our father left for work.

"Hurry, Tadpole, hurry, fast as you can. We gonna be late," my sister urged, in panic.

At twenty past seven we invaded the kitchen. Sampson cooled our porridge so we could gulp it. We grabbed our sandwiches, shouted goodbye and flew down the front veranda steps. In Roberts Avenue the progress of other children indicated how close we were to the ringing of the school bell. We were half a mile behind.

"Run Tadpole, run for your life," Maudie yelled.

Pink days were not as hectic. Green days were sane. When orange days dawned, we were ahead of schedule. In summer, by the time red days came around we vacated our beds before our father came to wake us. We had projects going in the backyard, like the commencement of the tree house. These works in progress required inspection, planning and discussion. Maudie and I were in the yard as early as five a.m.

reviewing our previous day's work and deciding what had to be done that afternoon when we got back from school.

The morning after Bliksem relieved himself on Mr de Beer, Maudie opened the living room door onto the side veranda. The sun broke the urban horizon and she noticed Joseph kneeling in Trixie's garden.

"What you think he's messing with now?" she asked, peering over the parapet.

The old mariner crouched on the ground. His shack door stood ajar in the first rays of early sunlight. The main house was shut up like our other neighbours. The occupants would be stirring. By six-thirty the first Detroit engine grumbled into life, followed by the entire street. By seven the last front door was flung open and a hung-over dashed for his tram.

Joseph knelt where he divined for water the previous Sunday. During the week Maudie and I watched him taking levels, making notes and marking out his proposed waterways.

In summer the old man went barefoot. He wore a canvas waistband, something he'd stitched himself. His trousers were unbleached ducks cut off halfway down his shins. His white cotton shirt was a loose affair he'd designed and sewed himself. He was seldom without his panama.

"Tadpole, look at Old Joseph over there. He got something under his shirt these days. Seems blinking funny to me. What you make of it?"

"Dunno. Never seen it before. He got something on that thong dangling inside his shirt. But search me, Sis, I haven't a clue."

"I think we better go check what he's up to," Maudie prompted.

We got to him as he was bending over an excavation. Maudie tiptoed behind him but he cautioned her with a hand. I peered past his arms to see what he was doing. He spoke soothingly.

"Come my little one," he murmured. "Don't be afraid. I shan't hurt you. Join your babies so I can move you together." He clicked his tongue in a coaxing lullaby.

"Sh-h..." my sister warned me.

I craned my neck. Joseph's spade had uncovered a nest of infant field mice. The mother a tawny rodent with a walnut stripe down her back, abandoned her brood and took refuge under a garden shrub. She peered up at Joseph, her tiny nose twitching the air. In his right hand he held her nest cradling her litter. His left was extended, palm up toward the mother but she was too suspicious to go near it.

"Come on then," he crooned, "everything's all right. Just hop into your nest with your babies and I'll find you another little hidey-hole where you can nurse them without being disturbed."

The mother inched forward, sniffed his fingers and darted back. Joseph left her. He eased himself to his feet and carried the young mice to his conservatory. There, he found a concealed nook in his rockery. When he came back, the tawny mother had returned to the old site of her nest. Joseph squatted casually letting his left hand fall near her. She scurried away but when he did not move she came seeking her youngsters. Quick as lightning Joseph thrust his hand into the hole and grasped her in his fingers.

"Careful Old Joseph," Maudie warned, jumping up and down. "The mouse'll bite you. I'm telling you, Old Joseph she'll bite you damn sore."

He flinched, bit his lip and muttered something under his breath.

"I told you Old Joseph. You wouldn't listen. I told you she'll bite you. Now you learned your lesson good."

He laughed and, grimacing from needle sharp teeth, carried the mother to her new home and carefully placed her in the nest with her offspring.

"Yes you're right, my little girl. She did bite me darn

sore."

"What you digging this hole for, Old Joseph?"

"For water, remember. Have you forgotten me telling you about the underground stream?"

"Nah," she drawled. "You had your stick thing and you walked round and round Trixie's garden and when you got here your stick thing bent down and you couldn't stop it."

"It's called dowsing for water, Maudie."

"*Dowsing*? How's it work, Old Joseph? How's your stick thing know where the water is?"

Joseph chuckled. "Maudie, I don't really know. Maybe God does. It's one of those intuitive things living beings have in them. The divining rod works for some people, for others, not. Even with me it doesn't always work. It's a mental reaction rather than a physical one."

"Yah, I s'pose so."

"When you grow up Maudie, you'll find you have a sixth sense that men don't have. You'll just know something is so without reason. It's a secret guidance from the great truth. That's how water divining is accomplished."

"Amazing. I'll hafta remember that."

"In fact any divining, Maudie. How do you think African inyangas and sangomas divine for their patients? Or isanusis smell out witches and sorcerers?"

"I been trying to figure that out, Old Joseph. I guess it isn't easy."

"Like the prophets of old, these shamans use a third eye which we all have but mankind in general hasn't learnt to master yet. Maybe it will take him another hundred thousand years."

"I don't see any water in this hole, Old Joseph."

"That's because you don't believe, my little girl. I can see it. It's there all right about three foot further to go. When you get home from school today, I'll show you. At the bottom of this hole there'll be a little spring flowing past. To tap the spring all I need is a length of

Trixie's hose."

"Trixie's gonna yell at you for messing in her garden."

Joseph laughed.

"I merely want to see how much water is in the spring, Maudie."

"You reckon you gonna hit it lucky, Old Joseph?

"I must be sure the spring's not going to dry up in a day. That would be silly wouldn't it?"

"Yah, I s'pose so."

She stood hands on hips, her toes playing in the dirt. At the far end of the garden his dustbin lay on its side, the contents strewn along the fence.

"Why's your rubbish bin such a mess?" My sister wanted to know.

Joseph leaned on his spade and sighed. "Monkeys. Inquisitive vervets off the koppies who raid every dustbin they find."

"Ours is in the backyard. I think they scared of going there with Hobo about."

"Not when they discover her leg's in plaster and her head's in a seaside bucket," Joseph chuckled. "The troop's taken up residence on the koppie under the water tower. Sometimes they scramble down the ridge to Gillooly's. Probably follow their food supply. The last three mornings they've come down Good Hope Street, raiding dustbins."

Maudie giggled.

"Tomorrow however," Joseph declared, "I'll play a little trick on them."

"You gonna give 'em a surprise?"

Joseph grinned.

"You'll see, Maudie. Just be watching tomorrow morning when the monkeys come scrambling down the garden fences."

Chapter 15

That evening our father serviced our Chev. He would be driving the Proberts to their daughter's wedding the next day and didn't want the engine to play up. Maudie and I were in the fig tree working on our tree house when the slab sided bonnet of the car nosed up to the gates.

I slipped out of the tree first and raced down the drive.

Maudie came galloping after me.

"Wait! Tadpole! Hang on! Don't always run faster than me."

We swung open the gates and leapt onto the running boards for a ride to the garage.

My sister's crimson sign tacked to the fig tree infused me with a feeling of freedom. Amos was coming with Mr Sunshine to spend the weekend with his mama. Graham and Louis would be visiting the next morning.

Our father donned his overalls and opened one of the bonnet's skirts. Maudie and I scrambled onto the front bumper and peered over the radiator.

"Never tighten the plugs much more than finger tight," he told us so we would remember when we grew up. "It's not necessary and all you'll do is squash the compression washers."

"Uh huh Abe, sure thing."

He had his head over the engine, his fingers twirling a plug spanner, lifting out the six sparkplugs one at a time.

"Please don't drop anything into the engine." He indicated the threaded holes before carrying the plugs to the workbench.

He laid out a sheet of newspaper, emery cloth and his feeler gauges. In twenty minutes he had cleaned the sparkplugs and reset the gaps. Fifteen minutes later they were back in the engine only a touch harder than finger tight and he was unclipping the distributor cap.

"I don't s'pose you tightened 'em too hard, Abe," Maudie observed.

Our father's tools were ancient. I think he bought them second-hand. His toolbox was wooden. He didn't buy new tools if the old ones broke. He fixed them. Holding a file in two hands, he sharpened his saws, tooth by tooth. He did the same with drill bits, fastened them in the vice and honed their tips.

Snapped tools were shortened down, the fractured stump rounded off. He reshaped his screwdrivers, sharpened his plane blade and chisels, hammered bent nails straight and cut new slots into the heads of wood screws. His tools, scratched and scarred, had non-working edges rounded like the steps of an old building.

After he reset the Chev's points, Mrs Probert waddled up the drive.

"Hello Mister Frey," she greeted, pausing to catch her breath. He hated being called Mr Frey but was too polite to tell her.

"Everything ready for Ruth's wedding tomorrow?" he enquired.

"Oh Mister Frey, I'm so aggravated I can't tell you. I've had nothing but aggravation all week. If it's not cleaning and dusting the church, it's worrying about the flowers. I've been trying to see the minister for days now to go through the details with him."

"I wouldn't worry about that Missus Probert. I'm sure everything will go off perfectly," our father replied, keeping his head in the engine.

"Oh I do hope the ceremony is done properly Mister Frey. I'm not happy about the organist's dress but she says she hasn't anything else. I hope not too many people notice. Then there's the hall for the reception. I can't make up my mind whether the band should be on the left or the right of the stage.

"The left," our father sighed from under the bonnet.

Mrs Probert digested this. "I wanted a list of the music the band's going to play so I can tell them in what order to play the pieces, but the band leader says he can't do that."

"Tell them to start with the first piece, Missus Probert."

"Oh dear I know something's going to go wrong. I just know it. There are all the speeches to worry about."

"Are you making all the speeches yourself?"

"Oh it's all right for you, Mister Frey. It's not your daughter who's getting married."

"Worst luck," he muttered, glancing at Maudie.

"The most important event in Ruth's life, mind you. If something goes wrong, what will the guests say?"

"I don't think they'll even notice."

She smiled sweetly. "There are the in-laws to think of. I'm worried about the catering. That's a big thing on its own, you know."

"I'm sure your in-laws won't starve in a single afternoon, Missus Probert."

"I haven't finished my own dress yet. It was ready but now I've decided to drop the hem an inch. The bridesmaids are coming tonight for their final fitting. If their dresses are not right, I'll be sewing until after midnight."

"That's a good time to be sleeping."

"Tomorrow I have to make the posies. I hope the florist delivers the right flowers. Jack is bringing home the confetti today. I'd better go and check it's not the wrong colour."

"You worry too much, Missus Probert."

Her chest heaved. "I'm in such a flat spin, I'll be truly grateful when the whole thing is over."

"So will I," he responded.

"Is Babs home by any chance, Mister Frey?"

Our father shook his head. "Gone drinking with her flying friends. Said she'd sleep over with them."

"What about my limousine Babs is getting me? She promised a Chrysler or a De Soto. Something really nice, you know."

Our father sighed. "I'm sure Babs has arranged a nice bridal car for Ruth. You gave her five pounds didn't you?"

"Oh yes Mister Frey, last Monday evening. But I worry about these things, you know. I would really like a Chrysler."

"Well I don't know what make she has for you, but if Babs promised you a bridal car, you can be sure she'll have one." He folded down the side skirt of the bonnet and turned the locking handles closed.

"You worry too much, Missus Probert. Babs will have your car. She'll drive it to the church with Ruth in the back seat. White ribbons flying from the radiator cap to the windscreen." He wiped his hands on a wad of cotton waste.

Maudie and I were loafing on the front bumper when I heard an uproar from the front garden. The throaty Zulu voice of Amos. For a one-child-vociferation he kicked up enough racket to bring the neighbours rushing to their windows.

"Heavens above, what's going on?" Mrs Probert cried.

"Sounds like he has a tribe of Xhosa warriors after him," our father remarked.

Amos flew around the corner of the house, charging up the drive. He didn't see us in the garage and rounded into the backyard at full tilt. Sampson stuck his head out the kitchen window, but Amos's message was too important for Sampson. He wanted Maudie. Sampson pointed to the garage.

"Maudie... quick!" Amos yelled. "Hobo..."

My heart stopped. Hobo had wandered onto the street. She'd been run over. With her leg in plaster she never had a chance. Our father and Maudie jumped to the same conclusion and sprinted down the drive.

"Hobo my angel... not you Hobo... no..."

Maudie's dog however was lying lazily on the front lawn, scratching her neck just below the red, white and blue bucket.

"Aren't you gonna help her?" Amos hollered. "She got her head stuck right through that bucket and can't get it off. It's choking her to death."

Sampson wandered onto the front veranda to see what the fuss was about. He fixed his eyes on Amos and opened his mouth wider and wider until he shook with mirth.

"Humph," Amos snorted and climbed over the fence to see his mama.

Friday evening's Star reported scant news of the muti-murder. The police had made no progress with their investigation. There were no leads. Detectives surmised they might be looking for a killer who commuted between Sophiatown and Kensington. They assumed the perpetrator owned some form of transport. Even bottle-and-bag men had pushcarts, I thought.

Our father studied the report and warned me of the danger. "Son, I've already told you to keep away from the willows at Rhodes Park. On the koppies, stay in sight of the houses. The Foster Caves are out of bounds."

He didn't say anything about stormwater drains. Only Maudie and I knew what was in the culvert under the road.

Chapter 16

Maudie surfaced on Saturday morning happy as a lark.

"Yea it's Saturday at last," she cried, waking me at first light. "We made it, Tadpole. It tickles me pink, really it does. We made it to the weekend."

"I still sleeping, Sis."

"But what about the monkeys? Don't you wanna watch the monkeys? We can keep an eye on Old Joseph's dustbin from our window."

I had a hazy recollection of Joseph's upturned dustbin. Quarter of an hour passed.

"Hey, there's one coming now. Come see, quick."

Maudie spied a vervet scrambling along the fence. Three others followed. They owned the street, springing down to examine anything on the pavement, swinging into neighbour's gardens, lifting dustbin lids to investigate what was inside. When two or three perched on a rim, the bin capsized. They pilfered vegetable peelings and scattered everything else.

Joseph's bin awaited them. He hadn't told us he'd found a grass snake with its back broken lying on the tarmac. He'd tossed the corpse into his dustbin but that had given him an idea. He'd propped the jaws open with a matchstick, taken some thread from Trixie's sewing basket and suspended the dead snake from the lid. Anyone lifting the lid would assume the snake was rising up to bite.

Chattering sixteen to the dozen, the troop scampered along Trixie's fence. When they reached the dustbin the leader sprang down to investigate. He stood on his hind legs only inches taller than the bin itself his eyes level with the rim. He reached over the lid to raise it. The other three watched from the fence.

Maudie started giggling.

"He's putting on an act, Tadpole. Pretending he's important to impress the others."

Before I could answer, the leader jerked open the lid and froze clutching the handle, staring eye level into the gaping jaws of the snake. His legs crumpled and he sprawled on the grass in a faint. The lid clattered back in place.

"Well, I'll be blowed," Maudie giggled. "That's the darndest thing I ever seen."

"Yah, Sis. I guess the others're gonna tootle off home now."

"No, lookee there. They haven't seen what's inside Joseph's bin."

Chattering in noisy argument the troop delegated another member to investigate. The remaining two remained rooted to the fence.

The second vervet was better prepared than the first. He inched the lid up, squawked at what was inside, promptly replaced it, sprang away and leapt for the fence. The one collapsed on the ground, roused himself and shot onto the fence like lightning. There they sat, gesticulating and chattering among themselves.

My sister cracked up.

"Cool it, Maudie, else I'll hafta take you to the outhouse."

"I didn't wet myself. But look. They humming and hawing there. I believe they double daring one of 'em to go take another look see."

A third monkey eased himself to the ground and glancing back at the others, cautiously approached Joseph's bin. Those on the fence backed up a few yards. The nominee crept forward, lifted the lid an eighth of an inch and put his eye to the slit. He peered into the interior for less than a second before slamming the lid shut. The troop fled.

"Well what'd'you know? Fancy that. I bet they never

gonna raid Old Joseph's bin again."

"I reckon not, Sis."

The morning sun cleared the eastern horizon and lay eclipsed by rooftops. Sunrise cast a shimmering nimbus along the corrugated iron. From the top of Good Hope Street, I heard the agitated barking of dogs baring their disapproval at the troop fleeing along garden fences. The suburb slept. Friday was payday and Friday night, drinking time for men in the trades. In an hour they would be off to their Saturday morning stint.

Maudie and I lay on my bed competing with each other to sustain the longest outburst of mirth.

"Ah put a cork in it," Frog yelled from his room on the other side of the passage.

Our father came in to see what was going on with us. "Do the great unwashed know it's Ruth's wedding today?"

"Yah we do Abe and aw gee, children aren't invited."

"I dunno if I want to go to a silly old wedding," I interjected.

"Well I do." Maudie stamped her foot.

"Maudie sweetheart, a wedding's an adult affair. You'd be bored stiff. I have to drive the Proberts to the church. While I'm gone, I'd like you children to behave yourselves."

"But Abe, we always do."

"Well, I'm not so sure about that," he remarked, leaving us and hurrying through to the back of the house.

"You mustn't tell, Tadpole, but I got an idea what we can do this afternoon."

"What?"

"When Abe's left for the wedding, we can jol down the avenue. The Methodist's not far, twenty minutes at the most. We can watch from the pavement across the avenue and see Babs bringing Ruth in her limo."

"Not a bad idea, Sis. We got nothing else to do."

"After they married, we can watch 'em drive away in their swanky car."

"Yah, I wanta see the limo."

"I thought you didn't wanna go to a silly old wedding."

"I don't, but I wanta see Babs' limo."

"Yah, especially with white ribbons."

"So we going to Ruth's wedding after all."

"Sure looks like it," my sister giggled.

From the back veranda I heard Hobo's tinny bark. The milkman in white overalls came up the drive rattling his bottles. He knew Maudie's dog couldn't chase him. He placed our fresh milk on the back veranda, nonchalantly picked up our empties and tramped down the drive tinkling the glass.

Maudie and I wandered into the backyard and hung over the fence. Amos squirmed on a chopping block having his head shaved. He couldn't see us watching him fidget and fuss. Selina shaved his frizz with a piece of broken glass. She cut his hair every six months. Everything came off and he walked around looking like a convict.

"Shave him bald, Selina, like an old man," my sister encouraged.

"No Mama, please don't. You mustn't listen to her."

He howled under Selina's hold, twisting his neck to squint at us.

"Next time I think your dog's in trouble, I aren't gonna tell you."

"Hey Amos," I called. "You wanna see Ruth Probert's wedding limo? She's getting married at the Methodist today."

"Yah. That's why I'm having my hair cut. So they'll let me in the church."

He started giggling until Selina cuffed his ear.

"We not allowed in the church." Maudie said. "We just gonna mosey along the pavement and see what gives."

Chapter 17

Three years had passed since the collision on the farm road. Figs dropped from the tree and rotted on the ground. Graham tormented his brother Louis for picking up Davy's head. Louis became obsessed with washing his hands.

Our father still didn't know how Momma and Stanley could have been involved in such a monstrous accident. Maudie knew but trauma prevented her from talking.

Graham and Louis arrived as we gulped our porridge. "Hey chum," Graham chortled. "How many times you washed your hands since you picked up that *soccer ball*? Thousand, two thousand maybe? I reckon you gonna get gangrene. Your fingers just gonna fall off by themselves. No need to wash 'em."

Louis scowled and disappeared into the garage to scrounge for spanners.

Amos, sporting an ostrich scalp, clambered over the fence in time to watch Louis ride his bike to the top of the drive and career into the backyard past the fig tree. He back-pedalled to brake but nothing happened. "Damn it!" he cried in panic, ramming his big toe onto the front tyre.

The bike careened into Sampson's room on the far side of the yard. Graham let out a roar of derisive laughter. "That bike's prehistoric. The dinosaurs had footbrakes and they extinct ages ago."

Louis picked himself up, scowled and wheeled the bike into the garage. "How about you and me getting us jobs at the Rand Easter Show, Graham? We can get us enough boodle to fix the bike properly."

"You mean, Bro, how about me getting us both jobs at the show."

Louis grunted, dismantling the brake and schemed of earning pocket money at Johannesburg's annual agricultural and industrial show.

Amos unearthed a fence dropper behind the garage.

"Boy, I'm gonna make me a snazzy spear outta this," he chortled.

"You don't need this, chum, do you? Gonna fix my old cattie," Graham asked as he filched a perished tube from Louis's saddlebag.

Amos ground one end of the fence dropper to a point on our father's grinding wheel. He fetched a hacksaw and cut barbs in the shaft. On the other end he fashioned a handle by binding wire around the dropper.

"Say, that's great Amos," Graham exclaimed, reaching to get a feel for the spear. "Who you gonna kill with this? The Tokoloshe?" He made a playful lunge.

Amos snickered. "No, man. I gonna spear me a catfish down at the lake. I'll bring it home for my mama to cook."

We ran out of things to do until Graham suggested, "Hey, I got this great idea about us making like a internal combustion engine."

We allowed him to organize us into pistons and a rotor. Four of us were pistons. We stood in a row ready to leap up and down.

"The firing order," Graham explained, "is one, three, four, two. You go down on your haunches, leap up when you're the piston firing and drop down again. I'll give the count and see how high I can rev the engine. Amos, you the rotor, okay? You stick your arms out and spin round. The faster the engine revs, the faster you gotta spin. Understand?"

We tried this a number of times, the four of us bouncing up and down to Graham's shouts of, "One, three, four, two, one, three, four, two..." But every time we speeded up, the rotor collapsed. So we took turns to be the rotor.

On one attempt our human engine did extraordinary well.

"C'mon, faster," Graham yelled. "You getting two hundred revs a minute." We sprang up and down like crazy. Amos spun in a blur.

Mrs Probert waddled up the drive and stopped dead. Our engine lost enthusiasm and plopped down. She gave us a wide berth on her way to the back veranda stairs.

Graham belched. Amos thought this was hilarious. He rolled his eyes and squinted at his nose. Then filling his body with air he forced out a competitive burp, a long drawn out croak like the lowest bass on a church organ. Then Maudie tried. She was quite good but her performance didn't have the resonance of the boys. Not to be outdone Graham gave us another of his renderings. Then Louis joined in and our backyard sounded like a frog marsh on a summer's evening.

Clutching the sewing basket she'd borrowed from Sampson, Mrs Probert lumbered down the kitchen steps. With an incredulous expression she waddled past. As each of us caught sight of her, our contribution to the cacophony abruptly ended. All except for my sister who had her back to her and burped obscenely when Mrs Probert rounded the side of the house. Our neighbour retreated down the drive shaking her head.

"What about our boat?" Graham suggested. "Why don't we build our own boat like we said we gonna?"

"Yah, I forgot about that," Louis added. "With our own boat, we don't hafta pay."

"And we can spear a catfish," Amos pointed out.

"Or take it to Gillooly's Farm and paddle on the river," I added.

"Where we gonna get wood to make it?" Louis muttered.

"Not wood, chum. Look behind you. That sheet of old roof tin lying by the garage. We can fold that into a canoe."

Graham leapt up at his own genius and inspected the sheet of corrugated metal. It was ten foot long, more than twice Maudie's height and four foot wide. We extracted it from a tangle of scrap between the garage and the fence.

"Whad'we do about the corrugations?" Louis wanted to know.

"We leave 'em, chum. They make the boat strong."

"Yah, but what about the ends where we gotta fix 'em together?"

"You gonna hammer the ends flat, bro."

I lugged our father's sledgehammer from the garage and Graham coerced Louis to pound the corrugations flat at either end. To shape the front, we folded the sheet in half, leaving the rest lying flat. A search in the garage produced a strip of timber for the stem piece. We stuck this in the bow and nailed each side of the folded sheet to the timber.

It took us hours to shape the bow of the canoe.

"S'gonna leak plenty," Maudie noted. "We hafta figure out how to stop the water coming in."

"I'll work on that, Sis. Any ideas?"

"Uh uh, not yet. Give me time and I'll figure it out."

Louis discovered that if we folded the stern into a point like the bow, the canoe capsized.

"Gotta make it wide at the back like a rowing boat," Graham noted. "Maud, how about a plank from your tree house?"

My sister climbed into the fig tree to retrieve one of her precious boards.

"Perfect," Graham muttered, snatching it out of her hands.

He grabbed our father's ripsaw and cut her plank to make the stern wide enough to accommodate our buttocks. We rolled the sheet over and nailed the stern onto my sister's tree house plank. Nailing each side at a time, we folded up the two sides of the stern and fixed them to the transom. Graham sat in the dirt to watch.

Our canoe was shaped. It resembled a narrow rowing boat and to anybody else, looked like a piece of homemade junk.

"S'gonna leak like crazy," Louis grumbled, pointing to the gaps between the nails.

Maudie clicked her fingers. "Got it."

"Shoot, Sis."

"I been figuring it out, Tadpole. Abe's roofing pitch... You know that tar stuff he fixes leaks in the roof with."

I tripped into the garage and rummaged under the workbench until I came across a tin of old roofing pitch. The stuff was stiff as liquorice.

"Sneak it past Semp-Sonne and heat it on the Queen Mary," Maudie whispered.

It took us all morning to leak-proof our contraption. The time came when we stood back against the fig tree and appraised our work.

"It's a ocean liner from Southampton," Graham grinned.

"Nah, maybe a dugout canoe in the swamps of the Congo," Louis suggested.

"How about a English battleship blasting the enemy with a broadside?" I offered.

"Or a fancy motorboat?" suggested Amos.

"Maybe a paddle steamer on the Mississippi? An Injun canoe in the Wild West?" I proposed. "Or even a dandy sailing yacht?"

"Nuh, Tadpole," Maudie argued. "S'Old Joseph's square rigger rounding Cape Horn in a sixty knot gale, running for her life in front of the greybeards with Old Joseph at the wheel."

I grinned at my sister. She was so happy about our boat.

"What we gonna call it?" Louis asked. "All boats got names, you know something like Cap'n Hook."

"*Her* Bro," Graham emphasized. "Not *it*. Boats're

women."

"Then you gotta give her a girl's name," Maudie pointed out. "How about Hobo?"

"That's your mongrel's name," Graham protested.

"Louise," Louis prompted. "She looks like a Louise."

Graham shook his head. "Nah s'not good enough."

"Babs," I suggested feebly.

Graham remained deep in thought.

Amos stopped polishing the point of his spear and put the weapon down.

"We must name the ship, Nkosazana," he stated solemnly.

Graham glanced up. "Incausa-what? Are you crazy? I mean what the hell's that? Jeez, nobody gonna understand a stupid name like that."

Amos drew himself to his full height. "Nkosazana means a beautiful unmarried maiden just like our ship."

Graham sucked his teeth. "Nah, it's no good. We need something grand, a name that's gonna make people stop and take notice, something royal."

We stood around, scratching our heads.

Graham clicked his fingers.

"I got it. We gonna call her The Vale of Belvoir, after a castle in England. Tadpole, see if you can find some paint and a brush. We'll paint the name on right away."

The Vale of Belvoir. The grandest sounding name I'd ever heard. Maudie came to me while I was searching for paint.

"The Vale of Belvoir is a green sounding name, Tadpole. You gotta find the dark green paint Abe uses on the drainpipes."

The only green paint I found was so old and stiff, none of us could stir it.

"Tell you what," Graham said. "We can stir it up with a power mixer."

"What power mixer?" Louis asked, searching the workbench.

"We just take part of this old eggbeater here,"

Graham explained, "stick it into their old-man's electric drill and presto, we got ourself a power mixer." He fitted the bottom part of an ancient eggbeater to our father's Millers Falls drill.

"Here Bro," he said, shoving it into Louis's hands, "mix the paint for us."

"You reckon it'll work?" Louis eyed the contraption dubiously.

"Course it'll work, chum. Just stick the eggbeater in the paint and away you go."

When Graham flicked the switch, all hell broke loose. The eggbeater thrashed at unbelievable speed. In three seconds it probably turned as many times as it had in forty years of hand usage. It operated so fast, Louis couldn't control it. He reached to switch off the power but the paint tin snagged on the eggbeater and started spinning on the end of the drill. It spun crazily, splattering paint everywhere.

"Turn it off, Graham, turn it off," Louis screamed, getting covered in paint. He tried lifting the drill out but the tin was stuck on the eggbeater. He couldn't put the drill down but the longer he held it, the more paint flew out.

I managed to wrench the plug from the socket. Louis's face was covered in green paint. Graham rolled on the ground under the fig tree splitting his sides.

"I dunno that it's so funny," Louis complained. "Seems to me, it was your idea."

Graham couldn't talk, he doubled up again. It took Louis half an hour to clean up the mess.

As my sister was good at lettering, she got the job of painting the impressive title on the bow.

We were standing back admiring our work when the Chev pulled up outside our house. We left Maudie's sign-writing to dry in the sun and traipsed into the kitchen for a bite of Sampson's lunch.

"You children go wash outside," he admonished. "You not coming in here looking like that." We humbly washed under the garden tap before he allowed us into his kitchen.

A polite knock on the screen door prompted us to look up and discover Mr Sunshine beaming down at us. He wore one of his immaculate double-breasted blue suits. The cuffs of his silk shirt showing past his jacket sleeves were fastened with gold cufflinks. His red and blue striped tie held in place with a gold tiepin was fastened in a Windsor knot. A crimson rosebud adorned his lapel. His patent leather shoes shone like mirrors.

"Lordy! Lordy, folks. Good afternoon Mister Freyer." His warmth swept over us.

"Lordy... I'm indeed sorry to disturb you good people. I was wondering if Miss Babs was home yet?"

"She won't be home today," our father explained. "Leaving straight from work for a wedding. Has to chauffeur the bride."

Mr Sunshine looked crestfallen but his radiance returned.

"Oh Lordy! Well, not to worry. I was hoping to see her. We have a little business between us. If you don't mind I'll spend some time with Sampson." He bent down and hefted his suitcase.

"Hamba kahle, Mister Sunshine," Maudie called after him. "Go well."

"Is Babs buying clothing from Mister Sunshine?" Our father wondered. "I think not."

This wasn't the first time Mister Sunshine had asked for Babs. What was our aunt buying if not clothing? The question occupied my thoughts as I ate my lunch.

Chapter 18

Mrs Probert, robed in a pink gown that reached to the pavement, came out of the gate with her husband. Our father was not finished dressing. The Proberts decided to wait in the Chev parked in the street. We children hung around the front veranda.

Presently our father came out of the house, strode down the garden path, climbed into the Chev and we watched as complete with the Proberts it rolled away down Good Hope Street.

The Methodist church was situated halfway down Roberts Avenue hill. Thirty aged cars were parked outside. One or two postwar models stood among them but the majority were from the thirties, straight sided Fords, Dodges, Plymouths, Hudsons and Chevrolets like our own. All flat-roofed saloons with the middle of the roof made of rubber. They'd come painted black from the factories, some more drab than others.

We pranced down the pavement and clustered under an oak tree opposite the Methodist. Louis collected acorns for his catapult and Maudie gazed across the avenue, eyeing two bridesmaids waiting with Mr Probert and a man with a box-camera. The rest of the guests were already in the church and the organ was playing.

"Whadya reckon happened to the limo?" Maudie wanted to know, hitching up her cords.

"Maybe Ruth's taking her time getting dressed, Sis. After all, it's her big day."

"Yah, I spect so. I s'pose she'll take ages to get ready."

Graham pulled the live cartridges from his pocket.

"Jeez, I got a snazzy idea for shooting these bullets on the koppies. You all gonna mess your pants."

I saw no sign of the bridal limousine and those across the road started looking at their watches. Inside the church the bellows organ began pumping out hymns already played. Each time a motorcar came down the hill, necks were craned and when it continued down the hill out came the watches again. A tram moaned its way past.

"Ruth's awful late," Maudie pointed out.

I heard cheers from the pavement opposite. A spanking new 1947 Chrysler shining regal black and sporting the whitest of white ribbons over the bonnet was cruising down the hill. Mr Probert glanced at his watch and stepped to the kerb.

"Wow, look at that everybody," Maudie cried. "Babs got the fanciest limo I ever seen. Loopity-loop, spanking new. See the ribbons, Tadpole."

The Chrysler, whitewall tyres and all, really was magnificent, the stateliest limousine I had ever seen. The bride veiled in white, sat in the back. Mr Probert held his hand out ready to open the door for his daughter.

The Chrysler cruised right by us with no attempt to slow down. It disappeared down the hill with everybody gaping after it.

"What's going on?" Amos asked. "Why didn't they stop?"

"Yah, what's Babs doing?" Maudie added. "She knows it's the Methodist."

"Another wedding," Graham answered.

Across the road the organist began playing music I'd heard twice before. Mr Probert studied his watch.

We lounged under the oak tree with our feet in the gutter. Maudie sighed. Graham skimmed an acorn across the tramlines.

"Just think, Maud. One day you'll have a fancy wedding like this."

"Uh uh, Graham. Not me. I tell you, when I get big

I'm not gonna fall in love or get married. That's kids' stuff."

"You're joking. What'll you do?"

"I been thinking about that. I wanta be a real lady. So I'm gonna get me a horse and a guitar and I'll ride round every day singing Don't Fence Me In."

"Good thinking," Amos agreed.

Another vehicle rattled down the hill, a rusted Dodge one-ton breakdown lorry. When I looked closer I saw it had a '39 Ford with a smashed radiator hooked up behind. I watched the two vehicles approach. The breakdown lorry's brake pads squealed as it pulled into the reserved parking space in front of the church.

Mr Probert waved it away. When the lorry wouldn't move, he became angry and cursed the driver. I didn't know he knew language like that. Babs swung the door open and climbed out. Mr Probert stopped shouting. Our aunt strolled around the lorry and opened the passenger door.

Ruth sat there in her wedding gown, her feet up on a coil of grease stained rope. Babs helped her down, extricating her gown with only minimal stains. Mr Probert stood back, his jaw fallen. Babs slipped a flask from her pocket and took a slug. She rummaged in the back of the lorry, dragging chains out of the way and retrieved Ruth's bouquet. Then standing back, she let Mr Probert take his daughter's arm.

Someone signalled the organist to start playing *Here Comes the Bride*. The group hurried to comply. We plopped down on the kerb with our feet in the gutter and tossed acorns across the tramlines.

"That's some bridal limo standing there," Graham snorted.

"What'll Missus Probert say when she comes out the church with her guests. And they see Ruth and her husband drive away in a breakdown lorry?" I asked.

"Maybe they gonna ride in the prang hitched up at the back," Maudie giggled.

Chapter 19

There was a cat that lived under the jetty at Rhodes Park, a Manx cat Maudie nicknamed Tsotsi. An escaped house cat, Tsotsi fished at the water's edge crouching as close as he could without falling in. The more engrossed Tsotsi became the lower his face dropped to the surface. His right paw crept toward the water and his claws fidgeted out of their sheaths. I watched him scoop a minnow, take mock fright and spring away. The more the fish floundered the bigger Tsotsi's frights. Then the poor minnow began to suffocate. Tsotsi encouraged it with his paw and when that failed, bit the head off and sat down to lunch.

"I s'pose Tsotsi will be real pleased to catch a fish bigger than a minnow one day, hey Tadpole?" Maudie giggled.

Sunday morning found us launching *The Vale of Belvoir* on the park lake.

"We gonna get in trouble," Maudie warned. "Abe told us to keep away from the willows."

"Nah, it'll be all right, Sis. Won't go near the willows. That's scary. Any case, Graham and Louis're with us and they twelve years old."

"Yah, I s'pose you right. I frightened of the scary side."

"Okay, I'm first," Graham declared, grabbing the canoe.

Our contraption floated low in the water. He pushed himself off and paddled by hand.

"Hobo can be our ship's dog when her leg gets better," my sister laughed. She clasped her hands in front of her and gazed at our canoe dreamily.

"What you thinking about now? Sailing round the world?"

"Nah. The Vale of Belvoir's too darn small. Our arms'll get tired."

"Well what would you choose to go round the world?"

"Me? I'd get a battleship, Tadpole. They the best. You don't hafta paddle."

Graham brought the canoe back to the shore to fetch Louis.

"You gonna get your trousers wet, chum. This thing leaks like a sieve."

Louis climbed in, slopping water over the sides. They paddled to the middle and returned half an hour later. When they nosed onto the bank, *The Vale of Belvoir* was awash. I had a vision of it sliding to the bottom of the lake and lying with other terrible things down there. I didn't say anything to my sister.

"We can hardly keep it afloat," Graham complained. "My bro will hafta fix it."

They dragged the canoe out the water and rolled it over on the grass. Amos stalked the shallows, looking for catfish.

"I seen where they are," Maudie piped.

She showed him where the bank overhung the water.

"If you lie on your tummy, you can see catfish underneath. They looking for old fish bait that floats in."

She watched Amos for minutes before anything happened. Then a catfish appeared. It approached silently, hidden beneath the surface until it was under Amos's nose. Because the water was shallow under the bank its back broke the surface. I gaped at its size.

"A real beauty."

Amos stifled a Zulu war cry and began raising his spear. The catfish was more out of the water than in. It was the ugliest fish I had ever seen and I couldn't imagine anybody wanting to eat it. Its skin was black like a shark and had no scales. The eyes were set on the top of the head and I suppose this meant it was a surface feeder coming up and swallowing its prey from below. The mouth was enormous with fleshy whiskers growing out of its muzzle.

I watched in fascination. Amos positioned himself. He raised an arm preparing to strike but this spooked the fish. Its tail swept the water in a flourish and the prize was gone.

"Ah, forget it. They too fast for you. You never gonna catch one," Graham sniggered, going for a walk.

"I gonna try again," Amos hissed.

Tsotsi joined Amos, crouched with his head over the bank. Amos perched on a knee his spear ready.

I couldn't tell whether the same catfish came back. It happened too quickly. Amos detected movement under the water. As the fish surfaced, he plunged his spear toppling into the water and screaming his head off.

"Yeeowee... I got him."

The fish went berserk. Amos hung on, hollering at the top of his voice. His spear went wild. He gritted his teeth. He had pegged the catfish through its tail. As the two struggled in the water his spear started working free.

"No... oooh."

In desperation he bent down, thrust his arms under the surface, scooped the fish up and heaved it onto the bank.

When the catfish arced over Tsotsi's head, the Manx raced after it. The fish thrashed on the bank turning head over tail. Each time it landed, Tsotsi darted in. When the fish cart-wheeled into him, Tsotsi skidded sideways to get out of the way. He began licking his chops. Amos watched wide eyed. The catfish thrashed for ten minutes, its body heaving and contracting. I thought it was spent. So did Tsotsi. None of us knew the primitive species could survive out of water.

When the fish rested, Tsotsi sprang. Claws

unsheathed he landed with all fours on top of what he thought was going to be his supper. The catfish was the same weight as the cat. It would be the biggest meal Tsotsi ever had in his life. When he sprang, the catfish lashed with more power than before. Its tail sent the enmeshed pair tumbling over. Each time they hit the grass it thrashed itself into a frenzy. Cat and fish rolled over and over in the grass.

"Hey quit it, that's my property," Amos sobbed, too frightened to rush in and separate them.

Tsotsi soon abandoned the idea of dining on catfish. He now tried to disentangle himself. He'd hooked his claws into the fish's skin and they wouldn't come loose. The fish cart-wheeled both of them. Tsotsi landed upside down with the catfish on top. He kicked with all fours to keep the monster away. Somehow he freed his claws and flew helter-skelter behind Maudie's legs for protection.

"Enough, enough," Amos bawled, "There soon be nothing left for my mama to cook."

It was time anyway to carry our canoe home to plug the leaks.

On the way home I heard Graham snickering to Louis.

"You take a dekko at that African guy following us in the park, Bro? Walked funny like. Gone now. Just disappeared."

"Nuh, didn't see."

I remembered Maudie's description of her giraffe man, I wanted to question my cousin but thought better of it. My sister's nightmares scared me.

"Let's go on the koppies," Graham suggested that afternoon, "I'll show you how to fire bullets without a gun."

"I getting scared of the koppies," Maudie confided.

"S'okay Sis. Daddy said to stay in sight of the houses."

She whistled up Amos and when we looked over the

fence, saw he'd filled a galvanized tub with water. His catfish floundered in that.

"When's your mama gonna cook it?" Graham asked.

"When she gets back from church. Hasn't seen it yet."

Louis pumped his bike's tyres.

"I planning to go riding on the koppie paths. Be just like riding a bronco."

"You ride over any thorns and get another puncture, chum, you can fix it."

Amos got the giggles.

"What you grinning at?" Graham demanded.

Amos pressed his lips tight. Muted explosions of mirth rocked his chest. His body shook. Maudie and I took up the sniggers. Graham strode on ahead pretending not to hear.

Across the street Mrs Probert's curtains were drawn. Her house was in mourning. Before the wedding she hinted to anyone who would listen that she'd hired a Chrysler. She'd got the shock of her life when she marched out of the church. It wasn't clear why a dilapidated Dodge breakdown lorry with grease stained ribbons and a Ford with a smashed radiator hitched up behind, were parked there. Our neighbour retired to bed with a headache for three days.

Joseph watered his conservatory plants. He had marked out his waterways and dug the first two ponds. An interconnecting canal was taking shape and a spade leant against his walnut tree.

"How you gonna fire those bullets, Graham?"

"That Bro, is a secret."

Louis scratched his scalp. Amos's homemade wire motorcar got stuck in an outcrop of kikuyu grass.

"When's your mama gonna cook your catfish, Amos?" Maudie asked.

He grinned at her, tugging the toy free. "Tonight. I'll hafta get her to bang it on the head and cook it in a pan." He patted his stomach.

At the top of Good Hope Street we ducked under the dead-end barrier and sauntered along a koppie path.

"I just thought of something," Graham remarked. "If we took The Vale of Belvoir up the mine-dumps, we could ride it like a sled. I mean they like big sand dunes. Probably do thirty miles a hour. Would be terrific."

Louis sighed. "Not bad. Yah maybe you're right. We can give it a try."

The mine-dumps are very lonely, I thought. Nobody goes there.

Maudie pranced in front of me. "Tadpole, I been worrying what Mister Sunshine wanted with Babs yesterday?"

"Dunno Sis. Business I s'pose."

"Yah, but what business?"

I shrugged.

"Why don't we find out? Why don't we spy on Mister Sunshine?"

"Spy on him?"

"Yah, maybe we can find out what he really got in his case."

Graham came to a halt.

"Bro go grab some twigs and dry leaves, will you? You others go help him. They gotta be dry. I don't wanta make smoke."

He built a miniature fireplace that resembled the inside of a volcano. We handed him our kindling which he packed into the furnace hole. Then he struck a match and tossed it in. The kindling flamed with only a suggestion of smoke. As it burned down, the ashes began glowing. He took a live cartridge from his pocket and dropped it into the fire.

"You got seconds to get down before that thing goes off," he chortled, diving into the grass.

I didn't see which way the bullet pointed when it landed in the fire.

"Maudie," I yelled, grabbing her hand.

We fell in the grass and buried our heads under our

arms. We waited. Nothing happened. Maudie lifted her head and at that instant there was a report from three feet away and a piercing whine as the lead slug hurtled past her.

"Blast you Graham." Louis protested. "That's damn dangerous."

"The second one's going in now," Graham retorted, diving for cover.

Maudie was out of reach. I started running. I rugby tackled her and we went down together. A second later the bullet whined over our heads.

"Now you learned how to fire a bullet without a gun," Graham hooted. "I gotta try that on The Bear one day. It'll scare him silly."

"He'll do more than phone the fire station, Graham. The old geezer'll call the police."

"Heh heh, probably pop his whole bottle of pills all at once."

Louis picked up his bike. "Where's this path go, Tadpole? I wanna ride somewhere new."

"Wait for me, chum. You can give me a lift."

The path skirted a boulder and disappeared down the koppie.

"Where's it come out?" Graham enquired, rocking his twin backwards and forwards on his bike.

"At a stream down the bottom. There's a log damming the water. Maudie and me sometimes go swim there."

"C'mon Bro, let's go see. I feel like a swim."

He climbed onto the cross bar and Louis kicked the bike forward.

"It's steep," I warned.

Maudie and I started running ahead. Amos followed. Graham gave a whooping war cry as Louis pedalled to pick up speed. The twins were on their way. We leapt onto a boulder and viewed the valley below.

"Oh, lookee there," Maudie cried. "They got a church in the river."

Twenty or thirty African people crowded the bottom of the path. Their pastor wearing running shorts stood waist deep in the water, preaching to his followers. He clasped a woman who fidgeted nervously. Then he arched her backwards and ducked her under the surface. The crowd murmured in wonderment. Maudie giggled. The convert surfaced spluttering but saved. The minister led her to the bank where a man and woman in white and blue vestments enticed the next recruit into the water.

The twins were picking up real speed now. Balanced on the cross bar Graham twisted forwards, hanging onto the handlebar. Louis crouched over him barely able to see past his brother's head.

"Lickity-lick," Maudie cried. "Graham and Louis sure going flat out now."

"Brake!" I yelled after them. "There's a church service down there. You gonna ride into the middle of it."

"I can't." Louis wailed. "The foot brake's gone soft again."

"Your toe," Graham hissed. "Shove your toe on the front tyre."

The bicycle shot down the path with Louis trying to stop it with his big toe. He could hold it on the tyre for only a fraction of a second. Then the friction burnt him silly and he howled in protest. Graham cursed him every time he took his toe off the tyre and Louis bellowed every time he put it back.

"Those people down there sure gonna get a surprise," Amos predicted.

"They gonna get a revelation," Maudie added.

At the sound of cursing the pastor glanced up. He waved his arms to shoo the bicycle away. His congregation turned to see Graham and Louis bearing down on them. Those in front backed into those behind and those on the bank toppled into the water. Graham was yelling at Louis when the front wheel hit a rock and they flew over the handlebar knocking a buxom matron into the stream.

The twins landed in the water among the congregation and surfaced face to face with the pastor. About twenty members of the congregation had fallen into the stream. The bicycle landed upside down with a portion of tyre showing above the water. I couldn't hear what was being said but there was a lot of fist shaking and angry faces.

Graham scrambled ashore. Louis cowered before the pastor taking the brunt of the censure. He extricated his bicycle and heaved the wreck onto the bank. When he managed to join his brother, the congregation members were shouting and gesticulating. The twins lost no time in lugging their bike away. When they reached the top of the path Graham decided it was time to go home.

Louis dumped his wreck in the garage and hiked back to Kiewietjie with his brother. Amos climbed over the fence to prod his catfish. Maudie took her silver sign off the fig tree while I dragged my feet up the back veranda stairs to feel the Queen Mary's feeder tank.

While I sat on the edge of the bath with my feet in a bucket of tepid water, attempting to scrub my neck without squeezing anything down my back, Selina next door started screaming blue murder. The first piercing shriek came from just beneath the bathroom window and jolted me into emptying the contents of the sponge down my spine. Her screams rose three octaves. I slid along the side of the bath and stuck my head out the sash window.

Below in our neighbour's yard Selina was backing away from someone I couldn't see. She held her arms out to protect herself and didn't stop shrieking for half a second. Then Amos came into view. He had his catfish clutched to his chest and was hanging onto the whiskered monster for all his life. It wriggled and squirmed and flapped and jumped so, that he was barely able to keep hold of it. And he was trying to get close to his mama so that he could give her the catfish to dispatch.

"Please Mama," he begged. "It's for our supper."

Selina would have none of it. She kept backing away, shaking her head non-stop. They went in circles, Amos advancing and she retreating, wailing and calling him all sorts of names in Zulu. Maudie came out in her pyjamas and hung over the fence below me.

"But Mama," Amos pleaded. "All I want you to do is kill it and cook it for the two of us."

Selina shook her head vigorously. All the time she backed away from her child until he must have realized that never would she so much as touch the catfish, let alone kill it. He didn't know the first thing about cleaning and cooking a fish anyway, so he must have also realized that not in a thousand years was he going to eat of its flesh.

His good intention turned to one of torment. He deliberately backed his mama against the fence, advanced until she pleaded with him hysterically. Then he flung the catfish at her.

There is no musical instrument that can reach the note that Amos's mama did. And no batsman more adroit at hooking a ball. She jerked her head sideways, screwed up her eyes and flung out her arms to ward off the gaping mouth and fleshy whiskers coming her way. Her reactions were slow and what she really achieved was to hook the catfish over Maudie's head into our backyard.

She turned on my sister now, threatening her with all sorts of reprisals if the fish came back over the fence.

The catfish thrashed in the yard. I passed my bucket down to Maudie who scooped up the wriggling monster and held onto the bucket with both hands.

"Stick it in the fridge, Maudie."

She struggled up the back veranda steps and lugged the bucket into the kitchen. I ran from the bathroom to help. We opened our old Kelvinator. Inside was a freezer compartment which didn't get much colder than the fridge. Except for some ice cubes, it was empty.

It took both of us to keep the catfish from escaping as we shoved the fish in with the ice cubes and closed the door.

Maudie started giggling.

"Semp-Sonne's gonna get the fright of his life when he opens the door."

Chapter 20

The summer of '47 was long. It arrived in September snatching the season from spring. Spring didn't come gently. Amid blustering winds, buds and blossoms appeared before sunset. They were not there when we rose. Then a dull summer was with us. Insidious weather. After a desolate winter, the drought began.

Gardens painted themselves crazy. Birds abounded. Trees clothed themselves. The need for water was great. Every morning a sapphire sun journeyed from the Sahara Desert. In the afternoon it sank to a horizon reddened by dust.

Maudie's and my hair matted. Dust clung to motorcars. Red corrugated iron became grey. As the dirty summer took hold, thermometers rose to their maximum. We opened windows at night. Screen doors kept flies out. Lizzie took washing off the line before it turned brown from a street dug up, or yellow from sand blown off mine-dumps.

Threats of rain came with October. Dry thunder storms. Windows rattled. The Impundulu Bird aloft, beat thunderous wings, laying her eggs in the flashes.

At five o'clock the rain came like a grey wall. Falling three thousand feet onto steel roofs. Lying on our windowsill, Maudie and I watched neighbours' houses obliterated. Rain swept across our garden. It pounded our roof and we had to shout to be heard.

Then it was gone, clouds and all. Good Hope Street steamed. Trees were stripped, gardens flattened, birds' nests lay on pavements and cats ate the fledglings.

"C'mon Tadpole, hurry. The gutters are flowing. We better go dam 'em quick."

I raced to get rocks, stones and soil from our front garden so my sister and I could build a dam in the street gutter.

"More soil, Maudie. The dam's leaking over here. Go get some more while I hold my hand over the leak."

"Okay, looks fine to me. I'll run and fetch woodchips from the coal shed for our boats."

In town there was a terminus for the four-wheel electric trams. From there the double-deckers began their swaying careering journeys down the middle of the main streets to the suburbs. Downhill travel was a delight to children and a nightmare for adults. A wild, waltzing ride, the motorman clanging his bell. Passengers who pulled the cord were treated to a fiery display of sparks from the wheels and a pealing of brake shoes.

At the bottom of Roberts Avenue the rails came to an abrupt stop. But a number of trams didn't.

An old Palestinian man came with his horse and cart, selling eggs but they were more often bad than fresh.

"No, no." Sampson shook his head and declined to buy from him.

Indian hawkers came around with their one-horse carts, offering greens. They hawked firewood from carts too and there were horse-drawn milk floats. There was no shortage of horse manure on the streets.

"Maudie sweetheart, please fetch a spade and bring in the droppings off the street. Spread them on the garden," our father called through the window.

My sister was busy in her tree house.

"Who, me, Abe?"

"Yes please."

Silence. No action.

"Why can't Frog go shovel it up?"

"Because I asked you."

"Humph..." She climbed out of the tree, found the garden shovel and carried in the horse dung hot and fresh, her face long and terrible.

"Yuk. S'not fair. Frog's not done a job for a million years."

It wasn't always my sister. More often, me. Our father couldn't let a coal lorry deliver without worrying about the remnants scattered in the street.

"That coal can't go to waste. I want it brought in. Now son, please."

"Tee-hee," Maudie giggled. "You gonna get in big trouble if you don't do what he says."

Before the dung session, my sister grabbed my arm.

"Quick, Tadpole. We gotta water that horse. You get Semp-Sonne's bucket. Hurry, before it's too late."

"And you?"

"I gonna sneak one of Semp-Sonne's carrots when he not looking and feed it to the horse."

I lumbered the bucket down the front path while my sister fed the horse from the palms of her hands.

Everyone knew that Mr de Beer's wife had run off with another man. So when the housemaster invited a young woman to Kiewietjie for afternoon tea, Graham wanted to pry. The fact that she was a newly certificated teacher seeking advice, didn't occur to him. When The Bear led his guest into his private suite and closed the door, our cousin became curious. The suite was on the upper level which made it difficult to see through the windows from the lawn.

"Bro," he called, "get seven of the guys and fetch blankets off our beds. We gonna make us a trampoline. I want to go shooting up to the first floor."

He laid the blankets one upon another on the lawn below the housemaster's windows.

"Okay you guys. I gonna be the first man on the moon. When I lie on the trampoline, you grab the corners and edges and pick me up, see. Then you bounce me, catch me in the blankets and shoot me up again. Get it? I hafta see what the old boy's doing with that dame up there."

They bounced him up. Graham tumbled over the heads of his accomplices and glimpsed the inside of the suite.

His first sightings proved unrewarding because he started outside the wrong window. The team shuffled their way around the corner of the hostel until they were below the living room. Mr de Beer sat with his back to the window, sipping tea. The young teacher faced him cradling her saucer.

Outside the window Graham's head or sometimes his feet if he was tossed upside down, bobbed into sight. When it was his head, he peered through the glass. At first the young woman didn't notice Graham's face or sometimes his feet appearing at the window every few seconds. However soon she couldn't help but see him. She half-listened to what the housemaster was narrating and half-stared at the face popping up at the window. Mr de Beer cleared his throat.

He then realized something was going on behind him. He coughed and carried on lecturing. But she was more interested in Graham's flights up to the window. He spoke louder, then leapt out of his chair and spun around.

Graham was on one of his ascents. Halfway up he realized Mr de Beer was watching him coming. The twin could do nothing to reverse his upward flight. When he arrived at the window he grinned sheepishly before beginning his descent.

"Not again," he yowled at his accomplices below.

"Hot. Again," they heard and bounced him higher. At the top of his ascent he grinned at the housemaster. The woman smiled and waved. The boys on the ground couldn't see the adults and bounced Graham up twice more before he catapulted himself sideways into a rosebush.

"Jeez, straight into the thorns, you idjuts."

It took half an hour to doctor his wounds. He looked like an Indian brave when summoned to the housemaster's office.

"Two weeks detention you little hooligan. You and your brother. Both of you. All free time cancelled. The pair of you will attend to your school work for a change."

Sampson (we never learned his tribal name, as he became coy when Maudie tried to prise it out of him) complained of feeling ill.

"Sampson," our father soothed, noting his fever, "Here are two aspirin. Take them with a mug of water and go to bed until you're better."

The aspirin had no effect and our housekeeper woke on Sunday morning, feverish and dehydrated. Being Sampson he didn't say a word and went about his half-day chores.

Trixie came in to give him a hand. While setting the table in his feverish state, Sampson let a porcelain meat dish slip from his fingers. It shattered on the floor. She was touchy when it came to waste.

"Sampson!"

Our housekeeper stood shivering with fever.

"I'll tell Mister Freyer to deduct the cost of that from your wages. Then what'll you do, huh, Sampson?"

Now this was a scene Trixie enacted from time to time in our household, but never followed through. We existed on an income of fifty pounds a month and succeeded because we wasted nothing. Our father's suits were shiny. Trixie sewed her own clothes. Frog saw new clothes once in three years and handed his old ones down to me. Maudie accepted what she could get.

Our father made his shoes last seven years. For Maudie and me this was not possible. Within six months we presented ourselves to the Scots shoemaker at the Fairview shops. When our footwear could no longer be repaired, Sampson claimed them for a black child. With awl and wire and canvas casing from an abandoned car tyre, the child's father stitched a new sole to the uppers and got a year's service out of them.

And I thought we were poor.

"Abe's paying Semp-Sonne five pounds a month," Maudie confided. How she found this out, I'll never know. Sampson had two wives and seven children in Zululand. He might have had a city wife too, but that would have been one of the things Semp-Sonne would never have admitted.

When the meat dish shattered at his feet, the first effect he had to suffer was a highly strung scream from Trixie. That was her natural reaction and didn't have anything to do with her temper. Nevertheless it rather made your hair stand on end. I had never seen Sampson's frizz actually stand up, but the cumulative effect of breaking crockery in our household must have made him the straightest haired Zulu in the country.

Barely having recovered from that shock he was then asked a question for which he had no answer.

"Why did you break that meat dish, Sampson?"

Our poor housekeeper pondered why he had dropped the crockery. That Sunday morning however, Sampson had tears in his eyes and Trixie thought she had gone too far. She then discovered he was running a temperature.

"Off to bed with you, my man. Here are two aspirin. I'll take over in the kitchen."

On Monday afternoon, still feverish, Sampson left his sick bed. He went on a mission to the koppies. An hour and a half later, my sister spied him reading in his room. He was poorly educated and I selected books from our school library for him. Some of them were difficult for me to understand so I could only trust he found them helpful.

The post arrived.

"The postman, Tadpole," my sister cheered, sliding down the Fig Tree to race me to our letter drop.

I heard the brass flap in our front door snap shut as letters fell to the floor. No one wrote to Maudie or me, but we slid out of the fig tree and hared into the house to collect the mail.

"Lickity-lick, I gonna get there before you," my sister hollered.

There was a letter for Sampson, a purple envelope addressed in clumsy printing. Maudie snatched the letter triumphantly.

"Semp-Sonne... Semp-Sonne... I got a letter for you from Zululand," she hollered, flying down the back stairs.

As Sampson never received mail from Pondoland or Swaziland or Basutoland or any other land, this last piece of information was superfluous. He sat at a little wooden table our father carpentered for him. The afternoon sun streamed through his door. Maudie crowded him while he read his letter, but he declined to give anything away.

"Aw gee Semp-Sonne. I'd really like to know what's going on in Zululand. You keeping it a big secret?"

While he read, she noticed he had not taken his aspirin.

"Semp-Sonne? Why didn't you take your medicine like you supposed to? You gonna get in big trouble with Trixie, you know."

Sampson knew. He shrivelled his nose.

"Not strong enough, little madam. Maybe for Europeans, but no good for Zulus."

"But... Semp-Sonne, you were sick Saturday night. Yesterday you had a fever. What did you do about your headache?"

He sighed.

"Maudie, I starved my body and slept. That is the best medicine. When my head pain didn't go away, I bought strong muti."

Maudie inspected the foul smelling powder in a twist of newspaper. It was ox-bile.

"Ugh," she pulled a face. "Where'd you get this muti, Semp-Sonne? S'gonna make you sicker. Tomorrow you gonna croak. We'll hafta bury you under the fig tree."

Sampson chuckled. "I had one dose and already I feel it working in my body. Tonight I'll take more and tomorrow morning I'll finish it. Then I'll be strong again." He patted his stomach.

"That aspirin medicine," he wrinkled his nose scornfully, "is no good for black people."

"This muti's horrible," Maudie countered, taking a not too close sniff at it. "Where'd you get this, Semp-Sonne?"

Her innocent questioning embarrassed our housekeeper, but he had a big grin on his face. "From the sangoma who passes on the koppies, little madam."

"Humph," my sister responded.

We left him reading his letter and clambered up the fig tree.

"You know Tadpole, Semp-Sonne's bonkers. I'd rather take aspirin than that horrible yellow powder stuff."

She pondered a moment. "And I aren't afraid of a silly old catfish like all those washerwomen were."

My sister's remark referred to what Lizzie told us. After my sister and I shut the fish in the freezer compartment, Sampson discovered it the following day, a big, frosted, black face staring at him with a frozen gape.

"Hau..." was his shocked reaction before slamming the door shut.

"What's up with you?" Maudie wanted to know.

"You put that thing in the freezer?"

My sister nodded.

"Zulus will not touch demons like that. Take it out

now or no supper for you."

"Ah, c'mon Semp-Sonne, Abe won't let you starve me, you know."

"Out, little madam. In the dustbin in the yard."

She shrugged, removed the frozen body and carried it down the back steps. Lizzie saw what she was about to do.

"Ah but Mozambique people live by the sea. We eat fish all the time. That'll make a good meal. It will feed me and my daughter and my daughter's children." She took the catfish from Maudie, wrapped it in newspaper and popped it into her carrier bag.

At four o'clock Lizzie made her departure. She pulled her shawl around her shoulders, picked up her carrier bag and let herself out the front gate. In Roberts Avenue she boarded a tram carrying other washing and ironing women home. As the lower deck was full, she climbed the narrow spiral staircase to the upper deck. There she managed to find a vacant seat. She didn't know the fish was still alive and thawing.

Halfway home her carrier bag resting on her knees twitched. She thought it was her imagination until the bag shuddered. Bemused, she made the pretence of looking ahead, while watching the bag out of the corner of her eye.

Then the bag jumped and the washer woman next to her saw it too. It was bad enough that her bag was moving around on her lap, worse that she didn't know why, but what worried her was that other passengers were noticing too.

She rested both arms on her bag, staring ahead as if nothing was amiss. She sat petrified. Her fingers felt the thing moving inside her bag.

On either side of the aisle, washer women were staring. Others further down the aisle turned around to see what was going on. Lizzie felt obliged to look inside her bag. With half the upper deck watching, she opened it.

Inside, a thawed catfish tried to free itself from the newspaper. It was making a mess of Lizzie's other possessions and she gingerly lifted the parcel out. With that, the fish jerked itself out of the newspaper and this time, Lizzie got a fright. She didn't want to touch the thing now that it had come back from the dead. She sprang to her feet and heaved the catfish away. It landed on the heads of the couple ahead of her.

Twenty people screamed at once. They leaped up, looking to see which way the catfish was headed next. Some scrambled from their seats and fled downstairs. The couple who received the fish about their ears whacked it away with flailing arms. It flew through the air landing on other passengers equally anxious not to touch it. By the time the wriggling monster dropped to the floor, the spiral staircase was packed. Those who hadn't made it to the stairs, stood on their seats.

The motorman realized something unusual was going on above him. First screams and shouts, then a commotion of passengers spilling down the stairs onto his driving platform. Thinking there must be a fire, he slammed on the brakes.

Upstairs, the catfish was full of life, swiping its tail and flipping itself across the floor. When the motorman braked, the offensive fish rolled to the front of the tram and slid down the stairwell onto the heads of passengers jammed there. Pandemonium broke out. It affected the passengers on the lower deck who wanted to know why the stairwell was crowded with people wanting to leave the tram.

The motorman brought the tramcar to an abrupt halt by ramming the electric motor into reverse. The wheels screeched on the rails. Passengers poured out, most not knowing why but anxious not to find out either. Traffic in both directions was stopped by the emptying tram halted in the middle of Main Street.

The passengers congregated on the pavement, more than half of them unaware of the cause of the exodus.

Both conductor and motorman flew upstairs and found not a fire, but ten or twelve washer women including Lizzie, sitting contentedly, waiting for the vehicle to continue its journey. They didn't want Lizzie to get into trouble with the crew of the tram, so no, they didn't know what all the fuss was about, they hadn't been able to see what caused all the panic.

When the motorman returned downstairs to his station, he found the ugly fish on the floor where he normally stood. He took a well aimed kick and sent it flying across the street into the gutter where it dropped into a stormwater drain. His passengers returned now, bringing their parcels and bags with them. He stood clanging his bell while they boarded. A few minutes later they continued their journeys home.

"Yah, I s'pose Sampson's funny sometimes, Sis. I wouldn't take that ox-bile stuff and I'm not frightened of a catfish. Though maybe I wouldn't wanna swim with 'em."

"And I aren't frightened of witches," Maudie declared, nearly falling out of the tree as she fought to wrestle a new plank into position for our tree house.

"Amos is different," she continued. "He takes aspirin when Selina gives it to him and he wasn't too scared of his catfish."

"Yah, you right, Sis."

"You think he believes in witches?"

"Maybe, Sis. That's cos he hears big people talking about superstition. At school, Amos is taught the opposite. He must be plenty confused."

"Yah, Amos was born in Jo-burg. Semp-Sonne and Selina and Moses came from kraals and hardly even went to school."

She pondered the progress of our tree house.

"What about old Sunshine? Where's he fit in?"

My sister posed a difficult one. Mr Sunshine was unique and I wasn't sure how to take him.

"You reckon he's covering up, Tadpole?"

"Not sure Sis. He's rich and talks real good. I don't think he's superstitious."

"Maybe he uses superstition to fool ignorant people?"

"Probably Mister Sunshine is very clever but he don't let other people know how clever..."

"He's hiding something that's for sure. But what?"

"Maudie, where's he get all his boodle? Sampson says he's a travelling salesman. People pay him lay-bys. And he brings 'em what they bought."

"So that's how he gets his dough."

"But he can't make much selling clothes, Sis. And he got a Chrysler."

"So what's he doing to make him stinking rich?"

"Something bad."

"Like what, Tadpole?"

"Like kidnapping little children and selling them to sorcerers."

The words were out of my mouth before I could stop them. Maudie screwed up her eyes and went back to hammering her end of the plank into position.

"I wish Amos was here to help with our den," she sighed.

That night I regretted what I'd suggested.

Maudie woke in terror.

"Lemme out... lemme out... lemme out..." her voice was muffled and faraway.

I padded across our room to find her lying upside down in her bed, her feet at her pillow and her head under the blankets, down at the bottom.

"Sis, you crazy or something?"

I grabbed her ankles and slid her out. She flung her arms around my neck.

"S'only a dream, Maudie," I whispered. "Go back to sleep now."

"No Tadpole. He gonna get me."

She was not fully awake.

"What happened, Maudie?"

"A man... locked me in his case... I couldn't get out. I called you, but you didn't hear me..."

I sat with her in the dark, stroking her hair. Then someone walked over my grave.

"Tadpole, one day 'tis gonna be for real. I'll call and you won't come..."

"I'll always come for you, Sis."

We fell asleep holding onto one another.

Chapter 21

The school term drew to an end with Maudie and me reluctantly engrossed in year-end examinations. Frog became impossible to live with. He always had a textbook under his nose, learning, reciting, demanding quiet, getting us into trouble for making noise.

"Can't you two shut up?" he yelled every fifteen minutes.

At six a.m. the milkman shattered the peace, rattling his spike against the bottles, driving Hobo mad. The dustmen humped everybody's dustbins onto their shoulders. They chanted a war cry to keep the neighbourhood dogs at bay. Cats disappeared, not many, but enough to keep alive the suspicion that the dustmen stole and ate them.

The bottle-and-bag man trundled his handcart up our street, collecting almost anything offered. He traipsed through town to the produce market, where he sold his stuff. Parents frightened their children with stories about him and small children hid themselves when they heard his pushcart.

The day came when Hobo's plaster could come off. Hobo knew something was in the air. She limped into the house that morning, thumping her plaster cast, wagging her rear end and shaking her head so vigorously, that the designs on Maudie's bucket blurred. She waited at the gate the whole day for our father to finish work. When she heard the Chev she galloped around the house, banging her plaster into shrubs and rose bushes, tearing across the lawn and nearly knocking Abe over when he opened the gate.

"My goodness," he grinned, "what's got into you?"

Maudie told everybody that Hobo was a lady dog. The only time Hobo was not a lady dog, was when a large male dog took an interest in her. The larger the dog, the more volatile Hobo became.

As we held the screen door of the vet's waiting room open for Hobo with her metal bonnet to limp through, I caught sight of the biggest Great Dane I had ever seen. Our father reached for a magazine and sat down while my sister and I looked after Hobo.

"Watch out Tadpole, that damn dog's gonna come sniffing Hobo," Maudie warned.

We had barely sat down when the Dane began whining and pestering his owner to free him. Hobo turned her head away. The Dane's owner sniggered and released his animal from its leash.

"Idiot," Maudie pronounced. "Now he gonna make trouble for us."

The Dane came sliding over the linoleum and began examining Maudie's dog from head to tail. With her leg in plaster and her head inside my sister's seaside bucket, there was nothing she could do.

The Dane sniffed her all over, careful not to put his nose near the wrong end of the bonnet. Maudie shoved the big dog away but he kept coming back. Hobo bristled. The Great Dane became excited. Maudie fended him off.

"Don't blame me if my dog bites your dog," she warned the owner.

"Not much chance of that my little girl, is there?" he smirked.

He stood up to fetch his Dane. Before he got there, his clumsy brute knocked over our lady dog, the bucket ringing on the floor and a furious growl coming from within. Our father clouted the Dane with his magazine.

"Hey mister, don't you dare hit my pet," the owner objected. "I'll see you outside if you like."

He was grinning his head off when he retrieved his dog. Hobo struggled to her feet and retreated between

Maudie's knees.

My sister's dog had two phobias. One, she was frightened of the dark when there was no one with her and the other, she was terrified of the vet even with the whole family surrounding her. We could never get her to walk from the Chev to the waiting room. She glued herself to the back seat and it took both Maudie and me to lift her.

If we put her on the ground she made a U-turn. So we carried her across the parking lot. She would only enter the waiting room if we assisted with a bit of pressure behind her rump. Going the other way wasn't a problem. She could easily pull Maudie and me out of the surgery, through the swing doors, all the way to the Chev.

In the waiting room, her teeth chattered so loudly, people turned to look. When we lifted her onto the examination table, she stood shivering nervously, shedding her white hair like a snowstorm. The vet we consulted this time, was a man.

"Go easy now. She's nervous," Maudie warned.

He must have thought the danger was she might bite him and she couldn't do that because of the bucket. He hadn't bargained for her other end.

"You look like you've recovered very well, Hobo," he sang, grabbing her plaster and prodding her back leg. Maudie's dog's bowels and bladder voided themselves. It was a quarter of an hour before he came back, washed, scrubbed and wearing a clean white coat. This time he approached our lady dog from the front.

"Her leg has healed perfectly folks," he told us after he cut away the plaster cast. He examined the limb. "It's a little thinner than its counterpart, but she'll put flesh on it within a week. It just needs exercise."

With the bucket removed Hobo was a brand new dog. She had a head and a neck and ears and eyes and her little tongue came out gratefully. Except for the vet, she wanted to lick all hands and faces that surrounded her. The stump of her tail agitated so fast, her whole body wobbled. She couldn't wait to get out of the surgery.

Her back leg was stiff, but Hobo was mobile again. She shook herself, glad to be free of the bucket.

"Giddy-up my angel, you can run gallopity-glock now," Maudie cried.

Hobo wagged her stump.

We followed her down the passage until she saw the Great Dane standing in the waiting room, gazing through the screen door while his owner paid his account. Hobo broke into a gallop. By the time she reached her top speed, she couldn't stop on the linoleum. She came up behind the unsuspecting Dane, lifted her head and snapped her jaws shut over his nether regions. The resultant yowl of pain turned every head in the waiting room.

"Go Hobo, go my angel," Maudie cried.

With my sister's dog hanging on behind, the Great Dane sprang through the screen door. Locked together, they bounded across the parking lot, the Dane fleeing and Hobo still flying along behind. I don't think her feet touched the ground. She only let go outside the parking lot and came trotting back, quite pleased with herself. She made for the Chev and waited for us to let her in.

"Now you see! You wouldn't listen, would you?" Maudie piped as the owner chased after his Dane. "I told you my dog'd bite your dog."

Chapter 22

Gillooly's was very popular when we were children. Wild enough for endless adventuring. African veld grass covered the farm. There were fir trees at the picnic spots and willow trees overhanging the watercourse. The far side of the river was deserted. We swung from the willows, often falling in, leaped from rock to rock and crossed to the opposite side. There lay a great pasture for romping; trees and thickets for hiding and the Linksfield Ridge koppies for climbing.

"Aw gee, Abe. When you taking us to Gloolies again? Haven't been for ages." My sister chirped. "I'm dying to go."

"Not this weekend, sweetheart," he answered, poised at the top of his stepladder, holding a paintbrush.

"C'mon, Abe. When?"

"Maybe next weekend. We'll see."

"I gonna remind you Friday."

Gillooly's was popular because in spite of its secluded setting, it was close to town. For families with fifteen-year-old cars or couples on motorcycles, this was important. Fathers spent Saturday afternoons fixing their cars or working on their houses. Mothers caught up on housekeeping.

Maudie only remembered on Sunday morning.

"S'not fair, Abe. Last weekend, you promised next Sunday. Remember? Well, it's next Sunday now, you know."

He chuckled.

"All right, my girl. The great unwashed wins again. You better get ready. We leave in half an hour."

"Yea... and The Vale of Belvoir also," my sister interjected, getting as much out of him as possible. "We can fold the luggage carrier down and tie our canoe on."

"Yes, if you wish, Maudie."

"And Amos, Abe. He's coming also."

Our father knew when he was trumped. He chuckled and climbed down from the ladder.

I didn't take part in this coercion because of my stutter and didn't have my sister's temerity. Maudie's near drowning in the Gillooly's River haunted me. It was eighteen months since I pulled her out and I couldn't forget seeing her eyes under the water watching me.

"Hey Amos," Maudie called over the fence. "Tell your mama you coming to Gloolies with us."

While our father brought the picnic basket and rug down the back stairs, I tied our canoe to the luggage carrier and Maudie, Amos and Hobo ensconced themselves on the back seat. Frog decided to stay at home and swot.

"Have you brought your swimming costume, Amos?" our father teased. He knew Amos didn't worry too much about costumes. Occasionally Frog could hand him down something, but by then it had already seen most of its days and Amos was so rough on it, he wore holes in the seat as big as saucers.

Amos giggled. He was in-between costumes and hadn't had one since he wore the previous pair out by sliding down our neighbour's roof on his buttocks.

Sunday afternoon was a great day for the African people of Kensington. They donned their best and paraded up and down the pavements. In pairs and groups, they strolled for miles through the suburbs, the women with their parasols and the men in their summer hats. There were young men who loved music so much they took it with them. They stepped along, playing concertinas, accordions, guitars and fiddles.

On street corners, other musicians set up bigger instruments; marimbas, an indigenous xylophone played with the fingers, and basses made from a tea chest, a shaft of timber and a length of heavy twine kept under tension by the player.

In Roberts Avenue I noticed Moses from next door boarding a tram. Sampson strolled with his roadster bicycle, Selina and other friends. Amos waved frantically through the rear window but she never looked in the Chev's direction.

"Hey lookee there," Maudie cried, "Old Joseph riding his Harley Davidson in front of us."

If our father drove slowly, Joseph rode his silent motorcycle combination even more leisurely. He idled along in top gear, the big vee barely ticking over. I kept my eyes on him and thought we would pass him until he turned down a side street. His panama lay on the sidecar's seat.

"That's one of the ways to the Foster Caves," Maudie blurted.

"Yes, where the great unwashed are forbidden to go," our father added.

"Yah we know, Abe. It's just that if you were going to the Foster Caves, you could get onto the koppies at the top of Good Hope Street... or you could also go the bottom way like Old Joseph."

She stiffened.

"The giraffe man..."

"Where, Sis?"

"What's this about a giraffe?" our father asked.

Maudie pulled a face, glanced at me and pointed through a side window. We passed the spot and I missed what she saw. I tried catching a glimpse through the rear window but it was small. All I saw was Mr de Beer's man Friday Lukas standing under an oak tree. There was no giraffe man.

"I didn't see him, Sis. I never seen your giraffe man."

She rolled her eyes at me.

Amos stared at her quizzically. He knew nothing about my sister's giraffe man. Our father was bemused but didn't press her. He thought my sister and I imagined things.

Hobo sprang out of the Chev the moment the car came to a standstill, bounding and romping through the grass. We three got busy untying our canoe and dragged it down to the river.

"Heck, the water's down," I pointed out, "we gonna get stuck on the bottom and won't get through the rapids."

"Well why don't we go upstream to the old tree trunk?" my sister suggested.

"So far, Maudie?"

"C'mon man, zoom-zoom, lickity-splick. Don't be so lazy. We can't canoe here. Let's go, Amos."

We hauled our boat upstream past the tree trunk that formed a weir. Amos launched it in deep water.

A minute later he knelt on the bank, laughing and rolling the canoe side to side. A grass snake had fallen off the bank into the canoe. It was angry and wanted to escape. Every time it tried to get away, Amos rolled the canoe. The poor creature rolled upside down and untwirled itself. It glowered at him and struck at his hands, but the lunges fell short, resulting in more ribald laughter.

"What'sa joke, Amos?" Maudie called.

He flicked the canoe and the snake found itself upside down, furiously trying to right itself. Amos was in hysterics.

She grinned and sneaked up behind him. Then shoved him on his buttocks.

"Yeowee," he yelped, toppling off the bank into the canoe. Now he was all arms and legs, scrambling to get out of the snake's way. The canoe capsized throwing both of them into the water. They surfaced face to face and swam off in opposite directions.

I dived in and grabbed our canoe before it sank.

"What's going on over there?" My sister pointed to wagtails swooping low over the river.

Racing inches above the surface, four wagtails zoomed and dived. Three crowded the fourth. They screeched and careened to and fro over the water. The fourth got the worst of it. Each time he tried to escape, they dived on his back. When he made for the bank, they flew in his face, forcing him over the river.

Then he smacked into the water and was down. The others gained height, let up on their chatter and settled on a willow branch. The one in the water climbed onto driftwood and launched himself into the air. Wet, he could not fly properly. His attackers dived, driving him back in the water.

"Aw gee," Maudie sobbed, "he's gonna drown."

"Which is what the others want, Sis."

She pushed me into the canoe and we paddled to rescue him. Crying pitifully, the wagtail climbed into Maudie's cupped hands. She cradled him in her lap to keep him warm. His feathers clung together. I saw from his wounds that he had been pecked.

"I'm taking him back to the car," Maudie said, stroking his feathers. "At home, I'll make a nest out of cotton wool and feed him worms and things."

"Howdya know wagtails eat worms?" I asked.

"All birds eat worms."

While she tramped back to the Chev, Amos and I paddled *The Vale of Belvoir* upstream. But then I thought of my sister on her own with a long way to go through the willows.

"We should go back," I blurted in alarm. "Maudie's on her own."

Amos had no time to answer. We never saw the squall. Wind struck without warning. I visualised my sister tramping alone under the willows and through the long grass of the pasture and a chill went through me. A second gust scattered leaves and debris across the water. There was no thunder. It was as if dusk fell and I worried again about Maudie on her own. I glanced through the tops of the trees overhanging the river. A black mantle lay across the heavens.

Then a real blast of icy fierceness struck. The storm was about us. Real storm wind under a storm sky. Stinging sand blew off the bank, blinding me. Branches groaned and dried twigs came down. Then rain came from behind, pelting our bodies. A grey curtain closed around us, the rain flying horizontally before the squall.

"Maudie's in this, all alone," I whispered.

A rotten tree snapped. The crack as it gave way was ear-splitting, making it seem it was on top of us, but it fell far away. The rain made it impossible to see. It swirled in a mist obscuring the riverbanks on either side. It blinded me and I kept my eyes fixed on the river.

The old tree trunk forming the weir loomed indistinctly. Behind us the trees along the river and the koppie beyond, disappeared in a shroud of grey. The rain swirled about our heads, my hair clung to my scalp and Amos's clean-shaven scalp shone wet.

We beached the canoe half full of water. Amos and I rolled it up the bank. We kept our backs to the wind and huddled to shield our faces.

"Amos, what we gonna do? Make a run for it?" I shouted.

"We hafta," he cried, wiping the streaming water from his face. "This rain's here the whole afternoon. S'not gonna let up now."

I snatched the bow of the canoe. Amos grabbed the stern. We held it upside down over our heads and scrambled downstream through the grass. I was frozen when we reached the Chev I looked for Maudie. She was there with her wagtail. With the rain streaming down, we tied *The Vale of Belvoir* onto the luggage carrier. Then we dived into the Chev and wrapped ourselves in our towels. Our father drove us home and I watched my sister cradling her wagtail. It had been a hell of a Sunday afternoon.

That night as Maudie writhed in her sleep I found myself hearing her cries. The pendulum clock in the passage ticked. Tick, tick, tick. I was sleeping, but also listening to my sister's agony.

She called out, squirming in her sleep. The carillon sounded. Then the hour. Two a.m.

Maudie started speaking.

"Johan... he caught you... you tied... here am I... up above..."

I didn't know any boy called Johan and neither did my sister.

"... he taking you..."

"... the koppies..." I heard her murmur.

"... dark in there..."

I was awake now. And cold.

"... he got a knife..."

I listened.

"... no... don't..."

I slipped from my bed and padded across to my sister. I put a hand on her arm.

"... s'not fair, Tadpole... Johan's cut... lying under rocks... his soul's gone..."

"Maudie?" I whispered.

"Whazzzz...?" she slurred.

"Are you awake?"

"... Tadpole..." she responded and started snoring.

Chapter 23

I surfaced on Monday morning as the sun crept over the corrugated iron roofs of houses across the street.

"You gotta wake up Sis," I whispered, shaking her shoulder.

"Wozzatime?"

"Six. Daddy's already having his breakfast."

"Ugh, school, oh puke."

"Maudie, who's Johan?"

"Johan? Dunno any Johan. What you talking about now?"

"You don't remember? You didn't dream about a boy called Johan?"

"Nope, I just told you."

The day passed without event until The Star landed on our garden path. Maudie, Hobo and I raced to get it. My sister snatched the paper, keen to turn to Curly Wee, but stopped short.

The report stated that detectives were investigating Johannes' disappearance. The family was frantic. The phrase *muti murder* hadn't been used. "Another school child missing," read the headline across the front page.

"Lookit this, Tadpole... happened here in Kensington."

I scanned the report. The previous day a local child, Johannes Rabie, disappeared in Roberts Avenue. It gave the time and his route.

"We were passing in the Chev when he was snatched, Sis."

"Doesn't say he was snatched. Just that he's missing."

I knew different. Johan's gone, Maudie. Been cut up

like Davy. You saw everything in your dream, only you don't remember.

The day started with Hobo getting her revenge on the milkman. He was more boy than man and got a kick out of terrorizing Maudie's dog. He would tiptoe up the drive, quietly deliver the new milk and retrieve the empties. Out of the corner of his eye, he checked where my sister's dog was and estimated his chances of escaping if he rattled the empty bottle on his return down the drive.

He made sure he was within reach of the gate. If Hobo was on the front lawn, she could be on the drive in seconds. But if she was at the far corner of the back yard, he would start clanging his bottles while still next to the house before running like blazes.

With Hobo immobilized, he mocked her, laughing and rattling his bottles while still on the street. Then he rocked the latch back and forth. Up the drive he chanted insults, accompanying himself with metal spike and glass bottle.

"Heavens, what a racket," our father sighed. "If we get much more of this, I'll complain to the dairy."

On Monday morning the young milkman rendered his ear-splitting performance. He didn't know Maudie's dog having shed bucket and plaster cast had crept into the garage behind the Chev and now lay in wait.

"Hobo," the youth sang, "I coming in. You like my ting-ling Hobo? Here I come now. Watch out, Hobo. Ting-ling."

Hobo didn't move. No one knew she was in the garage. She let him latch the gate behind him and make his torments up the drive and across the yard, stamping up the back veranda stairs with the new milk for the day and down the stairs with the empties, rattling the glass and bawling insults.

I was in the pantry wrapping Maudie's and my

sandwiches and saw the look of disbelief on his face as Hobo came out of the garage at full gallop.

In an instant, his discordant symphony ended.

His jaw dropped.

"Hauauauauau...!" he yowled.

He flung his metal spike in one direction and the empty bottle in the other. It landed in the compost heap.

He turned and made for our neighbour's fence. The corrugated iron sheets dividing the properties were five foot high, but he cleared them, ripping the crotch of his coveralls. Hobo shot through the gap in the bottom of the fence.

"Ayeeayeeayee..." he hollered, vaulting himself back into our yard.

This gave him a few seconds start, because Hobo didn't realize what had happened to him. She thundered through the fence again. The boy made for the fig tree, climbing into the fork of the bole. A smirk appeared on his face. Hobo's onward rush didn't falter. She made a flying leap onto Maudie's treads. With a strangled cry of disbelief, he scrambled into the branches overhanging the roof of the house.

As the eighteen-year-old youth clambered higher, my sister's dog negotiated the familiar bough after him. Among the secondary branches, the unfortunate boy lost his hold and tumbled onto the veranda roof. The crash brought Sampson and our father rushing out of the kitchen.

"My God. What's going on?" our father yelled.

Maudie giggled. Sampson began shouting advice. The milkman and Hobo had eyes only for each other.

Balanced on Maudie's treads, Hobo judged her distance and sprang onto the veranda roof. As she landed, he was halfway up the pitch toward the apex. There, he lost his nerve. With Hobo starting up after him, he retraced his flight down the corrugated iron, passing her going in the opposite direction. He hit the veranda roof with a force that shook the rafters.

"Get down off there," our father ordered.

The boy hesitated, eyes transfixed on the gap separating him from the garage. Hobo nipped him on his buttocks and the gap was no longer a problem. He landed on all fours on top of the garage, made for the adjoining back wall and clambered onto the compost heap.

At this stage, he took leave of his senses. He was so pleased with his return to *terra firma* that a sheepish smirk spread across his face. He dusted himself off and grinned at Maudie's dog stuck on the edge of the veranda roof. With a howl of rage, she backed up and leapt the intervening gap. He needed no further warning as Hobo clattered down the garage roof above his head, making for the compost heap.

Holding his buttocks, he took off across the yard. The way to the drive was open and he pounded down the hard earth, glancing back in time to see Maudie's dog come flying around the corner of the house. She was gaining, allowing him no time to undo the latch. With less than two yards separating them, he vaulted the gate.

We never saw him on our route again.

Chapter 24

"Why you always whispering that name?" Maudie frowned.

"What name, Sis?"

"You know... Johan or something."

"Dunno, Maudie. Maybe I was thinking and it just slipped out."

"We don't know anyone called Johan."

"The boy who was murdered..."

"That's Johannes, silly, not Johan. Any case he's not killed, only missing."

"You don't remember your nightmare, Sis?"

She stuck her tongue out.

Mrs Probert waddled across the street to borrow a cup of sugar from Sampson. It was five o'clock, an hour before our father would return from work. Our neighbour had further modified her trodden down man's shoes by cutting holes to ease the pressure on her small toes too. Sampson was in the kitchen preparing supper.

Mrs Probert had not recovered from her shock at Ruth's wedding when everybody saw her daughter's bridal limousine.

"It'll take me years to live it down, Mister Frey," she confided in our father.

An electrical storm skirted the koppie above the house. The lightning struck the top of our street and the boom of thunder drowned her monologue. She was about to repeat herself louder, when a glowing sphere emerged from the kitchen wall.

I was so shocked, I didn't believe what I was seeing

and clamped my mouth shut.

What appeared through solid brick and plaster, was bright orange in colour, perfectly round and about fourteen inches in diameter with the consistency of an opaque cloud. I couldn't see through it, but on the other hand it didn't look solid. It emerged from the wall in ghostlike fashion as if it had entered from the outside and was passing through. It had a floating quality, wasn't moving fast, but wasn't staying around for anyone to make a grab for it either.

From where I was sitting, the orange sphere came through the wall behind the Queen Mary and entered the slow combustion stove. Sampson saw it for the first time as he bent down to open the oven.

"Hau! Tokoloshe!" he yelped, snatching his hands away and dropping a pan of roast potatoes.

Mrs Probert woke up late to the fact that there was a strange phenomenon in our presence. She half turned her head in mid conversation when the roast potatoes splattered the floor and glimpsed the ethereal giant apricot heading for the kitchen table. She didn't really want to see it and snapped her head away.

"Oh my God. On my oath, it's Judgment Day. So soon."

She held her hands over her face so she couldn't see the sphere. But also gawked through her fingers so she could.

Sampson grabbed hold of a broom and peered into the oven to see whether any more phenomena were coming out, getting ready to swipe them with the broom if they did.

The orange ball floated toward the kitchen table and passed between her and me. She swallowed hard before snatching the tablecloth away in case it caught fire. She kicked her heels into the linoleum, skidding her chair away from the table, putting another two feet between her and purgatory.

The table cut the sphere in two, so I could only see

the top half as it passed between us. When it floated free, it became complete again.

Maudie sauntered out of the passage into the kitchen.

"Ooh! What a pretty balloon. Why didn't you tell me you had a balloon in the kitchen, Semp-Sonne?"

Sampson was falling over himself to knock the thing out of the air with his broom. He was obsessed with obtaining mitigating evidence that the roast potatoes spread over the kitchen floor were not the result of carelessness.

"No, Semp-Sonne, no. Don't pop the balloon. It's beautiful..." my sister cried, jumping up and down. She caught herself in mid sentence when the sphere disappeared through the wall into the pantry.

Sampson charged after it. He caught sight of it passing through the breadbox into the wall backing the living room.

"Maudie, quick!" he urged.

My sister sprinted down the passage to see it float across the living room and vanish through the next wall into our bedroom. She reached the front of the house and pivoted into our room to watch it coming out of our cupboard. It passed over her bed and vanished through the window. She raced to open the front door, but by then the thing was heading across the street.

"Tokoloshe," Sampson panted.

"No, Sampson. It was a fireball come to warn us," Mrs Probert proclaimed.

"We'll have to hurry. The house could be on fire inside all the cupboards. Open the lot. Quickly."

She waddled to the pantry and flung open the two cupboard doors.

None of us knew any better, so we joined her, searching for evidence of singeing or charring. Sampson took advantage of the reprieve to scrape the mess from the kitchen floor. He had a good look inside the oven to check there was nothing further lurking there. Then he joined us in searching the house.

"Look everywhere, Sampson," Mrs Probert insisted, throwing open the linen cupboard and hauling out sheets and blankets, "you can't be too careful, you know."

"Did you say your prayers last night, young man?" She questioned, turning to me.

I hesitated.

"Well? Did you say them or didn't you?"

That put me in a spot and the only way to extricate myself was to lie.

"Yah, Missus Probert," I mumbled, hoping the powers above didn't quite catch what I said.

"Where are those wretched twins?" she asked.

"The way those two blaspheme, it's a wonder we haven't been visited by the Angel of the Bottomless Pit."

She hurried through the house, going from room to room, throwing open cupboards and searching for fires that may have started inside.

"It's a warning I tell you. Mark my words this is not the end of it. It's a warning from The Lord."

"Hmpf," she snorted when, rummaging through Babs' clothing, she found a quarter bottle of brandy. From our father's bedroom, I heard the final reason the fireball entered the house.

"I thought so," she exclaimed, waddling into the passage, "I've always warned that mirrors should be covered and scissors put away when there's lightning about."

She must have forgotten about the cup of sugar she came to borrow, because she started aligning the path the orb had taken across Good Hope Street.

"Oh my God, no..." she spluttered and pounded down our front steps and across the street where her own property might burst into flame at any moment.

When our father returned from work, Maudie told him what had happened.

"Ball lightning sweetheart," he explained. "Probably static electricity. Hasn't been fully explained. Did it burn anyone?"

I shook my head.

"Semp-Sonne reckons 'twas the Tokoloshe, Abe," Maudie said.

"Oh, he would."

"And Missus Probert's sure it's a warning from heaven."

"Tee-hee. That figures."

When my sister and I were alone, I had another thought.

"The Impundulu bird, Sis. Remember what Isanusi told us? The lightning bird that lays its eggs in the flashes? Coulda been an Impundulu bird's egg."

"Yah, maybe, but where's it gonna hatch?"

I shrugged and she rolled her eyes at me.

We had supper, after which Maudie and I lost a battle with Frog over whose job it was to clear the table. Our father retired to the living room where he read the front page report about Johannes Rabie going missing in Roberts Avenue. He called us into the living room.

"I don't want any of you alone on the streets," he instructed.

"Whether you're going to school or coming home, you are to walk in a group. At least two together. Never alone. Do you understand?"

He glanced at Maudie and me. "You two should get an older child to accompany you."

"Yah Abe," Maudie replied. "We promise. Swear to God and hope to die."

I shivered.

My sister woke in the small hours of the morning. At

first I thought she was having a nightmare, but her stomach was playing up.

"Tadpole, pleeze... s'urgent... I need to do number two."

I rolled onto the floor in a stupor, staggered to my feet and followed her into the kitchen where I unlocked the back door. While my sister eased her running tummy, I waited at the compost heap. Hobo investigated a rustling in the side lane.

"Aren't you finished yet?"

"No-oooh... Pleeze wait for me."

The veranda light bulb blew. Maudie whimpered.

"You still there?"

"I can't wait forever, Sis."

The jangling of the overhead cast iron cistern was enough to waken the dead. We had the whole yard to cross. I wanted to make a dash for it.

"No, Tadpole, walk slow. My tummy's gonna run again." She clung to my hand.

When we reached the back veranda, I heard the front gate latch being lifted. In a panic, I dashed through the kitchen door, pulling Maudie after me and turned the key in the lock.

From the bathroom window, we peered down the side of the house. Babs staggered up the lane. Maudie's dog wasn't so sure and backed into the coal shed. Hobo the heroine, unafraid of Alsatians, Great Danes and milkmen in broad daylight, was slightly more cautious of long leggity beastlies in the middle of the night.

The figure coming up the lane held its arms out to fend off the house on one side and the fence on the other. As Babs approached the coal shed, a nervous rumbling erupted in Hobo's throat. Maudie started giggling. In the dark, the dog was a faint patch of grey. When her rear end reached the shed, she reversed up the coal. Babs staggered onward. Hobo retreated down the other side, where she hid with only her eyes peering over the top of the coal.

"Shush, Sis," I whispered. "Stop giggling, otherwise your tummy's gonna act up again. Then you can go back outside by yourself."

Hobo must have been desperate when the figure staggered to the shed and reached into the rafters. As Babs raised the bottle to her lips, the poor dog must have concluded it was being wielded as a club.

She howled her anguish, a cry that startled our aunt out of her wits. Hobo took off over the top of the coal and bolted between Babs' legs.

"What the hell...?" Babs' bottle flew into the air as she staggered backwards. Hobo shot around the corner of the house to the safety of the drive. Our aunt made a grab for her brandy bottle, missed then snagged it between her arm and chest as she hit the ground on her buttocks.

Hobo waddled up sheepishly. Babs hugged her and emptied the bottle.

Sadly, Maudie's wagtail died the following morning while we were at school. Sampson made the inexcusable mistake of throwing her bird into the dustbin. Sampson always learned the hard way.

"Semp-Sonne!" The house shuddered. "Semp-Sonne!"

"Yes, what is it little madam? I can't come now, I'm busy."

"Where's my wagtail, Semp-Sonne? What've you done with my sick bird?"

This exchange was taking place between Maudie's and my bedroom at the front of the house and the kitchen in the back.

"I threw the stinky thing away."

"What! How can you do that, Semp-Sonne? My patient was getting better."

"No Maudie, he was getting worse," he chuckled.

"When he died, I threw him in the dustbin."

"Semp-Sonne! I gonna kill you. How can you throw my patient in the rubbish bin?" She flew out of our room and confronted the villain himself.

Sampson had one hand on a hip and pointed with the other to the bin under the sink. "I was going to burn it in the Queen Mary, but maybe the smell would have been too bad."

Maudie nearly choked. She rummaged through the refuse and retrieved the corpse.

"We gotta have a proper burial," she insisted, taking her wagtail down the back stairs.

"Not where people gonna walk on him," she insisted, looking for a suitable site in the back yard.

"And deep enough that some people's dogs won't dig him up," she added, pushing Hobo away from the corpse. Her dog had been sniffing the dead bird and was about to chew on it.

Babs came up the drive and offered to give us a hand. "Where's the coffin?" she asked.

"Don't have one, Babs," my sister replied. "I'll just stick him in the ground."

"You can't do that, Maudie. Let's do it properly." Babs fumbled in her jacket for her cigarettes, emptying them into a pocket. She handed the carton to Maudie.

Maudie laid her wagtail in the cigarette box. It fitted but made the cardboard bulge. She placed the coffin in the little hole she had dug and covered it over.

"Why'd you always drink that brandy stuff, Babs?"

"Oh, I just do."

"Yah, but it smells terrible. Don't it ever make you sick?"

"Sometimes."

"S'worse than castor oil."

"When people grow up Maudie, they sometimes have problems they're not strong enough to handle. Alcohol makes it easier."

"Worse than school?"

Babs laughed. "Yes, Maudie. During the war we used to dig graves in the desert, real ones for real people. There were no coffins. We dumped our friends in the same hole and covered them with sand. We used bulldozers to bury them."

She patted the mound while Maudie broke off a pansy and laid it on the grave.

"That and a few other things which you wouldn't understand," Babs concluded.

Maudie glanced at her, but our aunt wouldn't enlarge.

"I hope you grow into a proper lady one day," she smiled.

"By the way, we're going to have an air show at Rand Aerodrome during the Christmas holidays. A bit of trick flying, some parachute jumping and so on. You're always asking to see the aeroplanes. Talk to your father. I'm sure he'll bring you along."

It was the best invitation Maudie and I had had in our lives.

Chapter 25

Saturday afternoon found us atop one of the mine-dumps that towered to the south of our suburb. It was Graham's suggestion.

"How about we carry the Vale up a mine-dump? Boy, we'll have a snazzy time sliding down the sand. They five hundred foot high, you know."

The mounds of yellow sand were the residue from the process of gold extraction. I got the impression that one ounce of gold resulted in forty thousand tons of mine-dump sand.

"You mean like a toboggan, Graham?" Maudie frowned. "Not so sure about that. Nobody there. Lonely."

What she said was true. The dumps were beyond the suburbs on the far side of the railway lines where there was nothing but deserted scrap yards and abandoned machinery from times gone by. Had our father known about our plans to go there he would have stopped us.

"Nah," Graham argued. "You with Louis and me and we're big."

I told our father we were taking our canoe to a friend's house in Malvern and would play with it in his yard.

Climbing the mine-dumps did sound like a good idea. From the top, we had a view of the major part of the city. Other dumps stretched east and west along the Witwatersrand as far as we could see. The slope we had just climbed was so steep we had to scramble on hands and knees, dragging the canoe after us. Far below, next to the road, were sixty-foot pine trees.

"They look like miniatures," I mentioned to my

sister.

"We were followed," she murmured, scanning the road below.

"Howdya know?"

"Just a feeling when someone's watching me."

"Who's going all the way to the bottom?" Graham chortled.

I shook my head.

"Can't we find a shorter run?" Louis asked.

"Sissy. If you dragged your hands in the sand all the way down, maybe they'd be clean by the time you reached the bottom."

Louis examined the palms of his hands and wiped them on his trousers.

Graham liked the idea of a shorter run too. He found another slope about a hundred feet long, which ended in a terrace of sand.

"Okay you guys, Louis and me gonna go first. You three hold the Vale steady while we climb in."

"Now let's go," Graham whooped.

They started shoving themselves until *The Vale of Belvoir* gained momentum. The vessel took off on its own after that. Clutching the gunwales, they yelled like two Red Indians as they rocketed down. They found they could steer slightly by leaning to one side or the other. When they fetched up on the terrace below, they leaped out.

"Fantastic!" we heard them cry. They picked up the bow of the canoe and dragged it up the slope again.

"Your turn," Graham offered.

For us, it was a squash. Amos wanted to ride in front, I sat behind him.

"I gonna keep my eyes closed," my sister admitted, climbing into the back.

Graham pushed us off so hard, Maudie fell over backwards and spent the ride lying in the bottom of the hull, her feet kicking my head.

"Aw gee, I never saw anything," she complained

when we got to the bottom.

"But you said you gonna keep your eyes shut," I reminded her. She retaliated with a punch to my ribs.

"Never been so fast in my life, even on a tram down Roberts Avenue," Amos giggled.

"Now for the big one," Graham declared, reaching for the canoe and dragging it to the main slope down the front of the mine-dump.

"It's a long way down," I pointed out.

"Nah, it's no steeper than the little ride we had now. Just means Louis and me gonna have a run four times longer. Meet you at the bottom."

When we let them go, they had to do some pushing to get *The Vale of Belvoir* sliding. But once underway, there was no stopping it.

"Sis, Amos, let's chase after them," I cheered.

We began leaping and sliding down the yellow sand.

Graham's and Louis's chorus of laughter began the moment they picked up speed. Their vociferation didn't get much fainter as they scorched away from us. What they hadn't bargained for was the effect friction had on the underside of the hull on such a long run. Now they were yelling in complaint at the heat being generated under their buttocks.

The canoe wasn't even halfway down the mine-dump and at the speed they were travelling, they couldn't get out. They protested their discomfort in desperation, but besides Amos, Maudie and myself, the only ears to hear them were those of a couple of pigeons circling below.

Then their problem was solved in a manner they weren't expecting. Halfway down the mine-dump, the slope changed its angle, levelling off abruptly and then dropping off again. Almost like a small terrace that had been rounded off by rain and wind. Almost like a ski-jump.

Yowling louder than ever, the twins ramped off the

jump and became airborne. They never got very high, but because the slope dropped steeply away, they covered forty yards before making contact with the sand again.

When Graham and Louis landed at such speed, Amos folded over with mirth. Afterwards, he couldn't look either twin in the eye without doubling up and going into hysterics. Whenever he saw them coming up the street, he jumped over the backyard fence to have uncontrollable giggles in his own yard.

When the twins shot off the ramp, the back of their improvised toboggan came off askew. They arched through the air, The Vale of Belvoir swinging sideways. They plummeted onto the slope in a cloud of sand and for a moment were lost in the havoc. Graham flew clear and we witnessed a windmill of legs and arms and an occasional glimpse of his head as he cartwheeled down the slope.

"Where's Louis?" Maudie hollered. "Don't see him nowhere."

We plunged down the side of the mine-dump to find him. When the canoe landed on the slope sideways at such speed, it rolled like a barrel and looked like a ten-foot cigar spinning down the mine-dump.

Near the bottom we overtook Graham. He was plastered in sand. To a stranger he might have been buried for weeks, tunnelling his way out. When he saw us, he was attempting to brush sand from his eyes and out of his ears. He favoured his left leg as he staggered along.

"What happened to Louis?" we called.

Graham pointed to the canoe. It had rolled to a stop thirty yards below us. The spinning down the mine-dump folded the two sides of *The Vale of Belvoir* over to meet each other. One could no longer have got into the canoe. Or out for that matter. It did resemble a giant cigar now, even at close quarters.

Coming from inside was Louis's bitter complaining.

I could see a foot sticking out. A hand was trying to prise open the two gunwales that had closed over like an iron maiden. Just visible inside this instant sarcophagus, was Louis's tousled black hair plastered with yellow sand.

"Graham. You there Graham? Darn it. Can you hear me Graham? Get me out. You and your confounded ideas."

Louis's voice was muffled. He struggled so much that the canoe rolled upside down and then he sounded even further away.

It took all our efforts to bend the gunwales out again. Louis was black from the battering he had received. He was so confused by vertigo that he was unable to stand.

"Why's it always me who comes off second best?" he demanded, trying to stand but having the ground come up to meet him. He remained sitting, holding his head while the world merry-go-rounded and see-sawed around him.

"We sure gonna have to fix our canoe," Maudie observed.

I looked at our beloved *Vale of Belvoir*. It needed straightening. I would have to wash off the mine-dump sand before our father noticed.

"T'wasn't such a good idea after all," Graham admitted, letting an avalanche of sand spill from his ear.

"It was a good idea," Amos guffawed. "Never laughed so much in my life." He took off before Graham could grab him.

Unfortunately, the condition of our sand-caked boat was the first thing our father noticed when we arrived home.

"Where on earth have you lot been?" he asked, inspecting the canoe.

"Playing on a pile of building sand," was my quick reply. He seemed to accept that quite readily which made it easier for me to lie in future.

My sister and I were threatened with dire consequences if we came into the house before cleaning ourselves up.

"The great unwashed have really excelled this time," our father said, shaking his head but also grinning. "Here's a bucket, soap and two floor cloths. Go and bath under the tap in the yard before you put a foot into the house. Then you'd better have a real bath."

While my sister was washing sand out of my hair, she warned, "Someone's following us. All the way home, I just know."

"You see him?"

"No, just a feeling. I can tell when someone's watching."

Chapter 26

"I getting bored again," Graham grumbled. "Why don't we do something different this afternoon, like exploring the Foster Caves?"

Maudie glanced at me with big eyes.

"S'out of bounds Tadpole. Abe warned us to stay away."

"S'okay, Maud, don't panic, you gonna be with me and my bro," Graham said.

I nodded. "Yah, Sis. I wouldn't mind seeing inside. But don't let Frog find out. He'll report us to Daddy."

The caves were concealed in a ravine on the koppies below Rockey Street. Once there, you couldn't see the houses above. Or be seen, for that matter. Those houses below in the side streets off Roberts Avenue, were hidden under their roofs.

In 1914 the Foster Gang terrorized Johannesburg with robbery and murder. They made the caves their hideout and vowed the police would never take them alive. It came to a sticky end in a shootout when the gang committed suicide inside the caves. I was too scared to go there on my own.

"Make us a snazzy den," Graham encouraged. "Can do a bunk from school, explore and muck around you know. Maybe find something the gang left behind."

Sunday afternoon found us hiking along a path on the koppie below Rockey Street. I told our father we were going to a friend's house. Hobo trotted in front, flushing out grasshoppers and butterflies. My sister howled in anguish and rushed to grab her by her collar.

"Ooh, the python. I forgot about what Mister de Beer said happened to his Pekinese."

"Yah, Maudie. Better keep Hobo close."

Amos picked up a stick and Graham guffawed. The path led us to an outcrop of rock overhanging the entrance. I looked down. A cigarette butt lay in the dirt, a bully-beef tin rusted and the remnants of a cooking-fire blackened a rock.

"C'mon, let's go down," Graham urged.

We followed him, squatted under the overhang and peered into the Lilliputian entrance.

"That's a blooming small hole to crawl through," Maudie complained.

"Nah, s'not the original way in," Graham explained. "The cops blocked that ages ago with rocks."

I gazed along the koppie. To the east, it stretched away. On the western slope, the nearest houses were a quarter of a mile off, hidden behind hedges. The Rockey Street houses above were out of sight. Below in Roberts Avenue, all I saw were corrugated iron roofs.

"Let's go in," Graham prompted.

He crouched on hands and knees and shuffled into the fissure. Louis followed. Amos was next, then Maudie prodding Hobo. I slid in last. After the summer sunlight, I was blind and made my way by feel. The rock pressed on my face. Maudie halted in front of me and pulled back against my knees.

"Don't move," I heard Graham's thundering whisper. "Our eyes gotta get used to the dark."

"We shoulda brought a candle," Amos protested.

Gradually, I began making out the slab above my head. Bat and rock-rabbit droppings stuck to my hands and feet.

"I found a hole we can crawl through," Graham told us. "I bet you it goes down to the cave."

We shuffled on our haunches until Graham reached the fracture in the rock. It was too tight to shuffle through.

"You gonna hafta wriggle through on your bellies," he muttered.

"Who's going first?" Louis enquired and immediately shut his mouth.

"I'll send the smallest to look round,"

"I aren't going in there," Maudie objected.

"Nah, but Amos is. Aren't you, Amos?" Graham prodded him.

Amos muttered under his breath in Zulu, refusing to tell Graham what it meant. He lay on his back and squirmed feet first.

"I worried about snakes," he protested.

"Whadya see?" Graham pressed.

"Nothing... too dark... lemme out now."

Graham blocked the hole. "You next Tadpole," he ordered.

I squeezed through and crouched with Amos in the dark. It was worse here than back in the tunnel. Louis squirmed through next. Then I heard Maudie's voice as she wriggled through, followed by Hobo. Graham was last.

We squatted on a ledge with a void below. If there was a cavern down there, I couldn't see it. I didn't know how high we were.

"Chuck a stone down, Bro," Graham instructed.

Louis felt for a pebble and let it clatter down the side of the rock into the cavern.

"Maybe eight feet."

"Picture-rail height," I thought.

"Sis, hold Hobo. If she falls, she's not gonna get out."

A glimmer of light came from the fissure we'd wriggled through.

"Arghhhhhhh," Amos squawked, swiping at something that flew into his face.

"Better come back another time," Graham decided. "Be crazy to climb down there without a light."

"Any case, what we gonna see?" Maudie added.

Four days later, school broke up. Graham and Louis entrained for Middleburg to spend Christmas on their small-holding with Phoenie their mother.

"No more school, no more books," Maudie chanted, "No more teachers' dirty looks."

But when she thought our father wasn't listening, she altered the ending.

"No more teachers' dirty broeks." Broeks being Dutch for knickers.

"And no blinking Mondays now we on holiday. Only Saturdays and Sundays, every day. Yea."

"Sis, it can't be Saturday or Sunday every day."

"Okay then I hafta make us a brand new holiday sign. This old one's no blooming good any more. 'Tis torn and full of holes."

"I reckon Hobo's been chewing on it."

She lettered a new sign for the fig tree. Coloured silver and gold with judicious care of grey, white, yellow and ochre crayons, it read *On Holiday.*

"How about taking The Vale of Belvoir to the park?" I suggested on Monday morning.

"S'long as we keep away from the scary side."

"Yah, maybe Amos can come along also."

He crawled through the fence and we lugged our canoe down the drive. Joseph worked on his miniature waterways. He had lined his canals with cement. Meandering through Trixie's garden, they looked wonderfully picturesque.

"Hello Old Joseph," Maudie sang.

Joseph glanced up from under his panama. His leather thong dangled inside his shirt.

"Where are you three ragamuffins off to on this magnificent Monday morning?"

"Aw gee, Old Joseph. We aren't really ragamuffins. We're on holiday."

"Oh all right then, Maudie. Where are you three holiday-makers off to?"

"Rhodes Park, to paddle our canoe. When're your

rivers gonna be full of water, so we can come play, Old Joseph?"

"Oh, I haven't finished by a long chalk. Next week perhaps. How do you like them?"

"Beautiful. If we make toy boats, can we come sail 'em on your lakes?"

"Of course, Maudie. On the little rivers too, for they are really going to flow."

"How, Old Joseph? How they gonna flow if they got nowhere to go?"

"Ah. Haven't you seen me with my spirit level and tape measure and string tied between pegs all over the garden?"

"Yah, I seen you messing in Trixie's garden."

"Well, the canals connecting the lakes are on a gentle slope, just enough to keep the water flowing. The siphon will feed the system, the rivers will flow from the top lake down to the next and so on. When they find their way to the bottom lake in the conservatory, a little electric pump will feed the water up to the top again."

"That means our little boats can sail from one end to the other?" Maudie schemed.

Joseph nodded.

"What happens if your electric pump stops, Old Joseph? All your water's gonna drain into the conservatory and you'll have a flood bigger than Noah had."

Joseph laughed. "Not at all. The lakes are twelve inches deep, but the rivers are only four inches deep. When I switch off the pump, the lakes will act as sumps. Each river will drain into the lake below and so the lakes will stay full. Otherwise my goldfish would die."

"But what if a goldfish got caught halfway when you switch the pump off?"

Joseph shook his head. "I'll make certain the fish are in the lakes first. If it did happen, the fish would swim with the flow. They'll be quite safe."

"You got it all worked out Old Joseph, haven't you?"

He chuckled, turning back to his work. "If I find time later, I might take the Harley down to the park to see how you're doing. Don't drown in the meantime."

"Aw, we can swim," Maudie assured him. She whistled for Hobo.

When we rounded the corner into Roberts Avenue, I glanced back and noticed the front wheel of Joseph's motorcycle combination nosing out of Trixie's drive.

There were not many visitors to the park on a Monday morning. We kept away from the jetty and launched *The Vale of Belvoir* among scattered clumps of reeds.

"Lookit Tsotsi there," Maudie giggled, pointing at the scruffy Manx crouching behind a fisherman, devouring his bait. Maudie and I were lifting Hobo into the canoe, when I heard a caterwaul. Tsotsi had been walloped across the ears. The fisherman packed his gear and went home. I saw him later with fresh bait sealed in a honey jar.

We took it in turns messing about in the canoe. When we weren't canoeing, we sat on the bank with our feet in the water, mindful of the catfish and the crabs. I didn't see any.

"Let's all go together on the lake," Amos suggested, munching one of Sampson's sandwiches.

"What, all three of us?"

He stuffed half the sandwich into his mouth.

"And Hobo also," Maudie added. "It's gonna be fun."

"I dunno if we'll fit, Sis."

"Course we'll fit." She prodded my ribs with her toes, "Hobo don't weigh much. She can sit on my lap."

I slid the canoe onto the water. We did fit, even with Hobo. But it was a crush and *The Vale of Belvoir* floated low.

"Summer holidays are snazzy," Maudie sighed.

"Yah, Sis. We can come to the park every day." We paddled to the middle of the lake.

"Hey, lookee there, now," Maudie cried. "That fisherman what Tsotsi got his bait... look, he caught something."

His red and white float bobbed in the water. Tsotsi noticed it too and bounded along the bank for his share of the catch. Hobo wasn't a cat chaser. So why she showed an interest in Tsotsi racing along the shore, I can't imagine.

"Sit still my angel, you gonna capsize us," Maud warned.

Hobo lurched off my sister's lap and over the gunwale. Our pride and joy rolled once. Amos hollered in panic. The side dipped under the water and the hull filled. Hobo doggie-paddled for the shore. Amos followed. He was not a strong swimmer.

Maudie and I treaded water, hanging onto the submerged hull. I was frightened of letting go in case we never saw our beloved boat again. It pulled us down and I didn't think I could hang on much longer.

"My hand's hurting," Maudie sobbed, kicking furiously to keep her head above water. She choked up a mouthful of lake.

I remembered her eyes in the Gillooly's River, watching me and changed my grip. I was finished too.

"Drop it, Sis. We'll come back tomorrow with some sash cord. Maybe we can dive for it."

"We never gonna get our canoe back, Tadpole." She started crying.

"Yah but we gonna drown if we don't let go. It's pulling me under."

We let go and started doggie-paddling for the shore. I found it hard going. The exertion brought on a migraine and my vision wavered. White flashes blurred my sight. Before we reached shore, I was blind.

"Maudie," I called in panic. "Help me. I can't see. I got migraine real bad this time."

"Here's my hand, Tadpole. Don't worry. S'not far now."

Flickering images pulsated inside my eyes. Molten-steel-white, quivering like a mirage. I could see nothing. My sister guided me to the bank.

We started for home without *The Vale of Belvoir*. Maudie led me. She laced her fingers in mine and warned me about the kerbs when we crossed streets. Amos kept an eye on Hobo. We made slow progress.

Halfway up the avenue, bile erupted into my throat. I put my hand to my stomach and my sister showed me where the edge of the pavement was. I lay in the dirt and grass with my head in the gutter, voiding my stomach and shivering with the filth of it, but it was the only way to regain my sight.

Abruptly, the juddering images disappeared and I now shivered with fear because I knew what came next. A monstrous headache exploded above my eyes. It pulsated as if the arteries in my head would burst. I felt washed out, like an old man wasting on his deathbed.

"C'mon," Maudie whispered. "Lemme take you home and put you to bed."

That evening, Mr de Beer invited himself to supper. The twins, along with the other boys, were home for the Christmas holidays. Neither my sister nor I enjoyed having the housemaster visit our father. He had a habit of reminding us that there was no future without learning. No future without work. I was nervous in his presence and my replies to his questions were incoherent.

At least I didn't have to sit at the same table as him, although Maudie was obliged to. I heard Sampson rattling the coffee cups. Then what I dreaded, my father brought the housemaster to see me.

"How are you, son?" Mr de Beer asked.

He fingered a phial of prescription pills, extracted one, placed it on his tongue and swallowed it.

I grinned feebly.

He reserved a special voice for pupils when they were accompanied by their parents. As soon as the other adult removed himself, so did the housemaster remove the warmth from his voice.

"I been vomiting," I mumbled.

"Well, we can't have that, can we? Not during the holidays. Get better, son."

I shivered.

Chapter 27

I was sick for two days. Resting in my bed the following afternoon, I heard the paperboy pedalling down the pavement followed by the plop of The Star on the veranda steps. He had excelled himself.

Hobo came pelting down the drive, followed by Maudie.

"No Hobo... me first... wait for me... Hobo-oh, wait. Ah phooey on you."

Why Hobo wanted The Star, I could never figure out. But she also raced my sister to answer the telephone and didn't know what to do when she got there first.

"Now, gimme the paper. I s'pose you think you smart?"

She spread The Star on my bed so we could read Curly Wee. I noticed a brief report about the missing children.

"The police aren't making any progress, Sis. Davy and Johan're still gone. Nobody knows where to look."

"Still missing?"

"Yah, that's what I said."

"Probably bunking school. They gonna be in big trouble when they get caught."

"Maudie, you know what happened to 'em. You could tell the police."

"Tadpole, sometimes I reckon you plumb crazy. Tell the cops what?"

I stared at her. She knew but she didn't know. I was too scared to tell our father what was going on. She stuck her tongue at me.

"And you seen a giraffe man, Sis."

"Yah, he put his hands on my neck. Smelled him

also."

"I never seen your giraffe man, Maudie."

"Heck, that's cos he vanished like he was wearing chameleon juice. Maybe Mister Isanusi gave him stacks of muti."

I squinted.

"Swear to God and hope to die, Tadpole. I seen him vanish before my eyes."

Five days later, we salvaged our canoe.

"C'mon. I reckon we better go'n pull up The Vale of Belvoir from the bottom. It's gonna be real yucky."

She dug out twenty feet of old sash cord from under our father's workbench. I tied one end to a wooden plank to keep it on the surface. The other, I looped into a lasso which I planned to dive and fasten around our canoe. Maudie put a leash on Hobo and whistled up Amos.

At the park, a strange sight met our eyes. The authorities were draining the lake. Glistening mud flats lay exposed and birds waded and poked their bills in search of food. Tsotsi padded in the mud too, investigating anything left high and dry. Frogs and crabs everywhere. A net stretched across a corner of the lake where a pool of water seethed with fish.

"What's going on here?" Amos quizzed us.

Maudie held up a hand to shield her eyes and examined the shore where the willows drooped.

"The cops..."

I followed her gaze. Four men in gumboots waded in the mud. They stooped, searching the bottom. Beyond, two police vans stood under the willows.

"They looking for clues?" Amos asked.

I stared at the scene. Amos knew nothing of what my sister witnessed in her nightmares. And I couldn't talk in front of her, because she denied it.

"Check the papers, Amos, they aren't making any progress are they? I mean, they got no suspects. Have they arrested anyone...?"

"Nuh, they city police. Don't know much about tribal things."

I didn't reveal what my sister knew about Davy Nguni and Johan Rabie.

"C'mon, let's go find our boat."

Hobo streaked for the bank but when she got there she hesitated, puzzled. The mud was black. It oozed. It breathed. Air holes broke the surface. They wheezed and sucked as if the mud was talking.

I shielded my eyes, staring across the morass. *The Vale of Belvoir* looked as drab as the morass it lay in.

"We won't have to dive for it," Maudie said.

"Race you, Sis. Last one's a rotten tomato."

I sprang into the ooze, expecting to sprint for our boat. I sank halfway to my knees.

"Sez who? You the rotten tomato now. I the king of the castle and you the dirty rascal."

Maudie and Amos stood on the shore splitting their sides.

"S'not funny," I complained. "You two gonna hafta get in here also if you wanna fetch the Vale. Then we'll see who's laughing."

Maudie rolled up her cords and gingerly lowered herself into the filth. Amos followed. Hobo sank to her stomach and made progress in short bounds. My sister's white mongrel bitch was a now black mongrel bitch.

We rolled our begrimed boat over to empty the water and dragged it to the shore. Hobo dug frantically, her head immersed in mire.

Maudie glanced at her in disbelief.

"Leave it, my angel. You not gonna get lucky. Jeepers, how'm I gonna getcha clean?"

Her black dog ignored her, sending a shower of mud through her hind legs. A catfish flapped out of the hole, startling Hobo into springing away. The monster didn't wait around to be investigated by an inquisitive dog. It floundered across the mud to the pool where other fish were trapped. Hobo bounded after.

"Hey quit it now," Maudie yelled. "Who'dya think's gonna wash you?"

We looked like sodden chimney sweeps. Under a park tap, we undressed and scrubbed ourselves, our boat, our clothes and Maudie's dog. We were partially successful.

My sister was disgusted.

"This isn't much good to us, we oughta take The Vale of Belvoir home. Can't canoe here till they find what they looking for."

"They not gonna find it, Sis."

She glanced at me in a funny way.

"Yah, any case," Amos lamented, "the lake'll take week's to fill up again."

"We just hafta find something else to do," I concluded.

"Like what?" Amos demanded.

My sister amazed me sometimes. For some reason known only to her, she took it into her head to tease Amos about his superstitions.

"Amos, are you frightened of the Mamlambo Water Spirit? Or the Impundulu Lightning Bird? The hairy Tokoloshe perhaps?" she quizzed, pushing her face into his.

"What if I am?" he retorted, pulling himself up to his full height and wrinkling his nose. "Why?"

"Cos I just remembered what we can do." She folded her arms triumphantly.

I was puzzled and glanced up from scraping mud under my nails.

"I not going near any Mamlambo Snake, and no Impundulu Bird and I don't wanna even see a Tokoloshe," Amos asserted. "If that's where you and Tadpole're going, then I'm on my way home to my mama."

"Crikey, you a scaredy-cat, Amos. We aren't gonna visit any of those silly old things."

"They not silly, Maudie. They real. My mama warned me about 'em."

My sister started to giggle.

"That's ancient legends from the Stone Age, Amos. You shouldn't listen to 'em. They belong in the bush where they come from."

Amos raised his eyebrows and rocked on his heels.

"Anyway," Maudie continued, "we aren't going anywhere near those things if it makes you feel better. But we can go visit someone who knows a lot about 'em."

"The sangoma?" I queried. "Isanusi?"

"Why?" Amos asked uneasily.

"I seen him back on the koppies."

"And then? What business we got with a sangoma? He'll turn us into hyenas, Maudie."

I guffawed at the thought of Amos in the shape of a hyena, pleading with his mama to be let into her room.

"He didn't last time Tadpole and me paid him a visit. He was actually very friendly and showed us his bones."

She stopped short of telling Amos the shaman threw the bones for us.

"You want him to tell us more bad things, Sis?"

She pulled a face at me.

The koppie's grass stood tall, hiding granite outcrops. It was mid-summer now. Wild flowers, yellow, white and pink, competed for space. Many insects and little creatures were about. Field mice scurried through the grass. Butterflies aplenty, frozen to flowers. Stick shaped grasshoppers; Maudie tried to catch them but they sprang away. Geckos sunned themselves on rocks. Bird calls all around us. Rustlings in the grass.

"You hafta pretend they mice in case they snakes," Maudie warned.

At the bottom of the path, we found Isanusi squatting under a thorn tree.

"Isanusi sees you," he greeted.

"Sakubona umfaan," he added for Amos' benefit.

We returned his greetings politely. Hobo lay down behind her mistress. The sangoma's sack worried Maudie's dog.

"What is it that brings you children here? And your friend?"

"Mister Isanusi remembers the bones he threw for us?" Maudie reminded him.

The shaman pulled at his chin with his left hand.

"Pleeze Mister Isanusi. We come to ask if you can tell us more about what you saw in your bones."

"Isanusi remembers the bones as if they were lying before him now."

"Well?" Maudie pestered.

The old diviner let his gaze fall on Amos. "Who is the little umfaan?"

"He's Amos," Maudie told him. "He's our friend, Mister Isanusi. He and Tadpole and me, we stick together."

"Why should two European children befriend a Zulu umfaan?"

Maudie put her hands on her hips. "Cos he's all by himself, Mister Isanusi. Tadpole and me the only children in the street his age."

The sangoma turned to Amos and quizzed him in Zulu. He asked questions which my sister and I didn't understand. Amos answered nervously.

"There are other things Isanusi has smelled out," the shaman said. "They are strange."

"In his visions, he's seen writing in black. A black Monday."

I glanced at Maudie. Her signs in the fig tree.

"There is a house burning. A woman entombed. She has been there many months."

Maudie rolled her eyes at me.

I didn't speak.

"Tobacco ground into powder. Isanusi smells snuff. Why a giraffe? It puzzles me."

We listened intently.

"A Mamlambo snake has entered a persons body... now they Mamlambo's slave, they cannot help what they do."

I listened in silence. Amos shook.

"In the night, a motorcar lies on its back."

This startled me. Momma and my sister in the farm pickup. But that didn't happen at night. Was it going to happen to Maudie again?

"There is a place Isanusi cannot see into... the lair of the ant-bear."

I shivered.

"And a strange tool from the sea."

"From the sea, Mister Isanusi?" my sister asked. "What tool from the sea?"

The shaman shrugged.

Hobo growled. She clambered to her feet. Someone on the path approached.

Isanusi glanced up.

"That is what Isanusi tells you children. Look for these signs. You will know them when you see them."

An old African woman approached.

"Hambani kahle, children," he cautioned, dismissing us. "Go well."

"Sala kahle, Mister Isanusi. Stay well," Maudie responded.

Amos was so nervous, he shook.

"I shouldn't of come with you. I done nothing to upset nobody. I'm going home."

"You threw your catfish at your mama," Maudie reminded him. "I bet that took ten years off her life. Perhaps this is her way of getting you back."

"I already got a beating for that. With the end of a rubber hosepipe. Didn't you hear me screaming? My mama was killing me. And if I remember right, there was chuckles coming from the fig tree."

"What about those washer women on the tram you scared half to death with your catfish when it jumped out of Lizzie's bag? The whole of Main Street came to a standstill. Maybe one of 'em was a witch and now she's after you."

"Very funny," Amos retorted. "What about you two anyway? You were stupid enough to ask a sangoma to throw the bones for you. I wasn't even there. All I gotta worry about is hanging round with you." He bounded away and kept his distance fifty yards in front of us.

"Whadya think about those things Mister Isanusi saw, Tadpole? He knows about our signs in the fig tree."

"Yah, Sis... the Monday one..."

"But what house is gonna burn down? And something about a lady? What lady?"

She pulled a face. "And a giraffe?"

"I dunno, Maudie. Could be making it up. Maybe he's been smoking dagga."

"What about snuff? Who'd we know sniffs snuff?"

"We gotta be on the lookout, Sis."

"A snake inside a person? A Mamlambo? Can't be Tadpole. Perhaps he's inventing it."

"Yah, Maudie. It's a load of rubbish. He just trying to frighten us."

We hiked in silence. Amos kept his distance.

Maudie touched my arm. "You know, I been thinking. The other evening when you were sick in bed, Mister de Beer told Abe that Mister Sunshine's clothing business is a cover for what he really does."

"You mean he's crooked?"

She stubbed a toe on a tree root pushing up through the sidewalk.

"Ouch, damn it," she cussed, leaping up and down on one leg. "Why don't they make the darn pavement smooth?"

Amos was so far ahead, making sure that whatever evil surrounded me and my sister wouldn't touch him, he didn't notice the song and dance.

Nor did he hear her suggestion.

"Tadpole let's spy on old Sunshine when he comes round again. Perhaps we can look inside his suitcase."

Chapter 28

The air show Babs told us about was going to be held the following Saturday afternoon and I forgot about Isanusi's warnings. Maudie and I had never been closer than ten thousand feet to an aeroplane.

"Can you two keep a secret?" Babs whispered.

"Cross my heart," Maudie promised.

"Well, I'm going to make a funny jump. I'll open my parachute which won't excite the crowd. They always lust for something to make their blood curl."

"So what you gonna do?" Maudie enquired.

Babs laughed. "I'm going to deliberately jettison my parachute."

"But you can't do that. You'll get killed."

"That's what I want them to think. I'll start screaming and waving my arms and legs helplessly."

"And then?"

"I'll let myself fall a few thousand feet."

"No Babs, please."

"When I'm just above their heads, I'll open my auxiliary chute."

"You're clever, Babs. They all gonna die of shock."

Babs grinned. She never told our father what she was going to do.

Our father was funny with the great unwashed. He didn't actually promise to take us to Rand Aerodrome. Maudie fretted.

"Aw, c'mon Abe. Aren't we going now? Babs is flying her Tiger Moth, you know."

"Really, sweetheart? First time I heard that. You must have long ears."

"Humph," my sister sulked. She knew all about hares with long ears.

Fifteen minutes before it was time to leave, he chuckled, "All right, we're going now."

"Aw, Abe."

Chaos as we scuttled to clean up our mess in the backyard and scrub ourselves under the garden tap. Amos transformed himself into a frenzy of diving through the fence and urging his mother to find something better than his play rags. Frog had made himself neat an hour earlier.

Spectators were not allowed onto the aerodrome. An area against the perimeter fence was marked off. Thousands of cars from the thirties and early forties, three and four deep, were drawn up at the fence. Families brought picnic baskets. Some lowered their cars' luggage carriers to form a table for their plates and food. Others spread their picnics on their cars' bonnets. We'd eaten an early lunch and wandered among the cars, eyeing and sniffing what other children were scoffing.

"Hot dogs, Tadpole. Lookee there, they got hot dogs. We better tell Abe to ask Semp-Sonne to get us hot dogs next time."

"Yah, Sis." I kept my eyes open for the signs Isanusi warned us about.

An army Dakota glided toward the airfield, throttled back, making a silent approach. The crew threw out a thunder-flash and an enormous explosion jolted the crowd into craning its gaze upwards. Young children ran for protection. Fathers laughed and quaffed their beer, peering up at a purple parachute-flare giving off smoke.

"An Impundulu bird laid an egg," my sister giggled. "Look, there it is, coming down by parachute."

"Don't say those things," Amos warned. "A real

Impundulu bird will carry you away to its nest."

I shivered as we threaded our way back to our old Chev.

We watched the Dakota as one after the other, twenty human bodies tumbled through the hatch. A murmur went up from the spectators. Canopies opened and filled the sky with wartime chutes. The crowd broke into spontaneous clapping when the last parachutist landed, rolled out of his fall and sprang up to control the billowing cloth.

We were still eyeing them furl their gear when a low-level fly-past came by, slow and steady at sixty feet, a column of aircraft in line astern. They crossed in front of us, Ansons, Beech Craft, a Dragon Fly staggered wing bi-plane, Pipers, Taylorcraft, Moths and Harvards droning noisily. They circled, formed up in line abreast and returned over the aerodrome, their engines reverberating on our eardrums. Then, regrouping in pairs, they made their final approach, landed en masse in front of the spectators and taxied to the hangars. The crowd clapped its approval and men reached for their beer.

A fabric covered bi-plane with radial engine taxied onto the grass.

"There's Babs," Maudie whispered. "She's gonna do her trick now."

"Uh-uh, Sis. Only one-up. No figure in the front cockpit, only the pilot's head behind the aft windscreen."

"Yah, I s'pose you right."

The bi-plane taxied toward the crowd and opened its throttle. It rose sixty feet and rolled onto its back. I gasped. I was positive the wings had touched the ground.

"How about that?" Maudie blurted.

Then the pilot flicked the plane over again. He rolled the plane until it overran the perimeter fence. Then he climbed steeply. Within minutes he was back, performing aerobatics, rolling, then a spiral corkscrew. We applauded.

The little plane soared and came back in a shallow dive, then steeply into a climb making the engine struggle. As it stalled, he looped the plane and put it into another dive. When he pulled up, the aircraft climbed vertically until it stalled and the crowd gasped. The plane toppled over and started spinning out of the sky, smoke streaming from the cockpit. A murmur came from the crowd. The plane spun lazily, twirling like a leaf, its engine dead. A woman screamed.

"He's had his chips," Amos yowled. "I got my eyes closed."

"Not so sure," Maudie answered, screwing up her eyes. "I think he's trying to fool us."

I watched in horror as the craft fell.

When I thought it was too late, the motor roared into life, the bi-plane pulled out of the spin and whizzed across the field in front of us. People started laughing nervously. They were on their feet clapping and cheering. There was a final display of aerobatics, the old aircraft making its landing approach upside down. It approached in a long glide, the motor throttled back and levelled off as it passed over the fence. Halfway across the aerodrome, it flipped right way up so close to the ground I thought the wings had touched. Then it was down, the crowd roaring its approval and drinking beer. We learned later that the pilot was an ace who had taken part in the Battle of Britain.

"This is exciting Abe," Maudie said, jumping into his arms and hugging him.

The full-blooded roar of a Rolls Royce twelve cylinder Merlin engine filled our ears. A Spitfire streaked toward us at three hundred miles an hour. Another throaty bellow made us swing around to see a Hurricane approaching from the opposite direction. They flew directly at one another, making us hold our breaths. At the last instant, each flipped onto its right hand side and peeled away, climbing for the heavens. We craned our necks. They began a game of tag.

"Dog fight," I told Maudie and Amos.

Chased by the Hurricane with only fifty yards separating them, the Spitfire dived and yawed to shake off its attacker.

The fighters rolled, banked and twisted across the sky. The leader rolled onto his back and dived away upside down while the other plane searched for it. Then the Spitfire latched onto the Hurricane's tail in renewed dog fight. They clawed their way across the sky, falling and slipping, spiralling and rolling, diving and racing, the howl of their engines rising in high crescendos. We watched spellbound. Then, as if tiring of the play, the two aircraft flew slowly over the aerodrome. Their cockpit canopies were open now and the pilots gave victory salutes to the spectators on the ground. Their home base must have been at another aerodrome, for they flew sedately away and diminished to two black specks on the horizon.

A Tiger Moth taxied onto the runway. It was yellow and I made out two little brown blobs in the open cockpits.

"That's Babs," Maudie shrieked, jumping on the Chev's bonnet and causing people to turn and stare.

"It is," she insisted.

We watched the Moth trundle down the runway, lift its tail and rise into the air. It climbed slowly, circling in front of the crowd and spiralled until it was thousands of feet above us. Then we saw a narrow white band stream from behind the tail.

"A Mamlambo snake being born," Maudie chortled.

Amos glanced at her uneasily.

It grew longer and longer and turned out to be a roll of toilet paper the crew unreeled in the slipstream. The crowd laughed. The paper was jettisoned and floated like a silken scarf in the sky.

"A long white Mamlambo snake," my sister teased.

"No," Amos implored. "You say those things, a real Mamlambo will come and get you."

Maudie laughed.

The Tiger Moth circled and angled in at the paper. It cut it in half with its propeller. Except for some debris, there were now two scarves undulating in the sky. The plane banked, came back and attacked them, leaving four strips plus some scrap behind it. The crowd now understood what the objective was: to leave no ribbon intact by the time it floated to earth.

Spectators urged the plane on with their cries. On the next run, the Moth managed to cut only three pieces in half and had to search for the missing section. Now there were eight ribbons floating among the debris of confetti in the sky. The plane dived to attack the remaining strips. With the exception of one, the roll had been destroyed. The last ribbon was low, fluttering only forty feet up in the breeze. We watched rapt. The plane banked and dropped onto the airfield, its wheels skimming the grass. It aimed at the tiny length of paper and rose to devour it. The crowd went wild. Spectators began blowing their cars' hooters to show their approval.

"See, Amos," Maudie taunted. "No more Mamlambo."

Amos scowled.

While everybody cheered and clapped, the Tiger Moth began climbing.

"Now she'll do it," Maudie blurted. "She's gonna pretend to fall out of her parachute."

"Sh-sh-sh," I warned. "Daddy doesn't know."

"He sure gonna get a heart attack."

Above us, the yellow Moth levelled off and circled the aerodrome. Our eyes were riveted on the plane. A figure in flying leathers, clumsy with parachute harnesses, stood up in the front cockpit and began climbing onto the wing.

"Your aunt?" Amos asked.

My sister nodded. "Yah, she's got a surprise up her sleeve."

I'm sure Babs hadn't meant to jump then. Still only half onto the wing, one leg reaching for a footing while the other straddled the cockpit coaming. The Tiger Moth lurched, Babs lost her balance and let go the wing strut. Blown by the slipstream, she tumbled off the wing and became entangled with the tailplane.

"Oh my God," our father cried.

Around us, people gasped, their eyes fixed on the figure ensnared in the tailplane control cables.

Babs struggled to free herself, but her parachute harness had snagged the control wires. The pilot no longer had control and was standing up in his cockpit, looking back.

"Oh Babs, oh heavens," our father murmured.

Our aunt's parachute blew out of its pack. It streamed back and filled with a thunderclap. Worse off now, she was strung between the parachute and the snagged control wires.

"I don't think she gonna come loose," Maudie predicted.

The sudden deceleration threw the pilot forward. The plane was no longer flying, but dragging the parachute down through the sky. Then the engine cut out. An eerie silence fell over the airfield. All eyes were fixed upwards on the crippled craft with the figure in flying leathers snagged on the tail, pulling an opened parachute through the sky.

It took only moments for the Tiger Moth to lose flying speed and dangle straight down. From where we were standing, it looked as if Babs was holding the plane by her toes, but there must have been a control cable hooked onto her harness to take such a weight. They were coming down fast.

"They're both going to be killed," our father exclaimed.

I couldn't see what the pilot was doing in the

cockpit, but he must have been strapping himself in and bracing for the impact.

Then Babs' auxiliary parachute opened. It blossomed from the leather clad figure, snaked upwards and filled with a cannon shot. The crippled plane seemed to float, suspended by both parachutes, but its descent had only been slowed. It was less than two hundred feet up now.

A siren began wailing as an ambulance and a fire engine barrelled from a hangar across the field to where the crash was going to take place. A car left the vicinity of the control tower and chased after them. Spectators stared in hushed silence. There were only a few seconds left.

The nose of the Moth struck the grass and we saw pieces of propeller and yellow wreckage fly off. Then came the dull crunch of collision between earth, wood and metal. The pilot, strapped in his cockpit, must have hit his head. The tail, supported by the two parachutes, wavered for a few seconds. Then slowly flopped over, bringing the Tiger Moth to rest upside down. Babs was still snagged.

We watched as the ambulance, an old '42 wartime Dodge, careered to a standstill next to the amazingly intact bi-plane. Four ambulance men leapt out. The Moth lay on its upper wing. Two of the rescue team crawled under the fuselage where we could see the pilot's head protruding. The others sprinted to the tail. The fire team arrived and began spraying foam onto petrol leaking from the tank in the wing.

A cheer went up from the crowd. Babs had been released from her harnesses. She was limping, but able to stand unaided. She pushed her way under the plane where ambulance men struggled to free the pilot. They released his harness and he fell from the upside down cockpit. Babs helped drag him free. When he pulled off his flying helmet, long hair tumbled down and the crowd went wild, whistling and cheering with approval.

The pilot was a woman.

Two ambulance men tried winding a bandage around her head, but she didn't like this treatment and we saw her protesting and waving them away. Then, shakily she climbed to her feet. Babs put her arm around her shoulder and they linked arms. To the cries, whistles, cheers from the spectators and hooting of cars, the pair limped around the plane, inspecting the damage.

"Thank God they're alive," our father murmured.

Amos reproached my sister. "You see what happens when you don't show respect for the spirits?"

Maudie laughed.

"Best damn stunt I seen in my life," a man near us enthused.

Chapter 29

Six days before Christmas, I heard Mr Sunshine coming up Good Hope Street. The Zulu who drew his rickshaw, wore sheepskin anklets with sleigh bells that jingle-jangled like a tambourine. As the poor man met the hill of Good Hope Street, they mimicked a dying steam engine.

"Shsh... it's him," Maudie whispered.

"It's who?" Amos mumbled, stuffing a fig into his mouth. "Who you talking in secret about?"

We spent the morning lying in the fig tree, stripping fruit. Figs rotted on the ground. Amos ate three to Maudie's and my one.

"Figs're good for my guts," he mumbled, his mouth full.

"Well, I don't wanna be round when you gotta go," Maudie retorted.

"And I weren't talking in secret. I just heard old Sunshine's rickshaw, that's all." She aimed a fig at Hobo sprawled in the shade below, hitting her dog's jowls. Hobo lifted her head and looked about in bewilderment.

"Yikes, him? Hasn't been round for ages. I sure see him plenty times in Sophiatown. Gave me a ride in his Chrysler. That's some car."

He tossed a fig skin into the yard.

"My mama, she won't buy anything from Sunshine. Reckons he's a crook, up to no good."

At the sound of the driveway gate latch, Hobo lifted her head. She clambered to her feet to investigate and returned to the shade of the fig tree. We lay among the branches, eyeing the homburg, the immaculate double-breasted suit, silk tie and gold tiepin, the patent leather shoes and the suitcase big enough to squash a child into, coming up the drive.

"Keep cavey, everybody," Maudie whispered, "the cat's in the gravy."

I didn't think he could see us through the leaves, but before he rounded the corner of the house, Mr Sunshine spotted me.

"Lordy... Lordy, my children," he beamed, when he caught sight of Maudie's cords. He put his suitcase down and rubbed his hands together. "What a way to spend your time, loafing up a tree."

"It's school holidays Mister Sunshine," my sister retorted politely. "We can do's we like during holidays."

"So I see, my children."

Only now did he catch sight of Amos lying dead still in the branches.

"Aha," he observed, stabbing a finger at him, "so you are here after all. Loafing too, I see."

"Yessir," Amos stammered.

Mr Sunshine picked up his case, dusted off the bottom and told us, "Well, I've got business with Sampson. Then with Moses next door. How's Miss Babs? I should see her sometime too."

"Didn't you know, Mister Sunshine? She crashed her biplane... but she got out alive," my sister answered.

"I heard something about that," he nodded, climbing the back veranda stairs.

"C'mon," Maudie urged when he was out of earshot. "Now's our chance." She began sliding down the fig tree.

"What's going on?" Amos asked. "What're you two planning?"

"Get down immediately. We got work to do."

Amos followed us across the yard to the outhouse abutting Sampson's room.

"Tell me what you up to," he grumbled.

"You'll see inna jiffy," Maudie told him. "Give me a foot up and stop complaining."

Amos helped us onto the back wall and we pulled him up after us. We scrambled onto the flat roof of the outhouse. A low fire-protection wall separated the roof from Sampson's and we crouched behind this.

"What we doing up here?" Amos questioned.

"We gonna spy on old Sunshine," Maudie confided. "Don't you wanna know what business he got with everybody?"

"You'll get me in trouble. I shoulda stayed in the fig tree."

"Didn't your mama say he's crooked?"

"Yah, but she says he getting rich from selling to pore people. She don't think anybody should get rich that way."

"Maybe it's not clothes he selling."

"Then where'd he get his dough?"

"That's what we gonna find out."

Sampson came onto the back veranda. I spied him from the roof behind the firewall as he and Mr Sunshine crossed the yard and disappeared into Sampson's room below us. They closed the door. We lay with our heads overhanging the gutter. Amos was closest to the fanlight.

"Whadya see?" Maudie whispered.

"What I s'posed to see?"

"What's he got in his suitcase?"

"I dunno. The fanlight's covered in newspaper."

"Well find a hole, silly," Maudie urged.

Amos wormed his way so far over the gutter that my sister had to hang onto his legs to stop him falling off the roof.

"Now can you see anything?" she pestered.

"Yah, old Sunshine got his case open... he taking a catalogue out. Sampson undoing a cloth... he got boodle folded in it... now he taking notes and giving 'em to Sunshine."

"He owes him money." My sister made it her business to know everybody else's.

"He paying him one pound and ten shillings," Amos noted. "Sunshine put it in his wallet. Now he standing in the way. Can't see properly."

Amos squirmed further over the edge. "What's happening now?" Maudie demanded.

"Sunshine unpacking leather samples. He getting near the bottom of his case... showing Sampson."

"Perhaps he's interested in shoes."

"No, something else in the bottom of his case," Amos whispered, "... brown paper parcels."

"What can they be?" Maudie whispered. "Muti?"

"Dunno. Can't see... Sunshine packing it away. Pull me back before they see me."

We hauled him onto the corrugated iron. Sampson and Mr Sunshine opened the door, strolled across the yard and parted at the corner of the house. Hobo sat up and gazed at us suspiciously.

"We didn't learn much," Amos complained.

"Sez who?" Maudie whispered. "We now know he got something suspicious in that case."

"Hang it, Maudie. Where'd it get us?"

"Lessee what happens in Moses' room."

Amos snorted. "This's getting bad. If they catch us, I gonna tell 'em 'twas your idea."

We squeezed through the fence into Trixie's garden and sneaked up to the walnut tree. The branches stretched over the glass conservatory, toward Moses' room.

"We betta watch out for Joseph," I warned.

"He's cooling down in his shack," Maudie whispered. "Gets hot working on his rivers and lakes and things."

We shinned up the old tree and crouched in the fork to see what was going on in the backyard. The top of the homburg was visible. Moses and Mr Sunshine conversed on the other side of the conservatory. A minute later, they disappeared into Moses' room and closed the door.

"Quick, now's our chance," Maudie whispered, urging Amos up. He scrambled into the branches ahead of her.

Lying among the leaves overhanging the conservatory, I peered over the top of cardboard partially covering Moses' window. He and Mr Sunshine were chuckling.

"He going straight for the bottom of his case this time," Maudie whispered.

Moses stood back while Mr Sunshine delved. He pulled out catalogues and samples, enabling us to see into the case.

"There the parcels I told you about," Amos whispered.

I moved a walnut leaf out of the way. Five or six objects wrapped in brown paper stood in the bottom of the suitcase. They looked hard and square shouldered. I had imagined them to be soft parcels.

Mr Sunshine lifted one out, a large, square medicine bottle. Moses screwed off the top and sniffed the contents.

"Whadya think it is?" Maudie asked.

"Muti, I bet..." Amos declared. "Probably strong muti. He selling bad muti to everyone."

As he uttered these words, he rolled off the branch and plunged through the conservatory roof.

The crash of breaking glass was deafening. One moment Amos had been perched on the branch ahead of my sister. The next, he had overbalanced and was reaching to grab at empty air. Plunging willy-nilly through the glass, shattering panes in every direction Amos plummeted to the earth floor below and began crying.

In his room, Moses hurriedly hid his muti or whatever it was. Mr Sunshine packed his catalogues and things back into his suitcase. Maudie and I froze.

Joseph opened the door of his shack and caught sight of us. Moses and Mr Sunshine came out the back room on the other side of the conservatory and stared at my sister and me cowering in the tree.

"What on earth happened?" Joseph demanded. "How did you children come to be up my walnut tree?"

He eyed the state his glass roof was in. "Who went through the conservatory roof? Amos?"

I nodded miserably.

"We real sorry, Old Joseph," Maudie pleaded. "Twas an accident."

He dashed into the conservatory to check on Amos. Maudie and I pretended we didn't know Moses and Mr Sunshine were staring at us from the backyard.

Amos was a mess, cut from head to toe. He'd got such a fright he couldn't talk. He sat on the conservatory floor with his head against his knees, clasping his body.

"Mix a glass of sugar water in my shack," Joseph instructed me.

He stared at the shattered glass covering his plants and then studied the fractured wooden framework above our heads. "Just what were you three doing up there?"

Maudie smoothed the dirt floor with a toe. She hooked her thumbs into her pants pockets.

"Aw gee, Old Joseph. Just looking for walnuts, that's all. 'Twas a genuine accident."

"You sure caused a lot of damage. It'll take me a week to fix this lot. You children are going to have to help me."

We spent the afternoon and the next three days in the conservatory. Amos grew a bump on his forehead the size of an orange. We picked up thousands of shards of glass from pot-plants, ferns and the earth floor. Joseph started work repairing the wooden framing. He counted thirty-six panes that needed replacing.

"Don't touch the new glass," he pleaded.

We sat on the earth floor while he balanced on a ladder, fitting the new glass into the frames. That was all the help he would allow us to give him.

Maudie amazed me sometimes.

"Do you think Mister Sunshine's a crook, Old Joseph?"

"No, Maudie. Why?"

"Amos's mama thinks so."

Joseph paused with a pane of glass in his hands. "Mister Sunshine is what I would call an entrepreneur."

"A troppra... what?"

"En-trep-re-neur, a person who finds out what other people need and then goes about supplying them just that."

"Would they buy strong muti from him, Old Joseph?"

"I suppose they would. But I think you'll find, Mister Sunshine deals in clothing, not muti."

Maudie rolled her eyes at me.

"Talking of muti," he added, "When I was strolling the koppies the other day, I saw you three with the sangoma."

"We just ran into him," Maudie explained.

"He's a harmless enough old character. In his own way he's an entrepreneur too, supplying Africans with what they want... traditional methods of healing ailments. He certainly doesn't want for patients."

"He threw the bones for us."

Joseph turned around, astounded.

"Really now? That's exciting. What did they reveal?"

"He saw a warning in the bones, Old Joseph, and told us to watch our step, especially where we not gonna expect it."

"Aha now," Joseph laughed. "Wouldn't you think that perhaps he's just pulling your leg? Probably chuckling his head off at you right now. Unless it's his way of getting rid of a bunch of inquisitive children, hoping you won't be back to get more so called bad news."

"Leastways we won't worry him again. We got much better things to do, Old Joseph, like exploring the

Foster Caves."

"I'd be careful of going there," Joseph cautioned.

"We went with Graham and Louis, but 'twas too dark to see anything."

"You need a lamp, rope and a stick to chase any snakes. The koppies are their last refuge. You're the intruders not them. So don't hurt them."

Amos's eyes widened.

Joseph added, "Rumour has it there's a secret entrance, but I've never been able to find it." He adjusted the leather thong around his neck.

"Where are those terrible twins anyway," Joseph asked. "I haven't heard Graham's belches in weeks.

"It's school holidays, Old Joseph," Maudie reminded him. "They gone back to their mama's farm in Middleburg."

Joseph fitted the pane of glass then glanced at my sister.

"I wouldn't worry about looking out for anything as the sangoma told you. It could be a mistake to watch for imagined danger in one direction, when the real danger like a speeding car could be bearing down on you from another. Would you like me to tell you a story illustrating what I mean?"

"Yah sure, Old Joseph, that'll be snazzy," Maudie said for all of us.

He smiled in amusement.

"Well, I'll tell you. Back in 1902, I was crewing on a square-rigger bound for Valparaiso to load fertilizer nitrates. We were still in the Atlantic and had yet to double the Horn. Nobody on board looked forward to the Cape. It's freezing in the Southern Ocean and the cape difficult to round in the face of continual gales and heavy seas. Forty foot is conservative. If the wind gets up to sixty knots, those seas rise to seventy."

"So you were all panicking about Cape Horn? Nipping straws before you even got there?"

"Quite so, Maudie. We perceived danger from one

direction when all the time it was sneaking up from another. We should never have bothered about the Horn, or the dangerous nitrates we would be taking on board at Valparaiso in the Pacific. Our voyage down the South Atlantic was progressing well, with winds favouring us. That numbed us into a feeling of false security."

"Until one night," he paused, "off the coast of Argentina. The south-easter was moderate and when I came on watch, loath to leave my warm berth below, the first mate ordered us seamen to get more sail on. Shivering and wishing I was back in my berth, I joined them aloft to break out sail. The ship was heeling to starboard. I went out on a yard to leeward, over the swell."

He paused.

"Now which of you thinks my warm berth down below was the safer place?"

"You chaffing us, Old Joseph? Inside the ship was the place to be," Maudie piped, putting her hand up, followed by Amos, then myself.

"In fact, Maudie, it was the other way around. Within fifteen minutes, every soul down below was going to meet his Maker. Being aloft in the rigging saved my life."

"With nice wind?"

He nodded. "You see, there is an unpredictable squall called the Pampero, which blows off the Andes between Argentina and Chile. It's violent beyond belief, rises without warning and tears out to sea. The captain estimated we were far enough offshore, so didn't anticipate it. The squall came from the opposite direction to the south-easter that had been blowing for weeks. It took us aback at over a hundred knots."

"Sure glad it wasn't me," Maudie said. "You shoulda been on a battleship, Old Joseph. They the best."

Joseph shivered.

"When I went up the mast, the ship was heeled to starboard. That was the side I was sent to, the leeward side. I heard the Pampero coming when it was two miles away. I shouted a warning to the deck and furled my sail as best I could. The blast struck like an express train. Billowing canvas, flailing sheets and halyards knocked my mates off the yards. Their cries disappeared in the night. The fury of the squall was deafening. I hung on. I refused to let go. It was mayhem up there."

"The ship was driven over to port, so I was now high in the air with sails and spars below me. We were totally overpowered. The squall rolled us flat. Masts in the water, hatches ripped off by seas that flooded the holds. She lay pinned like that in the chaos and fury for perhaps twenty minutes. The howl of the tempest, shrieking at a hundred knots was ear piercing and I heard no more shouting. The foundering ship was no longer beneath me, for I myself was now only a few feet above the sea."

"The deck, more than half submerged, was somewhere to weather, but I couldn't see it in the turmoil. Spindrift whistling through the air made it almost impossible to breathe. I had to face downwind in order to gasp air into my lungs."

Joseph came out of his trance.

"I didn't have time to think about what was happening. The ship sank, taking everyone with her."

"Everyone except you?" Maudie asked.

"Yes. The last I saw of her were her masts and starboard yardarms protruding through breaking seas. They were pulled down by the hull and I was alone in the Atlantic Ocean in the middle of the night."

"You hadda think fast, Old Joseph?"

He sighed. "My child, I felt like giving up right away, so I wouldn't have to suffer. I thought, if I breathe out and dive as far as I can, my lungs will breathe in water and it'll be over in a second."

"I s'pose so. I woulda done the same."

"Aha, Maudie, but this is the point. I didn't do that. I fought back. Something inside me told me to challenge the situation."

"How can you fight the sea, Old Joseph?"

"Mentally," Joseph answered, "you can fight anything. I asked myself whether I could tread water for an hour and my answer was, yes. So I huddled my arms about my body to keep warm and began treading water. Conditions were terrible. The wind shrieked and waves broke over my head. When I estimated an hour had passed, I put the same question to myself. Again, the answer was, yes. That went on for six hours. It was easier to think about staying afloat for only an hour than trying to survive the conditions the whole night."

"Yah, that's good thinking," Old Joseph. I better remember that."

"It also became a game. I was playing with the conditions, daring them to drown me. And me, defiantly staying alive. Anyway, the Pampero didn't last too long. Six hours later, about four o'clock in the morning, the sea was relatively calm and a light breeze began blowing."

"But you couldn't last forever?" Maudie pointed out. "You were stuck in the middle of the ocean with no lifejacket."

"The point, children, is, the rest of my shipmates gave up the moment they encountered adversity. They'd been dead for six hours. I was fighting. That's the difference. Do you remember Winston Churchill's nine words for success?"

"I guess we musta, Old Joseph."

"Never give in... never give in... never give in."

"Heck, that's no more'n three words."

"But don't forget them, children. They could save your life. Let me tell you what happened. Around four in the morning, I saw the navigation lights of a steamer approaching. I had given myself the chance of being rescued. My shipmates hadn't."

"It was chance the steamer came along?"

"Yes, that was sheer chance, Maudie. The fact that I was still treading water was deliberate. You understand that? Success is often the coming together of effort and luck. The steamer was no good to my companions. It passed swiftly in the dark, doing ten knots. The helmsman didn't see me in the water. The engine made such a racket, my voice wasn't heard on the bridge. I kept shouting for help even when the steamer was gone."

"What? They didn't stop to pick you up?" Maudie exploded.

Joseph chuckled. "I'm about to tell you. The cook was getting breakfast ready in the galley. He opened a porthole to dump refuse and thought he heard something, but saw no light. By this time the vessel had passed. There was a following wind. Only after the steamer passed and was downwind, did the cook hear my shouts. If I had stopped calling, I'd have committed myself to a watery death. That's the importance of never giving up, even when you think it's no use."

Maudie stared at him, her mouth open.

"Twas the same when the lion knocked you off your horse, Old Joseph. If you didn't fight back, you wouldna have a chance."

"Exactly. You've hit the nail on the head, my little girl. You children remember that. What I'm trying to teach you, is the single most important lesson in life. The secret is never giving in. No matter what happens, no matter how bad things seem, use your brains to fight back."

Chapter 30

"Leastways, we found out Mister Sunshine's doing something not proper."

"You can say that again, Maudie."

"I been thinking, you know. Remember the day your migraine was so bad, you couldn't come to supper?"

"Yah, when The Vale of Belvoir sank. I went blind and you led me home."

"Mister de Beer told Abe at supper, old Sunshine's using his clothing business as a cover for something else."

"We got proof now, Sis."

"And what'd Amos's mama say? Hang it, she said he's a crook."

"Yah, when Amos crashed through the glass, Sunshine got the fright of his life."

Maudie hitched up her cords.

"I reckon we better keep an eye on him Tadpole."

The rapture of Christmas escalated. My sister and I couldn't think of anything else and could not open our mouths without bringing the subject around to the time of the year.

Amos did not share this ecstasy. He was indifferent and I couldn't fathom why. I didn't realize we were ten times better off than African families. Our father was a working man and he budgeted. But there was enough to go around. In order to have one thing, we made do without another. African families did not enjoy that luxury. They went without both.

Our father took time and effort to make Maudie's and my Christmas happy. Frog's too, but this year he was at school camp at Scotborough and would wait until January to see what he'd got. Our presents were not expensive, but they were what we wanted. There were extra ones too, usually practical like clothing, but exciting to receive.

Amos's mama was a domestic. He never mentioned his father and I was too frightened to ask, in case his father was dead. I didn't know about illegitimacy. When Amos's mama came to work next door, it took me two years to realize he didn't get presents. Our father sent us next door with a packet of sweets for him. The next year we wrapped some cheap toy cars. He looked after them as if they were made of gold.

By Christmas Eve our excitement built up so, that Maudie bit her dog and our father had to take Hobo to the vet for stitches. It happened after he told my sister and me he wanted some jobs done in the garden. We were to water the flowerbeds with the hose and the pot plants with the watering can.

"Please use the sprinkling rose," the great unwashed was requested, "I don't want my plants washed away in the Big Flood."

"I got the hose," Maudie chortled, making a grab for it.

"You got the hose last time, Sis. Now I gotta lug the watering can backwards and forwards."

"Finders keepers," she chortled. "Losers weepers."

I went in search of the galvanized watering can.

Our pre-Christmas tomfoolery rubbed off on Hobo. She sensed the excitement and joined in the high spirits. Whatever Maudie and I got up to, Hobo made a game of it. My sister encouraged her. This morning however, she was piqued at having to water the garden. As she directed the hose, she stood scowling at the rose bushes.

"Get out of it, Hobo," she grumbled. "I hafta water the darn flowers. Now don't get in my way."

Hobo fooled around the lawn behind her, snatching the hose in her jaws and fighting it. Then she dashed past my sister's ankles, making gyrations on the lawn and circumnavigating the flower bed at full gallop. A white mongrel bulldog with its squat body and stubby legs at top speed, moves in short jerky motions, throwing its backside into the air and is a ludicrous sight.

"Hobo, shoo. You asking for trouble."

Her dog wanted Maudie to sprinkle her with the hose, so she could pretend she was escaping from some dreadful attack and have an excuse to tear around the lawn again. Maudie was having none of it.

"Hobo, you messing with the wrong person. Now scat."

I lumbered the watering can to two oil drums planted with hydrangeas at the bottom of our front stairs. Hobo grabbed the hose and tugged it out of Maudie's hands.

"No-o-o-o... stupid dog. Stop acting," Maudie shrieked, aiming a toe at Hobo's rump and snatching the hose back. Her dog discovered a new game now, *possession of the hose*. I put the sprinkler into the hydrangeas and turned to watch.

"Hobo, leave it. You soon gonna get in big trouble."

Her dog was very good at the game. She fought the part lying on the lawn as if it was a serpent, rolling upside down and getting entangled in its coils. Then she broke away and attacked it closer to Maudie.

"No, no, no. I'm watering the flowers, not you," she objected, taking a firm grip of the nozzle. She held onto it in both hands and leaned forwards. Her dog leaned back. Hobo slid her muzzle up the hose until she was close behind my sister. Then she tugged back. The more Maudie leaned forward, the more Hobo leaned back. The moment my sister turned her head or prepared to aim a jab with her toe, her dog bounded away. She was hoping her mistress would spray her so she could feign a frenzy of escape and race around the house a couple of times.

"I'm not playing, dum-dum. Can't you see I'm working?" Maudie muttered, intent on finishing her chore as quickly as possible.

Then Hobo achieved what she had been aiming for all along. She came flying past my sister, leapt into the air and snatched the nozzle out of her hands.

"Ayeeeeee." Maudie stamped her foot and made a grab for the hose. Hobo pulled away and galloped in a circle. The nozzle gripped in her mouth sprayed everything within range.

"You in big trouble, I tell you," Maudie yelled, making a flying dive for the hose. Instead, she got a face-full of water.

Now she was in a rage and Hobo would have done best to call off her tug of war. She had the nozzle and Maudie had the hose lower down, trying to wrestle it back. Hobo shook the hose vigorously, spraying her mistress from head to toe.

"Look what you done, you crazy dog. Lookit me now. I'm wetter than the flowers."

She rugby-tackled her dog, landing on the lawn with her chest over Hobo's body and her arms around her head and rump. Hobo grunted from the impact. She squealed like a pig, catapulted herself away from underneath my sister and galloped up the drive to the backyard.

"I told you. Now you learned your lesson," Maudie called after her triumphantly.

My sister had bitten her. She had put her teeth over Hobo's back and clamped hard. What she didn't realize was that she'd drawn blood. We carried on watering the garden while Hobo retired to her box to lick her wounds.

Our father noticed Hobo bleeding in her box and came to question us.

"What happened to poor Hobo? Was she in a fight

with another dog?"

"No," I answered. "She was in a fight with Maudie."

"Well, she's bleeding. We'll have to take her to the vet. She needs stitches."

Maudie was crestfallen.

The vet asked the same question.

"Lady dogs don't fight," he commented as he sewed up the wound. "Strange bite actually. Must have been a brute of a dog that did this."

"Twas me," Maudie whispered, fidgeting with the pockets of her cords.

The vet looked at her oddly. I don't think he believed her.

At Christmas time, the municipal workers who provided the suburb with services, came around the houses, asking for Christmas boxes.

"Chrismis missus, chrismis missus, chrismis missus."

They were joined by retailers' delivery boys. There were dustmen, milkmen, newspaper boys, greengrocer boys, gardeners, butcher boys, bottle-store boys, painters, street sweepers, postmen, assistants and so on ad infinitum. Sampson made a list and crossed off their names when they came for their bonsella. Our father gave the good ones a half-crown and the not so good ones, a shilling. This wasn't bad considering most people gave less and at some houses they got nothing.

Often though, one of them would pull a fast one. He collected from the route he'd served and then also collected from houses that weren't on his route. When the genuine worker pitched up, his service had been ticked off and Sampson described the conman.

"Oh, yes. That's Philamon who been cheating me. I'll get him." And off he went to get his money back.

The following year the same thing happened.

Sampson discovered that the conman and the claimant were in cahoots, on the off-chance they would be paid twice.

"Semp-Sonne oughta be mighty pleased, this year," Maudie whispered. "Abe gave him a bonsella same as his wages."

"Maudie, you've got long ears," our father chuckled.

She ran to our bedroom mirror to check.

"No, Abe. Same as always."

A few weeks before Christmas, our father made the family a Chinese Checkers board.

"What you doing now, Abe?" Maudie asked.

"The great unwashed are going to have to find that out for themselves, my little girl."

"Yah, but... Abe?"

When he traced the design on a sheet of hardboard, I couldn't figure what he was making. Maudie watched him and rolled her eyes. He drilled two hundred holes where the marbles would rest. I couldn't figure this out. My sister was itching with curiosity.

"Pleeze, Abe... don't be so stingy. I hafta know what you doing."

"Sweetheart, I'm making a colander for Sampson to drain spaghetti," he teased.

We were so gullible; we believed him and lost interest, which is what he wanted in the first place.

In the shops, checkerboards had marbles of white glass, green glass, red glass, blue glass and so on. Our father painted ordinary marbles by hand. That's eighty marbles. He did this in secret, because my sister would have questioned what he was doing with children's things. We had the best Chinese Checkers set in the neighbourhood. There was no television then and that board game entertained the family through long winter evenings, until the end of our father's life.

This year, Amos got a football. That was a difficult decision for me. For it was one of the requests on my list. Our crafty father scanned my list and complained it was too long.

"One of these things, you'll have to give to Amos," he told me bluntly. It was a toss up whether I got the football or the pocketknife.

Maudie was lucky, there was nothing on her list suitable for Amos. One item she didn't ask for, a vanity set, gave her and Hobo hours of fun. My sister wanted a kite, a baseball bat and ball, a cowboy suit, a magician set, a pocketknife, marbles, crayons and a spinning top. She didn't get them of course.

"Hr'm," she muttered to herself when she opened the vanity set. She inspected it, pouting her lips. It was six o'clock on Christmas morning. The summer sun, shining through the door leading onto the side veranda, reflected off the vanity set's mirror.

"Say, this can be quite handy," she squealed, seeing its purpose at once.

Mischievously she flashed the mirror in our father's eyes and when he asked her to stop, she picked on her dog. When Hobo caught sight of the reflection skimming across the floor, she chased it.

"Tee-hee, my angel, you funnier than a circus dog," Maudie giggled.

She made Hobo run for her life and a new game was born. It might have been called, wear out Hobo chasing the reflected light while Maudie sits on her bottom, endlessly moving the mirror backwards and forwards, giggling like an idiot.

Hobo loved the game. Maudie was ecstatic. They played it for hours. Whenever we weren't building our tree house, my sister and Hobo played *mirrors*. You always knew when they were playing it by the way Maudie giggled like an idiot. They spent whole afternoons playing it. Maudie laughed so much she nearly fell out of the fig tree playing *mirrors*. She sat up there in the sun and directed the reflection up and down the backyard, particularly in the shade where Hobo could see the flash more easily.

Hobo was insane enough to hare after the reflection. Up and down the backyard she raced, until she was so exhausted, she turned her back and trotted off to find her water-dish. Then as soon as she caught her breath, she chased it again. Maudie and her dog loved that game.

Chapter 31

"Tadpole, I think I smell snuff," my sister whispered the first time she visited Kiewietjie.

She also embarrassed our father by locking Mr de Beer out of his hostel. It started with Hobo holding the housemaster at bay for five hours on a Sunday afternoon. He came around to invite us to Kiewietjie on Old Year's Night and pitched up on the off-chance the family would be home. We had gone visiting and left Hobo to guard the property.

The housemaster strolled up our front path, climbed the stairs to the veranda and pressed the doorbell. Hobo was sleeping in the backyard. She came charging down the drive. When she saw the housemaster standing on the veranda, she sat down at the bottom of the stairs to guard him.

When nobody answered our doorbell, he started down the stairs. Hobo stood up. Her lips curled. She growled convincingly and he had second thoughts about coming down the stairs. So he rang the doorbell again. Maudie's dog sat down once more.

Mr de Beer didn't have all day and he tried coming down the stairs a second time. With the same result. He tried jumping off the parapet onto the driveway, but Hobo galloped around the corner of the house to head him off and he jumped back onto the veranda. When we arrived home, it was nine o'clock that evening. The housemaster sat sulking on the veranda.

"Your confounded dog is vicious," he complained to our father. "You should have it put down."

Maudie glanced at me, appalled.

Our father handed Mr de Beer a tumbler of brandy

to soothe his nerves. I was astonished he still asked us to Kiewietjie on Old Year's Night.

"That's very kind of you," our father responded. "We'll come around, but only for half an hour, as we have already accepted another invitation."

The evening spent with the Proberts was quiet, not like some of the parties that kept the city awake.

"Babs' gone to one of those sort of parties," Maudie confided.

At twenty-to-twelve, our father explained to the Proberts he'd promised Mr de Beer a half hour or so. We arrived a few minutes before midnight. Music blared and I heard fits of laughter,

"One drink only, then we're going," our father muttered.

The front door stood ajar and I heard music coming from the first floor. We went up. Maudie was last in and latched the door behind her.

"Tadpole, I think I smelt snuff downstairs," she whispered.

I frowned.

Upstairs we saw no one. We sauntered past the dormitories and went into Mr de Beer's suite where music blared. Signs of partying, bottles and glasses and dirty ashtrays, but no people.

"What the hell!"

Angry shouting downstairs and banging of fists on the front door. The housemaster and his guests had formed a human crocodile and weaved out the back door, the same time we entered the front. The housemaster had left his front door ajar so he could first-foot over the threshold when the New Year arrived.

The crocodile swayed around the garden and reached the front door only to find it locked. Mr de Beer was furious. By the time we went downstairs, the disillusioned revellers were wandering through the back door to refill their glasses.

Maudie unlocked the front door and stepped outside

to see who was banging. She found no one and stepped inside again. So at one minute into January the first, 1948, my sister first-footed across Mr de Beer's threshold and there was no point in him second-footing.

"Don't you ever try that again," he threatened.

A cold shiver crept up my spine.

When he wasn't looking, Maudie stuck out her tongue.

Our father had one drink and we left.

Chapter 32

"Help..." my sister moaned in her sleep. "... quick..."

I was alert in an instant and at her side.

"Tadpole, you gotta save me..."

"Maudie, wake up, I'm here, it's okay."

"He got a Mamlambo in his throat. I saw it. He was yelling at me for locking him out. That's when I saw his tongue... 'twas a Mamlambo snake."

"Wake up, Sis. You've got to wake up." I put my hand on her shoulder.

She surfaced in a sweat.

"You're okay, Maudie. Was only a dream."

I held her and she clung to me, shivering.

"I want crawl in with you," she pleaded.

I heard the carillon strike. It was three hours into January the first, 1948. We fell asleep holding onto one another.

Christmas and New Year passed. Amos had his football, I had my pocketknife, Maudie had her mirror and Hobo had her stitches taken out. Newspapers were a fraction their normal thickness. After the festive season, they carried little advertising. Editors and reporters were on leave and the media operated on skeleton staff.

Seven weeks had passed since our gruesome find at Rhodes Park and four weeks since seven-year-old Johannes Rabie disappeared. The press forgot about them. My sister knew where both boys were interred, but only subconsciously.

Four weeks slid by since Maudie's last sighting of

her giraffe man. I itched to catch a glimpse of him and back her up. Now that we knew about Mr Sunshine, I kept a wary eye on him. Maudie definitely kept out of sight of the bottle-and-bag man.

It was about this time that we discussed going back to the Foster Caves. Maudie was uneasy because our father had placed them out of bounds. We hummed and hawed for days in the fig tree.

"We got nothing else to do," I moaned. "We can explore the caves by ourselves before Graham and Louis get back. It'll be our last chance to do what we want."

"Yah, maybe, but only if we got a lamp. Otherwise we gonna be stuck in the dark."

"You better not tell Sampson, cos he'll stop us."

"Yah, old Semp-Sonne's not gonna let us go near the caves."

Amos was not enthusiastic.

"Hmmm, maybe," was all I could get out of him. He had his football up in the tree, resting his head on it. He opened one eye and squinted.

"But this ball's staying here. Otherwise we'll kick it all the way there and all the way back and there'll be nothing left."

I nodded. "Sure, Amos, but I'm gonna take my pocketknife. Might need it."

"And I not going in first."

"I reckon I hafta go first, seeing it's my idea, Maudie second and you last."

"That's not fair," Amos complained. "You'll be first with the lamp and me last in the dark."

"You choose, Amos. First or last?"

"Last in and first out?"

"Scaredy-cat," Maudie giggled.

My talk about a lamp was wishful thinking. The best I could do was filch a burnt down candle from the pantry. Sampson's matches were just about finished, so I took an old box our father kept on his workbench for lighting his blowtorch. I unearthed the sash cord we'd used to salvage our canoe. Maudie stole us three oranges from the pantry. She whistled up Hobo and I let us out the driveway gate.

With Hobo trotting in front, we trekked along the koppie to the caves and flopped down to suck our oranges. It was my way of stalling for time in case there were other school children bigger than me inside. There were no footprints at the entrance.

"C'mon what we waiting for?" Maudie asked, standing up.

Amos threw in a stone. It clattered against rock. I crouched on my haunches and shuffled through the first fissure. My sister and Amos followed and when Hobo found herself alone, she padded in after us. I couldn't find Graham's rat-hole, the tight fissure we would have to wriggle through in the dark. I set the half-candle down and felt for the matches. A rock lay in the hole. It hadn't been there before. I prised it out and with the help of Amos, dragged it away.

Maudie and Hobo waited. I lit the candle and pushed it into the rat-hole ahead of me, leaving my sister and Amos in darkness. Lying on my stomach, I wriggled through, struggling to keep the candle upright.

I was inside the cave. With space to sit, I examined my surroundings. Eight feet below, was a cavern. I crouched on a narrow shelf, looking down at wavering shadows. The cave was narrow. The crown sloped down to the floor. Maudie squeezed through, pushing Hobo ahead of her and nearly knocked the candle off the ledge. Amos kicked himself through, possessed. If the candle toppled into the chamber below, it would go out.

"Sure is scary in here," my sister stage-whispered, wriggling next to me while keeping an arm around Hobo.

Amos had a face full of dirt. He wiped himself and squatted next to us, scrutinizing the shadows below.

"I smell something," he muttered.

"Snuff?" I asked in alarm.

"Nuh... nothing like that... something I smelled before... dunno, can't think."

I glanced at him. "Dagga?"

He scratched his head. "Naw, not that. Maybe rats or rock-rabbits been messing up the place."

"I don't smell anything I haven't smelled before," Maudie whispered.

"I'll remember whatsit," Amos mused. "And tell you later."

We needed the sash cord for climbing down. I looped an end on a knobble of rock, flung the rest of the cord over the edge and slid down, burning my hands in the process. Maudie passed Hobo to me and shinned down. Amos dropped the candle into my hands. Paraffin wax spilled on my palms and I let the candle fall.

Now we were blind. Maudie whimpered. I scrambled on hands and knees, feeling for the candle and pulled the matchbox from my pocket. I found one and lit the wick.

"Man, you sure know how to scare a guy," Amos sniffed.

"Sorry, Amos. Was an accident."

"How many matches you got left?"

"Two. It's enough."

Amos scoffed.

"Ha, let the flame go out again, and we got only one to get us out of this tomb."

For the first time in the cave, I could stand upright. The flame made a halo around itself. The rock lay deep in shadow. I began exploring the wall opposite the ledge, while Maudie hung onto Hobo with one hand and me with the other. Amos stayed in the light. Hobo pulled free of my sister's grasp and disappeared into a crevice.

"No, my angel, get back here now," Maudie ordered. Hobo ignored her.

"Maybe she'll find a hidden passage, Sis."

Unhurried, we explored the cavern. I wanted to find the original entrance used by the Foster Gang and remove the rubble blocking it.

"We can make the caves a secret hideout."

"S'no good," Maudie concluded. "We aren't gonna find the old entrance."

We explored the side of the cavern under the ledge. I poked the candle into crevices. They were dead ends, too small for us to crawl into.

"I bet you these are tunnels leading into other parts, but been blocked with rubble," Maudie remarked when we found promising fissures in the granite.

"Yah, maybe you right Maudie. We hafta get a paraffin lamp and a proper torch."

I crawled along until the crown pressed against my spine. The fissures led nowhere and I lay in the dirt, watching the candle burn down.

"That smell again, real strong, man," Amos rasped. "We better go back." He crawled out of the loom of the candle.

"Yah, let's get out," Maudie urged, prodding me.

"Keep your shirt on, Sis, I first hafta check the other end where the roof's not so low."

"I wanna get out, now."

"Stay calm, Maudie. We can't leave so soon. You want to find the blocked entrance, don't you? There's enough candle for half an hour."

Under my breath, I cursed Amos for frightening my sister. Cupping a hand to protect the flame, I led them to the far end of the cavern. Maudie found an old sweet wrapping. The chamber narrowed and we halted by loose rock packed into a fissure.

"I bet you this is the old entrance," I breathed. "If we come back with a lamp, we can unpack this."

My sister didn't answer.

"... Johan... I feel him," she whispered.

I froze. With ice encasing my spine, I turned to her. Her face was blank. She had gone into a trance.

"What... did you say, Maudie?"

I put a hand out. The moment my fingers touched her, she snapped out of her stupor and gazed at me blankly.

Hobo appeared and my sister darted to her.

"My angel. What you got there? Well I never, Hobo, an old school cap."

Amos turned to look.

"Hobo been sniffing round in the dark and found this, Amos."

"Other kids. Probably same ones what dropped the sweet paper." He pulled the cap onto his head. "Look, it fits, Maudie. Maybe I can have it for school next term."

My sister frowned. "The candle's getting low."

"Sis, stand on my shoulders and get back on the ledge."

"Now you Amos." He climbed over my back and passed Hobo to my sister.

"Now the candle," I instructed. "And don't spill wax on me. It's blinking sore."

She planted the stub on the ledge. Amos, with his new headgear, shinned up next and once he made space for me, I clambered after.

"Let's get out of here quick," Amos urged. "There's something I don't like about this place." He reached for the candle, slipped and instead of closing his fingers around the stub, sent it flying over the edge.

"Darn it now," he cursed.

We huddled in the dark. Maudie started crying.

"Don't worry, I'll go get it," Amos fretted. I listened to him sliding into the cavern.

"How you doing down there?" I called.

"Can't find the damn thing."

"Feel with your fingers on the floor, Amos. Gotta be there somewhere."

"Shsh..." he hissed.

"Whatsa matter?"

"That smell again... there's something down here..."

I went cold. We were enveloped in black and needed the candle to find the rat-hole. It was our only way out.

"Amos, I can drop the matches down to you. Probably a field mouse you smell. It's their fur."

"No... ooo!" he insisted.

"Just find the darn candle, Amos."

He babbled nervously in Zulu, brushing the cavern floor with his hands.

"What's down there, do you think?" my sister whispered, leaning against me in the dark.

"Dunno, Sis. Hold Hobo tight, so she don't fall over the edge. Amos better find that candle fast."

Below us, Amos froze.

"What's going on?" I whispered.

"Shsh, I listening. Can't you hear it now?"

I heard nothing.

"It's coming for me. I hear it coming. And I smell it strong."

"Amos, the candle probably rolled away from the wall."

There was a garbled cry and I knew he'd found it.

"Get back to the wall, Amos. I'll drop the matches to you."

I fidgeted for the box and held them down to him. I let the box go and, amazingly, he caught them. The match spluttered and for a moment, I was blinded by the yellow. Then, as he held it to the wick, I made out Amos's features in the flame.

Maudie screamed.

An enormous snake slid toward Amos. Triangular head and black eyes, it was a python. The constrictor had been holed up in a cavity. It was in the cave when we entered and it was the smell of snake that Amos recognized. All the time he searched for the candle, the python was sliding out of its lair toward him.

When my sister screamed, I heard Amos gasp. He squatted on the floor, petrified. The python advanced. Maudie's voice jolted him into scuttling across the dirt to get out of the snake's way.

At once, the python was on him. I would never have believed a snake could move that fast. By the time I realized what was happening, it knocked Amos over, sending him flying. His legs kicked and his arms flailed until the reptile coiled its upper body around him. Amos hollered for his life, but didn't stand a chance. In seconds, the python pinned his shoulders and arms, the muscles in its sinuous body rippling and strangling. The cap Hobo had found, lay abandoned.

The constrictor coiled its lower body around Amos's stomach and tightened its grip. Amos blubbered and screamed without stop. Illuminated by the dying candle, our playmate lay face to face in the dirt with the python. Every time Amos struggled, the constrictor took advantage of his weakness by increasing its grip.

Maudie shook with tears.

"Help him, Tadpole, you gotta help him, quick, before it's too late."

I huddled, frozen.

"I dunno what to do, Sis."

I was terrified of the python and preferred to get out of the cave and run to a house up in Rockey Street to fetch an adult. Then, I thought of the rat-hole. No grown up could squeeze through that aperture. By the time they dug their way in, Amos would be dead. I watched our playmate lying in the snake's embrace, the python's head and neck only inches from his face.

"You gotta help him," Maudie sobbed. "In five minutes, Amos gonna be no more. Kill the snake, Tadpole, before it squeezes him to death."

"I dunno how," I whined.

"What about your pocketknife? Or tie the sash cord round its neck and drag it off him. Do it quick."

"Stay here with Hobo, Maudie."

I slid down the cord. My sister threw it after me. The candle burned to a half-inch stub. Now that I was down in the cavern, the python took an interest in me. Amos tried to free an arm but was held in a vice. I knotted a loop in the sash cord and advanced. The python stared at me with black eyes and prepared to strike. I hadn't bargained for this.

"It'll bite me, Maudie."

Amos glimpsed me from corner of an eye. He pleaded, but I didn't have the courage to go near. I froze with fear. Maudie yelled at me. The python increased its constriction.

"Help me, Tadpole. Please... can't breathe..."

I couldn't move. Amos and the python lay in the dirt, their heads touching. The sight made me want to retch up my guts. I circled, not knowing how I could get the big reptile off him. I was frightened in case the python left him and came for me.

"He's dying, Tadpole," Maudie warned.

Amos had no breath to cry out. The reptile's eyes, inches from his own, mesmerised him.

"It's gonna swallow him," Maudie cried.

Unprepared for what happened next, I gasped. Amos lunged with his head. He opened his mouth wide, exposing his strong teeth and clamped his mouth over the reptile's throat. He hung on, gnawing.

The python struggled. Its body rippled. Its jaws gaped, to savage anything within range. Amos's head was below their reach and he held on with his teeth. Maudie began hollering in anticipation of what Amos was doing. The python struggled. It writhed, trying to jerk its throat free. Amos clung with his teeth. He chewed into the flesh. The enmeshed pair rolled over and over on the cave floor.

I wanted to vomit, but stood with the sash cord, hating myself. Amos maintained his hold. The python writhed. Blood flowed from its throat and out of Amos's mouth. He bit deeper into the python's throat. The struggle seemed to go on for ages.

At last, the reptile relaxed its constriction. The head slumped. Amos held on with his teeth. Only now, did I have the courage to rush in and slip the sash cord over the head. I jerked the noose tight and held on with both hands.

Amos eased his grip and spat blood. He had chewed clean through the snake's windpipe. The reptile writhed in spasms, but the power to constrict weakened. Amos couldn't speak. He was exhausted. Slowly, he eased his arms from the embrace and pulled his legs free. He kicked at the tail with his bare feet when it slid over him. He crawled away and retched, again and again. I sat with him, wiping sweat from his face. He spat into the dirt.

"The candle," my sister pleaded.

Chapter 33

I glanced at the stub. It was a quarter-inch high and the flame danced erratically.

"We hafta leave it, Maudie. Can't pick it up. Just a wick floating in wax."

Amos tugged the cord to be sure the constrictor really was dead. The jaws gaped. The top of the body lay still. Only the tail twitched with muscular contraction.

"I taking it home to show my mama," he grinned weakly. He picked up the cap Hobo found and pulled it onto his head.

"Yah, good thinking, Amos," Maudie agreed. "I reckon everyone in Good Hope Street will wanna see that python."

"Even Joseph can't moan at us if we tell him how it darn near strangled Amos," I added.

We knotted the sash cord around the reptile's neck and climbed onto the ledge, hauling the python up. Hobo sniffed it suspiciously, the hairs on her back, rigid. Maudie giggled.

Below, the candle dwindled to a smudge of wax. The flame faltered. Up on the ledge, we were in dark shadow and crawled to the rat-hole. Amos left the box with the last match below. I pushed Hobo through to the outer chamber and urged Maudie to wriggle through.

"Hey, I'm not gonna be last," Amos agitated. "Yah sure, this is my python, but I'm not staying alone with it."

"Okay, you next. I'll be tail-end Charlie."

The moment his feet were clear, I dived through

with the sash cord and wriggled into the outer chamber. Maudie and Amos squatted in the gloom. I tugged on the sash cord and the python came sliding out.

On the koppie, the sun burned brightly and for the first time we had a proper look at our prize.

"You didn't horse around, Amos," Maudie chirped, glancing at me reproachfully. "I never seen anything like it. Not even in a circus."

"I was fagged out," Amos grinned. "But then I remembered what Old Joseph told us. Don't quit."

"Yah, I reckon he saved your life."

She glanced at me. "Been thinking, Tadpole, Mister de Beer moaned about a python swallowing his Pekinese. Must be the same one."

"I bet," Amos responded. "Next time he visits, you tell him we got his revenge. Maybe he'll give us something."

I snorted. "Fat chance. Old penny-pincher. Mean as a snake."

"Sixpence each?" Amos suggested hopefully.

"Huh. We'll get zilch out of him."

The python was so long and heavy, we traipsed in single file with it draped over our shoulders. Amos, wearing the tatty school cap, strode in front with the reptile's head dangling down his chest. I followed with the fat middle section of the body over my shoulder and Maudie took up the rear, supporting the tail hanging down over her back. Hobo trotted at her heels, excited at the trophy we were taking back to the suburbs.

It was like that, in bizarre procession, that we marched up the dirt driveway of the house next door where Amos's mama worked. The owners were on holiday. Selina wasn't in the backyard and as we noticed the kitchen door was open, we tramped up the back stairs in single file with the python over our shoulders and went into the house.

Selina was cleaning windows when we found her. She was in the bathroom with her back to us. She had opened the burglar proofing so she could reach the glass and had the sash window slid up. She was stooped, rinsing her cleaning cloth in a bucket of water when we marched in behind her.

"Look, Mama," Amos announced proudly. "Look what terrible thing tried to take your umfaan away from you. If it wasn't for Maudie and Tadpole here, your little umfaan would be no more."

Amos's mama, bending over the bucket, didn't need to straighten or turn around. She moved her head slightly and caught an upside down view of us standing behind her with the gaping jaws of the dead python hanging over her son's shoulder.

She jumped through the open window.

There was no word of greeting to her son, no maternal concern for the danger he had been in and no farewell as she departed. When we walked into the bathroom, she was rinsing her cleaning cloth. Approximately one second after Amos spoke to his mama, she was sprawled in a bed of squashed dahlias beneath the window. Her cleaning cloth had only got as far as the windowsill it now straddled, dripping water onto the floor and into the garden.

We followed Amos to the sash and looked down.

"But Mama," he pleaded, leaning over the sill. "Aren't you pleased to see your umfaan alive and well?"

Although Selina's mouth was open, she had not so much as uttered a word in reply to his questions. Surrounded by bent dahlias, she struggled to get to her feet and at the same time pluck the bottom of her dress over her knees. Her eyes, twice their normal size, were fixed on the python.

"It's okay Mama, it's dead. Look, I can show you," Amos said, trying to reassure her. With that, he began working the python's jaws open and closed.

Perhaps an animated dead python is more frightening than one that does what it's supposed to do: lie still. I don't know. Possibly at this stage, Selina was thinking of the catfish her son threw at her. Beneath the bathroom window, she was in a more vulnerable position. Amos was leaning above her. The python was as big as twenty catfishes.

Then the unthinkable happened. The python started sliding over our shoulders, down Amos's chest and out, over the sill.

Selina's legs jerked straight, driving her body away from the snake coming out of the window. She went backward through the dahlias and landed on the edge of the drive. She still hadn't said anything. Then she was on her feet and disappeared up the drive like an arrow shot from a bow. I heard her locking herself inside her room, bolting the door top and bottom and jamming a chair under the handle.

"I don't think my mama loves me," Amos sighed, wiping a tear from his cheek, "else she woulda take me in her arms. She don't care about that earthworm having her umfaan for supper."

The python caused a bit of a stir in our neighbourhood and a few people came to look at it. Our father did after I invented a tale that we'd found it dead on the koppie. Trixie refused point blank. After promising not to tell our father, Joseph listened to what really happened. He still wore his leather thong. Moses and Sampson wanted to see the corpse but only from the safety of the other side of the backyard fence. There was a lot of superstition about snakes.

"Sis, how we gonna get rid of the body? Smell's getting bad."

"Easy-peezy," she replied. "Hide it in our dustbin."

"Reckon it'll fit?"

"Squash it inside and cover it with rubbish."

That was a mistake.

The dustmen danced up our street, whistling and singing and chanting. I heard them coming, flinging off lids, banging the bins against the side of their cart as they emptied them and banging the empty bins back on the pavement. The python lay hidden. So when our zealous dustman snatched off the lid, the contents in the bin appeared normal.

He hefted the dustbin onto his shoulder and chased after the dustcart. Unfortunately, as he was pouring the contents from shoulder level into the cart, the python came sliding past his face. I don't suppose he was expecting this, especially at such close quarters.

"Hauauauyeowee..." His cry of anguish was one I had never heard before. It provoked the entire neighbourhood of dogs to break into a cacophony of barking and wailing. He flung the bin, spewing refuse and the twelve-foot snake, into the gutter.

Seeing what had happened, the rest of the crew dropped their dustbins in the street in case they had pythons in them too. They piled onto the dustcart and drove away, refusing to service our street until we got rid of our own pythons. The council sent an inspector to find out what the trouble was.

My sister, Amos and I were made to clean up the street. We spent an afternoon sweeping up the mess and shovelling it back into people's dustbins. The python's corpse was a problem because the inspector refused to have it removed. Maudie hit on the idea of dragging it down the gutter and stuffing it into a stormwater drain, in the hope that a rain cloud would come along and wash it away. At least it was out of sight in the drain beneath the pavement.

That January was dry and the python decomposed in the drain for three weeks before there were only its bones left.

Chapter 34

"Come here, little one," Selina called in Zulu to her unsuspecting son. My sister and I heard this over the back fence.

"There's a hole in your trousers, little Amos. I need to sew a patch on. So you must take them off and give them to me for a few minutes."

Amos did as he was bid and waited half-naked beside his mama perched on the chopping block with needle and thread.

"Got you!" she cried, leaping up. She nabbed him with one hand and reached for a rubber hose with the other.

"No Mama, no Mama! What I done now?" Amos screamed.

"I'll teach you for giving me such a fright I jumped out the window, you little monster."

Wham, bash, biff, she whacked him across his buttocks with the hose.

"Mama... Mama... Mama..." Amos blubbered, "Ow... ouch, you killing me, Mama."

"Everybody looking up my dress while I sitting in the dahlias. I'll do more than kill you."

"Mama, Mama, s'not fair. You tricked me. I can't run away with no trousers. I'll never do it again, I promise, Mama, I promise."

Still smarting from that beating, Amos was singing away in a galvanized washtub when his mama discovered what she thought was his school cap abandoned in the yard.

"Amos, you little brat. Look how filthy your new cap is. I suppose you think money grows on trees?"

Splat, she slapped him with her open hand across his back as hard as she could.

"Money grows on trees, hey?" she yelled, whacking him murderously again.

"I hope I killing you this time."

She was. His back stung so badly, he crumpled into five minutes of inconsolable blubbering.

"But Mama," Amos sobbed. "S'not my cap. Hobo found it."

"You lying to me are you?" She screamed, glancing at the soiled headgear. "I going to kill you again."

"No Mama, no Mama. Hobo found it on the koppies. Maudie told me I could have it."

Suspicious, Selina examined the cap. "Well... is a bit shabby and frayed round the peak. What's this red stain?"

Curious, she turned the cap over and deciphered indelible pencil on the lining.

"J. A. Rabie."

In our tree house, Maudie and I froze.

Selina brought the cap around to Sampson and the two of them discussed it. Sampson phoned our father at work and told him what had happened. Maudie and I were mortified. Our father phoned the police, arranged to leave the factory early and meet at our house around five o'clock.

The doorbell rang and Sampson showed two plain clothes detectives to the living room. He offered them tea while they waited for our father. My sister and I waited nervously in our bedroom until we were called down.

Selina arrived, dragging her son after her. Sampson handed the offensive headgear to our father. Everybody sat. Frog raised his eyebrows. Maudie, Amos and I fretted in the middle of the room.

"What's this all about then, Mister Freyer?" Detective Conradie asked.

"Detective, this cap seems to belong to Johannes

Rabie, the little boy who's been missing for weeks," our father told him. "Our children found it." He handed the cap to the police inspector.

"Well now, kids, where did you come across this cap?" he quizzed, looking at me.

"I... we... on the koppies... sir...." I stuttered

"Where on the koppies, boy?"

"Uh... you know, sir... up there on the koppies..."

"No sir, I don't know. That's why you're telling me."

"On... on one of the paths, sir... Yah, that's where we found it."

He frowned.

Maudie leaned against me. I glanced at her. She gazed at me strangely. Something was happening to my sister.

Detective Conradie prompted. "You know that Johannes Rabie has been missing for two weeks?"

I nodded. I wanted to vomit because I knew Johan was dead.

"Well, you will have to come onto the koppies with me and show me exactly where you found it, so we can search the area for clues."

"I... I don't think I can find the place again... sir."

He scowled, angry with me.

Maudie started speaking.

"Tadpole," she interrupted, staring into space. "It's dark. Light the candle." Her fingers reached for mine.

I put an arm around her. Her eyes misted.

"My sister's in a trance," I warned the detective. "Sh-sh..."

Our father stared at his daughter, his brow creasing.

"Johan is here. This is where I saw it happen."

I caught Detective Conradie's eye and put a finger to my lips. Our father peered at me, but I shook my head and touched my ear. I pointed to my sister.

"Tell me, Sis," I whispered.

"I did tell you... that night."

"What night, Maudie?"

"Don't you remember, silly? The day I saw the giraffe man. Johan was tied in the caves. I looked down. He was screaming. The sorcerer cut him and covered him with stones."

There was silence in our living room. My arm remained around my sister. I gazed at the detective and pursed my lips.

"In the caves?" Conradie murmured. I put a hand up. He sat open mouthed, but had his notebook out and scribbled furiously. Amos looked stunned.

Maudie started speaking again.

"The cap, Tadpole. Don't you remember? Hobo discovered Johan's cap in the caves and brought it to me. What a good finder she is..."

"Yah, Sis," I whispered, "Hobo's clever."

The adults stared, unable to speak. They thought we were play-acting. I believed my sister's visions were a result of Momma's and Stanley's crash. I decided to take things further.

"Davy Nguni, Sis?" I whispered. "What did you see?"

Detective Conradie's head came up sharply. He couldn't take his eyes off my sister.

"You know. I told you. The night before Guy Fawkes."

"What did you see, Maudie?"

"The stormwater drain by Rhodes Park. I looked down and saw him cut Davy bad."

I glanced at Detective Conradie and nodded. Maudie knew Davy's name before the head in the lake was identified. The adults watched my sister intently. Amos didn't say a word.

"Old Joseph found that thing in the water, Sis. And Louis picked it up. Where's Davy, Maudie?"

"You already know, Tadpole. The stormwater drain. Under the road to Sylvia Pass. In one of the pipes."

"My God," Conradie murmured.

"His clothes and things're by the weeds... covered

with rubbish."

Detective Conradie wrote furiously.

"Maudie," I squeezed her shoulder, "Perhaps you should go back to sleep."

"Yah, Tadpole. I s'pose…"

I led her to our bedroom, laid her on her bed fully dressed and pulled the cover over her. I drew the curtains and closed the door.

In the sitting room, Detective Conradie shook his head.

"I don't believe it, Mister Freyer," he spluttered. "It can't be true. Your little girl has seen these terrible things?"

"It's true sir. My sister told me this before. But only in her sleep. Please don't question her, sir. She won't know anything when she wakes. Go and look where she told you."

"Oh I shall, without delay."

"How long has this been going on?" our father inquired.

"Night before Guy Fawkes last year, Daddy. Maudie knew Davy was dead before the police did. And she knew what happened to Johan when everybody thought he was only missing."

"You never said anything?"

I looked at my feet.

He turned to Conradie. "Detective, I can't believe my daughter has dreamt all this. I hope my children are not leading you on a wild-goose chase."

"We'll have to confirm that, Mister Freyer."

"Maudie won't remember when she wakes up," I warned them. "She'll say we talking nonsense." They looked at me strangely.

"Mister Freyer," Detective Conradie began, "I don't think your daughter dreamt anything. I think she's gifted. I believe she may have been the recipient of telepathic activity in the minds of two highly stressed victims. But we'll only know once we find their remains."

He turned to Amos and me, his face serious. "Thank you... you two scallywags, for finding this cap. And to little Maudie for telling me what she witnessed while she slept."

"By the way," he continued. "Where exactly, was that dead python you found? I thought they were long since gone from the koppies."

"It wasn't dead, sir. Amos here, had to kill it with his teeth."

"Explain?"

"It went for him, sir. In the Foster Caves. Our candle had gone out. When Amos lit it, the python was on him so fast I didn't see. It twisted round him. And began squeezing until Amos couldn't breathe."

Conradie squinted at Amos, then me.

"You making this up?"

"No sir. It was strangling him. He couldn't breathe. I was scared to go near. Amos lay face to face with the python. He bit it in the throat and didn't let go. He chewed right through till the snake bled to death."

"Amos? I don't believe it," Conradie replied, shaking his head and beginning to grin. "Is this true, a little umfaan like you?"

"Yessir," Amos smiled. "We took him home to show my mama, but she give me a beating."

Both detectives chuckled, shaking their heads at Amos's audacity.

"Right," Conradie said, as they rose to go. "You three children have given us the lead we've been looking for. Thank you very, very much. We'll search the caves and the stormwater drain. But listen, it's not a good idea for you to venture anywhere near those places. Not until this muti-murder thing has been cleared up and the man responsible, behind bars. Be careful, kids, there's a child-killer walking the streets."

The interview was over and we didn't get into any more trouble. Maudie woke in time for supper. Amos complained to Selina about his second beating and showed her that his real cap was in good condition.

"Serves you right," she retorted. "That's for the next bad thing you do."

Chapter 35

Joseph filled his waterways from the siphon he'd taken off the underground spring. We lazed in his garden with our feet in one of his miniature lakes. The rivers fascinated me. They flowed slowly and majestically like real rivers, entering the lakes on one shore and leaving them at the other on the next part of their journey. We didn't have corks to make toy boats, so we floated chips of wood from Moses' chopping block, down the rivers.

"Can we bring proper boats one day, Old Joseph?" Maudie pleaded.

"I'll make them for you myself, ma'am," he offered, grinning.

We sat gazing at his rivers and the little pump returning the water to the top of the system.

"I'm indeed sad you children killed that python," Joseph commented. "They are lovely creatures. But I suppose, Amos, you felt threatened."

"He woulda swallowed me, Old Joseph. He wound himself three times round me and squeezed real bad. I couldn't breathe."

"Perhaps, had I been in the caves with you, I might have been able to coax the python back into its lair. Remember, you were intruding on its territory. It's not as if it attacked you in your own backyard."

He glanced at me and added, "I want you kids to promise you'll never kill another creature... ever again."

"I s'pose we hafta promise, Old Joseph. We'll gob on it for you, if you like," Maudie offered.

She grabbed Amos's and my hands and spat in our palms, then hers. Then Amos spat. Then I did. We rubbed our palms together as a pact.

"See, Old Joseph. There's no truer promise than that."

The 1948 school year opened on a pink day. There was excitement, moving up to a new class and my sister woke at five a.m. She packed her school haversack, made her own lunch, washed and dressed better than normal. Shortly after sunrise she took down our tattered *Holidays* sign and posted her pink *Tuesday*.

Frog was going on to high school, so we wouldn't be seeing him on our playground anymore. Graham and Louis were moving up to high school too, although they hadn't passed their exams. They were being sent there on trial. The primary school headmistress was only too glad to be rid of our cousins. The principal at the High would use his cane on the twins more than once.

Every year, Mr de Beer accepted about twenty new boys at Kiewietjie. And every year, the old boys subjected the new arrivals to initiation rites. So it was tradition that for the first ten days, new Kiewietjie boys were treated as morons. They took it like suckers, too timid to retaliate or complain, too afraid of the consequences of appealing to the housemaster.

They were known as Kiewietjie Convicts. The suburb of Kensington knew them as KC's. Shopkeepers, barbers, traffic officers, strangers on the street, delivery men, all knew who they were, because each Kiewietjie Convict had a cardboard sign hanging around his neck. Pinned to his breast pocket was a sprig of oak leaf to advise everybody what a greenhorn he was. They wore this garb at all times; in the hostel, on the street and in shops when buying stationery; except at school which wouldn't permit it. The sign and the oak leaf were removed when the newcomer lifted his feet off the floor to get into bed at night.

To drive home what cretins they were, Graham

forbade them to refer to themselves in the first person. The words, me, my, mine, I, our, were absolutely not to enter their minds. They were idiots of such lowly origin, they were told, that the only reference they could use to refer to themselves was, *it*.

Everybody else in the world was superior to them and had to be addressed as, *Sir*. This meant everybody, whether man or woman, young or old, street sweeper or principal. Ordinary citizens encountering a Kiewietjie Convict must have wondered slightly about his sanity.

"Good afternoon, Sir," a KC would address a female counter assistant. "It would like to buy a geometry set."

Things at the hostel were insane.

"What's wrong with its foot?" Graham demanded of a limping arrival.

"I sprained my..."

"*It*," Graham corrected. "It sprained its what? And remember to address this illustrious senior as *Sir*."

The boy blinked. He opened his mouth three or four times to speak. "Sir," he spluttered, "it sprained its ankle last week. I, er, it thinks it's nearly better. Its limp won't last long, Sir."

"Let me have a look," Graham insisted. "Kiewietjie Convicts got no brains to tell the difference between unscathed and mortally wounded. Did it hear that last year one of our KC's kicked the bucket and didn't know?"

"No Sir, it wasn't aware of that, Sir."

"The idjut kept coming to the eating hall although it'd been extinct two days. I hadta lock the doors to keep it out. Then cos it'd missed its own funeral I gave it the tram fare to the cemetery. They wouldn't let it in either, so I took it on again as a zombie. Now lemme check that ankle of its."

While he examined him, the boy was foolish enough to flinch.

"Jeez, see what I mean?" Graham crowed. "This foot's about to fall off with gangrene. And here it was, thinking it was getting better. Ten days immobility for that ankle. Everywhere it goes, it's gonna be pushed in a wheelbarrow by one of the other convicts. Take its shoe and sock off. I'll scrounge bandages from the sick bay."

After school, Maudie and I stopped by at the hostel. This was her second visit to Kiewietjie and except for our cousins and Mr de Beer, she didn't know anybody. She hadn't met any of the staff. Louis lounged on the unkempt lawn. The property was ramshackle. The new boys changed out of their school clothes and stood barefoot in khaki shorts and shirts. Their sprigs of oak were pinned to their breast pockets and each boy had his cardboard sign hanging around his neck.

"Stand to attention," Graham ordered.

"No, no, idjuts, not like that. Kiewietjie Convicts haven't got the brain to do things right. Hunch its shoulders, put its toes together and spread its heels. Yah, that's right. Now, clasp its hands in front to protect its nuts in case it loses 'em."

The new boys looked humiliated. Maudie started giggling and I put a hand over her mouth.

"I realize," Graham continued, "that standing attention is tiring. So how many of its wanta sit at ease?"

Foolishly, they all put their hands up.

Graham grinned. "Lazy jerks. I never found a Kiewietjie Convict that didn't wanta sit on its butt all day. Well now it can. I can show it how." He squatted on his haunches and held his arms out. For thirty seconds or so, he balanced on tiptoe.

"C'mon convicts," he bawled, "Sit at ease now, all of its. I doing it the best way, so just copy me."

He held the position until they imitated him. Then he stood up. "Don't get up," he warned. "It's privileged to rest like that. First five to fall, gotta get up an hour early tomorrow to weed this lawn. You can see, there's more weeds than grass."

There was agony in their faces as they competed to hold out. A minute went by while Graham walked up and down. Those who'd chosen to let their bodies sag, were instructed to raise them. At six minutes, the first boy collapsed into the weeds. When another four followed, the rest fell over, moaning and groaning.

"Up, up, up," Graham implored. "We got five volunteers. Now back to attention. I got some exercises to keep its fit."

He gave them two bricks each and told them to do a hundred press-ups while he counted. The groans came at fifty. At eighty, sweat poured from their faces. At ninety-nine, he started counting backwards. When he reached a hundred, they fell down. He gave them fifteen seconds rest and berated them to their feet.

"Please Sir," a timid hand was raised, "it needs to go to the bog Sir."

"How urgent?" Graham demanded.

"Now Sir, it's desperate."

Graham made him step forward. "Now, this is something Kiewietjie Convicts gotta be taught. They too stupid to know it by itselves. A KC wanting to go to the bog is in a extremely dangerous condition. It might explode any second."

The newcomers kept deadpan expressions on their faces. Graham had a punishment for laughing.

"The resultant world devastation's gonna be too terrible to contemplate."

He strolled over to a corner of the hostel and fetched a twenty-foot bamboo pole with a square of red material tied at the top.

"This is the danger signal it's gotta carry to the bog. Hold it high so everybody can see it and get out of the way in time."

He handed the pole to the boy but stopped him from rushing off to the outhouses behind the hostel.

"Another thing, some citizens not gonna see the danger it's putting 'em in. Could be looking the other way. So it's gotta holler, "Danger beware, danger beware," on its way to the bog."

The boy, almost jumping up and down now, nodded enthusiastically. He ran with the flag, crying out the warning every two seconds.

"When it comes back," Graham bawled after him, "it's gotta holler, *the danger is past, the danger is past*, got that?"

A worn tyre with a section of tread missing, lay under the hedge. Graham sent the boy in the wheelbarrow to fetch it. He was carted back clutching the tyre in his lap.

Maudie stiffened and her fingers reached for mine.

"I suddenly gotta awful feeling, Tadpole."

"What's wrong, Sis?"

"That old tyre..."

"Just a tyre, Sis."

She relaxed.

Graham spoke to the new boy.

"What's it got there?"

"A tyre, Sir."

"Lyre!" Graham bellowed.

"No sir, it is not a liar Sir. This is a tyre, Sir."

"It's a idjut. Can't tell the difference between a car part and a musical instrument. That's a lyre," he emphasized, prodding the tyre. "It's a ancient kinda harp. Hold it properly and play it. I wanta hear how it sounds."

"Sir, it doesn't know how to play a lyre."

"Same's a harp. Hold the lyre in its arm and stroke the strings with its fingers." He stood back to listen while the boy mimed playing invisible strings.

"I don't hear anything."

The boy looked nonplussed and began humming a tuneless falsetto up and down the scale as he plucked imaginary strings.

"Much better," Graham encouraged. "We got music now. You other idjuts gotta fall in behind our troubadour in the wheelbarrow."

He stood back.

"Its are going in for tea now. The injured troubadour in the wheelbarrow gonna entertain its with music and another gonna wheel it into the eating hall. After tea there's a hour-and-a-half prep."

My sister and I ran all the way home. It was ten blocks to our house. We were not allowed on the streets after sunset.

Chapter 36

It did not occur to me that I might know Maudie's giraffe man by name. However, my sister and I never saw him at the same moment. He always disappeared by the time I looked for him. Could he make himself invisible?

"I'm getting big now," Maudie confided. "Going up to standard one. No more just a kid in junior grade."

"Yah, Sis. We were all juniors once."

Even though I disliked school, I was excited about moving up to a new class. There were new faces, new friends to be made, a new teacher and unfortunately, new bullies. I was rid of Miss Meldrum who imitated my twitches and stammering. My new teacher was a spinster, a Miss Olds who came from Canada and told us she was of the family that founded the Oldsmobile factory. Miss Olds took care to ensure we understood what she was teaching us. My marks went up and the principal wrote on my term report that I was applying myself. That wasn't true, but I was happy for everybody to believe it.

Maudie, to my disgust, was naturally clever at school. But when she sat next to a boy who pulled her hair, she kicked him on the shin.

"Don't go crying to your mama now," she warned.

We were into the second half of summer, approaching Easter. My sister's giraffe man disappeared. The weeks went by. On weekends, Amos joined us. The municipality filled Rhodes Park Lake and we spent lazy hours in our canoe. Amos teased the catfish with his spear, but declined to catch one.

"Nah," he explained. "Next time I do that, my mama

gonna kill me proper."

Detective Conradie uncovered Johannes Rabie's mutilated body from a mound of rock in the Foster Caves. Just as my sister in her trance, told him.

Forensic detection showed that Johannes was taken there alive and suffered ritual murder. Vital organs were cut out while he still had breath in his body. What Maudie witnessed, was correct. The police stated the atrocity was the work of an African sorcerer. The organs made potent muti for casting spells and turning clients into superhumans, invisible, invincible, omnipotent.

My sister's prediction of where investigators would find David Nguni's remains was correct too; in the stormwater culvert, under the road to Sylvia Pass. David's bloodied clothes were discovered under refuse dumped on a weed-ridden lot abutting the drain. Consciously, Maudie knew nothing of this.

Our father accepted that my sister and I were telling the truth. But he found the strangeness difficult and did his best to hide newspaper reports.

He worried a lot.

"If ever you children visit the Foster Caves again, or the Bezuidenhout Valley stormwater drain, I'll confine you to our yard, never to venture through the front gate."

This became the sword dangling on a hair.

"We not gonna tell him about the giraffe man," Maudie whispered, "Cos you still gotta see him yourself."

Louis spent a Saturday afternoon fixing his decrepit bicycle. He spread parts all over our father's workbench. After the twins' collision with the Pentecostal congregation, he unthreaded spokes, straightened the rim and rebuilt the front wheel by hand. Ten spokes were missing.

"Damn it," he mumbled, "the front wheel wobbles like crazy." The parts strewn on the workbench were from the brake inside the rear hub. They were so old and worn they didn't work anymore.

Graham skated up the driveway into the garage where he belched.

"Jeez Bro, what's wrong with you? Not got the bike fixed yet?"

Louis glowered at him beneath his eyebrows.

"The brakes are kaput. Can't fix 'em no more. Gotta get new parts."

"How much?" Graham belched.

Louis scratched his forehead.

"Probably a pound. Plus new spokes and a few other things. Make it two. Can't do it. We broke."

Graham thought for a moment.

"I got it," he exclaimed. "Our old lady knows a coupla cattle farmers. Mister Basson for a start going to be at the Rand Show here in Jo'burg, Easter holidays chum. I'll get us jobs. Maybe look after his cattle for him."

Louis pursed his lips.

"Be the only job we can get, any case."

Graham belched.

"Leave it to your younger bro. I'll fix us up good."

Louis hung the bike in the garage rafters and wrapped the dismantled parts in a cloth. The agricultural-cum-industrial show was five weeks away.

"Old Sunshine's back," Maudie revealed one morning. "I seen him in Roberts Avenue in his rickshaw."

The travelling salesman returned early February, making his rounds to the African people in our neighbourhood, collecting money and showing his catalogues. If he still had square shouldered medicine bottles wrapped in brown paper at the bottom of his suitcase and was secretly selling them behind closed doors, we didn't know.

The day school broke up for the Easter holidays, except for the twins who were staying behind to work at the Rand Show, the boys at the hostel packed their suitcases and left for home; some were fetched by their parents from nearby towns. Others caught trams to the city centre, traipsed down Eloff Street to Park Station and entrained there.

Seeing there were no classes the next day, our father allowed us to wander down to Kiewietjie after school broke up.

"I'll fetch you in the Chev at nine o'clock this evening. You are not to walk home after dark."

At Kiewietjie, Maudie trilled, "Ah goodie, I gonna look for four-leaf clovers in this weedy old lawn."

I went round the back and strolled through the kitchen entrance.

"Howzit, Lukas?" I greeted. He grinned at me and continued tidying up. Next morning, he would be on leave.

I wandered through the hostel to the front veranda decorated in Victorian style. To my surprise, Maudie found her clovers, three of them. We trotted up the wooden staircase connecting the entrance hall with the first storey.

In a dormitory Graham stood on a tallboy next to Louis's bed, drilling a hole into the ceiling.

"Wotcha up to Graham?" Maudie quizzed.

"Working on a surprise for my bro, Maud. He gone to a matinee and when he gets back I wanna frighten him good."

"Where's Mister de Beer?"

Graham sniggered.

"The Bear, Maud dear, is gallivanting with a lady friend. He won't be back till after midnight."

"Yah but why you drilling holes in the ceiling? You making a awful mess."

"I gonna tie my bro's bed up here."

He enlisted our help to lift Louis's bed complete with mattress and blankets. We rested one end on top of a cupboard and stood the other on the tallboy.

"Wait here you two," Graham instructed, "while I go up in the ceiling. When I stick wire through the holes, you take it round the frame of the bed and poke it back. Savvy? I'll pull the bed up and fasten the wire."

Twenty minutes later, Louis's bed was fixed against the ceiling.

"You gonna get in trouble, Graham," my sister warned.

"Nah, Maud. It's just a surprise." He closed and latched the windows.

"Tadpole, you go to The Bear's rooms and bring his pipe, tobacco and matches. Yah, and half a dozen cigarettes also."

When I returned with these, he bared two electrical wires and tied one strand to the other.

"Not live, yet," he explained, "but when it is, my bro gonna mess his pants."

He closed the door, lit the cigarettes and left them burning in saucers around the dormitory.

"We gotta create a fog," he explained, "I'll get The Bear's pipe going in a minute, just soon's I finished wiring my bomb."

Maudie glanced at me in alarm.

"Time to be going," she said.

"Daddy's only fetching us at nine," I reminded her.

She rolled her eyes.

"Don't panic, Maud," Graham interjected. "Just a little thing the guys in the science lab taught me."

With cigarette smoke contaminating the air, he took a phial from his pocket and showed me the saltpetre mixture inside. He inserted the electrical wires, replaced the cap and rolled the phial in a wad of pulp magazines. Then he bound the magazines with string, so they wouldn't unwrap.

281

"Heck Graham, you gonna get in darn big trouble this time," Maudie predicted.

"Nah Maud. Just a bit of fun that's all. My bro likes being ragged."

He continued binding his device with string until it was solid. It looked like a real bomb.

Graham hid it under a dormitory bed in a corner and led the electrical wire to the fluorescent fitting in the ceiling. He fiddled with the neon tube, removed the starter and fitted the tube into place.

"When my bro turns on the light switch, my bomb's gonna go off and that neon's only gonna flicker. With this smoke, he won't see proper. Will look like the dorm's been hit by World War Three."

Maudie glanced at me. Graham stuffed the housemaster's pipe with tobacco, lit it and blew pipe smoke into the air.

"Ugh," he spat, turning the pipe back to front so he could cup his hands over the bowl and blow smoke through the stem. Louis's bed floated in smoke.

"Time to be getting out," he urged, switching off a table lamp.

We exited the darkened dormitory and closed the door. Graham nailed it to the jamb with four-inch nails.

"You two, check the front windows. Warn me if my bro comes in the gate."

He crouched at the door, with the pipe's stem in the keyhole, blowing smoke into the dormitory. Eventually he muttered, "Okay let's get rid of this." He pulled the pipe out, plugged the keyhole with a wad of paper and dashed to the showers where he emptied the pipe and returned it to the housemaster's suite. Out on the pavement, Louis opened the gate.

"Quick, in here," Graham urged, pulling Maudie and me into the prep room. "We can watch the fun from here."

Louis didn't come upstairs right away. He made a detour via the kitchen to scrounge a snack.

"What's keeping the blockhead?" Graham hissed.

Outside a car pulled up.

The wooden stairs creaked. Louis reached the top and sauntered to the bathroom. I heard water running. Then he was in the corridor whistling softly to himself, strolling toward the nailed door. Graham chuckled. Maudie held her hands over her mouth.

Lost in thought Louis sauntered to the door, reached for the handle, turned it and tried entering the dormitory all in one smooth movement. The door remained shut and he stumbled, rebounding into the corridor. His whistling came to an abrupt stop as he stared at the door. Graham began snickering. His brother tried the door again and put his weight against it. Nothing happened.

Just then, I heard the housemaster's voice from the top of the staircase.

"What seems to be the matter, Louis?"

Graham drew in his breath.

"Kee-riced. What's the old sod doing back so early? His girlfriend musta dumped him." He edged forward for a better view.

In the corridor, Louis tried the door again. Mr de Beer came up to him.

"Here, let me try, boy. Probably a bit stiff." He rattled the handle and put his shoulder to the door. Then he stood back and hurled himself at it.

Graham's nails pulled out and the door flew open. The housemaster lost his balance and stumbled into the dark interior, landing on his hands and knees on the floor.

"What the hell's going on?" he muttered.

Louis helped him to his feet.

"Where's the light switch, boy?"

He must have found it, for a half second later Graham's bomb under the bed went off. The explosion would have been heard on the next block.

"God Almighty!" the housemaster wailed,

staggering backwards out of the dormitory.

A weird light came from within. Mr de Beer peered in, not sure whether it was safe to enter. The air curled with smoke he thought had come from the explosion. Thousands of shreds of paper and string carpeted the floor. The flickering fluorescent tube in the ceiling haunted the dormitory with an eerie glow.

Louis squeezed in next to the housemaster. As they stood gazing at the littered floor and peering into the fog, they glanced up at Louis's bed floating against the ceiling.

Mr de Beer put a hand to his forehead.

"Oh my God. The explosion's blown that bed right up there."

"Yes, sir," Louis agreed, not taking his eyes off his bed.

"Get the windows open, boy."

The smoke began clearing. They found a light bulb and fitted it into a socket. Then the housemaster noticed the electrical wire leading from the fluorescent light to the bed where the paper bomb had exploded.

"Graham!" he yelled. "It's Graham. Where's your brother, boy?"

"I dunno, sir," Louis answered, his eyes still on his bed.

"Find him. Now."

Graham left Maudie and me in the darkened prep room and marched into the chaotic dormitory.

"April fools!" he pronounced, with a broad grin on his face.

Mr de Beer was flabbergasted. It took him seconds to respond.

"Is this... this mess and destruction... your sadistic idea of a joke, boy?"

"Not meant for you Sir," Graham apologized. "Seeing it's the last day of term and tomorrow's April the first and my bro and me'll be working at the Rand Show, I thought I'd pull his leg. I didn't count on you walking into my little surprise Sir."

The housemaster exploded.

"This is the last time, boy. Do you hear me? The last. The absolutely final time. Do you understand? One more fire, one more bomb, one more anything and out you go. And good riddance too! Both you and your brother! I won't have it. Do you understand, boy? I've had a goddamned enough."

"Yes, Mister de Beer. I'll clean up the mess right away."

"One more time," the housemaster repeated.

"And we out on our ears," Graham finished the sentence for him.

The housemaster nodded. I saw the rage he was in as he stalked out the dormitory. He fumbled in his jacket pocket for his phial of pills, selected two and popped them into his mouth.

"Ah, why me always? S'always me." Louis grumbled.

His younger brother laughed.

"Ah nuts, chum. I just gave him a scare that's all. Probably messed his trousers when my bomb went off."

"What about me?" Louis retorted.

Graham snickered. "Do me a favour, Bro. See if you can find a broom. I better sweep up the mess. You take your bed down from up there."

At one a.m. the next morning, I woke to the Big Ben carillon, followed by a single chime sounded by the clock that ticked in the passage. Our father wound it once a week. Maudie called out in her sleep.

"Tadpole, come help me," she moaned.

I shook off my blankets and padded across the room. I didn't want to startle her, so I caressed her arm.

"I need you. Where you?"

She grimaced in her sleep.

"Aren't you gonna help?"

"Yah, Sis."

She sat up in shock and clung to me. I felt her heart pounding. We stayed like that a long time before she was able to whisper what her nightmare was about.

"Why didn't you come? Just me and the sorcerer in the Foster Caves. He made me drink muti and threw me down."

The passage clock ticked.

"Twas horrible. I couldn't move."

"You're okay now Sis."

"He sharpened his knife."

"S'okay Maudie. S'only a dream. Everything's alright now."

"You never came, Tadpole. I looked down and saw you sleeping here in our room. You shoulda come to get me."

I held her close and brought her in with me. I tucked the blankets around us and didn't hear the carillon again.

Chapter 37

Every year, the Ferris wheel standing high among the swings, rides and side-shows was what we made for.

"Abe, 'tis Easter Holidays you know and the Rand Show is on," Maudie schemed.

"Really Sweetheart? I wasn't aware of that."

"Well it's true and we need money."

"Did you complete the chores I set you?"

"You know we have, Abe. We worked a whole week getting them done."

"How much did we agree on?"

"A pound? Wasn't it ten shillings each?"

Our father chortled. "That's a good one. Perhaps the best. No, it was ten shillings in total Sweetheart."

"Oh yes, I remember now."

"Five bob for each of you is enough. I'm uneasy about you going to the show in the first place. There are bad types there, so I want you to promise me you'll stick together."

"Swear to God and hope to die, Abe."

She came to me with a big grin on her face.

"I got us boodle for five rides each, my sister chortled." She persuaded Sampson to give us tram fare out of housekeeping.

Selina only had two shillings to give to Amos.

"I'll just watch you after my dough's finished," he lamented.

"Give me your two shillings, Amos," Maudie instructed. She pooled the silver.

"Now, lemme see. Twelve shillings between us. That's four rides each."

"Can't do that," Amos protested. "It's your dough.

You can get five rides each."

"Take it," Maudie ordered.

"No."

"You wanna fight?"

"You just a girl. I can't fight you."

Maudie bunched her fist and jabbed him in the eye.

"Ouch, that's blinking sore," Amos howled,

"Take the money or I'll whack you again. I'm not just a girl."

Her balled fist walloped him on the ear. Amos howled and staggered out of range.

"If you don't take your share of the twelve shillings, me and Tadpole will go to the show on our own. Then you won't go at all, cos you're not allowed on the streets by yourself."

"Okay I give in. Yea, yea, yea, I get to have four rides." He danced around the yard, kissing the coins.

Maudie squeezed past the turnstiles by mingling with a group of children. She found a discarded ticket in a waste bin and passed it through the fence to Amos who walked the wrong way through the exit gate, waving the ticket, pretending he had already bought it. I approached a turnstile, thrust the used ticket into a man's hands and dived through before he had a chance to examine it.

"There's the cattle section," I pointed out, thinking about our cousins. "The dairy hall's over there."

"Later," Maudie insisted. "Let's go see the funfair first."

Most of the exhibitions were in permanent buildings, but there were marquees with banners and bunting. Outdoor stands were decorated with flags and striped canvas. Loudspeakers blared, some pouring out martial music. Public address systems announced events at the main arena where show jumping was taking place. Now, I remembered how my sister knew enough about dressage to train Hobo.

"There's the big wheel," Maudie pointed out.

Half-full, the Ferris revolved lazily. The occupants seemed to go endlessly around from ground level to eighty-feet high in the sky.

"They must have a view right across the show grounds," Maudie said. "Good place to be if you watching somebody."

"We better keep an eye out for your giraffe man, Sis."

She rolled her eyes at me.

For an hour, we wandered around, getting our fun from the cries and screams of others.

"We still got dough in our pockets," Maudie grinned.

The figure-of-eight roller coaster produced terrified shrieks. Some women put their hands over their eyes the whole ride.

"I can never understand that, Sis, paying good money for something and then not see what you getting."

"Lookee over there," she pointed out.

The man at the test your strength stand, hefted the wooden mallet. He swung it with style sending the shuttle whizzing up the pole to strike the bell at the top.

"Who wants to test their strength?" he bawled.

A tough looking guy holding a girl around her waist swaggered up and paid his money. He rolled his sleeves and spat on his hands. Maudie giggled. The crowd stood back. He checked the weight of the mallet and its balance. He caught his girlfriend's eye.

Then he paused before raising the mallet. He brought it down with fury, striking the rubber cushion hard. The shuttle stopped halfway up the pole at *not enough muscle* and came down again. Maudie giggled. The crowd tittered. His girlfriend smiled at him.

"Try again," the man running the stand said. "You get three tries for your money."

He did. He hit the cushion so hard his feet came off the ground. Maudie guffawed. *A miss is as good as a mile* the sign-writing on the pole read. He didn't look at his girlfriend. Nobody besides Maudie laughed. The tough guy scowled at her, tried again and threw the mallet down in disgust. He stalked off with his girl.

The man running the stand picked up the mallet and sent the shuttle to the top.

"Who's next to test their strength," he bawled.

"I seen that tough man before somewhere," my sister murmured. "Can't think where."

We wandered over to the Dive Bomber a heart stopping contraption that revolved ten times faster than the Ferris wheel. It had open cockpits taking you up in the air, over the top then diving for the ground. Amos and I gave up our first shilling for a ride. Maudie watched.

"I'm not going on that thing," she protested.

A man in front of us vomited his Coke and hotdog onto another man on the ground who threatened to kill him.

Two-stroke motorbikes rode the wall of death, whizzing around the cylindrical wall. Maudie wasn't interested and Amos and I only had three shillings left.

As we gawked at the activity of the funfair, Maudie reached for my hand.

"I got a feeling we being followed. Someone's watching us."

I turned a slow circle, scanning the mass of bodies around us but it was difficult to see over the heads of adults.

"Let's go see the dodgem cars," she urged.

On the way, we stopped at The Whip. Men, women and children hung on for their lives, shrieking and screaming. Amos and I blew our next shilling on The Whip. Maudie kept her money. The Whip wasn't as good as The Dive Bomber. Nobody was sick on The Whip.

The Rotor was a big wooden cylinder. Everybody got inside and stood against the wall. Then the cylinder began revolving. As it speeded up, they were pinned to the wall by centrifugal force. Then the floor began dropping away leaving the people stuck ten foot up the wall. Women began screaming and men laughed nervously. Then when someone started being sick, The Rotor slowed down and everyone slid down the wall. Women's dresses got pulled up from sliding down and everybody laughed. People walked as if they were drunk. Amos and I asked Maudie to come with us on The Rotor. She didn't. She watched us part with our money again.

At the dodgem cars, Maudie was happy. She hung onto the fence, watching.

"Aren't you going for a ride, Sis?" Amos and I had only one ride left. She had four.

"After I've watched awhile."

At last she said she would have her first ride.

Amos and I joined her in the queue and when our turn came, we each ran to a car. My idea of driving a dodgem was to bash as many people as I could. I drove around looking for Amos and Maudie. Amos had the same idea. Each time we collided, we laughed at each other. Then I saw my sister piloting her car. She gripped the wheel with both hands, steering to avoid colliding with anybody. I came in from the side and bashed into her. I expected her to laugh, but instead she got angry.

"Don't do that," she screamed.

I laughed and was going to bump her again, but she gave me a dirty look.

"Can't you see? I'm learning to drive."

I didn't understand why she wanted to spend her shilling on the dodgem cars and then not get as much fun as possible. I went looking for Amos, When the power was turned off Amos and I dragged ourselves off our dodgem cars. We'd spent all our money.

Maudie came running behind us. "I'm going again."

We hung on the fence, staring at the dodgems. My sister raced a seventeen-year-old boy to get the same car she'd had before. She got there first. I watched her drive. It was terrible. She sat bolt upright, clutching the wheel as if piloting a bus and avoided colliding with anybody.

I got mad with my sister then, paying good money to have fun and then not having any.

"You wasting the money Daddy gave us," I chastised when she came off.

"He gave it to me. It's my money now. You spent yours. I'm learning to drive properly."

She went back to the queue and Amos and I watched her having her third turn. I wished she'd told me earlier what she was planning to do. Each time she ran to the same car. When she came off the rink for the third time, she still had a shilling left. But now she didn't want to spend it too quickly, so Amos and I waited around while she stood at the fence and watched six rounds of cars being driven by other people.

"Can't wait any longer Sis. We gonna leave you here."

"No... oh. I'll get lost. Just once more."

We waited miserably, hanging onto the fence while she had her fourth turn.

"I know how to drive now," she announced when she came off the rink. "I think I'll be a good driver on our box-cart."

I scoffed and she stuck her tongue out at me.

We smelt the cattle section before we got there. The dairy building was at the top of the show grounds, opposite the arena. Behind the arena were stalls, pens, kraals, paddocks and judging rings.

"Phooey," Maudie said covering her nose to keep out the stench of dung, wet hay, mud, body odours of pigs, sheep, cattle, poultry and horses.

We found Graham and Louis behind railings attempting to put a halter over the head of a big red Afrikaner bull.

Maudie caught her breath and froze. She reached for my hand and started crying. I led her aside while she buried her face in my shoulder.

"What's the matter, Sis?"

She shook her head. "Can't tell you. Gimme a minute... I'll be okay."

We climbed the railings. The twins, clad in overalls and gumboots, were smeared with mud and ankle deep in excrement. The tips of the bull's horns were docked, but dangerous to anyone who got in the way. Louis brought the animal to a walk by running alongside and throwing his arms around its neck. He let his knees sag and dragged his boots in the mud. The bull came to a standstill, stamping the ground. Louis hung like a leech, his hands clasped and his body suspended under the bull's throat.

When Graham approached with the halter, the Afrikaner tossed its head. It backed away, trampling the earth and dragging Louis. He felt for the buckle and hurriedly fastened the halter. Dodging the horns, he stood up and made a grab for a rein. He held it short. Graham darted underneath the bull's head and snatched at the other rein. They had the animal between them and tried to walk it to their bucket of cleaning water, cloths, grooming brushes and currycombs.

"Hey Graham, Louis, over here," Maudie called.

While they tried to groom him, the animal shuffled backwards, forwards and sideways. The twins tripped in unison, dragging their galvanized bucket, dodging horns and jumping out of reach of hooves.

"How's it going, Louis?"

"Can't you see? This one's a real bastard."

"You been sleeping at Kiewietjie every night?"

"That a joke? This job's twenty-four hours a day, seven days a week. Graham and me sleep in the stalls. Gotta start work at sparrow fart. Shovel the stalls, walk the animals, water 'em, feed 'em, wash 'em and groom 'em. This bastard's raw. Just come from the bush-veld and goes on show tomorrow."

"Better you than us."

"C'mon, give us a hand," Graham called, bending over the animal's rump, brushing its hindquarters.

"Both my hands are staying with me," my sister giggled.

The bull arched its tail and defecated, splattering Graham in the face. He swung his foot and kicked it in the stomach. The animal whipped its head around, jerking the rein out of his hand, backed and feinted at Louis.

"You kicked him Graham, not me," Louis screamed.

The bull tossed its head and charged. Louis dropped the rein and fled. He cleared the railings in one movement. The bull snorted and came back for Graham who dived through the railings. He reached, snatched a rein, caught it and wrapped it around the rails.

"Get the other one Bro, quick. I got him tied here."

Louis scowled and made a grab for it. They pinned the animal's neck between their bodies and began polishing its horns.

"He wants to be left alone to graze," Maudie commented.

"Maybe Maud, but Mister Basson wants him cleaned, groomed and taken for a walk. That'll help tame him so he can be handled tomorrow for judging."

They tightened their hold on the reins and coaxed the animal toward the gate.

"You gonna let him out?"

"Have to. We gotta take him to the bottom paddock and walk him there."

They coaxed the animal to the gate, but couldn't open it as it hinged inwards.

"Hey, Tadpole, give us a hand here. We'll hold him back while you swing the gate open."

I glanced at my sister.

"Rather you than me, boy," Amos remarked.

I jumped down and began opening the gate. The beast took off and charged for the opening, yanking Graham and Louis after it. I ran with the gate, swinging it wide.

Louis hung on, hopping and running. The bull careered into the railings, squashing Graham against the gatepost. He lengthened his rein, running at the animal's flank. It gave the bull freedom.

"Slow down," Louis yelled.

The animal put its head down and careered between kraals and paddocks. Show-goers scattered, fleeing down exit lanes, finding refuge behind corners and posts, fumbling for gate latches and climbing fences.

Louis jerked his rein, pulling the bull's head to one side, but that steered the animal into the railings and he found himself bounced between the bull's shoulder and the railings. He yelled louder than ever.

As they swung around the corner of the dairy building, crowds coming in through the entrance to the show grounds opened a path for the threesome. The Afrikaner put its head down and leaned to the left, its horns scything the ground. Louis was knocked flying by the animal's shoulder. He tripped and stumbled, somehow hanging onto his rein.

When the animal wheeled to the left, the impetus whipped Graham off his feet, skidding him into orbit over the ground. A path opened. Graham dragged behind digging his boots. Louis collapsed at the end of his rein, sliding over the ground.

A group of farm boys came out to watch and laugh. Ten of them fell on the animal's neck, forcing it down. The Afrikaner slowed to a halt, snorting and puffing and stamping.

Louis eased himself up, wiping mud from his eyes. Graham untangled his body from his rein and lay in the mud.

"Check his boots," Maudie giggled. "They got more holes in 'em than Missus Probert's velskoens."

The farm boys laughed and joked. They led the bull back to its kraal. Louis ran his fingers over his ribs. Graham limped.

"How'd your little walk go?" Amos ragged. The twins glowered at him. "Who was taking who for a walk? You got more exercise than the bull."

He lost his footing on the railings and fell into the mud. Without a word, he dived through the rails to put distance between himself and the twins. However, our cousins were too bruised and aching to worry about Amos.

On the way home, Maudie whispered, "We been followed the whole day."

"How'd you know?"

"I just know."

"You see who?"

"No."

"The giraffe man?"

"Not sure. Maybe somebody else."

"Who?"

"Somebody, that's all."

Chapter 38

"Aw gee," Maudie complained, "Lookit my Holiday sign. Falling apart. All my work for nothing."

"Nuh, not nothing Sis. Been there for weeks. You're a good artist."

Her *Holiday* sign in the fig tree was tattered and wouldn't last another week. Amos scrambled over the fence. Hobo lazed on her back in the autumn sun, opened an eye, inspected the upside down Zulu child, wagged her tail and went back to sleep. Amos joined us in the tree.

By the end of April the autumn soakings came to an end and a dry winter set in. Johannesburg's atmosphere became laden with the smoke of coal fires lit in people's stoves. My sister and I made a journey onto the koppie to a distant fir grove and collected pine cones lying under the trees.

The sun descended into the northern hemisphere and our days shrunk. It was barely light when we woke in the morning. Afternoons ended too soon and creeping cold chased us indoors. Johannesburg is six thousand feet above sea level. Leaves fluttered from branches and our world turned bleak. Snow covered the Drakensberg and Cape mountain ranges. Southerly winds blew through the peaks to plunge our nights below freezing.

"Abe, why we gotta have winter?" Maudie sighed. "Hasta be the worsest time of my life."

"If we didn't have winter, Sweetheart, we couldn't have summer could we?"

"Yes, but... aw Abe, you foxed me on that one. Gotta think about it."

The square of lawn in the front garden deteriorated from green to brown. Leaves littered pavements. Across the street, an oak tree shed its acorns. At night I snuggled under my blankets, listening to acorns pinging onto the tin roof of a shed. The winter wind bustled around corners. In our yard, *The Vale of Belvoir* lay upside down against the back fence, accumulating grime.

Lack of food brought rats from the koppies into the yards of the houses. Our father set traps. If he thought he got rid of them it was because they advanced into neighbours' yards. They made determined attempts to get into our house under the kitchen floor. But no colony of rats lasted long against a berserk Zulu. Sampson chased them with his broomstick, clubbed them, poisoned them and caught them in traps. When we were out of rat poison, ingenious Sampson doctored a piece of cheese with ant poison and got his rat that way. He chuckled for a week over his deception. Maudie wasn't impressed.

"Semp-Sonne, s'not fair to trick a rat like that. God's gonna punish you good 'n proper."

Then one bitterly cold afternoon toward the end of May, my sister caught sight of our friendly clothing salesman.

"Hey lookee over there, Tadpole. Isn't that old Sunshine's fancy car parked near our house?"

"Yah Sis, I reckon. Lets go see."

My sister and I were dancing home from school, keen to pat Hobo and retire to the fig tree. A shining black Chrysler was parked across our street. I don't think I'd seen a Chrysler in Good Hope Street before. If Mr Sunshine gave Amos a ride from Sophiatown, he dropped him off in Roberts Avenue.

We stopped to inspect the car, a late 1947 model with whitewall tyres. The paintwork and chrome sparkled. The interior leather had been waxed and polished till it shone.

"I can tell it belongs to Mister Sunshine," Maudie murmured, running her fingers over a mudguard.

Like his rickshaw and the way he dressed, his car was immaculate. The vehicle might have been on display in a showroom. It put our drab '34 Chev to shame. Maudie and I leaned against the windows admiring the interior, when a voice startled me.

"Lordy, Lordy, children. You like my car do you?"

I jumped back, as if caught snooping. He stood behind us, suitcase at his feet.

"Want to come for a ride, children?"

I hesitated. Maudie spoke for both of us.

"What you done with your rickshaw today, Mister Sunshine?"

He laughed self-consciously.

"How do you children like my car?"

My mouth must have been hanging open, for he waited with his hand on the door handle, beaming at us.

"Too cold this morning for the rickshaw. Any case I've been sick with the 'flu."

"Is it really yours, Mister Sunshine?" I asked.

He looked embarrassed.

"Lordy, Lordy. Yes, children, I operate the Chrysler as a taxi. Has to earn its keep, you know. Normally my partner drives it. But there's not much business in the middle of the day. That's why I'm using it myself now. Taxi business is early morning and late afternoon when people need to get to work and get home again but missed their train."

"Gee, Mister Sunshine, must be the smartest car I ever seen," Maudie enthused.

"Oh it doesn't stand round idle, child. On Saturdays it's a wedding car and Sundays I use it for, ah... other things."

He unlocked the boot and dumped his suitcase inside. Then he slid into the driver's seat, beamed at Maudie and cruised away.

"Wonder what he got in his case this time?" she pondered.

On weekends with no Sampson around, the Queen Mary went out. By Saturday night, the hot water tank was tepid. I hated sitting naked on the edge of a metal bath with my feet in a bucket of lukewarm water, washing with a cloth. My sister and I went about barefoot and came to the bathroom with rings of dirt around our necks. Our water ended up cold and brown.

Mid-winter holidays arrived and Maudie unpinned her crimson sign on the fig tree. She pulled a face when she saw the condition of her old *Holiday* sign.

"Phooey. Lookit this. S'no damn good. Been torn and the colour's all wrong. S'not gonna give us a good feeling, is it?"

She found her orange and pink crayons and carefully lettered a new two-tone notice. As it didn't rain in winter, that sign stayed in the fig tree our whole school holiday.

Sampson went home that July. Zululand is sub-tropical and warm in winter. He started getting ready three months early. Clothing bought at jumble sales for his wives and children, was aired and ironed. He folded and packed them into the metal trunk he kept under his bed. Hand mirrors and combs, needles and cotton, material for his wives, were packed.

"It's a big to-do, getting ready, isn't it Semp-Sonne?" Maudie told him.

When the day finally came, he and our father grappled with his trunk to get it closed. Then there was his blanket roll and carrier bags. Our father strapped the trunk onto the Chev's luggage carrier. Sampson climbed into the back with his carrier bags and blanket roll. He sat like royalty while our father chauffeured him to Park Station. We weren't going away this year there wasn't any money.

"You children had two weeks at Umhlanga Rocks last year," our father reminded us. "Perhaps next year we can afford a holiday."

"We'll just hafta play in the backyard, Abe."

For three months now ever since the Rand Show, when my sister and I were on the streets, she experienced the sensation of being watched. Sometimes, she'd spin round to catch the voyeur out.

"Whatsa matter, Sis? Someone walk over your grave?"

"S'nothing. I just got a feeling, that's all."

Detective Conradie made no progress with his investigations. Newspapers washed their hands of the crimes. Maudie and I were banned from our favourite adventure grounds. But I didn't respect the ban if I thought we could get away with it. My sister's nightmares persisted.

Joseph's miniature waterways attracted us. On Monday morning, Amos, Maudie and I hung over our driveway fence watching the old mariner at work in his front garden, until eventually he put down his garden implements and invited us over.

"I've never made those cork boats I promised, have I?"

"No, you never done that, Old Joseph," my sister agreed.

None of us knew how to make cork boats that would sail. Our efforts ran to chips of bark that floated like flotsam down his rivers and lay dead on the little lakes. We soon tired of these make-believe boats.

"Real boats that truly sail Old Joseph? You promise? You not chaffing us?" Maudie persisted.

"If you three will be patient while I fashion them for you, I'll show you how. They're straight forward really."

"Swear to God and hope to die?"

"Yes, I suppose so Maudie," he chuckled.

He led us to his garden shed where he'd stashed four champagne corks for us.

"A bit of trade with the bottle-and-bag man," he commented. "Now Maudie, you slip home and fetch writing paper for the sails, nail scissors to cut them out, a pencil to outline the ensigns and your crayons to colour them."

He asked me to scrounge eight matchsticks for the masts and four used razor blades from our father's and Sampson's razors for keels and rudders. He'd only come up with one blade himself.

"No boat can sail without keel or rudder," he explained.

Resting a hand on Amos's shoulder, he said, "Amos, you stay and watch, while I get my knife out and shape the boats' hulls. Then you'll know how to do it next time."

My sister and I left them in the shed and dashed home to get the things he wanted. After we scrambled back through the hole in the fence, we found that Joseph had neatly sliced the corks down the middle.

"We'll start with a fleet of four ships," he explained. "The flat part made by my fillet knife is the deck of each ship."

He took an ancient knife from his Cape fishing days and shaved a sliver from the underside of each hull.

"We can't leave them altogether round underneath. With no ballast, the ships will roll over. How many masts do you want on your ships, one or two?"

"Two, Old Joseph," we chorused. They would look more like real ships with two masts. We understood from him that a proper full-rigged ship has three masts, but the corks were not long enough, so we settled for two.

"Very well," he answered. He pierced the decks with an awl and planted the matchsticks, pushing the heads into the cork because it expanded over the heads and held the masts firmly.

"Now for the sails. I'll cut square sails like the old windjammers used to have. But we can only have one sail on each mast as it's not long enough for more. With two masts and a square sail on each, they'll look pretty good." He reached for Maudie's scissors and snipped out the sails.

"What ensigns would you like on the sails?" he asked.

We shrugged.

"How about a red Maltese Cross for your first ship?"

We nodded, although we didn't know what an ensign or a Maltese Cross looked like. When Joseph outlined the design onto two sails with my sister's pencil and coloured them in with her crayons, we were impressed.

"Now, what about your next ship? What about blue scimitars?"

We were loath to show our ignorance, so after glancing at each other, we nodded. When Joseph coloured the paper with the broad-bladed, curved swords, the sails looked very smart indeed.

"Make the next one a pirate sail, Old Joseph," Maudie suggested eagerly.

He chuckled his agreement and obliged by drawing a black skull and cross bones, shaded in pink, onto the next suit of sails.

"That's gonna be my ship, Tadpole," Maudie chipped when I reached to touch the sails.

Joseph laughed.

"I'll have the sword ship then," I countered.

"What about you, Amos?" Joseph enquired. "Is there anything special you'd like on your sails?"

Amos frowned. For a moment he couldn't think what he'd like.

"An Impundulu Bird," he blurted.

I laughed.

Joseph grinned, picked up Maudie's pencil and sketched the outline of an eagle with wings outstretched, sending down forked lightning. He shaded the bird brown and the lightning yellow. It was magnificent, like a coat of arms.

"That's really snazzy, Old Joseph."

He copied the design onto the second square of paper

and carefully fitted the sails to their masts by piercing the matches through them. The sails took on a billowing shape.

"They look good standing on the table," Joseph said. "Even I'm impressed. But they won't sail because we haven't fitted keels and rudders. Now where are those razor blades?"

"Here, Old Joseph." He examined them while deciding how he would attach them to the hulls. Then he snapped each one in half and fitted one half to the underside of each hull by pressing the sharp edge into the cork. The little boats would no longer stand upright, but lay on their sides on the tabletop.

"The keels will stop the vessels from making leeway," he explained.

From the remaining pieces of blade, he broke off four little squares and pressed them into the back of the hulls for rudders.

"Now, they'll sail in a straight line, instead of around in circles," he told us. "Take them and try them out."

We ran to his biggest pond and carefully launched our sailing ships.

"Wowee, look at 'em go," Maudie cried as the fleet edged its way across the water. "Our ships're really sailing. Good thinking, Old Joseph." We stood fascinated until the little craft fetched up on the opposite side and we ran to bring them back again.

Joseph came and stood with us. He held the ship with the Maltese Crosses on its sails and watched for a while.

"Children, your ships are only running before the wind. You can do better than that. Let me show you how to make them reach across the breeze."

With a finger, he angled the sails forty-five degrees across the decks of his Maltese Cross ship and launched it. I was astounded. Instead of running with the wind as ours had done, his vessel reached across the breeze. When it fetched up on the other side, he angled his sails the other way and put his ship back on the water.

Amazed, I stood and watched it sail on a reciprocal course.

"Well, I'll be blowed," Maudie cried. "You darn clever, Old Joseph."

She adjusted her skull and cross bones sails, so her pirate ship could do the same thing. She set it down in the water and gave chase to Joseph's vessel. Amos and I watched. Soon, we had all four sailing ships reaching backwards and forwards across his pond.

"You the best teacher we ever had," my sister enthused.

We spent our July holidays lazing next to Joseph's waterways, sailing our little ships. With Joseph's tuition, we re-enacted Trafalgar, the Spanish Armada, pirates of the Caribbean, the great grain races and even the American war of independence, when French vessels ambushed English men of war in the Chesapeake.

"These stories're really exciting, Old Joseph," Maudie declared. "Nobody teaches us history like this in stupid old school."

Chapter 39

The day dawned when the giraffe man caught up with Maudie and me. Flouting our father's restrictions, we were tramping the koppies far from home, when he came after us.

It would never have happened if it wasn't for the marshmallows. Uncle Ira came to visit one evening. He didn't come often, but Uncle Ira always gave Maudie a brown paper packet of sweets. He never brought anything for me or Frog. We had just finished our supper, when Uncle Ira arrived. He had a singular habit of jingling coins in his trouser pockets. To Maudie and me, they sounded silver and not copper.

"Uncle Ira's got plenty dough," Maudie whispered.

Uncle Ira smiled and gave her the packet of marshmallows.

"Sweetheart, I'm confiscating those for the time being," our father intercepted. "You've just eaten supper and your stomach's too full for sweets. Keep them for tomorrow."

"Humph," Maudie retorted. "S'gonna be a long night."

The next morning, Maudie and I were alone under the fig tree with her marshmallows. Sampson had gone to the shops and Frog was visiting a friend. My sister wanted to share them with Amos, because they were a lot of marshmallows, but he had been carted off by his mama to visit her sister.

"They real beauties, might's well just scoff them ourselves," I hinted.

"T'will be snazzy if we toast them," Maudie suggested, opening the packet and counting them.

"What? In our toaster, Sis?"

"No, silly. Where you been all my life? We hafta make a little fire under the fig tree. Then we can stick a fork in the marshmallows and hold 'em over the fire till they toasted."

I don't remember why we used our father's decorative pine cones to make our fire. Something to do with a debate whether pine cones made a good fire or not. Anyway, they did. The result was that as I sat poking the dying embers and feeling bilious, the realization hit me that we had better replace the cones before our father noticed his decorative ones had gone up in smoke.

"We'll hafta take my box-cart," Maudie declared, "and collect new ones from the pine grove far side of the koppie."

"S'pose you're right, Sis. There's no other way."

"My cart'll hold much more than we can carry by hand. One of us can ride there and maybe even ride back atop the cones."

I liked the idea.

"I'll fetch Hobo's harness. She can pull the box-cart," my sister concluded.

Hobo was a little surprised at being harnessed to her mistress's cart, but it didn't take her long to realize we were going on an expedition. Maudie tied the steering ropes to her dog's harness and climbed into her cart.

"Mush, mush!" I shouted. Hobo got such a start, she charged out of the yard and down the driveway, towing Maudie in the box-cart. I raced behind.

To stop from running her dog down when they reached the gate, my sister dragged her feet on the ground and hauled on the brake. The brake was a wooden lever nailed to the side of the cart. When you applied it, the lower end dragged on the road. If you wanted to stop any quicker, you used your feet as well.

Moses had just let himself out of Trixie's front gate and was trudging up the hill toward the koppie. I kept us waiting at the bottom of our driveway, pretending I was having trouble with the latch.

"Whatsa matter Tadpole? You worrying about something?"

"Nothing much, Sis. Sick from those marshmallows. Got a strange feeling."

Hobo needed help in hauling our box-cart up Good Hope Street with Maudie sitting in it. I pushed and we made it to the top and turned into Rockey Street running below the koppie's ridge. I scanned the traffic below in Roberts Avenue. A tram made heavy work grinding its way up the hill. Another barrelled downhill hell for leather, yawing left and right, the motorman clanging his bell continuously.

To reach the pine grove, we left Rockey Street and branched onto a two-wheel track that led us beneath the old water tower.

"Getting rough here. Steep also. Gonna hafta help Hobo with the cart."

"Yah Sis. I'm giving her a hand by pushing at the back."

Under the water tower, we stopped to rest. We left the track and made our way along a footpath over the crest of the ridge, down toward the Bezuidenhout Valley face of the koppie.

This side was deserted. There were no houses up here and those in Rockey Street were out of sight over the southern slope of the ridge. The pine grove lay a quarter mile further on.

"I reckon we can let Hobo run free," Maudie suggested, untying the steering ropes. She hauled the box-cart herself, following her dog who raced ahead, chasing flying insects and sniffing out geckos.

When we reached the grove, Maudie whooped. "Wowee. Lookit these cones lying round. Better pick the best ones for Abe."

She darted from cone to cone, checking each one and loading those that met her approval.

I felt sick.

"Sis, I got a migraine coming. I'll just sit under a tree."

She frowned at me, muttered something and continued collecting cones. I felt bilious and shivered. An omen crawled through my stomach.

"I reckon I got the ones I like," Maudie called from the other side of the grove.

I looked up and detected movement on the koppie below us. My sister noticed it too. She tiptoed through the pines for a better view. I didn't see that well, but she spotted a figure squatting under a bush.

"I think we better go," she murmured.

"Want me to help with the cones?"

She shook her head, packing the last few into her box-cart.

"Tadpole, we gotta go now."

I whistled up Hobo and we hauled the laden cart out of the grove. The path was narrow and rough and we made slow progress. I tramped in front with the steering rope, towing the cart. My sister pushed from behind, coaxing the wheels to stay on the path. Hobo followed at her mistress's heels, but once she realized we were headed home, she brushed past and galloped ahead.

As I struggled with the cart, I heard my sister's voice trying to attract my attention. I glanced back but she urged me to keep going.

"We being followed," she warned, pushing faster. The rope became slack in my hands.

I increased my pace but it became hard going on the rough terrain. The box-cart bounced over stones and Maudie had to grab at her cones to stop them spilling out.

"Who's following us?"

"Back there. That man under the bush. Soon's we left the pine grove, he came after us. Must have heard you whistle for Hobo."

I glanced down the koppie. An African man

scrambled through the pine grove. He worked his way straight up the koppie to intercept us below the water tower. I couldn't see his face because he was distant and the brim of his hat low. He loped like a giraffe. I wanted to retch and my vision wavered.

"He'll cut us off, Maudie. We hafta turn round and go down instead."

"What about Hobo?"

"Hobo's okay. She'll come looking for us."

I dragged the cart around and trundled it back down the path, toward Bezuidenhout Valley.

"Pray he don't see what we doing before he gets to the water tower. Give us a bit more lead."

"Yah, my cart's real heavy with the cones."

Hobo came hurtling down the path, kicking up dust and sending stones flying. We ran with Maudie's box-cart now, in spite of our cargo of cones. Hobo's stump of a tail wagged furiously when she caught up. She darted past and raced ahead until she came to a fork in the path.

"Can't stay on the koppies, Tadpole. Gotta get down to Bez Valley, fast," Maudie called.

Hobo was off like a hare. We fled further and further from home. Above, our pursuer reached the water tower and looked around. He was too far away to see his face and my eyesight blurred with migraine. It took him seconds to realize we had doubled back and he started after us again. The path angled around the side of the koppie and I lost sight of him. I couldn't tell how fast he was gaining.

Hobo darted onto a granite outcrop, lost her footing and slid over the edge. I heard her whimper as she disappeared. Then a howl of agony as she plunged into a rock cleft, jammed tight, her legs hanging free. I couldn't see over the edge where she had fallen and her howls of distress didn't cease.

"Sis, we gotta leave her and get off the koppie fast." I was all for abandoning my sister's dog and racing to the safety of Bezuidenhout Valley where there were people and motorcars and houses.

"Nah, Tadpole, never. We hafta rescue her. I not gonna leave her here."

She clambered down the rock and came out under the ledge. I slid off the path, dragging her cart after me. Pine cones spilled out and I packed them back. We found Hobo wedged in a cleft. She was pinned by her shoulders and buttocks. Her legs hung loosely and she wouldn't stop howling. I tried pulling her free but she wailed even louder.

"Just lie with her, Tadpole. The giraffe man's coming. Pat her and whisper to her. We gotta be quiet's a mouse."

A crunch of footsteps on the path above approached. We lay under the outcrop. Above us, stones flew. The footsteps passed and receded up toward the ridge.

"He's gone up the wrong path," Maudie whispered. I didn't move.

"We hafta get off the koppie, Sis."

"We aren't leaving Hobo here."

"But we're cut off from the water tower. Can't go home."

"Be quiet and lie still. Pat Hobo so she don't start yelping again."

We lay like that, under the granite outcrop for perhaps twenty minutes. I squirmed across the rock to see what was happening above. Our pursuer slowed and I watched his back. He tramped up the ridge, searching. Then he abruptly turned and started down again. I pulled back and held up a silencing finger. Hobo licked my sister's face.

We lay in silence. Above us, our pursuer scouted the path, puzzled over what had happened to us. When I thought he was out of earshot, I edged out. He took a position at the top of the path and sat like a sentinel looking over our position into the valley below.

"Sis, if we're real quiet about it, we can start freeing

Hobo."

The migraine hovering over me would soon send quivering mirages into my eyes.

"What's he doing now?"

"Don't think he can hear us, Maudie. Too far away. Only thing, he's blocking our way home. Gonna see us for sure if we move outta here."

I pulled and squeezed and prised until Hobo whimpered in distress. She was wedged solidly. Maudie lay with her, whispering encouragement, but she also sobbed. I heaved with all my strength but couldn't budge her dog. I stopped to rest.

"S'only one way, Sis," I whispered. "I hafta jerk her hard's I can, harder than when she fell in. Otherwise she's stuck for good. She gonna croak here."

"Hang on, Tadpole, she'll yelp like crazy. The giraffe man will hear."

I took my shirt off, wrapped it around her dog's muzzle and knotted it. Hobo struggled. Maudie looked doubtful. I fingered the harness, which I knew was going to cut into her ribs.

"S'no other way, Sis."

Maudie wiped her eyes and prepared to stop Hobo slipping back into the cleft. I straddled her dog, bent down and gripped her harness in both hands. I breathed in and counted to three. Then I jerked upwards as hard as I could. Inside the gag, Hobo screamed.

"I gotta try harder, Sis."

Hobo wailed the moment I grasped her harness. Maudie whispered assurances. I gripped the straps, braced my legs and wrenched with all my strength. Hobo howled. The harness cut into her body. I didn't let go. I thrust my legs, straining my back. Maudie threw herself over her dog's head. Hobo struggled desperately. I heaved. Again and again I jerked the harness.

"S'nough, s'nough. You killing her," Maudie whispered.

With one last gut-wrenching effort, I jerked. Hobo pulled free.

I collapsed on the rock.

"You free, you free my angel, you free," my sister murmured, hugging her.

She unfastened the harness. Hobo lay bruised and bleeding. She smarted from her ordeal. Maudie unwound my shirt, to be rewarded with frenzied tongue kisses.

"We aren't out of it yet, Sis. Can't go back to Good Hope Street. Gonna have to get down the koppie to Bez Valley. It's miles and miles out of our way."

The first migraine spots flickered fire across my eyes. I cursed myself for gorging on Uncle Ira's marshmallows.

"I'm going blind, Sis... migraine. Can't carry on. You're on your own."

"Uh-uh. Not leaving you here. You coming with me. There's a concrete thoroughfare not far. Goes down to Bez Valley. Zillions of stairs, if we can only get to 'em in time. Darn long way to the bottom. Maybe we can do it."

"You hafta guide me, Sis. Can't see no more. What about the giraffe man?"

"I reckon we can make the stairs before him. But then we hafta get down real fast."

She jammed the pine cones into her cart and strapped them with Hobo's harness. We broke cover, my sister leading the way, pulling my hand and me hauling her laden box-cart.

My vision blurred. The terrain was rough. The wheels of her cart bounced over the stones. I slithered on loose scree, slipped and fell, but Maudie yanked me up and ran again. The further we careered, the worse my vision deteriorated.

"Keep going," Maudie insisted.

"How we doing?"

"He's coming."

"Where?"

"Where Hobo got stuck."

I couldn't see anymore and tripped over my feet.

"Leave me, Sis. I'm holding you back. You and Hobo get away."

"Keep running, Tadpole. I'm telling you. Keep running." She tugged me hard.

I stumbled onto the concrete thoroughfare and dropped her cart's steering rope. A juddering mirage blinded me.

"You're on your own, Sis. Take Hobo and zip down like mad. I'm not gonna make it down the stairs cos I can't see."

Maudie messed with her cart, dragging it around. I heard the giraffe man pounding down the stairs.

"What's going on, Maudie?" I yelled at her. "I told you to get out of here."

She grabbed my hand and pulled me down. I tripped over her cart and found myself sitting on the cones.

"Put your feet up," she commanded. "There's a bicycle ramp alongside the stairs."

I didn't understand.

"What you doing, Maudie? Why don't you go? I told you to run. Now get out of here."

"Quick, put your feet up and hold on."

I felt her box-cart bend under her weight as she climbed on behind me.

"We going down the bicycle ramp," she declared.

"Never! We'll never get out alive, Sis. You're crazy."

I'd seen these bicycle ramps. They were precipitous and you could neither ride up nor down them. They bypassed the stairs, intended for a bicycle to be wheeled.

"No, Maudie. Don't be stupid. You're mad. S'not possible."

She gripped the steering rope in her hands and kicked us forwards with her bare feet. We began rolling.

I felt the front wheels fall away and we took off like

a rocket. I saw nothing. I didn't know how my sister could steer at such speed. Perhaps her system of safely navigating dodgem cars at the Rand Show, taught her a thing or two. We hit the bottom of the first ramp so hard, I thought her cart would snap in half. But we kept rolling down the concrete path toward the next ramp.

Again, I felt the front wheels drop away. I heard Hobo scudding down the stairs trying to catch up. The plunge was sickening. The box-cart careered off the side of the concrete stairs but that didn't slow our descent.

Maudie hung on grimly. She crouched over my shoulders, gripping my body with her knees. My head was pushed down to my chest but I dared not raise it in case I upset her balance. This ramp was longer. We seemed to be accelerating all the time. Even for fun, I would never have brought her cart down here. It was suicide.

We hit the footpath very fast. I didn't want to see how fast we were going. The axles must have been red hot. At this speed the brake was useless. I left it dangling loosely. Behind us, I could hear Hobo tumbling down the stairs.

We plummeted down five ramps. The last ejected us into a cul-de-sac at the top of a side street and we ramped onto the tarmac swaying wildly. Broadway Avenue, crowded with cars, lay below. I heard the rumble of traffic. How my sister would stop her box-cart before we reached the intersection, I had no idea.

"Brake, Tadpole, brake," she yelled. "We gonna crash."

I grabbed the wooden lever with both hands and heaved. Pieces flew off where it dragged on the tarmac and I smelt burning wood. Traffic growled in the avenue below.

"Harder!" Maudie screamed. "We gonna go under the cars."

We hurtled down the hill too fast to drag our feet. Maudie threw her weight to the left, forcing me with her. She began swinging her box-cart in an arc. I leaned with her. The pram wheels squealed on the tar. We skidded. The tyres pulled off and we rattled on the rims. We shot through the gutter into someone's driveway and rolled upside down under a garden hedge.

"Well, that was that," Maudie giggled, picking herself up.

I sprawled with pine cones spilled on top of me. Hobo came bounding down the street. My blindness switched to devastating migraine. My skull burned.

"S'okay, I'll give you a hand," Maudie soothed, helping me crawl over the roots of a tree to the edge of the pavement. I lay with my head in the gutter, my hands clutching my temples. Maudie righted her capsized box-cart and wheeled it on its rims, out of the driveway. She searched for the tyres that had peeled off and retrieved pine cones from every which place. She came and sat with me and I felt Hobo nuzzling between us.

"What's happening with the giraffe man, Sis?"

She scampered into the middle of the street and sighted up the koppie.

"Don't see him. Musta made himself invisible. Gotta be up there someplace. But just before we started rolling, he was damn close. Got a proper look at him."

"Sorry, Sis, I couldn't see. Total whiteout. The marshmallows... I'm gonna be sick."

The biliousness in my stomach overcame the hammering in my head. I pulled away from my sister and retched into the gutter until I was turned inside out. I wiped my lips on my arm. My head pulsated and my face burned.

Maudie stroked my back. Then she started giggling.

"What's so funny?" I asked.

"You didn't see how fast we were going."

"Oh yah Sis, I could feel the way we bounced down the ramps onto the footpath. But you were good, Maudie. You were darned good. I dunno how you steered down those ramps. We could've capsized on the koppie. You handled the box-cart like a pro."

"I learned on the dodgem cars at the Rand Show."

I stared at her. She stuck her tongue at me, but she did it to hide her smile. I had made her happy and it reminded me of the time she first coloured the days of the week to be pinned to the fig tree.

"I just had to do it, Tadpole. What'd Old Joseph tell us about not giving in?"

"You took him serious like?"

"Couldn't leave you up there."

"You're the best, Maudie."

She helped me fit the tyres onto the rims. I repacked her box-cart. The brake lever had disintegrated. Hobo wouldn't follow, but insisted her mistress put her harness on her so she could pull the cart. We turned the corner into Broadway Avenue and started our trek along the pavement.

We had three miles to traipse home, along Broadway to Rhodes Park and then all the way up Roberts Avenue.

"Can always take a short cut over the hill, Sis."

She shook her head.

"Uh-uh. S'not worth it. Gotta stay on the pavement with people and delivery men and bicycles and horse 'n carts and cars going by."

"At least we got Daddy's pine cones."

"But the koppies're no longer safe."

"And I never got a look at your giraffe man's face, Sis."

"Yah, Tadpole. I reckon I still the only one who knows what he looks like."

Chapter 40

Before those July holidays ended, my sister and I took our last tepid bucket-baths ever. A cold front closed with Cape Town, bringing gales and rain to the coast and snow to the mountains. The Free State and southern Transvaal plunged to sub-zero temperatures. Our days were not much better than our frost-blighted nights. Each morning, Hobo found her water-dish frozen and trotted off to pester her mistress.

The fig tree offered no refuge against biting winds. Maudie and I took to playing on the side veranda, getting morning sun at one end and afternoon sun at the other. The Saturday before Sampson returned from sub-tropical Zululand, our father lit the living room fire early, the coal smouldering over a cheerless hearth.

At four o'clock in the afternoon, Maudie and I fixed ourselves bread and peanut butter in the pantry. I inspected the Queen Mary, which was choked with ash and dead since the previous evening. I felt the feeder tank.

"S'like ice, Sis. Bathing in the bucket's gonna be torture."

My sister pulled a face.

"We gonna perish from the friz. We'll hafta make our own fire."

"Like how, Maudie?"

"Scoop the old ash out and clean the inside of the Queen Mary proper. Start a brand new fire, Tadpole."

"Won't work, Sis. Smokes for ages. Takes a zillion years to get going. Water'll only be hot at midnight."

"That's cos old Semp-Sonne kills it with coal. I wanna clean the Queen Mary proper and start it going with plenty wood."

"Sampson's younger than Daddy, Sis."

She rolled her eyes at me and started work. I hitched myself onto the kitchen table to watch. She scraped out a bucket of old ash that had been there for years and lugged it to the dustbin in the yard. When she hurried back, she poked into nooks in the firebox and hooked out chunks of slag. Next, she cleaned the air vents with her fingers. My eyes were opened by my sister's enterprise. By the time she finished, she had cleared out three times more ash than ole Semp-Sonne ever had.

Our father came into the kitchen. "What's going on here?" he grinned.

"Gonna have hot baths tonight, Abe."

"Well, you certainly look like you're doing a good job, my girl."

She glanced at me and chuckled.

"Sis, I wanna help now."

"Uh yah. Bring lotsa kindling. No big hunks, hey. Small sticks, to burn real fast. Gonna pack the Queen Mary full."

I glanced at her in amazement. She crumpled newspaper and laid it in the stove. Down at the coal shed, I selected kindling as instructed. I took the axe to the fagots and split them in two. Then in two again. Then I pared them. I think my sister wanted the stove to take off like a bonfire. She opened the air vents, packed the combustion almost to the top with kindling and added a layer of coal.

"Double dare you to light this," she challenged, offering me the box of matches. "Probably burn the house down."

I glanced at her in alarm but she beamed as broadly as Mr Sunshine. I struck the match and held it to the paper.

Her kindling blazed. The Queen Mary sang. I glanced at my sister. She grinned at me.

"Never seen the combustion go like this, Sis."

We stood holding our hands to the heat. After three minutes, we were forced to back away. Our father came to see what we were doing and stood staring with his mouth open.

"Don't set fire to the house now, you two," he teased, striding to the stove to check for himself.

My sister's layer of coal glowed. She packed another. The stove roared. I helped her throw on a third layer. When that blazed crimson, she added another and kept increasing coal until the combustion was packed. We could hardly get near the stove. Babs and Frog came through to check what my sister and I were up to. The water in the tank gurgled. The pipes hummed. The steel chimney pipe glowed.

Frog ran to our father, "Stop them, Father. They are going to burn the house."

We didn't.

The family abandoned the meagre warmth of the living room fire and ensconced itself in the kitchen. No one could sit near the Queen Mary. Maudie giggled. We ate supper in the kitchen. Halfway through our meal, boiling water shot up the overflow pipe onto the roof and drained into the gutter pipes. My sister dashed to the bathroom, rammed the plug into the drain and opened the tap. Steam billowed out along with the piping hot water she had engineered.

"Well, I'll be darned," our father remarked. "Never seen the Queen Mary go like this. Maudie, would you come here a mo?"

He lifted his daughter to his chest, carried her to the kitchen sink and wet his fingers under the cold tap.

"I hereby re-christen this stove, The Queen Maudie, in honour of a very special girl," he declared, flicking water onto the stove. It sizzled in steam.

My sister giggled.

After supper, we filled the tub and everyone had hot baths. From that day on, my sister and I cleaned, packed and lit the Queen Maudie every Saturday and Sunday afternoon.

Shortly afterwards, I noticed a four-inch news item in the body of The Star. The report concerned two Cape Town men and was a reprint from a sister newspaper, The Cape Argus. What drew my attention was that I'd seen a library book with the same names printed in the headline.

"Jekyll & Hyde Sought."

I didn't know who these two men were, but Cape police had been seeking them for two years in connection with crimes they'd committed in Cape Town. The trail had gone cold and the Cape police were supplying information to Johannesburg detectives, asking for cooperation. I don't think our father read anything that happened in Cape Town. It was a thousand miles away, two days by steam train.

"What's your giraffe man look like, Sis?"

"Hmmm, African. But I don't think South African. Maybe Nyasaland... you know, somewhere up north."

Nyasaland was halfway up the continent and one of the poorest countries in Africa. South Africa accommodated two million illegal immigrants from the rest of Africa, so what my sister suggested was probably correct.

"Reckon he looks like a sorcerer, Sis? Remember, I never seen him."

"He don't look as bad's some bottle 'n bag men I seen."

"What about these two guys the cops are looking for?"

"You mean Mister Hyde and Mister Jekyll?"

"Yah,"

"English names. They gotta be European."

"Yah, maybe."

Spring commenced officially on September first when the municipality opened Rhodes Park swimming bath. Our father wouldn't let us swim until the first rains fell, because he believed rain washed polio away. That year an eleven-year-old girl in our street died of polio. It was the worst thing my sister and I had ever heard of and we fell into depression.

We sailed our cork ships on Joseph's lakes. We cleaned *The Vale of Belvoir* and paddled it on the river at Gillooly's Farm and Rhodes Park Lake. We kept away from the scary side.

Louis earned pocket money at the agricultural show and bought new parts for his bicycle. Graham spent his money on himself. The twins were about to turn thirteen and my sister was about to be abducted.

In September she turned eight, unwrapped some presents she liked and one she didn't. Mrs Probert had sewed her a bright yellow play dress in the hope that my sister would discard her corduroys. She didn't.

My birthday arrived in October. I turned ten.

"Double digits, now," our father teased me. "A stick and a ball."

After that, whenever anybody asked me how old I was, Maudie always answered, "A stick and a ball," leaving them scratching their heads.

Selina couldn't tell Amos exactly how old he was. As he was tired of being eight, Maudie made his birthday the day after mine. The three of us gorged ourselves on bread and peanut butter. Amos was much happier being nine than eight.

I still saw Mrs Probert with her toes sticking through her shoes. She supervised her husband in her garden. She could only garden in an upright position and not many flowers are five-foot-six inches tall. However, not since her daughter arrived at church in a breakdown lorry did she ever utter another word to Babs.

When warm weather came around, Mr Sunshine went back to cruising the suburbs in his yellow and red rickshaw. Every month, he collected money from Sampson and Moses. They paged through his catalogue and ordered more goods. Selina maintained he was crooked and turned her back on him.

On Mondays Lizzie came to do the washing and on Tuesdays her daughter Mary, ironed. Mary never asked if there were any more catfish to take home. And after she heard about Amos bringing his dead python to show his mama, she gave him a wide berth and avoided making eye contact. Amos countered by brushing against her whenever possible and looking up when they touched.

Then one evening in October when the weather began to warm, a constable in blue uniform and helmet, rang our front door bell. My sister and I raced to see who it was and found ourselves staring up into his face. I wondered what trouble we were in now.

"I would like to speak to Babs Thomas," he told us.

"I'll call Abe," Maudie blurted.

He came to the door and invited the constable in.

"No," the policeman answered, "I haven't the time. Babs Thomas does live here? This is the correct address? I have to serve her with a summons."

"Oh dear," our father answered. "Yes, you've come to the right address, but she often sleeps over in one of the hangars at Rand Airfield where she's rebuilding her biplane." He gave the constable Babs' work address at the garage. Our father questioned him what it was about, but his curiosity was met with closed lips.

After the constable went away, our father said, "You two are to keep your mouths shut. I don't want any neighbourhood gossip. You know what Missus Probert's like,"

"Yah, Abe," Maudie drawled. "We promise. Swear to God and hope to die."

Chapter 41

Maudie and I knew that the stormwater gulley that starts at Ellis Park, traverses the bottom of Bezuidenhout Valley and eventually becomes the Limpopo River was a dangerous place to play. More than one Johannesburg child had drowned there. And after Johan Rabie's remains were discovered in the drain, our father warned us to stay away. But that is where Amos, Maudie and I were when the first of the season's storms hit the city.

That it happened on a Saturday morning was strange because thunderstorms generally break in the afternoon. Amos had a wild notion about damming the gulley, building a weir out of rocks, stealing cement and making it waterproof. That way, he argued, we would have another stretch of water where we could paddle The Vale of Belvoir. At the time, it sounded fantastic. We each grabbed an orange from Sampson's pantry and sauntered down the pavement, sucking them.

"It's gonna be great," Amos said, spitting a pip into the gutter. "We just need a coupla rocks to build the dam inside the drain, say six foot high. That leaves four or five feet for stormwater to spill over the top. When the flood's gone, our dam'll be full."

"Dunno why we didn't think of it before," I responded.

"Lots of rocks all over the place. Right next to the drain. All we gotta do's pack 'em in place." Amos licked the orange juice running down his face.

"Gotta cement 'em pretty tight."

"Your old man's got half a bag standing in your garage. Just have to scratch around a bit."

We trotted down a Bezuidenhout Valley back street.

Side streets here came to dead ends and backyards looked over the culvert. We climbed through a safety fence into a no-man's land of weeds, overgrown kikuyu grass, broken glass, rusting tin cans and broken rock.

"Sure is big," Maudie observed.

"Ten foot deep and about twenty foot across, Sis. Let's go down."

Had we noticed the approaching storm clouds, we would have had second thoughts. An old willow branch rested against the side. We eased our bodies over the edge and let ourselves down until our toes touched the branch. Then we clambered down the bough into the bottom of the drain.

"This is where we gonna build our dam," Amos said. "Can't make it too far away, cos we gotta fetch the rocks."

We traipsed along the drain to inspect the site. "Seems good enough to me," I approved.

Maudie glanced up at the brim above our heads. "Gonna have to work like convicts."

"Yah, but we'll get a mile of water to paddle on. Can charge other people to canoe on our dam also. Boy, this is gonna be the best thing we ever done."

He dribbled a stone with his feet. "Let's see how far the dammed water's gonna reach."

"Yah, sure."

We sighted up the drain where it curved to the left and estimated the water would be four feet deep there. We strolled up the middle, leaping over debris and kicking at weeds growing through the concrete. At the bend we took a sighting on the next curve, putting the depth up there at about two feet. That was more than enough to float our canoe. Amos dribbled an empty baked beans tin up the gulley.

The third bend was three quarters of a mile upstream from our proposed dam.

"Look, an ess-bend up there, lets go'n see what's on the other side," I suggested.

A tongue of water rushed toward us.

"Just factory waste water," I said.

We skipped to one side and continued up the drain with the water racing down the middle. A minute later, the stream doubled in size.

"It's raining uptown," Maudie warned. "Just felt a fleck on my arm. Must be coming this way."

I followed her gaze at the heavens. The sky was half blotted out.

"Been pouring over the city for half an hour. Gotta get oughta here," she urged.

"No place to climb out, Sis."

Another surge caught us. No longer down the middle but spread across the culvert.

"Run, you two," I urged, grabbing my sister and shoving her ahead of me. "No way out. We gotta get back to the willow branch."

We had over a mile to cover. We dashed through the ess-bend. The drain stretched into infinity and vanished around a curve. Water swirled past our feet. Maudie held me back, but I slowed my pace to stop her panicking. Rain overtook us.

"Don't wait, Amos," I yelled. "We'll catch up."

He widened the gap and disappeared around a bend. Stormwater rose up Maudie's shins, slowing her down and I thrust at her from behind.

When we rounded the next bend, Amos was close to the willow branch. A wave broke behind my sister and me as a new surge overtook us. Maudie was up to her thighs.

I saw Amos reach the branch half-submerged in the tugging water. He struggled to climb onto it and as he did so, the bough toppled over and was swept away. Maudie tripped and went down. In a heartbeat, the stormwater began carrying her off. Her feet were all I could see in the broken water. I dived into the melee, making a grab for her ankles and gripping hard. The stormwater carried me too, dragging my feet over the bottom. With one arm around my sister, I crabbed to the side of the gulley, skidding on my feet and slowing our slide down the drain.

Ahead, Amos was stranded. The water was up to his waist. Clutching Maudie, I clawed at the wall. We didn't talk. The flood tugged at us mercilessly. When it reached our chests, we would be washed away. First Maudie, then Amos, then me.

"We not gonna get outta here," Amos bawled.

The rain poured down.

My ears caught a new sound, the muffled rumble of a Harley Davidson. The motor revved up. Joseph didn't race his engine like that. But then his bike appeared on the lip of the drain above us. Joseph leapt off.

"Oh Jeez," he cried.

He flung himself down on the brim and reached with his arms. Hanging onto my sister, I stretched an arm toward him. Amos did the same. We didn't close the gap by a long chalk.

"Hang on," Joseph called. "I'll get my pliers out of the toolbox."

He disappeared and I spread my feet against the rushing water. It had risen to Maudie's chest and above my waist. She climbed onto my back piggy-back style. Amos struggled to maintain his footing. There was no sign of Joseph.

"Just wiring the fence to the bike," he called a minute later.

The next thing, a section of diamond-mesh fence slid down the side of the drain.

"Hang onto that," Joseph called. "A makeshift scramble-net. Got it anchored to the Harley. Send Maudie up first."

"Go, Sis."

My sister peeled herself off my back and scrambled up the mesh. Joseph pulled her to safety.

"You next, Amos."

Our Zulu playmate needed no second bidding. He

clambered up the wire net. Then it was my turn. We huddled with Joseph well back from the edge and gazed at our recent prison. Amos spat into the weeds. It was raining harder than ever now, but we didn't care. We stood with Joseph, getting our breath back and watched the white water flash by. It climbed halfway up the drain and roared like an express train. We were cold and shivering. The water rose until it came within two feet of the brim.

Joseph glanced at us and we glanced at him.

"You're lucky," he murmured.

When I looked behind us, I saw where he had used his pliers to cut twenty feet out of the safety fence closing off no-man's land.

"We gotta thank you, Old Joseph," Maudie replied. "I was sure we were gonners."

Joseph nodded. "It was close. Come, Maudie, I'll take you children home on the bike."

"How'd you know we were in the stormwater drain?"

He chuckled but didn't answer.

"You been stalking us, Old Joseph?"

Chapter 42

The last Saturday of October found the three of us lounging dejectedly in the fig tree, swinging our legs and bemoaning the injustice headed our way.

"S'not fair," Maudie wailed, plucking an unripe fig and launching it at Hobo asleep in the shade below. She missed.

Amos and I had assumed we weren't allowed to take such liberties with her dog. Perhaps we were. She'd never said we couldn't throw figs at Hobo, but we had always chosen to take out our frustrations on the wall above the compost heap. That way, we didn't have to go around afterwards picking up rotting fruit from the yard.

"Oughta be a law against it," Amos bemoaned. "Only fun we get the whole year and they go'n cancel it."

"Yah, their nose in a rat trap..." my sister grumbled, "you know... squashed flat."

"Still a week left, Sis. Maybe they gonna change their minds and have it after all."

She aimed another fig at Hobo, hitting her in the stomach. The dog grunted in its sleep.

"Uh-uh, they not. Municipality's decision's final. Saw it in The Star."

We were deploring the fact that there was not going to be a Guy Fawkes display at Rhodes Park this year as there had been last year in 1947. I had assumed the exhibition would be held as usual. Then rumours started filtering through that the council would do away with it this year.

"Heck Tadpole, s'not right. Monday week's not gonna feel like proper Guy Fawkes if we can't watch fireworks."

I visualised my sister's *Monday* sign lettered in black.

"The whole year's wasted," Amos sighed.

We had just scoffed our lunch and were waiting for our cousins to come around from Kiewietjie. Year-end exam time approached and the twins were ordered to spend Saturday morning swotting up their work.

"Not even enough pocket money for a rocket," I muttered.

"Maybe we can get some crackers," Maudie moped. "I seen penny crackers quite big, and small ones, two-a-penny."

"Naw, s'not gonna be the same without rockets and Catherine wheels and Roman candles and things. Rockets cost a boodle. Sixpence or a shilling at least... two and six for a big one. And what about sparklers? We got no dough."

Hobo's ears pricked up the moment the driveway gate was unlatched. When she heard one of Graham's belches, she put her head down again. Louis rode his bicycle up the driveway and propped it against the fig tree. Graham skated into the garage, looking for a key to adjust his skates. Hobo's stub wagged a couple of times, showing them she was aware of their presence but too lazy to get up.

"What's the big discussion all about?" Graham wanted to know.

"The council's cheating us," Maudie moaned. "No fireworks this year."

"Yah, I heard, Maud. So I reckoned I can have my own display at Kiewietjie. All the boys hafta pool half-crown each. I oughta get about five quid to spend."

"Aw phooey, Graham, s'not fair. What about us? I gonna perish with no fireworks."

"No problem, Maud. If you wanta put two-and-six into my pool, don't see why you three shouldn't come along,"

"Yah, why don't you?" Louis asked.

"Not sure. Hafta ask our father," I wavered.

"Aw, c'mon Tadpole." Maudie chirped. "I'll speak to Abe if you worried he's gonna say no."

"What about Mister de Beer?" I questioned. "Didn't he moan about you shooting off fireworks at Kiewietjie?"

"Recited the riot act as usual. Said it was a Monday night and school next day. Wants everything over by eight-thirty. You guys coming or not?"

"Yah," Maudie sang. "Sure, Graham we gonna be there. I'll tell Abe and plead for the dough."

Amos started fidgeting. "I not allowed out at night, unless I with a big person. You know... this muti-murder thing."

Someone walked over my grave.

"Yah, Sampson said don't go out at night. The sorcerer makes himself invisible."

Maudie rolled her eyes at me.

"I'll beg Abe to fetch us in the Chev when the fireworks are over."

"S'pose so, Sis. But we can walk there by ourselves if it's before sunset."

And so it was arranged. My sister inveigled the money out of our father. With me, he would have started bargaining. Maudie told him what she wanted it for, inflated the figure and made a point that it included Amos who didn't stand a hope of getting anything from Selina. In the end, she made on the deal, for our father forked up three shillings.

"Yippee-yankee-doodle," she crowed, "After all our suffering, we done it. We gonna have Guy Fawkes after all."

I couldn't believe our luck when my sister showed me the money. From bemoaning the injustices of the world, I now began counting the days to Guy Fawkes. And those days got brighter. Black... pink... green... orange... red...

When Maudie's calendar reached gold, the police took Mr Sunshine in for questioning. It caused a stir in Kensington. Residents were shattered because his rickshaw was a common sight. It happened on Saturday morning, two days before Graham's proposed fireworks display. Returning from the shops, Selina noticed two plainclothes detectives apprehending Mr Sunshine at the corner of Good Hope Street and Roberts Avenue. Breathless, she hurried up the street to tell everybody.

We learnt about it because we heard her calling Sampson and Moses over the backyard fences and a three way conversation across our yard developed. She spoke Zulu and Amos translated for us.

"I've been telling you men for years. That shyster is no good."

"What happened?" Moses wanted to know.

"You men wouldn't listen to a woman's instincts. You had to keep looking at his cheap catalogues and buy his cheap blankets and things. You could have bought much better in town. But by dealing with him, you gave him reason to come back to our suburb every month."

"Has he been arrested?" Sampson asked.

"I, Selina, have never bought from him. Not a penny's worth. I didn't want bad types coming round here." She eyed Sampson and Moses disapprovingly.

"Just half-an-hour ago, I saw two plainclothes policemen take that tsotsi-no-good to the police station for questioning. Right here in Kensington. Not two blocks away. Now what do you think the police want with him?"

Sampson and Moses looked blank. Mr Sunshine had been with them only an hour earlier.

"Well, we'll find out sooner or later," Selina snorted. "He's been up to no good, I tell you. I got no time for him."

By Monday, I had forgotten about Mr Sunshine's arrest. We had another matter to contend with. The weather.

"It always starts raining on Guy Fawkes afternoon," Maudie sighed, dodging a drop of condensation from the back-veranda roof.

My sister was close to being right. I can remember few firework displays that weren't either washed out or held in sodden conditions.

"Didn't rain last year, Sis. I remember, cos that's when Old Joseph rescued the cobra."

"Yah, but it did the year before and it sure rained the year before that also."

"Last year won't help what Graham got planned tonight," Amos added gloomily. "This weather's gonna ruin everything." Amos should have returned to Sophiatown on Sunday evening, but he'd bullied his mama into letting him stay for the fireworks. In return she made him do extra homework.

Since early morning, a cool mist had settled over the suburbs. It drizzled all day. Water dripped from drainpipes and our backyard became a mud patch. When the chill breeze that brought the weather shook the fig tree, it made its own rain forest. Hobo retired to her box on the back veranda where she snuggled into her blankets.

Sampson summoned my sister and me for a snack supper and Amos hopped over the fence to see what Selina could scrounge for him. He returned wearing his school jersey pulled over his play clothes. Maudie and I were just finishing our bread and boiled egg.

"You children better wear your sandals," Sampson insisted. "And put jerseys on. It's cold for this time of the year."

We came into the kitchen to pass his inspection.

"Your father will fetch you at nine," he reminded us. "You are not to go on the streets after dark. Do you understand?"

As we let ourselves out through the driveway gate, I noticed Joseph fiddling with his waterway circulation pump. He glanced up and strolled to the fence. His leather thong hung from his neck, something dangling from it inside his shirt. Maudie and I still hadn't found out what that was yet.

"Where are you ragamuffins off to, this late in the afternoon and in such dreary weather?"

"Aw gee, Old Joseph, we aren't ragamuffins, Maudie retorted. "Graham and Louis got five quid for stacks of fireworks tonight."

Joseph raised his eyebrows.

"Five pounds, three bob," she grinned. "Tadpole, Amos and me put in the three bob."

"So that's why we going to their fireworks display," Amos giggled, "cos we paid our share."

A smile lit Joseph's face.

"Sounds interesting." He waved us away.

With the early evening coming on, it was nearly dusk when we turned out of McDonald street and skipped along the pavement to Kiewietjie. Street lights illuminated the fine, spitting mist in yellow arcs.

"It's gonna be one wet Guy Fawkes," Maudie said.

With less than two blocks to go, Mr de Beer's Morris Eight pulled alongside. "Want a lift?" he called opening the passenger door.

Maudie jumped in. I couldn't figure why he would give us a lift with only two blocks to go.

"No, Sis!" I hollered and yanked her out again.

"What's your problem, boy?" he growled.

He slammed the passenger door and roared off. I saw him turn into the hostel drive and I began to panic about him telephoning our father about my rudeness.

"Why couldn't I go with him?" Maudie complained.

I shrugged.

We let ourselves in through the front gate, a tall wrought iron affair. I sauntered up the overgrown path, dodging pools of water. The boys amused themselves with horseplay on the ground floor veranda. The drizzle transformed it into a skating rink and they competed for who could slide the furthest along its slippery surface. To the delight and cheers of the onlookers, most wound up on their buttocks.

"Jeez, the Bear arrived in a stinking mood," Louis commented. "Can't understand it."

I shuddered. The housemaster would get me into trouble with our father, yet.

"Ah forget it, Tadpole. S'not the end of the world," Graham grinned.

Mr de Beer closeted himself in his upstairs study. I noticed a light in his suite. He'd lit a fire in the grate and a wisp of smoke curled from a chimney pot.

In the lobby, Graham sorted fireworks. He spread boxes of them on a table and my eyes widened at the assortment. When I came in, he started an argument with Louis over who was going to fire off what.

Amos put his hands on the table and gawked.

"Is this what five pound's fireworks looks like? Never seen so much in my life." He reached over to handle an enormous rocket.

"Hey, don't touch that," Graham snapped. "Special star-bursting super-skyrocket. Cost a fortune. Could only afford three. They five shillings each. S'what a whole box of these ordinary firecrackers go for."

"Five bob? What they do for that sorta dough? Fly to the moon and back?"

"Gimme that," Graham hissed, snatching the rocket away. "These three rockets, dear boy, are the most powerful that moolah can buy. They reach twice the altitude of any other rocket invented. At the top, they burst like exploding stars. Not once, but three times, in different colours. Then, just when you reckon they burnt out, they explode with the biggest big-bang you ever heard. You gonna wet your pants."

"They fantastic," Louis chipped in. "I seen one before."

I watched while the twins sorted the fireworks.

"Put the sparklers together, Bro," Graham directed. "But separate small from big. We betta light the small ones first and keep the big ones last."

"Whatta I do with the crackers here?"

Graham glanced up from some golden showers he clutched in his hand.

"The same chum. Keep the big-bangs together and separate the ordinary crackers in one pile. You also got some jumping-jacks and a machine-gun there. Make a separate pile. I got a few here you can add to 'em."

Outside on the veranda, I heard a huzza of cheers as a new skating record was established. Graham sauntered out the front door to see where the day's record stood. He came back chortling.

"Benson fell flat on his arse. He done the best slide so far. But not's good's my record."

Louis pulled some flare type fireworks out of a box.

"Ah... was waiting for 'em to make an appearance," Graham said. "Put 'em with the Roman candles and Chinese lanterns."

There remained some Catherine wheels and a thing called a Zigzag because of the crazy antics it performed when ignited. The twins stashed them together and reviewed their assortment.

"Not bad for five pounds," Louis admitted. "Should have a two hour show with this lot."

Graham glanced out the window.

"Yah right, Bro, we oughta get going. S'almost dark and we hafta be finished by eight-thirty, maybe nine if we stretch it. Bear's not gonna notice."

"What about asking him if he wants to watch?"

"Yah, good idea."

While Graham took a Roman candle and an assortment of crackers onto the veranda, Louis charged upstairs. The boys arranged themselves on the parapet and stairs to watch. Graham selected a dry spot on the garden path for his display. The candle emitted a brilliant mauve light that lit up the front of the hostel. Everybody's face turned the most incredible colour.

Louis came down the stairs.

"Damn it, Graham. I asked him, but he's in a funny mood. Wouldn't even look at me. Just grunted."

"Leave the old sod then. Probably run out of his medicine and the pharmacy's already shut. Maybe I'll try later." He lit a golden shower and sprang out of the way.

Amos, Maudie and I found a place at the foot of the veranda stairs. Graham maintained a fast pace. There was always something glowing brightly, giving off a shower of sparks, jumping around crazily, or going off with a bang. Louis ran to and fro from the lobby, bringing his brother items he needed for the performance. Eleven or twelve strangers leant over the garden fence.

Graham launched one of his smaller rockets. Maudie giggled, rocking on her heels as it hissed away into the night.

"What's your case?" I retorted, digging her in the ribs.

"Don't you remember Hobo at Rhodes Park last year? She chased the rockets, but couldn't figure where they went."

"What about Daddy trying to catch her and everybody laughing at him?"

"Your father sure didn't think it was funny," Amos said.

"We shoulda brought Hobo tonight," Maudie grinned.

Graham launched three small rockets one after the other. Then he fetched a wooden frame he'd nailed together from a tomato box. He mounted Catherine wheels on the frame and lit them. His show continued without stop. At seven o'clock it was in full swing. There were more onlookers and strangers hanging over the garden fence now. They clapped and laughed and Graham rewarded them with comical bows.

He turned to the boys sitting on the veranda parapet.

"I hope you lads appreciate my show so far," he announced. "I still got a coupla boxes left, but I reckon its time to launch one of my special star-bursting super-skyrockets."

He pranced up the veranda stairs into the lobby.

"Lemme see if I can persuade The Bear to come down

and watch. I mean this is really special. S'not every day we spend a whole five bob on a rocket."

Two minutes later, he was back.

"Sod him. The bastard's acting up real bad just like a goddamn bear with a sore head. Sits huddled in his study with his fire going in the grate, gulping wine and reading a book. Something strange come over him. Never seen him like this. Wouldn't lookit me. Just like a animal. Growled something about not interested in my immature nonsense. Told me to push off. Swore at me also."

"Ah forget it," Louis commiserated. "We never gonna come right with him. Let's get our next rocket up, up and away, boys."

Graham grabbed the skyrocket from his brother and ran down the steps with it. He slid it into the launch pipe and stood back.

"Now watch, everyone," he called. "Let no one breathe or look away for a second. You about to witness the eighth wonder of the modern world... a triple-stage, multi-colour, star-bursting, super-skyrocket, all the way from Hong Kong."

"Let her go, Graham," someone cried.

He bowed, bent down and lit the wick. I held my breath, eyes fixed on the touch paper. Graham stood back. The propellant began hissing like a steam train. Hobo should have been there. The sibilance increased sharply and the rocket launched itself.

"Hey, that's real pretty now," Maudie sighed. "Specially cos it cost so much."

The super-skyrocket trailed a flaming tail and reached double the height of Graham's previous missiles. The flame burnt out and the overcast turned black. The pavement onlookers fell silent. Even I was startled by the brilliant burst of light that showered down like emeralds. Then another, this time copper and gold. I heard oohs and aahs of appreciation. The third starburst was a fire-glow of crimson rain. As the last of these vanished in the night, the rocket exploded with a thunderclap that set a baby on its mama's back, crying. The boys on the veranda began laughing and cheering and calling for more.

Graham grinned and beckoned the three of us to follow him up the stairs. Louis chased after us.

"I got an idea," Graham confided. "We can have a little fun with The Bear. But we hafta be quick. He gotta think we all down here letting off fireworks."

"You gonna get us in trouble," Maudie objected.

"Naw, Maud, it's nothing," Graham grinned. "You just stand on the balcony upstairs where you can see his French window. All you gotta do is signal what's going on inside."

"What you up to now?" Louis frowned.

"Not me. Us. You and me together, Bro."

He clapped his arm around his brother's shoulders. "I'm gonna get Benson to carry on with the fireworks so The Bear don't suspect anything."

Louis pursed his lips.

"You and me going on the roof with a tablecloth." Graham snickered. "We gonna play injun smoke signals with his chimney."

"Who we sending the signals to?"

"Idjut. We gonna smoke him out of his study, don't you see? If he won't come out by himself, we gotta do something different."

"Ah, he'll twig it's us, Graham."

"Naw, not if we do it properly. I want Tadpole and the others to stand on the balcony and signal when his fire starts smoking. I'll just take the tablecloth off his chimney. When the coast is clear, I'll cover the chimney again."

"He's gonna get real mad," Maudie objected.

"Let him. He'll just think it's the wind blowing down his chimney."

He ran his fingers over the remaining fireworks lying on the table and scooped up a selection including one of the super-skyrockets. He dropped them into a paper packet and tucked it under his arm.

"What you doing that for?" Louis asked him.

"Curtain call, Bro. Benson's got more'n enough here to finish off his show. I thought maybe we could keep some in reserve."

"You not taking them on the roof, are you?"

Graham nodded. "Sure am, Bro. Best place to see 'em."

As instructed Maudie, Amos and I climbed the old staircase and tiptoed along the upstairs corridor. We let ourselves onto the dormitory balcony adjacent the housemaster's suite. Standing at one corner, I peered through a French window into his study. A homely fire burned in the grate. The housemaster relaxed in his armchair, engrossed in a book. On a side table was a medicine phial.

A liquor cabinet stood against a wall. A bottle of sherry had been uncorked and was half empty. He drank from a wine glass. A cigarette burned in an ashtray. He reached for it and slipped it between his lips.

I pulled Maudie and Amos away from the parapet when the housemaster hauled himself out of his chair. He paced to his fireplace and prodded the coals with a poker. He stood there gazing at the glow, then picked up two logs and placed them on the coals. Below us, I heard Benson letting off fireworks. The housemaster topped his glass, went back to his armchair and picked up his book.

Graham and Louis were above us on the roof. From the end of the balcony, I made them out, crawling across the shingles toward the chimney stack. The housemaster settled in his armchair. A rocket took off from the lawn below and hissed its way past.

When the twins reached the chimney, Graham gave a low whistle to draw my attention. I waved to him indicating everything was clear. He bundled the tablecloth into a ball and thrust it into the chimney.

Inside the study, the new logs were beginning to flame. The moment Graham choked the chimney the flames went out. Wood smoke started filling the fireplace above the coals. Unable to rise up the chimney, the smoke eddied out over the hearth.

Mr de Beer sensed something was wrong. He became restless and turned around in his armchair. When he caught sight of smoke swirling into his study, he flung his book down and leapt out of his chair. I held up two arms to Graham, warning him to remove the tablecloth.

By the time the housemaster crossed his study the fire was drawing again. The logs kindled their own flames and the smoke disappeared back into the chimney. A remnant wafted above the hearth. He fanned it away with his arms and stared at the burning logs before returning to his chair. I waited for him to settle down before signalling to Graham.

Up on the roof, Graham jammed the tablecloth into the chimney again. In the fireplace the logs went from flame to smoke pouring into the study. I watched the housemaster engrossed in his book.

It took him a minute or so to realize his logs were no longer crackling. He turned his head and glanced out of the corner of his eye. I don't think he was expecting to see his study filling with smoke. He leapt up and faced the hearth. I held up my arms to warn Graham.

As if by magic, smoke was drawn back into the fireplace where it vanished up the chimney. The logs sprouted little orange flames. Mr de Beer stood staring at the phenomenon. He strode to his side table to fetch his glass, downed the sherry in one swallow and refilled his glass at the liquor cabinet. Glancing once more at the logs burning in the grate, he plumped himself down in his armchair and reached for his book.

Maudie and Amos were snickering so much I sent them to the other end of the balcony in case they could be heard inside the study. I waited a minute before signalling Graham again.

I saw the cloth being rammed into the chimney and went back to monitoring the study. The housemaster put his glass down, reached for a cigarette, slid it between his lips and lit it. Then he lifted his feet onto the arm of an adjoining chair and lay back with his book. His fire had been smoking for five minutes before he smelt the wood smoke.

Having settled himself so comfortably, he was reluctant to rise from his armchair this time. He hauled himself up slowly and stalked toward his hearth. I signalled to Graham. The housemaster took a poker and probed up the chimney. He bent down on hands and knees and peered up the chimney. The fire began drawing and he stood up, satisfied with his efforts.

Up on the roof, the twins waited for me to signal them. I shook my head and waved my arms in a scissors movement warning them to call it off. The housemaster was back in his chair, his fire crackling noisily.

Graham tossed the cloth past the edge of the gutter to float down to the lawn. Maudie, Amos and I were about to leave the balcony when the dormitory light was switched on and Lukas, the hostel's man Friday entered the room.

"It's him," Maudie squealed in fright, backing into me.

Lukas laid spare blankets on two of the beds, turned off the light and left the dormitory.

"S'okay Sis," I assured her. "Lukas didn't see us. We aren't gonna get in trouble."

My sister trembled.

"Whatsa matter, Sis?"

She backed into me and reached for my hand. Her body shook. She twisted her head to talk, but no words came out of her mouth. I had a flashback of when she fled the kitchen table and darted to the safety of the fig tree.

"You all right, Sis? Whatsa problem?"

"The giraffe man, Tadpole. That man who came in there. He's the one who touched me at Rhodes Park."

A chill swept up my spine.

"And was him standing on the pavement where Johan Rabie disappeared."

Lukas had indeed been standing under an oak tree when I'd looked through the back window, but I hadn't been looking for him. I'd been looking for a giraffe man.

"Lukas, Sis? You sure? Can't be. He's worked here for years."

"He's the one that chased us on the thoroughfare when we escaped down the bicycle ramp."

"Can't be, Maudie."

"I tell you, it's him. That's the giraffe man, Tadpole."

Chapter 43

My sister's words stunned me. I knew Lukas well, but had never seen her giraffe man properly. I hadn't noticed him at Rhodes Park. When I'd peered through the Chev's rear window, Lukas had been lounging on the pavement. But I hadn't been looking for him and so didn't make the connection. When we'd collected pine cones on the koppie, my migraine had all but blinded me.

Maudie had never seen Lukas before. The night she'd locked Mr de Beer out of his hostel, Lukas was at another party. The afternoon of the Kiewietjie Convicts, Lukas had stayed out of sight inside the hostel. And the evening Graham wired Louis's bed to the ceiling, I'd greeted Lukas when I went through the back while my sister brought her four leafed clovers through the front.

I trembled at Maudie's revelation.

An illegal immigrant from Central Africa practicing sorcery in the middle of Johannesburg using employment as his cover? It was not the first time witchcraft had come to a city. There had been a case in London where police had fished a child's torso out of the Thames.

My sister had assisted the police once. Was she now going to give them the name of the perpetrator?

"Stay close," I whispered. "He can't hurt us tonight."

Up on the roof, Graham opened his packet of fireworks.

"Damn it Bro," I heard him cuss.

An argument developed above us. I gathered that

Graham had left the matches behind and blamed Louis. He sent his brother to fetch them.

I did not see him take a sparkler from the packet and drop it down the housemaster's chimney. The fireplace in the study began glowing with an intense light that reflected on the ceiling. Mr de Beer didn't notice. He heard the hissing of the sparkler though. He glanced up and caught sight of the glare on the ceiling just as the sparkler went out. Frowning, he reached for his book.

"What's Graham up to now?" Amos whispered.

For a moment, I didn't answer. I had not recovered from the shock of Maudie's revelation.

"Dunno Amos. He's mad. When Mister de Beer finds out, he's gonna give him six of the best right up the jack."

Louis's twin selected another item from the packet and tossed it into the chimney. A firecracker exploded in the grate below.

"Good God," I heard the housemaster exclaim as he leapt up, strode to an open window and looked out. Down below, the boys were letting off their fireworks. They didn't notice their housemaster watching them. He left his window ajar and made his way to his chair. On the way, he caught sight of something lying on the hearth.

Standing on the balcony, I couldn't see what it was. He knelt and picked up the remains of Graham's firecracker. Now he was suspicious and stood staring at his fireplace. He let his gaze wander up the chimney breast. Above him, Graham laid the packet of fireworks on the chimney stack. Louis crawled along the roof with the matches.

Mr de Beer made up his mind to come outside and investigate. He disappeared into his bedroom to fetch his jacket.

Up on the roof, Graham cursed.

"Watch what you doing, you stupid blockhead. You knocked the whole blinking packet into the chimney."

"S'not my fault, Graham. Didn't see 'em in the dark.

Shouldn't of put 'em there."

I wasn't sure I heard Graham correctly. His packet was crammed with fireworks. The first one went off as the housemaster returned wearing his jacket.

Up on the roof, Louis had his fists up.

"You gonna tell The Bear 'twas you," he screamed. "I sick of getting in trouble 'cos of you."

Mr de Beer might have heard the commotion on the roof but as he entered his study, a firework known as a smoke-screen, ignited in the grate. It emitted a silver-grey fog that effused from his fireplace and rolled over the hearth. He stopped in his tracks, eyes transfixed. As he stared, his mantel disappeared behind a curtain of smoke.

Inside this fog, a Roman candle ignited. The walls of his study glowed pink.

Mr de Beer stood bemused. Possibly his brain was addled by his imbibing. A big-bang exploded in his grate, billowing black smoke over the hearth. He opened his mouth in disbelief.

In the next instant, a rocket burst out of the smoke. It shot under the coffee table, ricocheted off a ball-and-claw leg and headed for the housemaster's feet.

"My God!" he screamed when he saw it coming. He sprang into the air to let it pass under his feet.

I don't know what happened in the bedroom, but when the rocket hissed through the doorway, Mr de Beer dived after it. The soles of his shoes protruded from under his bed.

Another rocket ignited. It lodged in the chimney, its tail sending a shower of sparks onto the hearthrug. It freed itself, shot out of the chimney above us with insufficient speed to keep it flying and clattered onto the roof.

Firecrackers exploded in the grate. The housemaster emerged from his bedroom, clutching the remains of a burnt-out rocket. A jumping-jack bounded about the study, exploding each time it leapt into the air. He dropped the rocket and chased after this new arrival, but was apprehensive about catching it. He leapt around the study, trying to stamp it out.

Its last contortion took it across the room where it fell behind the cushion of his armchair. He wasn't quick enough to follow its erratic course and began looking for it underneath the chair instead.

Another rocket emerged from the fog of smoke. It roared into his chandelier, shattering glass lampshades and light globes. It became lodged up there, its tail spewing rainbows of sparks into the study.

"God Almighty!" he cried, diving for cover.

The only electric light illuminating the study now came from a solitary table lamp. The floor beneath the chandelier was littered with shards of glass. The darkened room lit up with the purple glow from inside the chimney. A Chinese lantern had got stuck on its way down and was spreading its bizarre light over the floor of his study.

Mr de Beer knelt on the floorboards, peering over the back of a settee. His face took on a purple hue. Another rocket banged about in the grate, finding its way into the room. Its wooden tail was alight. The flaming firework wavered toward the ceiling, lost power and dropped onto a pelmet.

I realized that fireworks had lodged halfway down his chimney. And now they were slipping onto the burning logs.

While the housemaster snatched away the rocket singeing his pelmet, a Chinese-shower dropped onto the logs. It gushed its fiery display into the study. A Catherine wheel rolled onto the hearthrug and spun erratically, singeing the pile.

Before Mr de Beer could save his curtains, two rockets took off simultaneously from the fireplace. One closely missed him standing on the sill and exited through the window. The missile arched across the street and disappeared behind the roof of a neighbouring house. The other rocket never left the floor. Its wooden tail was burnt off. It spun out of the grate in horizontal cartwheels, twisting across the study, singeing rugs and upholstery, finally disappearing under a settee.

It didn't matter now which twin had knocked the packet down the chimney. The study was in chaos. Mr de Beer swore, darting from one smouldering piece of upholstery to another. He rushed to the door leading to the corridor, flung it open, thought better of it and raced back to his study. Smoke wafted from under his settee.

He upended it and began ripping the lining away, when Graham's triple-stage, multi-coloured, starbursting, super-skyrocket, all the way from Hong Kong, slipped out of the chimney. It began to roar.

"Oh my God," the housemaster yowled.

Not taking his eyes off this new demon he clambered to his feet.

Graham's skyrocket took off, just as a machine-gun started shooting coals out of the grate. The housemaster couldn't decide which was going to cause more damage. The rocket ricocheted off the open door and shot down the corridor. Burning embers from the grate flew into his study rapidly as the machine-gun firework continued to go off. They landed all over the study. Mr de Beer held up his hands to protect his face and darted about the room stamping out what coals he could.

Careering along the corridor, the skyrocket ricocheted off a wall at the far end, twisted, contorted under power and came back again, clattering along the corridor's walls. It roared into the study as the first starburst exploded, showering the room with sparks. Mr de Beer dived into his bedroom. He was opening the door to see whether it was safe to come out, when the second starburst went off, filling his study with emerald light.

"Graham and Louis've had it this time. They gonna get expelled for sure." Maudie exclaimed, clutching my fingers.

The third starburst caught the housemaster trying to get out of his bedroom.

"I smell fire," Amos warned, "I mean real fire. Lookit the curtains in there. They smoking. Mama, I shoulda stayed with you tonight. We gonna get the licking of our lives."

Mr de Beer was halfway across his devastated study when the super-skyrocket gave its final performance. The explosion shattered windowpanes and a picture fell off the wall. The housemaster fell to his knees.

"Oh my God..." I heard his anguished cry as he clasped his hands over his ears.

Amos was right. It wasn't only the chemical reek of fireworks but the pungency of smouldering fabrics in my nostrils now.

"Yikes," Maudie pointed. "Those curtains are burning proper, now."

Curls of flame ate toward the pelmet.

"And there's smoke coming outta his bedroom window. A rocket musta set his bed alight."

Fires had started all over the study. The contents of a wire wastepaper basket were flaming; a file lying on a bookcase smouldered; burn marks in rugs glowed red; and the hearthrug was smoking. As I watched, the upended settee burst into flame. The curtains blazed now, the fire licking the wooden ceiling.

"Fire!" Mr de Beer screamed at the top of his voice. "For God's sake, fire!"

He glanced at the smoke coming out of his bedroom and raced to the door leading to the corridor.

"Fire!" he yelled down the corridor. "Fire, everybody!" He hesitated, peered down the corridor and spurted back into his burning study, making for the telephone. He tore the directory open, put his finger on what must have been the number of the fire brigade and spun the dial furiously.

"What do you mean last time was a hoax?" he screamed down the line.

"Yes, this is de Beer speaking. Yes, I am the owner of Kiewietjie and have been for two years. Yes, I did phone you about the same time last year. No, it wasn't a hoax last time. Or this time. There really *was* a fire last time, only it disappeared by the time you arrived. No, this one's not going to disappear too. I tell you, my whole suite is alight. No, I'm not imagining it. I can see the flames with my own eyes. Yes, I'll pay the costs if the fire's not here by the time you pitch up. Just hurry, damn it. Yes, you can phone me back on this number to confirm I'm still here. That's if the telephone wires haven't burnt through by then."

He slammed the receiver down, sprinted to a window, flung it open, leaned out and shouted, "Fire... Fire... Fire!"

Down below, Benson was setting off the last of his Roman-candles. He looked up casually, "Sir?"

"Fire! Damn you. Can't you see, boy?"

Benson took a pace backwards to get a better view of the upstairs windows.

"Good heavens, Sir. There's smoke coming out of your bedroom and your study curtains are burning."

"That's what I'm trying to tell you, boy. Are you stupid or something?"

The others jumped off the veranda parapet and joined Benson on the lawn. They peered at the burning suite.

"I'll save what I can," the housemaster yelled, "... throw my things over the balcony. You pick them up. The fire brigade'll be here any minute."

He fled into his study, grabbed papers and books, stuffed them into a briefcase and flung it straight through a closed window. Then he disappeared into his bedroom and came out coughing, dragging a suitcase. Clothing fell out. He crammed books and files into the case, struggled with it onto his balcony and heaved it over the railing. With that, he snatched at items randomly and flung them out the windows.

"Man, this's no place to be," Amos declared. "Reckon we oughta get out while the going's good. If that man sees us up here, he gonna think we'd something to do with this."

Amos had no inkling of what Maudie told me about Lukas.

"We up to our necks this time, Amos. All three of us."

"Yah, another reason to get out while the going's good."

The twins clambered off the roof. Keeping a wary eye out for Lukas, I led my sister and Amos through the dormitory and opened the door onto the corridor. Smoke swirled from a linen room. Linen smouldered, choking the room with smoke. I slammed the door and we raced downstairs.

Graham and Louis skulked in the lobby.

"Jeez, I done it this time," Graham moaned. "What the hell we gonna do?"

"Warn the guys to clear their things out the dormitories," Maudie urged. "The linen room's burning."

Amos nodded vigorously.

"That's right. Upper level's going any minute."

The boys swarmed upstairs. A glance into the linen room and they slammed its door. They raced to pack their paraphernalia. The staircase from the lobby became crowded with pupils lugging suitcases down and others hurrying upstairs for more. The heat drove Mr de Beer from his suite. Arms laden with possessions, he joined the boys.

The lawn became littered with belongings. Items dumped on the veranda were carried away from the building. The roof over the suite started burning and I changed my mind about returning inside. The boys held an impromptu roll call. Mr de Beer keened like a wild beast, holding his fingers to his temples. He looked like he was having a nervous breakdown.

"Never seen him like this before," Louis muttered. "Musta run out of his medicine."

I heard the fire engine's siren when it was still half a mile away. By the time the vehicle pulled up, neighbours crowded the pavement. Helmeted firemen leapt from the engine and sprinted to the corner hydrant. They unreeled hoses across Kiewietjie's weed ridden lawn. They connected a suction hose between the engine and hydrant. Pulling gasmasks over their faces, they raced up the veranda stairs. Water was turned on, the pumps started and hoses aimed through upper windows.

"You boys move everything on the lawn to the hedge," a fireman instructed. "Then, stand back."

Street spectators gawked over the fence. The place was in chaos. In the dark, I didn't know who was who.

A fireman holding a clipboard approached Mr de Beer, began questioning him and noted his answers. The housemaster was overwrought and the fireman crossed things out and wrote new answers.

Then they left him alone. He affected a curious posture, hunched and deformed, shaking his head in denial. I thought he might be arguing with himself. His hands kept fingering his face.

"Aw, shame," Maudie whispered. "I feel sorry for him cos Kiewietjie's really like his own house and now he's losing it."

The blaze took hold of half the upper storey. First to go was the study roof. It collapsed, exposing fiery trusses and progressed toward the dormitories and linen room. While firemen tried to save the dormitories, Mr de Beer's suite burnt. A rumour went around that they would preserve the ground floor. We huddled against the hedge, our faces red from the glow.

I hadn't seen the twins since roll call. There was chaos everywhere. Graham and Louis were on the street. They slunk through the garden gate at the bottom corner of the property, tripping over fire hoses.

Shaking his head, Mr de Beer caught sight of them. He waited for them to cross the lawn before accosting them.

"I've been wondering where you two hooligans were," he growled.

"Yes Sir?" Graham responded. He came to a halt and

lounged with his brother staring at his feet.

"This is your work, isn't it?"

Graham bit his tongue. He wouldn't look at the housemaster.

Louis glanced at his brother and began stammering. "No Sir, it wasn't us. Truly, it wasn't, Sir. We had nothing to do with it."

Graham still hadn't spoken. The housemaster dismissed what Louis said. He didn't look at him. His eyes were blazing and he kept them on the younger twin.

"I told you to answer me, boy," he hissed. "Now answer me, damn it."

I had never seen him this angry. Graham looked up, but didn't speak.

"You two arsonists were on the roof weren't you? You interfered with my chimney. That's why my fire kept smoking. Not so?"

Before Louis could make another denial, he stared him out and threatened, "I'll get a statement from you two yet. And I'll see the police get it. Then I'll charge you with arson. Your mother can sell her blasted smallholding to pay for my new hostel. I'll see you two little sods are sent to reformatory. Look at the soot on your hands. Where did that come from? Answer me, damn it."

"It didn't happen like that, Sir," Graham offered.

"So you were on the roof, you little bastard? It was your work? You've just admitted it."

"Yes, Sir," Graham replied, defeated. "But it was all a mistake, Sir."

"Mistake? You burn down my property and call it a mistake? Are you soft in the head, boy?"

The housemaster sneered. He became apoplectic. He brought his fingers to his temples and made his way to the fireman who questioned him earlier. They spoke for a minute and I noticed the fireman glance in the twins' direction.

"Big trouble coming," Amos murmured. "I sure'm glad I not part of it."

"You are part of it," I reminded him. "We all are."

"But Tadpole, we didn't know they were gonna knock those fireworks down the chimney," my sister defended.

The housemaster summoned Graham and Louis. The twins glanced at each other. Graham put his hands in his pockets and the two of them trudged across the lawn to where the housemaster and the firemen waited.

"Rather them than me," Amos breathed.

From what I could see, the fireman quizzed our cousins about how they started the fire. Mr de Beer stood to one side, while the fireman shot question after question and noted what Graham and Louis told him.

A gala night developed on the street. Hundreds of strangers gawked through the hedge and over the dilapidated wall. Others hung onto the fence at the side of the corner property. A group lounged in the middle of the street, talking and watching. Someone laughed.

The fire gutted half the first floor but the firemen prevented the blaze from spreading downstairs. They worked inside the building now, cooling down hot spots to prevent them flaring up again. I watched them going from room to room. One came out of the building and approached the housemaster. We edged nearer to hear what was being said.

"Mr de Beer," he reported, "this is a matter for the police. I'm going to call them in."

The housemaster nodded his approval.

Maudie pushed against me.

"Aw, poor Graham and Louis," she whispered. "What they gonna do to "em?"

I shook my head. "Dunno, Sis. I just dunno what's gonna happen. We shoulda stayed at home."

She began shaking. I put an arm around her. Amos looked morose.

Fifteen minutes later, a black van pulled into the hostel's driveway and two detectives got out. They followed the firemen up the veranda stairs into the semi-gutted building. We waited. Maudie snivelled. I recollected the Saturday afternoon in the fig tree ten days back, when Graham told us about the half-crowns being pooled for a momentous Guy Fawkes evening. Who could have known it would end like this? I had never felt so bad in my life.

One of the detectives came out of the hostel and strode across the lawn. As he approached the housemaster, I recognized him.

"Mister de Beer," he began. "I'm Inspector Conradie. You are Mister de Beer, I take it?"

"Oh yes, I'm de Beer. I'm the housemaster here. The boys board with me. This is my hostel."

"You own the property, Sir?"

"I certainly do. This fire is an enormous loss to me. You see, I'm not insured."

"How long have you lived here, Sir?"

"Two years. Ever since my wife left me. She ran away to Cape Town with some lover bastard."

Conradie drew himself up.

"Sir, the fire department made a curious discovery in your hostel. I'd like you to come and see for yourself, Sir."

"What discovery, Detective?"

"Downstairs, Sir..."

"The ground floor hasn't been touched by the fire, Inspector."

Conradie clasped his hands in front of him.

"Ah now Sir, the storeroom beneath the upstairs linen room. There's a wooden floor which is also the storeroom's ceiling. Do you understand what I'm saying, Sir?"

The housemaster put his fingers to his temples and shook his head.

The detective continued.

"Sir, that wooden floor burnt through and collapsed into the storeroom beneath. Nobody realized the downstairs room was alight because it was locked. Until about half an hour ago that is, when smoke was seen coming from under the door. When firemen broke into your storeroom, they noticed the heat had cracked new cement on one of the walls."

Conradie stared hard at the housemaster.

"Two-year-old cement, Sir. Not the same as the original when this building was erected sixty years ago. They discovered a false wall with a cavity behind it. Now do you know what I'm talking about, Sir?"

Mr de Beer didn't answer.

The detective paused. "A burning piece of timber, one of the joists I think, had fallen into the cavity and firemen were obliged to remove bricks to retrieve it. You know of course Sir, what they found behind the false wall?"

Maudie nudged me.

"What's happening?" she whispered. "Why's he talking about a false wall?"

"Shush, Sis, be patient."

As if in great pain, the housemaster held his hands to his temples. He shook his head, denying what the detective was revealing.

"You do know what they found don't you, Sir? A woman's skeleton. Your lack of denial is tantamount to admission."

Mr de Beer looked very tired.

Conradie continued. "Also black and white feathers together with smaller bones. An animal? A child?"

"That wasn't me..." de Beer protested.

"But you knew about them? Where's your African employee? Is it him?"

"I was being blackmailed. He knew about my wife."

"You'd better come to the station for a proper statement, Mister de Beer." Conradie extended an arm and led the housemaster to the police van.

"Tell me," Maudie whispered.

"Missus de Beer didn't run off with another man, Sis. She never left the hostel."

"You mean she's inside?"

"They think Mister de Beer killed her two years ago. But there's other stuff there also."

Our father arrived in the Chev and parked in the side street.

"Abe," Maudie cried and ran across the lawn to tell him what had happened.

He was late. It was after nine o'clock. Amos and I stood watching the firemen finish their work. They reeled in their hoses. A few made a final inspection of the first floor. The spectators on the pavement grew in number.

A commotion broke out on the driveway where the police van stood. In the dark, I couldn't see clearly. Torch beams played this way and that. Voices called to each other.

Two figures came racing in our direction.

"Bastard gave me the slip," Detective Inspector Conradie called. "Should've handcuffed him right away. But he can't have got far. Our van's blocking the driveway. Has to be on foot."

"Arrest his accomplice in the mean time," he ordered.

They disappeared in the dark, around a corner of the hostel to check the outbuildings. A few minutes later, I was astounded to see them returning with Graham's lyre, the Morris Eight's discarded tyre. A torch beam played on the section of missing tread .

"Matches the tracks we found at Rhodes Park," one of them called. "Confirms what we thinking."

A fireman helping the detectives came dashing around the side of the hostel.

"His car's gone. There's a hole in the hedge behind the garage. That's how he got away."

There was real confusion on the premises now.

"What about his man Friday? Gone too?"

"Lukas? Yah, must have escaped together."

"Get on the radio immediately. Call for a general alert. We're dealing with two killers here. The Jo-burg sorcerer and the Cape Town psychopath. We've got a muti-murderer and a multiple personality schizophrenic in cahoots with each other."

Our father, with Babs and Frog following, pushed through the crowd.

"Where's Maudie?" he asked, coming up to me.

"She went to meet you, Daddy." I answered in fright.

"I haven't seen her."

I froze.

"Maudie?" he bawled into the dark.

There was no answer.

He turned to Babs and Frog. "Spread out and find her. Check the street and the pavements. I'll go round the back."

Ten minutes later, they returned. There was no sign of my sister.

Police scoured the premises. Their torch-beams probed the property. An officer noticed our frenzy.

"What seems to be the problem, Sir?" he asked our father.

"My little girl's missing. She was here fifteen minutes ago. Now she's gone. Can't find her anywhere."

The officer stiffened. A look of alarm spread across his face.

"Leave it to me, Sir. We'll deal with it," he blurted and ran to inform the detectives.

Conradie glanced in our direction.

"Another child has been snatched," I heard him pronounce.

Chapter 44

Maudie was gone. My head spun. I felt dizzy. I thought I would fall. I was living in a waking dream. What was happening around me was fantasy. I floated around somewhere in the night air, looking down on the gutted hostel and the activity on the lawn, the firemen at their fire engine, the gawking crowds hanging over the fences and the frenzy of torch beams searching for my sister. A roaring in my ears made the commotion around me and the metallic exchanges on the police radio seem to be coming from another world. I heard a voice in the distance and was shocked to realise it was my own.

A manhunt was being put into operation. I couldn't face the horror that they were looking for Maudie. The shock hadn't hit me yet.

"It's time for us to go," our father murmured, touching me on my shoulder. "There's nothing more we can do here. The detectives are searching everywhere. A general alert for the Morris Eight and its number plate has gone out, and descriptions of the two men are being circulated."

I couldn't speak. We were abandoning Maudie. She was in the hands of two killers and we were walking away. I buried my face in my hands.

"The police will find her," our father murmured. "The police will find her."

Like they found Davy and Johan, I thought.

We bade an agitated goodbye to Graham and Louis who, with the other boys, were going to be temporarily accommodated by the local YMCA.

On the way to the Chev I rescued a torch lying on the rear bumper of a police van. It would have fallen off and been lost in any case as soon as the van drove away. Perhaps I was stealing it. It would be in memory of Maudie, a souvenir of this shocking night.

We were crowded on the back seat of the Chev, Babs, Frog, Amos and I squashed shoulder to shoulder. Our father was silent about anybody sitting in Momma's seat and we were silent too.

Would there now be an empty place where my sister used to sit? I wondered. And would we visit *her* grave on Sundays?

When we pulled up outside our darkened house in Good Hope Street, Babs oversaw Amos home to his mama. Our father woke Sampson and told him that Maudie was missing and that he was going to search for his daughter himself. He intended taking Babs and Frog with him. My elder brother was going on fourteen, old enough to help. If the night was too long, he could catnap on the back seat while Babs and our father peeled their eyes for a black Morris Eight.

Sampson was to give me breakfast the next morning and keep me at home, although it was a school day and exams approached. Father didn't know when he would return. The manhunt would cover likely places Maudie could have been taken to: the Foster Caves; Rhodes Park Lake; the adjacent stormwater drain; abandoned gold mine property; the mine-dumps with their lonely scrap yards at their bases; the Kensington koppies and the ridge overlooking Bezuidenhout Valley. The Chev would search cul-de-sacs, lonely streets and dark lanes.

I was put to bed and told not to worry. Before he left on his mission, my father assured me he would bring Maudie home.

Even at ten years of age, I was astute enough to know he meant her remains. I gazed at my sister's empty bed and cried myself to sleep.

Chapter 45

I wasn't conscious of any time lag between hearing the Chev drive away and opening my eyes in the darkness some hours later. When I woke, I glanced at Maudie's bed expecting to see my sister tucked up tight and serenely asleep. In the dim light of a street lamp, I made out the shape of her covers, flat neat and undisturbed. My sister was out there in the night somewhere.

The shock cut through me like a knife as the events of the previous night slipped into my memory.

"You gonna get us in trouble, Graham," Maudie had warned.

I was fully awake now. I got up, trying not to look at my sister's un-slept-in bed. I was alone. My father's room was empty and neither were Babs nor Frog in the house. They were out, seeking to bring home the remains of the youngest member of our family. As the clock struck four a.m. I became convinced I had to find my sister myself.

In the pantry, I found half a loaf of bread. Sampson kept a bowl of dripping in our ancient Kelvinator. I sliced a doorstep of bread and smeared it thick with dripping. In my mind, I saw my sister eyeing me in a funny sort of way, the way she did if I sneaked a delicacy for myself and didn't share it with her.

Hobo was awake on the back veranda. I went out, patted and stroked her, whispering soothingly. She wouldn't look for her mistress for another two hours. The fig tree showed gloomily in the light shining through the screen door. It was the first time that Maudie's black *Monday* sign had hung from the bole on a Tuesday morning. I swore a silent oath to my sister's memory that I would not remove it.

Sampson would sleep for another hour-and-a-half. By then I would long be gone. I closed the kitchen door and locked it.

In our bedroom, I pulled on my shorts and shirt. I didn't bother to wash for the job I was going to do. I switched off the lights; picked up the police torch I had appropriated and let myself out the darkened house. Except for the parts lit by streetlights Good Hope Street was impenetrably dark so I didn't feel bad about the torch. After all, I was going to do police work in bringing my sister's remains home. I was not afraid.

The night Graham wired Louis's bed to the ceiling, I'd woken to the Big Ben carillon followed by a single chime and Maudie calling me in her sleep.

Tadpole, come help me.

I remembered shaking off my blankets and padding across our room to sit with her.

I need you. Where you? You not gonna help me?

I remembered speaking gently and shaking her awake.

Why didn't you come sooner? Just me and the sorcerer in the caves. He threw me down.

I remembered the passage clock ticking.

He made me drink muti so's I couldn't move.

"S'only a dream," I'd told her.

You never came, Tadpole, you never came. I looked down and saw you sleeping here in our room.

Was that what my sister said? Or was she calling me now?

Maudie had been gone the whole night and I didn't think she would have lasted long in the hands of a man with a Mamlambo snake for a tongue and another who practiced witchcraft. But I knew where I would find her remains. I didn't want the police or anybody else touching them. That would be sacrilege. I would carry them home myself.

When Sampson woke, he would find my bed empty

and would be in a panic. I couldn't worry about that now. Good Hope Street was deserted and I broke into a trot up the middle. There were no cars to run me down. First light progressed to dusk. In Trixie's property, a lamp was on in Joseph's shack. I didn't want him to see me. I needed to do this job for Maudie alone and I hoped Joseph didn't come out of his shack and call me.

At the top of Good Hope, I swung into Rockey Street and after a while, turned down the lane that led to the southern koppie and the Foster Caves. There was no one about and with the narrowness of the lane, the closeness of the hedges, the overhanging trees and the morning dusk it was gloomily dark.

The first thing I found was the Morris Eight lying on its roof. Its tyres were smooth and the car had skidded over the edge of the embankment at the end of the lane and rolled onto the koppie. Both doors hung open and engine oil and radiator water were weeping out. I smelled petrol too. The wreck could not be seen from the road.

Twilight lightened the eastern sky. I padded barefoot down the path Maudie, Amos and I had taken to lug our overgrown earthworm to show Selina.

In the gloom before dawn, I discovered a new entrance since we were last here. This took me by surprise until I remembered the detectives who interviewed us, said we had given them a lead and they would search the caves. They had cleared the original opening. Loose rock previously dumped there had been unpacked, allowing me to enter standing up.

I switched on the torch and went into the caves. I could get much further this time. When I searched through the tunnels, I went cold. In the beam of light, was blood. Blood everywhere. Fearing to advance, but remembering Maudie calling me I forced myself to edge forward.

The further I crept through the caves, the more blood there was. Now further into the cave than ever, I stopped dead. The torchlight had found my sister's feet. I didn't want to look.

For a time I couldn't move. Somehow I forced myself to take a step nearer, then another, and a third, and a fourth. The light hovered over her bare feet. Slowly, I inched it past ankles, shins, knees, thighs, torso, not daring to shine it higher than her shoulders. Reluctantly, I brought the light onto her face. With shock I saw her eyes blink. Realizing she couldn't see who was behind the torch I shut my eyes and turned the beam so she was able to identify me.

Then I tiptoed toward her, shading the lens so I wouldn't dazzle either of us. She lay on a slab of rock, watching me come for her and I was reminded of her eyes under the water at Gillooly's.

All around her, the cave was splattered with blood. As I crouched next to her, the torchlight revealed Mr de Beer's body lying a few yards behind. We learnt later that he had cut his wrists. Beyond him was the bloodied body of Lukas.

"The bull, Tadpole," Maudie whispered.

I didn't know what she was talking about but thought, in the circumstances, I had better humour her.

"What about a bull, Sis?"

"The Afrikaner bull under the thorn trees. It charged Uncle Stanley on his motorbike. He fell in front of us. Momma tried to miss him, but we crashed, Tadpole, we crashed."

So now I knew what had caused the inexplicable accident that took Momma's life. I bent and hugged my sister gently.

"You been scoffing bread and Semp-Sonne's dripping," she reproached.

That made me chuckle. My sister smelt I'd been snacking and hadn't shared it with her. I would get into trouble yet.

"We going to Kiewietjie tonight to see the fireworks," she chipped. "I wanna see the fireworks real bad."

That brought me up abruptly.

"No, Sis, we saw the fireworks last night."

"You silly-billy. It's Monday. I haven't put my Monday sign in the fig tree yet."

I took both her hands in mine and asked slowly, "Maudie, don't you remember Kiewietjie burning down? Lukas and Mister de Beer snatched you last night and brought you here. Don't you remember all that, Sis?"

"You making it up, Tadpole. Stop teasing me."

"What do you think happened last night?"

"Aw c'mon, last night was Sunday, you know that. We packed our school things."

I shook my head.

"Why's it so dark? And watcha doing with a torch? Where'd you get it? Why you waking me so early? When the sun comes up, I'll pin our Monday sign in the fig tree."

I stared at her. She had no recollection of waking on Monday morning and pinning her black *Monday* sign to the bole of the fig tree. She had no idea she had been to school and could not recall the evening at Kiewietjie. Not the burning down of the hostel or her kidnapping. She did not know what had happened in the cave and wasn't aware of where she was.

"I guess we better get ready for school, Sis," I suggested, helping her to her feet. I needed to get her out into the morning light as quickly as possible and take her home.

There was a movement behind my sister. I raised the torch to see the bloodied apparition of Lukas towering above us, clutching a carving knife. I pulled Maudie away and started dragging her toward the entrance. She didn't know why and I wouldn't let her turn around. In the dark, I tripped on the rocky floor of the cave and fell backwards, dragging Maudie down with me. The torch clattered across the rock and came to a stop shining its beam on my sister and me. I couldn't see Lukas but I could hear him hobbling toward us.

The beam of another torch played on the walls of the cave. A few seconds later, it found Lukas.

"What the hell do you think you're doing?" I heard the outraged cry of Old Joseph.

He had seen me leaving on my mission and followed me to the caves, just as he had been shadowing us for months, I found out later.

I pulled Maudie's face into my chest and wrapped my arms around her head so she wouldn't see or hear the altercation between Joseph and her giraffe man.

Joseph fumbled with the thong around his neck and withdrew an olden-days marlinspike. Yowling an oath, the seventy-one-year-old mariner dazzled Lukas with the torch and attacked. Already injured, Lukas reacted slowly. Joseph fell on him. When he rose, the marlinspike was embedded in the sorcerer's throat.

I didn't want Maudie to see so I fumbled for our torch and shone it toward the exit, pushing my sister in front of me.

Out on the koppie, the sun peeped over the horizon, highlighting spiders' webs, droplets of dew clinging to grass and cradled in wild flowers.

"What's going on?" Maudie asked bemused. She looked at me curiously. "Where're we? What we doing on the koppie?"

"Be patient, Sis. I'll explain when we get home."

As she stood there, glancing around in confusion, a wrenching fear overtook me. What if I had not woken early this morning? What if Maudie had never confided in me about her nightmare of lying on a sacrificial slab in the Foster Caves while the sorcerer honed his knife?

If I had not come to the caves before sunrise, Joseph would not have been here either. When Lukas regained consciousness, he would have had Maudie to himself. I felt so bad I wanted to vomit.

"What's up with you?" Maudie wanted to know.

"You getting one of your migraines or something?"

"S'okay, Sis. Just thinking, that's all."

I bent down, dusted dirt from her clothes and straightened them for her.

Joseph limped out of the cave. Good Old Joseph, always cautioning us to let things live.

"Is she alright?"

I nodded. He wanted to ask questions, but I put a finger to my lips. Not now.

Joseph trekked with us along the path I chose to protect Maudie from seeing the wrecked Morris Eight. I was frightened it would remind her of Momma's and Stanley's accident.

"You like a ride in the sidecar?" Joseph offered when we reached Rockey Street.

"Sure, Old Joseph, that'd be snazzy. But something funny's going on. Dunno what. Maybe I better stay with Tadpole so's he can tell me what's going on here. You gonna walk with me, Tadpole?"

I nodded and took her hand. We didn't speak as we footed it, hand in hand along the rough pavement. Joseph idled along, a discreet distance behind us.

When my sister and I strode up our driveway and rounded the house into the backyard, Sampson shouted his glee and came dashing down the veranda stairs to see for himself that my sister was real. Tears streamed down his face puzzling Maudie even more.

"Maudie, Maudie. You are really you," he cried, picking her up and hugging her.

"Yah Semp-Sonne," she responded, frowning and eyeing him as if he was insane. "Of course I'm me. Who'd you think I am?"

Hobo was happy to see her mistress but as she hadn't known Maudie was missing, she wasn't as overjoyed as Sampson.

"Lookit your sign, Sis," I pointed, leading her to the fig tree and showing her our black *Monday* sign.

"Something funny going on here, Tadpole. How'd

that get in the damn fig tree? I sure didn't put it there."

She gave me a funny look and ran to check with Sampson.

"It's Tuesday today, little madam," he confirmed.

She dashed back, giving me another funny look. I think she thought Sampson and I were in cahoots in some sort of plot against her.

"What day's it Old Joseph?" He was sitting in the kitchen talking to Sampson about what he knew, awaiting the arrival of our father and police detectives.

"Why, Tuesday, my little girl."

"Something strange here nobody's telling me," she accused, looking sheepish.

Reluctantly, she unpinned her *Monday* sign and replaced it with her new pink *Tuesday* one.

"We aren't going to school today," I informed her, and was rewarded with a happier facial expression.

I left her messing about in the fig tree and waited at the front gate for our Chev and worse, the detectives, so I could warn them and ward off an inquisition which might send my sister over the edge.

The Chev arrived first. Our father looked like death. He was dishevelled and red-eyed from having been up the whole night searching for his daughter. When he saw me, he shook his head in defeat.

"We never found her," he confessed, before I could tell him otherwise.

"We searched everywhere. I've just come back from the police station. Maudie's gone." He was weeping.

I didn't know how to deliver the good news.

"There's someone waiting for you in the backyard," I told him.

He frowned and left me with Babs and Frog while he strode up the drive to meet his visitor. I think he thought a detective was waiting for him. Babs and my elder brother looked as frayed as my father.

"Maudie's here," I stuttered, "but she's lost her memory. She don't remember anything since Sunday night when she went to bed."

They didn't believe me, until they heard my father's euphoric voice in the backyard. He was laughing and crying at the same time as he strode down the driveway, clutching my sister to his chest. Tears streamed down his face.

Maudie was protesting,

"Put me down, put me down, Abe. What's all the fuss about?"

"Maudie's lost her memory," I warned him. "Don't ask her any questions. Old Joseph will tell you everything."

I got a funny look from him too, but he was crying too much to question me.

We went into the house where dear Sampson had tea and sandwiches ready in the living room. Joseph stood up and put his arms around our father. They stood like that for a long time.

Maudie hadn't eaten since her early supper the previous day, the one she would always deny having.

"Babs, I wanna check something with you," she said, while simultaneously munching two sandwiches, one in each hand.

Babs was taken aback.

"What did you get up to, that the police came round? They were looking for you, you know. You been shoplifting or something?"

Our aunt was stunned and her mouth grew taut.

"You'd better tell her," our father interjected.

"Oh very well then, Maudie. Everybody else has heard about it. Do you know what prohibition is?"

"Nuh."

"It's when the government forbids the sale of liquor."

"Oh yah, Babs, that's the black market thing."

"Well, not quite. The black market is the illegal selling and buying of booze."

"So?"

"Anyway," Babs continued, "I think even you children know, there is a law that prohibits Africans from buying liquor."

"That's good," Maudie interjected. "Means when Amos is big, he can't get blotto and make a fool of himself like I seen a lot of Europeans do."

Babs blushed.

"The truth is, Maudie, that African people drink just as much as if there wasn't prohibition. Except they're obliged to pay twice the price on the black market. It's a stupid law, really."

"Go on, Babs."

"Maudie, I'm sorry to admit that I was buying liquor on behalf of African friends," Babs said quietly.

"The police found out and charged me. I had to pay a fine, which I couldn't afford. That's why my Tiger Moth still isn't flying. I don't have the money to finish it."

"That's not fair," Maudie interrupted.

"The police also wanted to know who I was supplying the booze to."

"Who?"

"Mister Sunshine. He used to pick up the supplies at the garage in his Chrysler."

"That's why he's so rich! Wasn't only the catalogue stuff he was selling. Was getting rich on this black market thing."

"That may be," Babs agreed. "But you know that the police have also had a little talk to him too. So that's all at an end now."

"Why aren't you rich from this black market thing, Babs?" Maudie wanted to know. "You don't even own a car."

"I did it out of empathy, Maudie. I didn't make a profit out of it."

While Babs was talking, our father phoned the chief inspector working on the case and told him Maudie was home and safe. Detective Conradie came over immediately, but before he arrived, I inveigled my sister to give Hobo some exercise by shining her vanity mirror from the top of the fig tree.

I had to protect her from interrogation.

With all the adults frowning and looking at me impatiently, I stuttered through what I thought they should know. I told of Isanusi's divination and also my sister's nightmare of finding herself on a sacrificial slab and how I was certain I would find her in the Foster Caves.

"The caves?... the Foster Caves?" Detective Conradie glanced at our father in shock.

"That's the first place we investigated. We searched them around ten o'clock last night. One end to the other. Nothing there. I don't understand it."

He pondered for a while, searching for an explanation.

"de Beer and this Lukas character must have driven around and only taken your daughter there after we left. Very cunning."

I told them about the blood, but that Lukas was lying in it. The housemaster's wrists and hands were bloodied too, but my sister was unaware of the two men in the cave with her and unaware what had happened.

"The first thing Maudie said to me," I explained, looking at our father, "was about a bull charging Uncle Stanley on his motorbike. Maudie says he fell in front of Momma's pick-up. Momma tried to miss him and that's when they turned upside down."

Our father fixed his eyes on me.

"Maudie's known this for four years but couldn't tell us. She doesn't remember anything since going to sleep on Sunday night. Nothing about waking up Monday morning either. She doesn't remember going to school yesterday, the fireworks, Kiewietjie burning down, or being snatched. She can't figure how she got in the caves and didn't know it's Tuesday today."

Our father looked at me disbelievingly and started

to question me, but Conradie stopped him.

"Amnesia is not uncommon when the victim receives a shock they cannot handle. I've come across it more than once in my investigations. Trauma is overwhelming. Everything is erased from the conscious mind. In your daughter's case, it'll be for the best. The less she remembers, the better. We have a lady psychiatrist who works with us. I'll discuss it with her. She might want to talk to your little girl."

Joseph told Conradie what he knew of the matter. It was he, apparently, who had noticed the tyre tracks with the missing section of tread when he parked his Harley Davidson at Rhodes Park that night. After Johannes Rabie went missing, Joseph shadowed my sister and me for months. But he knew nothing about the giraffe man whom my sister had noticed on four occasions.

"You'd better keep this, Detective," he offered, handing over his bloodied marlinspike wrapped in a cloth. "Lukas was seconds away from using his knife on the children. I didn't have a choice but to take him out."

He told the detective where he would find the Morris Eight and what he would see in the caves.

Conradie thanked him.

"We're pretty sure de Beer is the Jekyll and Hyde the Cape Town CID are looking for. I don't know how he got involved with this Nyasaland sorcerer, Lukas. Possibly Lukas knew de Beer murdered his wife and was blackmailing him as he claimed. I really don't understand it."

"We need expert opinion on what might have happened in the caves. Perhaps Mr Hyde unexpectedly transformed back into Dr Jekyll who put a stop to what was about to happen. Without your daughter's evidence, we'll never know for sure."

He left us then and I decided not to return the police torch. It would be Maudie's and my memento.

My sister danced into the living room. "Hobo's had

enough exercise for a week," she giggled.

"Want to come and sail your cork square-riggers on the lakes next door?" Joseph asked.

"Good thinking Old Joseph," Maudie cried. "Lemme whistle up Amos."

Maudie is four, standing on the passenger seat of a battered farm pickup truck which has no seat belts. Her mother Doreen is driving. Ahead, the dirt road stretches in a haze of heat. A clump of blue-gums shimmers in the African sun. On the opposite verge of the road are clusters of flat-topped thorn trees. An Afrikaner bull is camouflaged by their shade.

Barrelling toward the pickup is a motorcycle, an old Royal Enfield thumper. Doreen's elder brother Stanley is astride the bike. He is wearing RAF goggles but no head protection because crash helmets haven't come into use yet. The engine is misfiring and Stanley fiddles with the spark advance and retard lever on the handlebar.

He doesn't get it right and the motor backfires. The startled bull charges onto the road, intent on doing battle with the Enfield. Stanley swerves. The bike goes down in an uncontrolled broadside into the path of the oncoming pickup.

Doreen swings the wheel way too much. The pickup begins to roll. Her door flies open pitching her into the dirt and the vehicle rolls on top of her. The bike tumbles with Stanley half-on half-off and slews under the bonnet of the inverted pickup into the windscreen. Hot engine oil and radiator water pour onto him but he doesn't know it. His neck is broken.

There is no breeze to stir the blue-gums. The bull ambles back to the shade of the thorn trees. A pall of dust lingers over the wreckage. The front wheels of the pickup spin lazily. Maudie is screaming.

For other exciting titles visit our website

endaxipress.com